WHEN HER WORLD WENT AWAY

ALEXIS L CARROLL

BLOOD BLOOMS PRESS

This is a work of fiction. All of the characters, organizations, and events portrayed in this novel are products of the author's imagination.

WHEN HER WORLD WENT AWAY

Copyright © 2024 by Alexis L Carroll and Blood Blooms Press

@Alexisxstetic

All rights reserved.

ISBN

Print 979-8-9915187-0-3

E-book 979-8-9915187-1-0

First Edition: November 21, 2024

Cover art/design by Fay Lane www.faylane.com

Interior graphics by Amanda Stockton @BatwoMANDA

No part of this book may be reproduced in any form or by any electronic or mechanical means, including information storage and retrieval systems, without written permission from the authors, except for the use of brief quotations in a book review.

01 02 11 20 20

Dedicated to the ones who dared to leave home… only to find themselves back where they started. Keep your head held high, for every step is your journey and no one else's.

CONTENT WARNINGS

Abandonment anxiety
Child harm (briefly described)
Depression
Explicit language
Explosion (off page, experienced)
Fight scenes with knives
Gore (descriptive)
Manipulation
Monsters (descriptive)
Murder/Death (on page, brief)
Sexual Assault (speculative, not talked about)

Romantic Intimacy:
Kissing
Light touching
Fade-to-black

"Where were you when it happened?"

Sairha pushed her hair back from her face and took a deep breath. Wolves howled far beyond the firelight of their camp, eliciting a shiver down her arms. Staring into the flames, she recalled exactly where she had been *that day,* the day the world went away...

CHAPTER ONE

"No!" Sairha cried out, bolting upright, heart racing. She clutched the bedsheet close to her near-naked body, gasping, trying to make sense of reality. Make sense of the unfamiliar room she was in.

"I'm here. I am right here, Sairha." The whisper came from beside her and an arm wrapped around her shoulders. "You had a bad dream. It's over now. You're safe."

The darkened hotel room sharpened and the images of bloody hospital walls faded away. It was only a work nightmare. "It was—was...so *weird*," she stammered. She gripped his arm tightly, as if anchoring herself to real life. That's right, she was in a rural part of Mexico, *Sabueso de Oro*. Studying abroad, a nursing program as far from smalltown Lake Haluhoe, California, *and* her family, as possible. More specifically, she was in Sven's hotel room, a handsome public speaker, also from California, whom she had spent the last two days with.

"Do you want to talk about it?"

"No."

Sven stroked her head and she focused on the feeling of his fingers through her hair, willing herself to settle down.

"Can you fall back asleep?"

The thought of falling asleep again seemed bleak. Having a panic attack, from her imagination no less, was not how she wanted Sven to remember their last night together. Souring the romantic fling. "Sorry I woke you," she whispered.

"You didn't. I've been awake for a while," he murmured against the top of her head. "I get restless at night. And you were thrashing around quite a bit, I was worried."

She tensed in his arms. "Sorry."

"Don't be."

Falling into a comfortable silence, it wasn't long before Sairha's eyes got heavy again. Cuddled up against his chest, held tight in his warm embrace, she felt enveloped in safety despite hardly knowing him. His scent was earthy, a mixture of ginger and pine, that reminded her of the woods back home. With his hand still stroking her hair, paired up with the steady beat of his heart, she became relaxed enough that her eyes shuttered.

"Sairha, wake up," Sven's voice pierced through the silence, urgency in his tone. "Something isn't right."

Hadn't she just fallen back asleep? She opened her eyes, at least, she thought she had. The room was pitch black. She closed and reopened them. Still dark. No light peeked from the curtains, no red glaring numbers from the alarm clock, the dim light in the bathroom gone. The air felt thick, like a heavy blanket had been tossed over them. About to question what happened, Sairha's thoughts scrambled as the room shook violently. A vase of fresh dahlias Sven had bought her crashed to the floor. A bedside lamp fell into her side, eliciting a yelp from her. The hotel shook harder. Sairha clung to Sven, as their mattress slid from the bedframe. A loud crash reverberated across from them, as the television tumbled from its mount.

Then it all stopped.

"Sven—"

A blinding, white light cut through the darkness and Sairha's words, and she buried her face into the crook of her arm. An ear-splitting explosion escalated into a high-pitched tone. She couldn't decide whether to keep her eyes hidden or cover her ears. Which sense could she live without? Sven's arm covered her exposed ear, pulling her head against his chest to shield the other. Who was this man that would protect her over himself?

What's happening?

As fast as it happened, it was over and they slowly unfolded from each other. Sairha looked at Sven, in shock, before a loud crack gave only a moment's warning. A chunk of the ceiling crashed on top of them, burying them. Ears ringing, Sairha's vision blurred. The last thing she remembered before passing out was the screaming, lots of people screaming.

"Sairha," Sven called to her and the heavy weight crushing her was lifted. She heard coughing amidst him calling her name again. Disoriented, she tried to respond but only a groan emerged. At last the final piece of debris was removed and Sven's strong hands pulled her free.

An unnatural glow peeked from behind the curtains. Resembling neither dusk nor dawn, ominous in nature. Sairha and Sven cautiously parted, taking in the damage.

"Careful," Sven said, offering Sairha his arm for support as she edged her way to the side of the bed.

"How long was I unconscious? What was that? An earthquake from hell? Do you think anyone was hurt?" Energy bubbled at her core, a familiar buzz she often got from being a trauma nurse. Grabbing her clothes from the floor, she slipped her black tank top over her head, her chin-length reddish blonde hair poofing up from static. Ignoring her hair, she pulled her jeans on quickly.

While Sairha was in a hurry to get moving, Sven sat speechless, watching her for a moment. She found his white button-up shirt on the floor, shook it clean, and tossed it to him. He caught it and quickened his pace to catch up with her. Sairha was lacing up her boots before he had his shirt pulled over his tan chest.

"I have no idea," he replied. "That was nothing like any earthquake I've been in. Had to be something else, something more serious." He ran his hand through his long black hair, then perhaps thinking better of it, tied it out of the way with a rubber band from his wrist.

"What could be more serious than an earthquake?" Sairha snorted, but knew there could be worse, much worse. She found her phone behind the nightstand. It remained black after hitting the homescreen several times. "Huh, my phone is dead. That's weird," she muttered, double checking that the charging cord was secured to the device. She looked over at Sven and saw him frowning down at his.

"No, no, no." Sairha panicked, picking her way to the table and dumping her messenger bag. She snatched her laptop from under a pile of her medical textbooks and notepads. Snapping it open, she waited for the screen to light up. She let out a loud, irritated groan when nothing happened. "All of my research papers! My studies! Gone!"

Sven rubbed his temples. "What is going on here?"

"This is starting to freak me out." Sairha sighed, closing the dead laptop. Then she remembered something, something more important, and her hand flew to her mouth in dismay. "Oh my god—Cassandra!"

"What? Sairha! Wait!"

Sven's words couldn't reach her; she was already running out the door.

The hotel hallway was disheveled with tables knocked over and the decor strewn across the floor. Sairha rushed down the hall, avoiding broken glass. The once beautiful landscape paintings she passed hung awkwardly off their hooks, another shake away from crashing to the floor. She paused in front of the elevator, distraught as the situation's seriousness became more apparent. Sven caught up to her, and she waved her hands at the doors. "Of course, if the power is out, why would the elevator work? Help me find the stairs."

They found the staircase on the opposite end of the hallway, its door jammed shut.

"Can you tell me what's going on, at least?" Sven grunted, pushing as hard as he could to get it wide enough to climb in.

"Cassandra, the girl I was with when we first met? Her and that guy from the bar, Greg or something, were staying here too. A few floors down from ours," Sairha explained, squeezing through the gap he had created. "I have to make sure she's okay." On the other side, the door had been blocked by a thick metal support beam wedged out of place. The only light in the stairwell came from skinny, rectangular windows, not wide enough for a child to get through, making their descent difficult. Wasting no time, Sairha began tiptoeing through the rubble.

Sven said nothing and followed her down. Once in a while they glanced back up at the shifty, loose stairs above them. *"A few floors down"* felt like it took forever to get to, but they eventually made it and had an easier time getting out of the stairwell.

Sven closed the door softly to avoid disturbing the structure, as it was their only way out. Sairha was ready to move, but he grabbed her elbow, concern and sympathy written on his face. "Sairha, you need to be prepared for..."

She shook her head. "Don't say that. Do not say it."

He released her, thankfully saying nothing more. She couldn't think about that possibility. She had to stay focused. She wished she could remember what room it was, as she passed by the numbered doors. "It's either 410 or 401. If my phone worked I could double check."

She stopped in front of the door labeled 410. With silent insistence across his demeanor, Sven pushed past her. The door locks were deactivated from the power outage, the handle turning easily in his grasp. Sairha stood close behind, watching, full of anxiety, as he entered. Three steps in, Sven started to gag. He tried to block her way, but she was ready and ducked under his arm.

Sairha froze.

The once nice suite had been ransacked, looking as if a bear or pack of wolves had torn through it. Furniture smashed, the bathroom contents strewn about. Shattered mirror glass littered the floor, worse than their room. What Sven tried to prevent Sairha from seeing was the gory mess on the bed; a vibrant shade of red soaking the center.

"Sairha, don't."

"Maybe I can help," she said quietly. Her eyes widened at the visual as she drew closer. Training as a nurse, she was used to seeing blood and broken bones; however what lay in the middle of the mattress no longer resembled a body. Bits of flesh were scattered about a decimated skeleton. The bones looked mangled, gnawed on, and broken in precise snaps.

All that blood. How was that possible?

Stomach roiling, Sairha choked back the bile that threatened to come up. The scene was too much for even her to handle. She threw herself into Sven's arms, closing her eyes tight against the image that would surely be burned into her mind forever. Sven kept a firm hold on her as he closed the door behind them, though she wouldn't have left his side anyway. It was hard to grasp what was real. *This wasn't just an earthquake.* Sairha swallowed a lump in her throat. *Something unspeakable, unimaginable happened in that room.*

"What was that other room number you said?"

She heard him but could not register its meaning. Her adrenaline was dwindling. Was that her friend? Was that Cassandra in there?

"Sairha. Sairha." Sven lifted her face to his, his light brown eyes hard and serious. "You need to pull it back together. We have to get out of here."

"Room—Room 401," she croaked

She knew she should let Sven do the searching but, because of what she had seen, or maybe because it was her friend, when they reached the room she wanted to be the one to go in. "Please, let me." She stared at him.

He took a deep inhale and then stepped aside, allowing her access.

Palms clammy, she gripped the handle. Every thump of her heart felt exaggerated and loud in her ears. The door slid open and bumped into something. A dresser was half off the bed and wedged against the wall, blocking their way into the rest of the room. Glass and pillow feathers littered the floor. No sign of blood. "Cassandra?"

The silence that followed felt cold, eerie. Cassandra was here, she was. She *had* to be.

"Cassandra!"

"Shhh, listen," Sven hissed, tilting his head.

Sairha couldn't hear anything past the beating of her own heart. She forced it to quiet down, trying to pick up whatever had caught Sven's attention.

Tap, tap, tap.

What is that?

The soft tapping was close.

They both looked at the wedged dresser, noticing that it wasn't against a wall after all. Rather, it was barring the closet door.

"Cassandra!"

Sven passed Sairha in a flash and pushed the dresser out of the way. It crashed to the floor and Sairha ripped the closet door open. A woman lay curled up on the ground, her soft tan face tear-stained, mascara running, and clothes haphazardly put on. Her curly brown hair was a matted mess.

"Cassandra," Sairha breathed, relieved.

Cassandra's hand shook as she reached out for Sairha's.

With a determined tug, Sairha pulled Cassandra out and straight into her arms, wrapping her in a tight hug. "Are you okay? Let me look you over." Sairha scanned the surface of her friend for any wounds, mental damage to be assessed later. There were some scrapes and bruises, but nothing that needed immediate attention.

Sven cleared his throat after climbing back over the dresser. His face was tight, somber. "No one else here. We really need to go, I don't think it's safe to linger."

Sairha looked Cassandra over once more, concerned. "Let's go, okay?"

Quietly they headed to the stairwell, Sairha physically supporting Cassandra. It wasn't difficult to avoid the wreckage of the hallway, but the stairwell would be a different story.

"Do you think you can manage on your own?" Sairha asked once they got there.

"It's a bit of a dangerous trek down." Sven opened the door just as gently as he had closed it. "One of the pillars has fallen. We need to be careful where we step. I'll go first to pick out the safest way, Cassandra you come second so I can steady you if you feel weak or stumble. Sairha will be right behind you." He nodded at them.

They returned the gesture in agreement, and he started down the stairs. Sairha couldn't help but admire how effortless it was the way he took the lead. Her foot slipped on a piece of debris and she had to catch herself from crashing into the wall. Long jagged cracks crawled up the wall, looking like just one touch would turn it to dust.

It became apparent, as they went, that Cassandra was not okay. With her arms wrapped tight around herself, as if she could stop herself from shaking, whimpers escaped her quivering lips.

Sairha frowned, sympathizing. How the room looked, it left a thousand questions of what had happened in its wake. She most wanted to know how Cassandra had become trapped alone in the closet. Where was the man she had been with? None of what Sairha had seen made sense. Weren't they just in some sort of earthquake or explosion? Where were the people? Once they were safe, she planned on inquiring what had befallen the couple. For now, she watched Cassandra the best she could while climbing down.

They descended with no problems until the second level when Sairha noticed something in her peripheral vision. A shimmer moved in the shadows above them and scattered when she tried to look directly at it. It wouldn't have been noticeable in the corner of the stairwell, except that it moved too quickly to be a shadow. Without it stepping into the light from the broken windows, there was no telling what she saw. A shiver rolled through her. However, before Sairha could call Sven, something else commanded their attention.

Screeching, metal grinding against metal.

"Run!" Sven and Sairha yelled at the same time.

The top stairwell groaned as it gave way, filling the air with vibration and clouds of dust. Cassandra shrieked, covering her ears and closing her eyes tight. Her frozen terror trapping Sairha behind her. Chunks of drywall crashed around them.

"Sven! What do we do?" Sairha yelled over the commotion.

He looked up behind her and then back at Cassandra. It took less than the blink of an eye for him to make a decision. In one flowing motion he was in front of Cassandra, sweeping his arm around the back of her and picking her up. He flung her over his shoulder like a rag doll, then hurried down the stairs.

About to follow, Sairha paused to glance behind, wondering if she would see some creature coming out of the darkness to grab her. Shadows shifted and a metal plate swung down. Sairha's eyes widened, spying something skeletal thin and gray in the dim light for a split second.

"Sairha!" Sven's shout released her from her stupor.

It was now or never, they needed to make a mad dash. Sairha nodded and hurried to catch up. No longer careful about their path, they leapt over the debris and broken steps as fast as they could. The door lay at the bottom of the stairwell, right in their sights. A loud crack echoed with a miserable, metallic whine. The top landing scraped along the damaged walls, filling the air with a white plaster cloud. Sairha's eyes burned trying to look through it, visibility near non-existent, and saw Sven running out of the building with Cassandra.

Another shriek of metal resounded.

Sairha wasn't sure she would make it, even trying as hard as she was. A loud crash was followed by a chunk of stairs falling in front of the door, as she got to the bottom. It looked like the end for her, but she had to try, had to give it her best effort. Reaching for the door frame, Sairha was ready to pull herself over when strong hands latched onto her and yanked her out with force. They fell backwards into the alley, Sven on the bottom with Sairha pulled close, wrapped protectively around her.

A deafening thud left Sairha's ears ringing.

"Does this make me like Indiana Jones now?" she asked, out of breath, the famous boulder-dash scene playing in her head.

Sven let out a hearty laugh. "Sure," he managed to gasp between accelerated breaths. "Absolutely." He gripped her face in his hands and kissed her.

CHAPTER TWO

"Fuck. I cannot believe we made it out of there *alive*."

Sairha gaped at the hotel's former exit after the dust had cleared. Blocked completely by debris, there was no way back in without a wrecking ball. *I could have been crushed,* she thought in awe, heart still racing. She looked down at her shaking hands. She had experienced adrenaline many times before but never like that. It was very different from the rush of the emergency room. This was the thrill of being alive when she probably shouldn't have been. It felt like she could run a marathon, leap from a building, hell, even put on a black bodysuit and crusade around the city. Stop muggers, fight bad guys.

Bad guys. What was that thing I saw? She scanned the building for a view inside. Whatever it was, it had to be dead now. Crushed. A chill slid down her spine.

"Sairha!"

Drawn away from her curiosity, she turned toward the end of the alley where Sven motioned for her to return. Upon reaching him, Sairha assessed the situation. Cassandra sat on the ground with Sven hovering over her, his brows knit together in concern. "So much...darkness...the noises...oh, the noises," Cassandra muttered, rocking back and forth.

Medical training took over and Sairha dropped to her knees, grabbing Cassandra's wrist into her hand, counting the pounding pulse under her fingertips. "She must be going through shock," Sairha sighed, releasing Cassandra's arm. She lifted Cassandra's head up, peering into her blue eyes. "Cas? Cassandra? Can you hear me? You need to breathe, okay? We have to calm you down."

Cassandra remained unresponsive, muttering to herself.

Sven shifted from one foot to the other, his arms crossed at his chest. "Will she be okay?"

Sairha took Cassandra's hands into her own and kept her voice poised, "Cas, can you feel this? Can you feel my hands holding yours?"

Cassandra stopped rocking. Her mumblings slowed. "It's all my fault...the darkness..."

"Nothing was your fault, honey." Sairha rubbed Cassandra's hands in hers. "It was not your fault."

"You—you didn't see it. You couldn't see it."

"See what?" Sven asked, an eagerness in his voice.

Sairha shook her head. It wasn't a good idea to force Cassandra to talk about what was upsetting her, not until she calmed down. Instead she brought Cassandra's hands to her face and flattened them against her cheeks. "Cassandra, focus on the feel of my skin. Focus on my face. Yes, that's right."

Cassandra stroked Sairha's cheeks, eyes refocusing, and her mumbling stopped. After everything that had happened, she sympathized with Cassandra having a mental breakdown, alone in a traumatizing catastrophe. They hadn't known each other long, having met a few months back in a club one lonely night. Cassandra had formed an almost instant attachment to Sairha, dragging Sairha along to parties and events in the small city any chance she got, the local socialite. The same could not be said for Sairha, an introvert through and through. Yet, seeing this woman before her slowly coming back to her senses evoked a tinge of protective tenderness.

The alleyway started to feel stuffy to Sairha, either from the lack of breeze or her shyness at feeling close with Cassandra she couldn't be sure. It was eerie enough how deserted the street beyond was, and Sven pacing like a caged dog beside them did not help. "What should we do from here?" she asked, trying to keep her words steady. Energy ebbing away, she wanted a plan that involved resting somewhere safe, until Cassandra recovered.

Sven stopped, his eyebrows raised like he might have forgotten why he was waiting. "Right. Let's get you both somewhere safe until we know more about what's going on. Whose place is closest?" He moved to the opposite side and pulled Cassandra's arm around his shoulder.

"Cassandra's." Sairha pointed with her chin. "That way."

They paused on the sidewalk, taking in the town square. Once a busy area, it was now deserted, not a soul to be seen. Litter from the surrounding affected buildings lined the gutters. The gray midday light revealed a large crack in the earth that ran the length of the street. Sairha followed its path across the square until it disappeared into the darkness of close together buildings.

"But where are all the people?" Cassandra asked, shuddering.

"Hopefully somewhere safe, somewhere far away from this place." Sairha patted Cassandra on the shoulder, but caught the grim look on Sven's face behind them.

Avoiding being too exposed to the open, they crept along. Once in a while, the sound of the ground crumbling drew their attention to the ominous black crack. Sairha held her breath so often she began to get a headache. "What's that?" she whispered, halting the group when she spied something moving in the shadow. Cassandra's grip tightened around them, a whimper escaping her lips. Sven hissed for her to be quiet and crouched. They watched as something swayed back and forth in the shadows, a low wheezing sound coming from it. Sven backed them as far to a wall as they could go. A blur darted, taking out the swaying figure, disappearing into a dark alley. A guttural shriek filled the air, sending goosebumps down Sairha's whole body. She couldn't tell if the sound was more human or animal; whatever it was, it was cut short. Sven turned them around, picking a different path.

They reached the marketplace where Sairha had enjoyed showing Sven the local artisan wares the day before. A colorful, festive place full of music and wonderful foods, the perfect date spot. Now in shambles. Carts were turned over and smashed, the string of multicolored flags and lights dangling haphazardly on their poles, the air stale. Sairha gulped, trying to fully grasp that this was real. She watched the ground as they picked their way through, afraid to trip, and paused before setting her foot down into an inky puddle. Following with her eyes the thin stream that flowed into it, she grimaced and closed them tight when she saw its source. A body lay crushed under a cart, pale and lifeless. Looking around, she shuddered, finding evidence of two others, their blood mingling, feeding into several smaller puddles.

Her heart pounded in her ears, driving that headache deeper into her skull. If she hadn't been helping Cassandra stay steady, Sairha was sure she would have had a tremor. The last thing her friend needed was to see the gruesome scene, so Sairha remained quiet and hurried with Sven to get them out of there.

Cassandra perked up as they approached her condo a few

blocks later. Sven and Sairha unwrapped her arms from around them, testing her stance. Finding her sturdy enough, Sven left the women and put his ear to the door. "Keys?"

Cassandra shook her head.

"Sorry about this then," he whispered. Shoulder against the door, he slammed into it, using brute force that splintered the frame. The door swung open. Once he deemed it safe, Sven stood aside to allow them in.

Instant relief washed over Sairha stepping into a familiar place. Not much had been disturbed, although a few framed photographs from the wall lay broken on the ground. Nothing compared to the town. Cassandra disappeared down the hallway, Sairha watching to make sure she was okay on her own. Satisfied, she went into the living room, relieved to find the worst damage was several books fallen off their shelves. She couldn't tell if the furniture was misplaced or not, having only visited on the rare occasions of dropping Cassandra off after long nights of drinking. Other than that, Sairha preferred her own shabby apartment and going to work.

She's my only friend here, she thought and plopped down into an armchair. *And my coworkers, I guess.* None of them she had truly bonded with. Nonetheless, she hoped they were safe with their families. "The hospital!" Sairha jumped from her seat, turning for the door. "They need me!"

Sven grabbed her arm. "Sairha, wait a minute. Calm down. Let's sit and talk before we go running off."

"But..."

There was an intensity in his gaze. He wouldn't let her hightail it.

"Okay."

"I'm sure they have it handled without you." He released her and motioned for her to sit again. "It's dangerous out there. You need to wait it out, maybe a few days. And I want to talk to you about something else. Something you won't like."

"Oh." Sairha sat on the edge of her seat, lacing her hands together in her lap. As much as she wanted to dash off to the hospital, Sven had sparked a sinking, terrible feeling inside her. And her body was becoming heavy with exhaustion. "Something I won't like?"

He sighed and glared up at the ceiling, rubbing his hand over his face. "Yes," he eventually said. He took up the chair opposite her, resting his hands on his knees. "This isn't easy for me to say;" he paused, took a deep breath, then blurted the next part out. "I can't stay here. You and Cassandra have a safe setup in her place and are far enough away from the main damage. I'll make sure you have plenty of food stored to tide you over until the military or something of the like comes."

Sairha's jaw dropped, eyebrows rising high in disbelief. "You want to leave us?"

He nodded. "I have to get back to my family. They need me. They'll be worried about me since I stayed behind when my elders left, to hang out with you. It would be best if I left now to get there faster."

"Get there faster? How are you going to get from the outskirts of Sabueso de Oro, Mexico to the middle of nowhere California?!" Sairha could not believe it. The idea sounded insane to her. Her chest tightened.

"Well...walk, I guess. It's not like I can hail a cab or jump in a plane to get home. Maybe another town will have a better way. I've got to try."

"And you just want to leave us? Here? By ourselves?" Sairha's voice rose as she spoke, panicking over his safety. And perhaps from the fear of being left alone. "Can't you just wait it out too?"

"No, I can't, Sairha." He looked away from her. "My grandfather is really old. If anything happens to him and I'm not there... You'll be fine indoors." He turned back, his features a mixture of determination and pleading, a plea for her sympathy, for understanding.

"Ah, that's better." Cassandra came into the room, looking like springtime in jeans and a low cut flowery top, inappropriate for the day they'd had, but casual for her. Mental breakdown be damned. Concern replaced her happy expression when she took in the tense atmosphere of the room. "What the heck is going on out here? Are you two arguing?"

Sairha jumped from her seat and traversed the small area in front of her chair, rubbing at her temples with both hands, thinking before she spoke again. She stopped and pointed at Sven, "He wants to leave. Without us. Just leave us here to fend for ourselves. Who knows what's out there!"

Cassandra's eyes widened and she looked at Sven. "And where the heck are you going?"

Frustrated, Sven stood as well. "I *have* to get home. I can't stay here with you ladies. I need to make sure my family is okay. You'll be fine without me." The look Cassandra gave him implied she was on Sairha's side. He pinched the bridge of nose, visibly stressed.

Sairha plopped down, stunned, a million thoughts running through her head. "You don't think it's like this... Oh god, *my* family." She hadn't even considered it could be global. Her family lived isolated in the California mountains, not that far from Sven's own family, according to him. With communications down, she had no way to contact them. The tightness in her chest squeezed harder.

"Sairha, I'm sure they're fine," Cassandra cooed, moving beside her. She rested her hand on Sairha's shoulder and gave it a reassuring squeeze.

Sairha shook her head. "What if they aren't? What if they

need me too?" She tried to breathe normally, to calm herself down. She wanted to know. She needed to know how her family was. The more she thought about it, the more Sven's plan seemed less crazy. The more it started to make sense. It might take them a while, but it was possible. Maybe it wasn't like this everywhere and they would find communication options or transportation somewhere else. She lifted her head to look him straight in the eye. "I'm coming with you. I need to see if my family is okay, too. You said the night we met that we are from around the same area."

"Me too," Cassandra said. "I'm coming too."

"Cas." Sairha looked up at her, shocked.

"What? I don't have any family here. My mom and dad went on a thirtieth-year anniversary cruise to Europe. Who knows if they'll make it back here. I want to stay with you, Sairha." She squeezed Sairha's arm again and they both looked to Sven for his answer.

Now it was his turn to look stunned, thick eyebrows raised. A few minutes of the silent showdown passed until he shook his head. "Sure, our homes are, like, sixty miles apart or so. But... No, absolutely not. Have you guys even done any long hiking? Survival training? Anything like that? It's too dangerous!"

"If you can do it, we can do it."

"Hey, speak for yourself." Cassandra tried to lighten the mood but it missed its mark with the seriousness of the situation. No one laughed.

"It's safer in numbers, Sven, you can't argue with that. We'd be better off all together. Look," Sairha paused, trying to steady herself mentally. "Just let us come with you up until our paths separate. If we find a working phone or transportation, you can go your own way. Please? Neither of us are prepared for something like this, but we can learn."

There was intensity in Sven's stare as he weighed her words. His breathing seemed to remain even throughout the conversation, much different than Sairha who swore her airway was being blocked. With a sigh, he conceded, "Fine, you guys can come. We're leaving tomorrow, soon as it's light."

Before bed, Sairha helped Cassandra clean up the broken frames. Together, they sat down at her small dining room table, surrounded by a handful of candles, and put the photographs into albums. It was surreal to do something as normal as scrapbooking when they knew the outside world was a disaster scene. It wasn't like Cassandra could take the books with her, but it was comforting to look at pictures of her family with her. She stored the albums in a trunk, with a few other mementos from Cassandra's childhood inside, and locked it. Maybe they'd come back someday. Or maybe it would become a time capsule.

Sairha wanted to talk to Sven, to patch things up between them, however, her pride whispered that she hadn't done anything wrong. Instead, the women retired for the night without another word spoken to him.

"You don't have to come, you know," Sairha said, pulling a borrowed pajama shirt over her head.

Cassandra adjusted her sleepwear, making sure her freshly managed curls were secured in a silk cap, and collapsed onto the bed. "Why wouldn't I come?"

Sairha shrugged, furrowing her brows after a moment's thought. "Well, first off, we don't really know him. You less than me. And I know you said that about your parents, but what if they do come back soon? What if this gets fixed tomorrow?"

Her friend mulled over the topic, nibbling on her bottom lip as she did. "He saved my life. And you trust him. So..." Cassandra smirked. "That means I do, too. My parents? Sairha, you know they pay for this place? I haven't had to really hold down a job ever because they give me everything I need. This is one thing they never gave me; time together. I don't want to be alone, Sairha...not again. And if this is fixed tomorrow, then we'll stay here and help rebuild the town or something humanitarian like that. But, as far as I'm concerned, you are my family now and I'd follow you through the desert, over the hills, and through the woods."

Sairha left it at that, dumbfounded by how easily Cassandra came to that conclusion. Maybe it was natural to want to remain close to the person, or people, who had saved your life. Maybe that's why she, also, trusted Sven enough to go on a journey together. Tucking herself into bed beside Cassandra, she leaned over and blew out the candle.

Hours passed and Sairha's thoughts were still running wild on whether it had been selfish to demand tagging along with Sven. Their families lived close, so it made sense to stay together. She was determined to not be a burden for him, but an asset. There wasn't going to be anyone telling her to hurry up or stop complaining. If Cassandra held them back, Sairha would help pick up her friend's slack too. Cassandra was slender, but also in shape. She doubted she would slow anyone down.

Sighing, she rolled over to stare at the ceiling. Her feelings about him were confusing. *Get a grip, girl,* she scolded herself. She wanted to be in his arms, to feel his chest rising and falling as they slept, to smell the ginger and earth in his long black hair. She kept reminding herself that she hardly knew the guy, and yet, there she was, unable to stop thinking about him. Even when she'd been so mad at him for wanting to leave. All kinds of emotions stirred inside her from just thinking his name. He probably didn't feel the same way.

Frustrated with the path her train-of-thought was going down, Sairha kicked her blanket off. *I am not weak. I do not depend on any man. And I am not obsessed.* A new mantra to reason with herself. *It was just a fling, a quick hookup. Who cares if he is charming? Handsome? A good person? He doesn't know me. I don't know him. This is ridiculous... I'll never get any sleep at this rate. I need some fresh air.*

Careful to not disturb Cassandra, Sairha got out of bed and stole away down the hallway. Maybe with the power gone she would see more stars than usual. It was one of the things she missed most about her rural mountain home. A clear, velvet blue sky with twinkling diamonds, more than the eye could see. She'd see it there again soon enough.

As hard as it was, she avoided looking over at the couch while quietly passing the living room. She wasn't sure she could resist going to Sven, if she caught a glimpse of him sleeping there alone.

Nearing the small kitchen, something felt off. A warm breeze flowed through the dining room, and Sairha proceeded with caution, hands clasped to her chest. Another gentle gust of wind blew the curtains back and forth. The patio door was ajar. Perhaps, she should have turned back and gotten Sven, or grabbed some sort of appliance turned weapon, but her curiosity was in control of her body, and she headed to the door. Her heart jumped into her throat, a dark figure stood at the railing. Palms clammy and nerves shot, Sairha cleared her throat. He turned around.

"Sven," Sairha breathed out in relief.

A pale crescent moon illuminated the surprise on Sven's face. "What are you doing up?"

Stepping outside, foolishness and uncertainty swirled

inside her. A sudden chill crept along her flesh, despite the warmth of the night air, and she rubbed her bare arms. Maybe it was the atmosphere between them that left her shivering. "I couldn't sleep," she confessed. "I came out for some fresh air, saw the door open, and..." Embarrassed that she had been spooked, she didn't finish the sentence.

His chuckle was low as he reached out for her, encasing her inside his arms when she neared. The heat that came off his chest calmed Sairha instantly, and a blush tinted her cheeks at being so intimate. Was he not mad about earlier? Or maybe he was showing pity for how pathetic she had made herself seem in that desperate argument. He snuggled against her and her racing thoughts fell silent. He let out a deep exhale and she allowed herself to gaze skyward, to stop wondering what-ifs.

It was a clear night, though the stars seemed distant and dim. They were still there, that's what mattered. A comforting sign of normalcy after the crazy, grey day.

"You are one of the most determined women I have ever met," he whispered. Then added, with a grin in his tone, "Other than Cassandra when she's preying on business men."

Sairha laughed. "Thanks, I think? I guess that's a pretty big compliment, for people who know her, that is. Hey, listen—"

"Shhh." He drew her even closer, his cheek brushing hers.

Her heart skipped a beat. Again, she wondered how something so new could feel so right. But she had to say something to him, to make up for earlier, and to ease her restless soul.

"I want you to know that...I'm not...I mean, it's not because of...I would want to go home to my family regardless of having ever met you. I'm not incapable nor a weak minded person."

Shit, that did not come out right, she stressed.

Sven tensed but didn't make any effort to pull away, to her relief. A star in the distance twinkled, as if trying to reassure her that it was alright.

"I know," he said after a while. "I can tell you truly love your family, and, in the heat of our discussion earlier, I realized how determined you were to get to them. It was a reflection of how I felt, am feeling inside, about my own family."

Sairha was speechless. The fact that he could acknowledge and relate to how she felt, that he had actually agreed to take them because of those feelings and not just because she was a whiny brat, amazed her. She was thankful above all else and leaned back against him in contentment. Perhaps she could get used to this, to her feelings for him, to being in his arms. Those butterflies would surely calm over time. Although, she hoped not.

"We've got a long, hard road ahead of us," Sven whispered.

Sairha froze. The pressure and heat of his lips on her neck, as his arms slinked lower down her waist, sent thrills throughout her whole being.

"We should probably rest up," he mumbled.

Goosebumps ran along her flesh when his thumbs stroked the bare skin between her shirt and pants. He kissed along her neck, suggesting that he had other ideas than actually resting. She couldn't help but melt against him.

"Yeah, rest," she breathed out. She fought hard to keep a moan back as the woman inside responded to the man against her. He turned her around. Sairha lifted her arms around his neck, tilting her head up. Eyes closing out the surrounding night, she pressed her lips to his.

CHAPTER THREE

Regardless of how tiny Cassandra's couch was, Sairha woke up well rested and snuggled in close to Sven. She took a moment to admire him and smiled at how peaceful he looked while sleeping, despite being squished between her and the couch. And though she felt a tad guilty about it, she awakened him with a soft kiss, before getting up to prepare for their journey.

They enjoyed a final hot meal, the 'Last Breakfast' Cassandra called it, thanks to a match and her stove being gas powered. Everyone had laughed at the joke, but as they ate migas, a fried tortilla and egg scramble, with a side of chorizo, a quiet calm fell over them. Perhaps savoring the warmth in their own solitude. Once done, Cassandra started loading her dishwasher. Sven and Sairha stared at her in silent amusement.

"What?" she asked, annoyed and defensive when she noticed them. "I want this place to look somewhat clean. Just in case someone else wants to pop-a-squat here. Or you know, when I return. If I do."

Sairha tried to smile with reassurance, but wasn't sure it

came through. A tiny voice inside warned that their journey was a one-way ticket. She shook it aside, hoping that once they got out of the area, the rest of the world would still be okay. They could call home, check in with their families, and Cassandra and her could take a plane home. Side-eyeing Cassandra, she briefly wondered how the party girl would enjoy the open expanse of her rural home.

"What's first?" Cassandra clapped her hands together, rejoining Sven and Sairha.

"Right, first we need to get supplies," Sven said, breaking his long silence.

"And I'd like to stop by the hospital, make sure everything is being handled, and tell them I'm leaving." Sairha stood up, ready to face the new adventure. "There's a decent store with basic necessities on the way."

Cassandra nodded, grabbed her cup of tea, and left the dining room. Once she was out of sight, Sairha turned to Sven, concerned about his pensive mood. "You alright? You've been awfully quiet."

"Have I? I just have a lot on my mind." He ran a hand through his hair, taking a deep breath with the motion.

"Anything you want to talk about?" She worried he was already regretting agreeing to take them.

He glanced at her, before wrapping his hair into a tight low ponytail. "Just...thinking about the road ahead. Keeping you two safe."

"Hey, I trust you." She patted his arm and smiled, though he did not return it.

SHROUDED IN DARKNESS, the store loomed like an ominous ode to the disaster of the day before. No movement anywhere. The outdoor lights were blown out and a 'Buy One, Get One' sign waved back and forth on its string, like a tornado had blown through. All that was missing was a tumbleweed.

"It looks deserted. I guess we could just...leave money on the counter?" Sairha glanced left and right around the surrounding area. The few remaining cars in the lot, covered in dirt but otherwise untouched, she guessed had been there since before the earthquake. Where were their owners?

"Let me go first. I'll try and find a light." Sven jogged ahead to the door.

"But how will you find anything past the window light?"

He turned and grinned as he tapped his nose, then winked before he slipped inside, disappearing from view.

"How did you end up with a guy like him?" Cassandra asked.

"I was wondering that myself," Sairha replied, staring into the store after him. The memory of when they met played out in her mind like a whirlwind romance movie.

Two days earlier, Cassandra had pleaded with Sairha to use her days off to go out. Cassandra the socialite, ever on the prowl for good-looking out-of-towners. Her favorite hunting grounds were public speaking events, full of "tasty treats in suits". Feeling homesick, Sairha tagged along despite preferring the solitude of her small apartment. When she locked eyes with the handsome speaker on stage it was like a magnetic pull summoning her to him, but she did not follow it. The moment was gone as soon as it had happened. She became another face in the crowd and Cassandra convinced her to grab drinks at a bar.

Later that night, Sairha had bumped into a man at the bar, spilling their drinks, and that was how she physically ran into the handsome speaker, Sven. They bonded over being from the California mountains, barely an hour's drive from each other. Sven talked about his work speaking on equality in small communities and traveling with his elders. She told him about needing a change of scenery, the hospital training, and ultimately feeling burnt out. His attentiveness to their conversation had made her feel safe and heard. Caution to the wind, she had allowed herself to be swept away by his charm, even if it was going to be a one night fling.

Watching him walk into potential danger now made her feel sort of funny inside, worried, forcing her to acknowledge that she liked him. A lot more than just a hookup. Perhaps it was kismet, considering what they had been through.

"Hey." Cassandra shifted her weight from one foot to the other, fidgeting. "Listen, Sairha. I never talked about...back in the hotel—"

"Shhhh. Wait."

A loud crash echoed through the store. Sairha's heart jumped in her throat and she prepared herself for a fight. Against what, she wasn't sure. Something black and figureless? An animal? A human? A flash of what she saw in the hotel came to mind, something she had blocked out completely until then. Something mysterious. It was thankfully only Sven that appeared in the doorway, setting her at ease.

Motioning them in, his smile dazzled in the light of a white candle that he held to illuminate the way. "Found an emergency kit," he said, his tone overly cheerful.

"What was that loud crash? Are you okay?" Sairha looked him over when she walked past to get inside, seeing no cuts or scrapes.

He shrugged and led the way down an aisle. "Got caught on something. All good."

He seemed off, weird, like his actions were forced. But then again, she was starting to internally freak out, so maybe he was too and trying to overcompensate. Sairha let it go. It wasn't like she knew him well, or for very long, to judge how he acted. They were in a new setting, everyone's nerves had to be shot like hers, right?

"I've never seen this place so empty. It's kind of eerie," Cassandra whispered.

"Me either, and I've been here in the dead of night after a hospital shift." Sairha glanced at the empty cash registers nearby.

Tiptoeing around broken packaging, empty boxes, and tossed aside items, they made their way through already looted aisles. Cassandra bent down and picked up a crumpled wad of money. "Um. What are we looking for?"

"Well, since electronics seem to be dead," Sairha said, recounting what they knew had happened so far, before sighing. "I guess flashlights and anything that requires batteries would be useless."

"Mostly lightweight things. All the matches and lighters you can find," Sven offered.

"Candles, right. As for food, canned stuff is our best bet... Unfortunately." As much as she hated its lack of nutritional value, canned food was preserved to last in situations as dire as theirs seemed. Who knew when they'd get another fresh bunch of broccoli or handful of green beans.

"Yeah, but cans are heavy!" Cassandra countered, grabbing a box from the floor. "How about these?"

Sven and Sairha both stopped to look at her, a box of yellow mini cream-filled cakes in her hands. The very idea brought out quiet laughter from both.

"How many books and television shows joked that these would survive the apocalypse? They knew what was up." Despite defending herself to their laughter, Cassandra had a large, goofy grin on her face as she wiggled her eyebrows.

"Leave it to you, Cassandra, to call upon fiction for survival guidelines." Sairha shook her head.

"All fiction is based on some level of facts, Sairha," Cassandra retorted.

"Let's go this way." Sven moved towards another aisle, stopped halfway, and inspected something.

Two hiking packs came into view when they arrived and Sven grabbed a khaki colored one. "This one looks like it's had a tough day, but I think we could just tie the strap off and it should hold." He handed Sairha a green pack and started to fix the broken strap on the khaki bag by candlelight.

Cassandra motioned for her to put the boxed cakes inside. Sairha smiled and opened one of the side pockets, "Put them in here, so they'll be safe from squishing. We'll have to pack the heavier stuff in the center."

"Come on, let's go find those cans and then some candles." Sven slung the fixed pack over one shoulder. He picked his candle up and led them past dark aisles, until they found the canned food. They looked through the cans, squinting in the dim light, searching out ones with the longest expiration dates.

Sairha noticed Cassandra being picky with her selection. "You'll be thankful for variety when you get tired of eating only green beans or corn every day, Cas." Sairha made a show of putting some canned beans into her bag, also her least favorite. The hairs on her neck rose, the feeling of someone watching her. She glanced behind and found Sven with a thoughtful expression. "What?" she whispered.

He shook his head with a soft smile. "Nothing. You just surprise me."

She raised an eyebrow in question, but he only shrugged.

"Hey, what about cereal? It's lightweight. Marshmallow sugary things, here I come!" Cassandra picked up the candle and, like a true junk food expert, navigated the group to the dry goods aisle with no trouble at all. Picking out her favorites put a smile on her face as she started discarding their boxes.

Sairha used the opportunity to pull Sven aside. "Hey, how are you doing? Are you okay?"

His face scrunched up in confusion. "What do you mean? Of course I am okay."

"I don't know. I haven't known you for long, but..."

"But what?" He sounded annoyed.

"We've been through a lot in the last twenty-four hours. It's normal to be a little...off or anxious."

"Sairha." Sven's tone was flat.

She waited in silence, perplexed she might have offended him, while all he did was stare at her. The sound of Cassandra ripping open boxes echoed around them. *I shouldn't have said anything*, she fretted, *mental health is such a personal thing.*

He sighed, then let out a low chuckle. "You're very observant. It has been stressful. But, it will all work out fine."

"Alright," she said slowly. That wasn't the answer she had expected. And it did not make her feel any better, but maybe he'd open up later, when they were somewhere they felt safe. "Come on, Cassandra. Let's find some candles now." She took the backpack from Cassandra, then headed to the next aisle.

The lighting area was more of a wreck than the rest of the store. All forms of light source had been looted. Flashlights, lanterns, batteries. Everything. Sairha picked up an empty lighter packet. Dismay with a touch of hopelessness crept in.

Sven came up beside her. "Guess I was lucky when I found this emergency light. Someone must have dropped it in their hurry."

"Well, now what are we going to do?" Cassandra huffed.

Sairha tapped her foot, searching for a solution. They

couldn't stop at all of the small shops in hopes of finding a candle or two.

"God, this place is a wreck." Cassandra kicked some trash away from her feet.

God?

"Prayer candles," Sairha muttered, a forgotten memory triggering an idea.

Sven rolled his eyes. "You really think prayer will help us now?"

"Not prayers. Prayer candles. Those big, long candles they light in churches, with saints on them? My mom used to get the blank ones to keep around the house for power shortages. We live out in the middle of nowhere so it happens often. They last forever." Sairha set off towards the home decor area as she spoke. "They might be a little heavy but it's better than nothing. And we won't need as many."

Sure enough, there were a handful left. Tall candles sitting on the very bottom of a shelf, unnoticeable if you weren't looking for them. Beside those were boxes of long matches. Dust covered, forgotten. They grabbed a few, found some water bottles, and left the store. Outside, Sven paused beside a car and pulled out a map.

"You can read that thing?" Cassandra peered over his shoulder.

"Yeah, I can. My grandfather taught me." He cleared his throat and leaned over the map. Producing a pen from his backpack, he traced a route to the border. Both women bent closer beside him. "It shouldn't be too hard, or long, for us to get here. Call it a hunch, but I don't think we'll have the usual difficulties at the border."

"The usual difficulties?" they said in unison.

Sven glanced up at them, then let out a sigh as he gestured

with his hands. "There might be...new difficulties there awaiting us. We should just be prepared."

"Like what, wild animals?" Cassandra grimaced.

Sairha shuddered, thinking about that dark creature she had seen, lurking, and that body that had been tackled into the shadows. She stole a glance at Sven and wondered if he had seen the mystery creatures too. He caught her, perhaps feeling her gaze upon him, and gave her another dazzling smile.

"Nothing we can't handle, I'm sure," he said with enough confidence to put both of them at ease.

Sairha considered speaking up, but she wasn't even sure exactly what she had seen. Maybe it was just a maned wolf or a felidae that had wandered into the city after the earthquake. No, she wasn't going to make Sven already regret choosing to take them along. For the time being, she'd keep that to herself, not wanting to sound crazy.

THE SUN BEAT down on them without mercy as they walked, the brightness painting the scenery in solemn shades of grey. Soaked in sweat, they were too overheated to talk. Cassandra fell behind Sairha, stifling grunts and moans. Sairha could tell that she was trying her best but Cassandra was quickly spent. Sairha was not faring much better, finding each foot step harder and heavier to pick up.

When the hospital came into view, Sairha's heart leapt at the familiar building and she headed toward it with renewed energy. As they got closer, however, it felt all wrong. There weren't any people coming or going, no ambulances with a team rushing someone in, or nurses on the side of the building having a quick smoke. It was calm, quiet.

"Maybe we should...skip this place?" Cassandra whispered, standing beside Sairha.

"I agree." Sven's brows furrowed downward, glaring at the building. "Let's push past it, Sairha."

Sairha scrunched up her face, irritated with their suggestions, and moved past them for the wide open doors. A foul stench of rot, tinged with metallic notes wafted out and forced Sairha to cover her face. "I have to go inside," she declared before the other two could stop her. The short walk to the door had her heart pounding at what she might find. She so desperately wanted this place to be safe, to be the pillar of hope she knew it to be, a place of healing. *Could I even leave if they need me, though?* she weighed, before entering. Blackness surrounded her, in sight and sound.

There was no one.

The front desk sat empty, papers and pamphlets littered around. And blood. So. Much. Blood. Sairha closed her eyes, fighting back the tears that threatened to come, and turned away. *What happened here? Why? All these people, the staff...* She opened her eyes to the lobby and gasped, taking an involuntary step away. Chairs lay in splintered pieces around the room, clothes and bedding ripped to shreds, all painted in dry blood. A massacre had happened there. This was more than an earthquake.

"Sairha! C'mon! Please, it's creepy out here!"

Cassandra's whining was the motivation she needed to leave. Sairha hissed, something inside her afraid of the silence being broken. Waiting a moment to see if anything came or called out, if there were people still alive. She hoped they were locked up tight. Safe. She did not want to go farther in, to see more lives lost to whatever had done this. Nothing happened and she backed up towards the door, unable to turn away from the scene.

"Are you okay?" Sven whispered to her once she was outside.

"I..." Sairha started, then shook her head, fighting the tears again. "I need some time to process." Her gaze fell on an ambulance haphazardly parked in the drive. Sairha went to it, wrenched open the door, and reached under a seat. A red first-aid kit was her prize and she shoved it into the backpack. They might need it sooner or later.

They left the hospital, but try as she might, Sairha struggled to also leave the visions of carnage behind.

STRANGE SHADOWS STRETCHED across the new town they entered as the sun set. Not a single light in a window nor person to be seen. Sombering their moods to see yet another place affected. Just like the last two towns they had walked through. The silence gave Sairha too much time in her own head. Four days ago she had been a nurse, studying abroad to escape her small hometown, suffering a mild mental burnout, a loner with one single friend in the area. Everything was normal, if not dull, until she had met Sven and said 'what the hell' to a little romantic fling. When they locked eyes, it could not have lasted much longer than a few seconds. The intensity of it had been so strong, so connected, it awoke something up in her. Something that had been hidden away while she focused on her career. And yet, it was just a moment, just one glimpse.

But who is Sven really...

It seemed easy for him to take the lead at the hotel and he had not shown an ounce of uncertainty when needing to make quick decisions. He was not military trained, but his survival skills seemed expert. A natural born leader, even in the face of disaster. A shiver ran down her spine when she recalled the earthquake that had started this new adventure together, if she could even call it an adventure.

"*Oof.*"

"Sshhhh."

She had collided into Sven. He tensed, squaring his shoulders, and crouched down. Looking ahead of them, his expression tightened. Sairha motioned back to Cassandra to stay quiet as she approached. When she gazed across, where his eyes were focused, she was surprised to find they had reached the border control.

Often full of people, coming and going in their cars and RVs, the checkpoint station was an empty ghost town. Usually a commotion was going on, now eerily quiet. Except... There was a faint clicking noise, if they listened hard enough. Like nails tapping on metal. Rhythmic, it echoed off the walls of the lone building.

Her heart sped up as she listened, igniting her imagination to create terrible images: a shadow monster, zombie-like human, or a large, wild animal. She dared not speak to ask what it was, afraid to give away their location, and instead placed her hand on the back of Sven's shoulder. Strong heat radiated off of him, she had never felt his muscles so taut.

The tapping noise stopped. A screech like a dying animal broke the silence.

Grabbing them both by their wrists, he pulled them away as quick as he could. Sairha was a fast walker but had trouble keeping up with Sven. The pace was too fast. In an agonizing second, her ankle betrayed her, rolling, and sent a sharp pain shooting up her leg. The pain was swiftly gone, but there was a soreness any time she put weight on it, as they hurried back towards the outskirts.

Hearts pounding, they locked themselves inside an abandoned tiny home they had found left wide open. Sairha attempted to catch her breath while Sven finished securing the door. After it had been calm and quiet for a while, she dared to test weight on her ankle and cried out. Regretting it instantly, she fell back onto the couch.

Sven's attention snapped to her, concern washing over his features. Crossing the distance between them, he knelt down by her legs and gingerly lifted the ankle she was glaring at. "What happened?"

"I rolled it. It's fine, really. Just sore from running on it right away." Sairha pulled her leg away from his grip, irritated at both the pain and being babied.

Eyebrows knitting together, he grasped her leg again. He narrowed his eyes at her, a silent dare to try and pull away again, as he removed her boot to massage the ankle. "Don't be stubborn," he said softly.

"Why did we rush away anyhow? What was it? A wild animal?" Cassandra asked.

"Don't know. But I didn't like being out in the open, so close to nightfall. How's that feeling?" He rubbed above Sairha's ankle with both hands, applying equal pressure.

"Good," she conceded and closed her eyes. The tender way his hands moved up her calf released the tension in the muscle, along with her irritation. She couldn't help the relaxed smile that sprung up. *He answered Cassandra pretty fast,* Sairha thought absentmindedly. *Like he didn't want to talk about it.*

Cassandra watched them for a while before she made a show of reaching up in a stretch, a small groan emitting out of her as she did. "I don't know about you guys but I am completely beat. Guessing... we'll be continuing in the morning?" She pointedly looked at Sven, a clear hint at staying there for the night. And that she was ready to get away from the two of them.

Sairha peeked open an eye, watching Sven's reaction when he thought she wasn't looking.

He nodded, momentarily pausing his massage, with a smile that seemed forced. "Yeah, that's a good idea. We can stay here for the evening. Sairha needs to rest before we start this...journey. Why don't you both sleep while I keep watch?"

"You don't need to tell me twice." Cassandra yawned and headed down the small hallway, clearly eager to get out of the room. She walked like she owned the place and wasn't a complete stranger in someone else's home. "Later, lovebirds."

After a moment, Sven turned his attention back to Sairha. That was it. There would be no pleading her case to keep going. They hadn't found a working car or phone. No people. Here was a man she was blindly following, entrusting him to get, not only herself, but also Cassandra, safely to her family. If her family was still alive. She wouldn't think of that, that what-if. Instead she reflected again on how little she actually knew about Sven. Could she really trust him? It was too late to turn back now, she had to trust him. She wanted to.

He caught her staring and smiled at her. Different from the forced one a second ago. It was soft and genuine, catching Sairha off guard. Her heart flipped. Slow, and a little shaky, she reached out and grasped a freed strand of his long, black hair. It felt like silk, as it slid away, and she moved her hand down to caress his cheek. A short caress like that warmed her from fingertips to palm. He was always so warm to the touch.

"How's your ankle now?" he whispered.

Letting her mixed thoughts rest, she gave her foot a wiggle. "Much better now. Aren't I supposed to be the healthcare provider here?"

He laughed. "But when the healthcare provider needs attention, who takes care of her?"

"You got me there."

He grinned still, though more tenderly, and leaned up to push some of her hair away. His thumb caressed her cheek and he moved in closer, his lips inches from hers.

Did he just steal my caressing-hair-swoop move? Her breath caught in her chest as he landed a subtle kiss.

"Tomorrow I'm going to start teaching you guys how to survive in this new environment."

"Wha—*woah!*"

With little effort, Sven slid his hands under her and lifted her from the couch. Her arms went tight around his neck automatically, terrified of falling, despite how strong he felt. The surprise subsided, and it dawned on her that he intended to put her into bed. It was a smart move on his end, since she would have fought to stay awake with him, pestering him with questions about himself and what he meant about teaching them. Now that opportunity was gone and she resigned herself to thinking teaching them survival skills just meant less stress for him, so that they could contribute rather than be hindrances.

He was careful when he laid her down beside Cassandra in the bed, who was in a deep slumber by the sound of her breathing. She noticed a small book on the night stand and picked it up. "What book is it?" he asked quietly, amused.

"Shakespeare," she replied, opening it to the red ribbon placeholder. *"If we shadows have offended, think but this, and all is mended. That you have but slumber'd here, while these visions did appear."*

"Fitting." Sven shook his head, then gave her a goodnight kiss on the forehead before he turned to leave.

"Sven," she called softly, feeling like a little kid asking for one more story. "Do you think the world will ever be back to normal?"

He paused in the doorway, thinking, and gave her a half smile. "Possibly."

But his eyes conveyed something different; *probably not.*

The night air was crisp, refreshing compared to the stuffy house. A slight breeze swept the last of the day's heat away. A lone figure stole across the land, his foot falls silent, his breathing shallow. A level of stealth that was second nature to him. Sven had patiently waited for the women to fall asleep before he had left the small home. It took a little longer than he had hoped. Sairha had been restless, tossing and turning. Either fighting to get comfortable or something heavy on her mind. The latter he assumed, given their situation. However much he wanted to go in and reassure her, put her at ease, there was a more pressing matter at hand. The women would be okay in there by themselves, would not even notice he was gone, and he would get what needed to be done *done.*

The checkpoint building was easy to get back to. He hid behind an abandoned car, peering over, searching. It would be near impossible to see the creature in the dimness of the night, but, with luck, Sven caught the slightest movement in a window. A shadow that didn't quite match its surroundings. Never in his life had he thought he would have to deal with one of those and alone, no less.

He crept closer and put his back to the wall, listening; breath shaky, his insides twisted in knots. A horrible stench forced him to lift his hand over his nose and mouth.

Now or never.

Sven straightened his shoulders and took a swift turn into the building, his fist balled tight until the knuckles were white. It had to be done. This was the sort of thing he was afraid would slow him down, having to protect the women. But when she smiled at him, with those eyes colored like the sweetest honey, that one look made it worth the hassle. He both hated and loved how weak she made him feel.

A low growl grew in depth, followed by a resounding clamor of metal and glass breaking, echoing in the night. A fight had started.

CHAPTER FOUR

Sairha stretched her sore muscles as she walked the narrow hallway, leaving Cassandra to sleep in. Dust outlines marked where old photos had hung, probably for years, now a blank spot left behind. She hoped the former tenants had found somewhere safe to evacuate to. When she reached the living room, she expected to see Sven asleep on the couch yet found the room empty. Panic crept inside her.

Don't freak out, she scolded herself. *He did not abandon you.*

A noise in the kitchen made her jump. It could be Sven, or it could be someone *or something* that broke in. She recalled how Sven had checked the houses before they had gone inside. As quietly as she could, Sairha leaned against the wall, before the kitchen entry, and peeked over. A quick scan, then a huge smile lit up her face when Sven straightened from looking in a bottom drawer. His long hair dangled to-and-fro, freely down his back, as he moved around. For a brief second, she wanted to ask if she could brush it for him.

Sven turned and caught her staring. "Hey! Good morning."

Sairha smiled to hide her blush. "Morning. Did I scare

you?"

He let out a small laugh but looked exhausted, like he had done more than see a long night of standing watch. "It will take a lot more than you sneaking about in the morning to scare me."

"Did you sleep at all?" she asked, concerned.

A brow raised and there was a twinkle of amusement in Sven's eyes at her question. Nodding, he lifted a box and popped open the lid to show her its contents. "I found donuts!"

Sairha's stomach growled in response.

Even though they were a little stale, the donuts were a nice surprise along with getting to sleep in. Assuming this would be the last time they slept in a bed for a while or got anything other than the food they had packed, she enjoyed the donuts slowly, sitting at the breakfast bar, appreciating every sugary bite. The desert stretch came next since there was no transportation to be found. Instead of worrying about that, she relaxed into her chair and talked with Sven who stood across from her. A serene moment, just the two of them.

Despite the exhausted, rugged look he wore, Sven was in a cheerful mood, and it was contagious. He made light hearted jokes and even talked about situations he had gotten into as a kid.

"Sounds like you were a bit of a troublemaker," Sairha teased as she pulled apart a glazed knot donut. Her favorite. It had been a real treat to see one hiding at the back of the box.

"Me? Naaah," he said lazily, then smirked. "Well, I guess if you compare me to my little brother. Then, yeah. I was the troublemaker out of us two."

"You have a little brother?" Sairha tried not to sound too excited, not wanting to scare him off the subject. He hadn't talked in-depth about his family, only a handful of comments about working with, and getting back to, them.

"Yep, a grandpa, mom and dad, a little brother. Aunts and uncles, a handful of *cousins*."

Sairha noted the odd underlying tone when he said cousins and lifted an eyebrow in question.

"More like extra brothers and sisters. Ones you never asked for but they're still family so you gotta love them." He shrugged.

A desire to see what *that* version of Sven was like sparked inside her. Carefree and surrounded by happy family members, rather than the disaster survival versions of themselves they were thrust into. Knowing she might regret it later, Sairha decided to say something anyway. "I'd like to meet your family someday. If they are anything like you, I bet it would be a good time."

Sven's expression was blank as he nodded. "Yeah, maybe someday."

He keeps his home life so carefully guarded. Sairha smiled politely, then thought to offer a little insight into her own. "I have a sister named Alison. She's younger than me but try telling her that. Ever since she could walk, she wanted to be like me. Practically my shadow. Pretty sure she gave my mom premature gray hair. Alison is always getting into trouble." She let out a soft chuckle, sadness edging its way in. "She took it the hardest when I announced I got the internship at the hospital. We had a huge falling out the month before I left, and we never really resolved it. I've been sending her letters and little gifts, but…" The sentence trailed off and Sairha swallowed back the bitter memories normally kept locked away. Sven laid his hand over hers, the gesture comforting and a welcomed distraction. A deep breath freed her of the past regret, and she gave him a small smile. "That's why I also need to get back home. To make amends."

"Hey, how come no one woke me? And for *donuts*?"

Cassandra stood in the entryway, wearing a groggy expression with wild bed head curls. They chuckled, and Sven pulled his hand away, their peaceful bonding moment over. Sairha pushed the box towards Cassandra. "Eat up, sleepyhead."

Cassandra let out a happy squeal and sat down at the breakfast counter, fingers wiggling as she scanned the options. In no time flat, the woman had devoured one donut after another, and sat back with a content expression. "What I wouldn't give for some coffee right now. Those were so good, but that staleness will haunt my mouth forever. What's the plan? I thought we were early birds on the run."

Sven pointed at both of them. "You did a lot of walking yesterday. In some intense heat. There's potential yet for you two to become decent long distance hikers."

Cassandra snorted, nudging Sairha with her elbow.

"We told you we could handle it." Sairha's tone dripped with pride. Yesterday was only the beginning, they had managed to keep pace and only needed one break. Hopefully they could continue to surprise Sven and be useful.

"Now that breakfast is over." Sven smirked, clapping his hands together. "Your training starts today."

"*Training*?" Cassandra asked, alarmed. "What training?"

"First, reading maps." Coming around to Sairha's side, Sven unfolded the large map and smoothed it out over the breakfast bar. "You see this spot? This is where we are and over here—" His fingers danced along the print as both women leaned in for a better view, "—is where we are heading."

"Well, fuck," Cassandra huffed. "That's kinda far."

It hadn't taken them long to get ready and out the door since they never unpacked. A fresh change of clothes, lace up the boots, and they were set for another day. Sven led them towards the checkpoint area again, less cautiously this time. Sairha noted the contrast in his demeanor as they neared, the subtle way his body carried less tension.

Cassandra, on the other hand, made a quick grab at Sairha's arm, chewing on her bottom lip as her eyes darted everywhere and nowhere. "Do you think the wild animal or whatever is still in there?" Her grip on Sairha tightened.

Sven opened his mouth to reply, seemed to think better of it, and instead pulled Cassandra closer to him. "Let's listen," he whispered. Together they crouched behind the front end of a dusty, black sedan. Sairha knelt on the other side of Sven. He put his hand on Cassandra's shoulder, his gaze stern but patient. "You need to slow your breathing down. Your heart and breath must be calm. Take deep breaths in through your nose. Out through your mouth."

The three of them quieted, one by one, as they focused on their breathing, the 'calming of their hearts'. Some sort of instinct inside made Sairha close her eyes. Her heart began to feel light in her chest, yet she was more aware of it than she had ever been before. She wasn't sure, but she thought she heard something. A gentle scratching. Or scraping.

Sand blowing on the wind.

It worked, she mused, taking a peek. A small breeze moved the dirt in tiny swirls near her feet. Determined, she concentrated harder, unclouding her mind of its excitement at this new skill.

Drip. Drip. Drip.

Tilting her head towards the sound, Sairha snuck a glance at Sven. Their eyes met. "Do you hea—"

"I don't hear anything. Let's go." Sven sprang up and adjusted the pack on his shoulders.

"I didn't either," Cassandra sighed irritably, standing as

well. "I don't think that breathing stuff really works. Maybe if there was actually something to hear. Or if you're some sort of superfreak with superfreak hearing."

Before Sairha could reply or argue that she had heard something, the other two were already walking away from the beat up car. Sairha shrugged off the bitter feeling of being ignored. *Sounded like something dripping into a puddle.* The more she thought about it, the more positive she was. It was a familiar sound. *I remember now.*

A hospital scene flashed in her mind. A limp hand hanging past a surgical sheet, red trailing down the fingers, dripping into a pool on the floor. The metallic smell. And the shouts that used to ring in her ears, both human and machine. The sounds of someone dying.

Sairha shook free of the morbid recollection and jogged to catch up. She decided to let it go, maybe she had only imagined it, or maybe she was paranoid. Suffering post-traumatic stress. Even before the earthquake, she had nightmares about the emergency room. She wasn't a 'super freak', maybe that hearing technique did or did not work. The only way to know was to practice it more, to be sure she was doing it right.

It was probably nothing...

Lips cracked and aching, Sairha ran her tongue along them, though it felt like sandpaper as well. Not even the gulp of water they had recently rationed helped. It had been four days since they had left the border town, four days of the same view on either side. Hot, desert sand, the sun so bright colors blurred into shades of grays. Her throat clenched up, spotting the water bottle in Sven's backpack ahead of her. It was hard to maintain a steady march while she was that parched.

Cassandra grumbling behind her did not help. Irritable beyond reason, Sairha had to fight herself to keep from snapping at her friend.

If Sven is even an ounce as exasperated as I am, he's doing a fantastic job of hiding it, she thought, jealous of his perseverance. *What was I thinking that I could do this? No turning back now.*

"Ugh, do you think we'll find a gas station or something soon? I am so thirsty," Cassandra whined, dragging her feet along the sand, leaving a cloud of dust behind her.

Sairha sighed, then wished she hadn't. The action made her throat worse and when she breathed in, her nostrils stung. Ignoring it was near impossible.

Sven turned his head to glance back as he spoke, sweat glistening down his temples. "I think we'll find one eventually today, according to the map. But, for now, the less talking the less dry your mouth will seem."

Sairha snorted.

Cassandra made a low complaint under her breath, about water and rude boyfriends.

All thoughts stopped, for that comment threw Sairha for a loop. *Boyfriend.* Her ears tingled from embarrassment at the comment, hoping he hadn't heard it. She wasn't sure what they were. They hadn't known each other long and it wasn't like he had officially asked her either. Yet, they did just go through a life changing event together, and he still acted interested in her romantically. And the feeling was very mutual. Thinking about it made her confused, and she was too hot and tired to be confused. She needed a break to clear her mind. "There isn't a lot around here, but a breather would be good for us."

There was a tall cactus, a short walk ahead, offering minimal but much needed relief from the sun.

"Better than nothing." Sven shrugged and led the way.

It was even less shade than they thought.

He plopped down, taking the least amount for himself, and the women sat as close as they could bare within the shadow. "It practically *is* nothing," Cassandra groaned. "Can't we drink from this thing? Like in old westerns. Chop off a cactus arm or something and the water pours right out?"

Sairha shook her head, mildly amused. "That's an old movie myth. I did read somewhere that there were some rare cacti you could, but hell if I remember what it looked like. Definitely was not this one." She looked up at the cactus above them and spotted a brilliant pink and yellow flower, its star shaped face seeking the sun. A rare miracle to see, considering the bloom only lasts a single day. She smiled, amazed that she could recall some of that at-the-time useless information she had once read from a book long ago.

"Here, drink up." Sven grabbed the half empty water bottle from his pack and tossed it to Cassandra. He flashed Sairha a quick smile, charming in spite of the sweat that dripped down his tan face.

That smile made Sairha's heart flutter, and she was temporarily distracted from the ache in her limbs. The moment was gone too soon when Cassandra handed her the water bottle. Sairha swished the lukewarm liquid around her mouth, then relieved her throat. Temperature be damned, it was refreshing to have a gulp of water after hours of travel.

"Why do we walk during the day instead of at night? It'd be cooler, and we wouldn't be sweating our asses off as much. Or need tons of sunblock." Cassandra smirked at Sairha, who stuck her tongue out in response. She pulled her hiking boot off and turned it upside down to let the dirt out. Sairha thought that was a great idea, and followed suit, her feet near sighing in relief.

"It's dangerous to walk around in the dark, and we need to preserve our candles. As well, there's things that stalk the night, Cassandra, things it would be better to face during the day, when you can see them for what they are," Sven said thoughtfully. "Such as coyotes or mountain lions."

"Scorpions and snakes," Sairha muttered, now wary of undesirable critters climbing into her boots.

Cassandra shuddered. "Yeah, those are nasty things. Night-time, daytime, all the time."

There was a long silence as they thought about the creepy crawlers of the night. With repulsion, the women both said, "*Tarantulas.*"

They hurried to put their shoes back on after that.

When it came to Sven's turn to drink, Sairha surveyed him. He was lost in thought, staring in the direction they were heading. Despite being drenched in perspiration, she noted that was the only sign of discomfort he showed. He appeared relaxed, like the miles of trudging was only an afternoon walk. *Shouldn't he be out of breath? Or vying for water like us?* she scoffed. She tapped his arm with the water bottle, startling him, but he took it and drank.

"Ah, you were thirsty after all," she teased, though noting he hadn't consumed much.

There was a twinkle in his eye as he looked at her. "Of course. Why wouldn't I be?"

She shrugged and dug into the pack for sunblock. "I am very observant, you know. You have to be when you are in the line of work I am." Her grin was playful.

"*Were* in."

Sairha and Sven looked over at Cassandra. She gestured with her hand to the land in front of them. "What? It's not like you'll be going back to the hospital if everyone is either dead or hiding now. We haven't seen a single person. Basically, like a zombie apocalypse. Our old jobs and old careers are useless. We have to start hoarding all the canned foods and toilet paper while we can. And it would probably be a good idea to have aliases."

"Oh yeah?" Sven laughed. "And what shall we call you?"

"Oh, DJ Caterina, of course." Cassandra blew kisses to an invisible crowd and did her best impression of manipulating a turntable, pausing to adjust fake headphones. "They really like me."

That provoked a loud bout of laughter from Sven and Cassandra joined in, easily able to laugh at her own folly. That was Cassandra's lifestyle regardless of any 'apocalypse'. Turn everything into a joke.

Although she joined in the laughter, inwardly Sairha was devastated. The countless hours of studying, leaving her home, the internship she had fought for; was it all for naught? The hospital had been in shambles, desecrated, and she wasn't there when the people needed her most. If the rest of the world was like this, she'd never work in a traditional hospital setting again. Bitterness formed a pit in her stomach, souring the relaxation. She stood. "Let's go. If we're going to be hot and miserable, I'd rather be moving and getting somewhere while we're at it."

"Alrighty then." Cassandra glanced at Sven. She stretched her arms up wide before picking up her pack to sling over her shoulders. Displeasure at leaving so soon pulled the corners of her mouth down into a scowl, but she said nothing else.

Sairha reached out her hand to help Sven up, hoping a forced smile would cover up the sadness she felt inside. They locked eyes, and for a second, she fretted he'd sense something was amiss. He said nothing as he took her hand. A quiet electricity ran between them. She withdrew, slung the second pack over her shoulders, and walked away in silence.

"It wasn't like the cactus gave much relief anyhow," Cassandra muttered under her breath.

Clank!

"Cassandra," Sven groaned.

"What? It's not like we've seen anyone for the past four days." She kicked the tilted, corroding metal again. Layers of sand slid off, revealing a white reflective sign claiming there was a service station ahead. "Oh! Can you believe it! I am so ready to raid their supplies for some snacks and, ugh, more water." Her laughter was giddy, somewhat delirious, as she all but danced past the road marker.

"Just be on your guard, Cassandra. You don't know what's out here," Sven called, picking up his pace to match hers.

Sairha glanced at the sign as she walked past but didn't register its symbols. She was on autopilot, while her mind wandered the vast emptiness she felt. It had proven to be too difficult to shake off the dire straits of their situation. Ahead of them, between blurry waves of heat, lay the station, yet she felt nothing, not even an inkling of hope.

"Oh. My. Gosh. We found it. We found the holy grail!" Cassandra shrieked.

Agitated by the outburst, Sven reached back and clasped Sairha's hand, practically dragging her up to Cassandra, then yanked Cassandra by the shirt closer to them. "Shhh! Are you crazy? Do you *want* to get us all killed?" He pulled them low to the ground, out of view of the windows. Survival mode activated, his hand wrapped tight around Sairha's as he glared across the desert at the lone building. "Keep quiet."

Sairha gave Cassandra a warning look to not speak, then

turned her attention to the situation. It appeared safe enough, if not abandoned. The tan walls were plastered with a dull, grayish-beige mixture of sand and garbage along the bottom, information signs haphazardly strewn about. She tried to see into the small windows but found them blacked out by newspapers on the inside. They would have to get closer to see through. She turned her gaze from the building to where a set of gas pumps should have been. One lay on its side, barely under the carport, as if the fuel pipe was the only thing keeping it chained down. The second pump had ceased to exist. To her, the place appeared abandoned, left for ruin.

Sven let go of her hand, a stern look on his face somehow conveying this was part of their training. Maintaining a low crouch, and smooth movements, he hurried to the side wall, then flattened against it.

Watching him in action was something to behold. His footfalls were assured, as well as light, barely disturbing the sand below. Nodding to Cassandra, Sairha did her best to scurry across the desert as quietly as him. When both women leaned back against the wall, she glanced over her shoulder to where they had come from. *We have a lot to learn,* she thought, watching the dust settling in big clouds over their footprints. *Nowhere near as stealthy as Sven.*

Motioning with his finger to his lips, then to his ears, Sven took a visibly deep, but silent, breath. He wanted them to concentrate, focus, see what they could hear. Like they had days ago at the border.

At first it was difficult, exacerbated from the sprint, but Sairha willed her breathing to calm down and her heart to slow. Her eyes closed in that sort of trance-like feeling she got from honing her sense of sound. And she listened.

Nothing.

Nothing but the sound of their own breath.

No dripping noise, no metal banging, no people. The place could be deserted after all.

Sven inched cautiously to the double doors, then darted to the other side of them. Sairha and Cassandra remained on the opposite side. He opened a single hand, palm out, and they understood to remain there. Slowly opening the door with his other hand, Sven peeked inside.

Regardless of her effort to stay calm, Sairha's heart pounded hard against her chest as the man she liked disappeared into the shop. Cassandra fidgeted beside her, anxious as well. Minutes, that felt like a lifetime, passed before he opened the door wide enough for them to enter. A small smile on his face gave her instant relief until a strong, pungent scent wafted out and she cringed. The store had been ransacked.

Stepping over a rotting cardboard display inside, Sairha slid on some discarded lottery tickets, nearly crashing into the check-out counter. She stabilized herself and was surprised to see the cash register gone, along with all the cigarette cartons normally locked up behind it. Turning away, her foot hit a hard plastic phone, its old curling cord leading back to a busted landline base. When she peered down the aisle in front of her, her heart sank. There was little left in the form of food and the back wall of refrigerators had been left open, emptied.

"Well, I hope they left something for us," Cassandra broke the silence. "Somewhere."

Sven headed to the left of the store, scanning the shelves as he walked by. Cassandra chose the other way, clearly on a mission to find something for herself, while Sairha stood a moment longer. Confused, and yet, in awe of the state of things.

"You have got to be kidding me!" A frustrated growl came from Cassandra's aisle. "No cake desserts left whatsoever? Not even a blasted ho-ho or cookie?"

Sairha snorted, shaking her head, and proceeded to dig around in the hope of finding things they could use. *Is this really the world now? Even here?* She fought back her previous feelings of hopelessness that had threatened to consume her.

The room's stillness was shattered with a piercing scream. Sairha and Sven raced towards the back of the store, towards Cassandra. They found her holding the bathroom door open, horror-struck as she peered inside. The smell was terrible, nauseating. Sairha covered her nose and mouth with a grimace.

Bloated and gray, a man in jeans and a flannel shirt lay sprawled out on the floor, bodily fluids oozing out of holes in his chest. His black hair was caked to his head and reddish orange foam was leaking from his mouth and nostrils.

"He's been dead for a while, it looks like," Sairha muttered. She spied a silver pistol, just out of the body's reach, in a pool of blood. "But, that's a shotgun wound."

Sven rubbed a hand over his face. "Looters."

"Should we...take the gun?" Cassandra gagged.

"No, don't touch it. There's all sorts of bacteria in there." Sairha turned away, motioning for Cassandra to close the door.

Sven sighed. "That is why we must be careful before entering any kind of house or building. You never know who, or what, is waiting for you to mess up."

The door closed with a deafening click, but the putrid smell and Sven's somber warning lingered in the air long after. It was otherwise silent the rest of their time inside, searching for anything to salvage. Outside, in the glaring rays of sunlight, an old RV came into view behind the station, its thin door left wide open. Sven crept towards it, Sairha and Cassandra close behind. No funny smells or liquids warned them to stay away.

"Let's check in here for supplies," Sven whispered, then

stepped up, turning his head left and right, inspecting the small space. "It's clear."

Glass and food crunched under their boots, the place not much different from the store. "Looks like a Sunday morning after partying all weekend," Cassandra joked as she strode past the two and began to rummage around the kitchen.

Sven nudged Sairha towards the front of the RV. When they were out of earshot, he leaned against the driver's seat, pinning her with a concerned expression. "Are you okay?"

"What do you mean?" The heat bothered her, her feet ached, she was so damn thirsty, and her stomach felt like it was eating itself, she was that hungry. Not that any of it compared to her intrusive thoughts of being useless, or the weight of defeat that sagged her shoulders, but she wouldn't tell him any of that. It was her own burden to carry.

"What she said the other day, it really got to you. I knew it as soon as she said it," he stated matter-of-factly, and it stung even more hearing him say it out loud. "Listen, I've been thinking about how to approach you and say this. Everything you've done up until this point was not wasted and definitely not nonapplicable in this time. I wanted to tell you right away, but gave you your space, in hopes that you would come to see it on your own."

"I feel like I've lost the biggest part of myself," she blurted out. Sven remained quiet, but attentive, making her feel secure enough to continue. "If this is the new world, where am I going to fit in? Who will I be now? My whole life was centered around being a nurse in the emergency room." She sighed, dropping her head in defeat.

"Sairha, are you kidding? You're going to save someone's life someday. Maybe tomorrow. Possibly next week. Or a month from now. Either way, the medical work that you are capable of will be so handy, so important. Anyone would be lucky to have you around in their group. You are a vast wealth of knowledge. Do you think—" he motioned towards Cassandra, who was still rooting around. "—she won't hurt herself? She's going to need you. And before you say it, I wouldn't know what to do if she broke a limb or had a concussion. You are over-glorifying my abilities if you believe that. Honestly, I know how to survive in the wild, in elemental extremes, but you..."

He reached out and squeezed her hand. Goosebumps trailed up her arm.

"You will do more than survive. You will persevere and ensure the people who are with you are doing more than surviving. They will come to you when they are sick, or when they feel weak from lack of iron or something, when they have a cut a little too deep to heal on its own. Hell! You will make sure bones are set the best way possible rather than letting them grow back all messed up. That's important stuff, you know! You are not defined by *where* you work, but how you do it."

She lifted her head, pushing her short hair behind her ears. "I guess I hadn't really thought of that." Maybe she wasn't the only observant one in the group. "I got so hung up on the fact that I wouldn't be a nurse in the traditional sense, in a hospital or doctor's office." She slid her hand into his, the warmth of his palm more than comforting. Even if they were both covered in sweat and grime, she welcomed the heat from his touch. The small gesture had both of them grinning.

"I found some chips!" Cassandra called with triumph. She bounced up, holding an unopened bag. "And half a jar of salsa along with one beer. It's warm, but hey. Now we've got a party."

Sairha and Sven rejoined Cassandra in the dining area of the RV, plopping down at the small table. Sairha crossed her arms and frowned at the beer. "Hate to be the bearer of bad news, but beer will only dehydrate us more than we already are."

"Shut up, Doctor Sairha. No one asked you." Cassandra stuck her tongue out.

"Yeah, shut up, Doctor Sairha." Sven winked at her, then snatched the beer up. He popped the cap off using the edge of the tabletop.

Sairha shook her head, chuckling, feeling a weight lifting from her. *Don't sweat the small stuff*, she guessed was another part of survival. She watched as Sven took a generous gulp of the beer, then handed it off to Cassandra. She couldn't decide what she wanted a long drink from more; him or the beer.

It was a short lived moment of peace, sharing the stale chips and a single beer between them, but it was needed. Both Cassandra and Sairha had a little more pep to their steps when they exited the RV, Sven close behind them. Cassandra stretched her arms up into the sky, a big smile on her face, and Sairha loved to see it.

"Hey." Sven placed a hand on each of their shoulders. "You ladies know how to ride a bike?"

On two trick bicycles they found, they rode across the desert until the first few stars twinkled. Cassandra had wanted to stay in the RV, in a musky small bed, but Sven insisted it was safer to be as far away from there as possible. Sairha took turns peddling with Cassandra riding behind her on the back pegs, then letting Cassandra peddle herself, while Sairha wrapped her arms around Sven. It was a weird adjustment, but they made it work, covering more distance than if they had walked, giving their worn boots some reprieve.

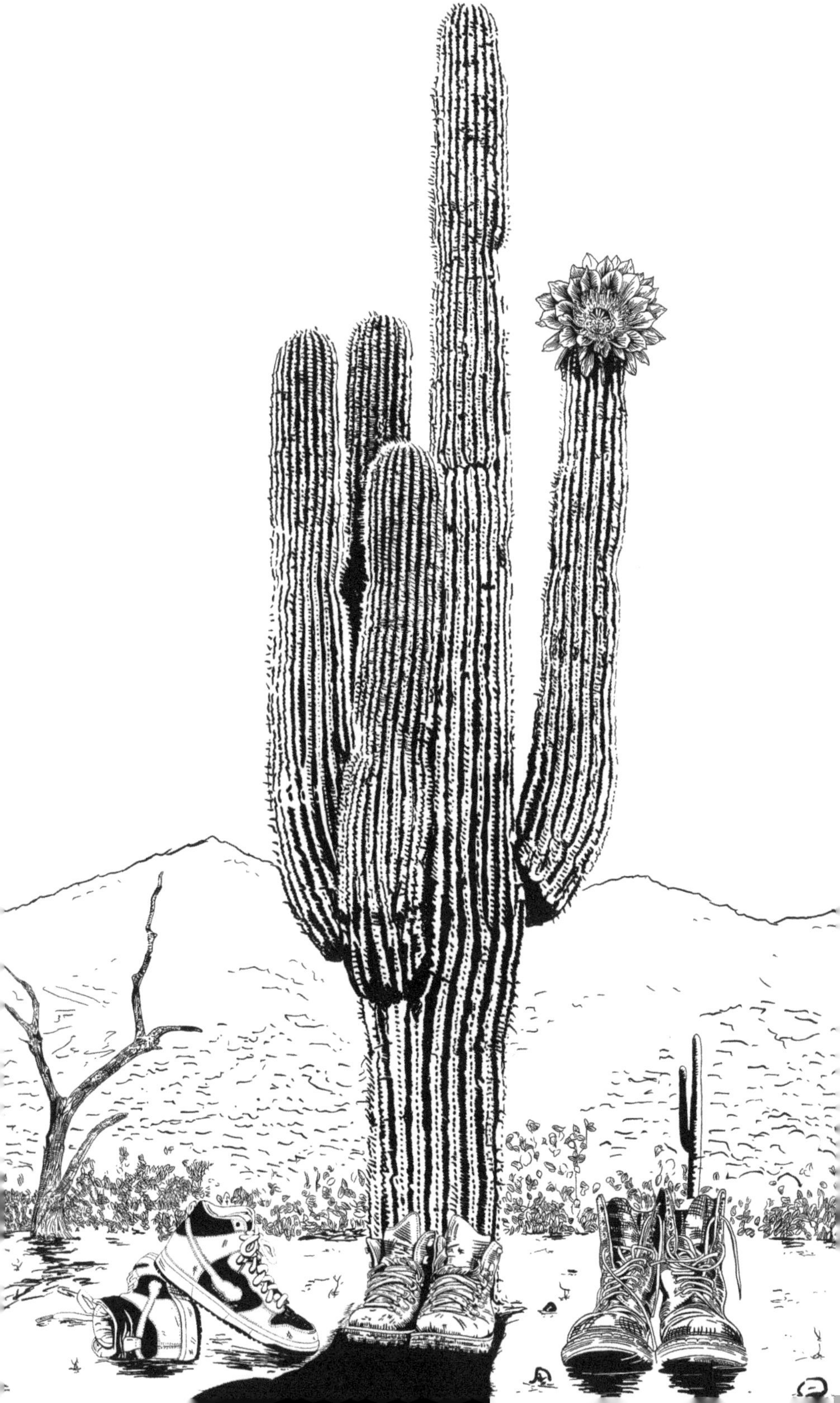

CHAPTER FIVE

THE TERRAIN BEGAN TO CHANGE AS THE DAYS ON THEIR JOURNEY blurred together. The flat desert land began to give way to soft dirt and green vegetation, more trees popping up than cacti, as they sped by on their bicycles. They stopped at one other rest station along their path and were lucky enough to find drinkable water. Other than that, Sven's planned route kept them in the wilderness, far from small towns. Sairha trusted his judgment, and in turn, Cassandra trusted hers. After all, he had gotten them this far. He explained it was to keep them safe and avoid any hindrances that would derail them from getting to their homes. He wanted to get back home as soon as possible, and so did Sairha. Every day she repeated to herself, *They are there. They are safe. They are waiting.*

Sven set a steady pace and never seemed to tire. Sairha and Cassandra, however, gave up the pace after a few hours. They tried to keep up, but being as tired as they were, he managed to get further ahead again and again. Once in a while he would veer off, look around at the new surroundings, and then circle back around to them. This continued well throughout the day, until they were unable to physically bear any more and got him to agree to a break late in a quiet field.

"What are you looking at?" Sairha leaned to peer over Cassandra's shoulder.

"Looking at the map," Cassandra mumbled between bites of her granola bar. She hadn't bothered to look up from the half unfolded paper resting on her legs.

"Ah." Sairha sat back against the dried up tree they were resting under, too tired to force more conversation. She willed a breeze to blow by, to rustle through the branches, and with any luck, cool them down. *You look as thirsty as I feel.* She patted the tree trunk, her gaze shifting to the dried up grass around them. *One spark and this whole field would go up in flames.*

"We have two full water bottles left, and we'll find more soon." Sven stood from rummaging through his pack and presented Cassandra with one of them. She pushed it away, still focused on the map, and he turned to Sairha instead. He held it out towards her, along with a smile.

Her muscles screamed in protest as she reached for the bottle. The ache wasn't so noticeable when they were actually moving, but whenever they took a break, her body was in agony. She tried her best to ignore the pangs as she took a gulp of water.

"You guys are doing really well." Sven took a step back to stand in the sun. His face and hair were soaked with sweat, and yet, he looked rejuvenated, ready to go another ten miles. "Making really great distance today."

Cassandra grunted in reply.

"Tell that to my bones," Sairha groaned. "Can't decide if my butt hurts more from the seat or my legs from when I'm standing."

The sunlight turned Sven's eyes into pools of molten chocolate as he gave her another brilliant smile and a thumbs up. "We'll stop for the night soon, I promise. Call it early. You both deserve it. I'll find somewhere nice to set up camp."

Camp sounded heavenly. Sairha wanted nothing more than to lie down and sleep for a few hours, days even.

"How about we push through to this town? It's only a few miles away. We could probably reach it by 'midnight'." Cassandra lifted up one hand and made air-quotations. Sven had been teaching them to tell time by the sun and moon positionings, and although she had been resilient to learning, she was actually pretty good at it.

"*No*," Sven snapped, sharp and direct.

It was so unusual to hear that level of forcefulness in his tone that both women looked up at him with mirrored confusion. A long silence passed between them without Sven providing a reason why. Cassandra huffed. "Why not?"

A flash of bewilderment crossed his features, and he spoke with his hands. "I thought you were tired! And that we agreed to stick to the outskirts plan, staying away from cities." He shielded his eyes, nostrils flaring, then wiped at the sweat dripping down his forehead.

Did his hand tremble? Sairha raised an eyebrow, suspicious. "Sven." She tried to keep her voice calm to ease whatever this new anxiety was he showed. "We need more food and water. And honestly, it would be nice to sleep in a *bed* again. I know you said we were doing good, but our bodies are suffering. Cassandra and I really need a good night's rest if we're going to continue like this. And I don't know much, but the bicycles are starting to look a bit worn down."

"Besides, you said we deserved it," Cassandra added, her tone full of pleading, probably not far from begging on hands and knees.

Sven pressed his lips tight, hands clenching and unclenching, then lifted them in exasperation. "But it's a *full moon* tonight," he cried out. "A full moon means a lot of visibility at night. Which might sound ideal, but you two—*we* do not have any idea what kind of...people are left there. Are they friendly? Or are they murderous assholes ready to rob us and do god-knows-what to you women? We'd be spotted before we had a chance." He took a deep breath then crouched down to their level, his expression more pleading than Cassandra's. "Please, let's rest early today. In a nice field somewhere, here even. I promise to take you guys into the town tomorrow, during the day, and we'll look for anything and everything you want."

There was a twinkle in his gaze, something unspoken that begged Sairha to understand. Never had she seen him act this way, desperate, erratic, maybe even... *frightened?* She wanted to ask, wanted to know if there was more he wasn't saying. If there was some*thing* out there, something less than human. Shouldn't they know about it? Instead, she remained quiet, not wanting to sound crazy herself, and yielded with a nod. She turned her head away from him, unable to tolerate that soul piercing stare any longer.

Cassandra huffed again, annoyed, and crumbled up the map. "Fine," she spat with venom. "You owe us."

"Great." Sven threw up his hands and stormed off.

Once he was far enough away, Cassandra leaned back against the tree and let out a low whistle. "Man, what's eating at your boyfriend? Mooooood swings."

Sairha bristled at the label. There it was again, that word. *Boyfriend.* He acted like it, or at least she thought he did. But was that how he felt about them? Did she even know how she felt?

Cassandra's mouth dropped. "What? No, don't tell me. Why else would we be following him around, across the freaking country, if he wasn't your boyfriend?" She let out a laugh and patted Sairha's arm. "What are you waiting for? For him to change his online status to 'in a relationship'? He's *your* boyfriend, Sairha, and *you* need to go talk to him."

"Hey, we aren't just *'following him around'*, okay? Just so happens he lives close to my family home, remember? ...And do I have to?" Sairha groaned. "I've never...asked a guy if we were official or not. You really think he was being moody?"

"Mhm." Cassandra nodded, her eyelids heavier with every second that passed. "Listen, I have a lot of experience with men. Earlier, he was like a spazzed out dog excited to go on a walk. After our talk just now, him snapping at us? It's like we cornered that dog and told him he has to be leashed."

Sairha waited for clarification, but Cassandra's eyes were closed. She marveled at how peaceful Cassandra, a self-proclaimed pampered princess, looked outdoors now. At least one of them seemed to be adjusting. With a sigh, Sairha set her sights on finding where Sven had gone. His dark clothed figure stood out across the dry field, wandering around without aim. A few paces, then he would stop and look in a different direction. *He is acting weird.* Sairha grabbed the water bottle and stood up. *What am I doing? I have no idea what I'm going to say to him.*

There was a noticeable change in temperature when she stepped out from the shade. A drop of sweat slid down her spine. Taking long strides, she waved to grab his attention. "Hey! What are you doing?"

"Oh." Sven glanced over at her, his eyes lighting up as he did. "Hey!"

Sairha's insides felt like they were melting under the heat of his attention. She wished she could figure out the right words to convey the feelings he elicited in her. Often, somehow, Sven seemed to know that she could not express them and would wrap his arms around her, as if to say he understood. That she didn't need to voice her feelings.

This time, however, he simply stared at her with a smile she wasn't sure was as sincere.

"Here." She offered the water bottle. "I thought you could use some more hydration." For a moment, she thought she might have to force him to drink it, as he stared at the bottle in her hand far too long without moving. Relief filled her when his hand brushed against hers, at last taking it.

Popping the lid off, he took two huge gulps then poured the rest on his face. Water went flying when he shook the excess off, causing Sairha to scrunch up her face. He laughed and wiped the rest off with the back of his hand. "What?"

"Nothing. I just... Well, are you feeling alright?" She was concerned, more than ever, after that. Wasting water was not something he'd normally do. "Feeling faint? Dizzy? The effects of dehydration are very serious if you let it go for too long."

Sven quirked his head to the side, holding her gaze. "Yes, I am feeling alright. Actually, I feel great."

"Well." Sairha debated how to explain that his erratic behavior was ringing all sorts of alarms in her. "You are acting sort of...delirious? Like happy-go-lucky, this is a great time, everything is unicorns and lollipops. How do you have so much energy when we are practically dying? And moments ago, what was that? You got really weird about us wanting to stop in a town for the night. Classic signs of dehydration."

"I'm fine."

"Normally you are Mister Serious, teaching us to be on guard, no goofing off, always look over our shoulder, sleep with one eye open type stuff. That is the *normal you* that we have gotten to know... you know?" Sairha felt foolish as the words left her mouth. They really did not know him well enough to pinpoint his behavior as off; she'd only spent a weekend with him before the big earthquake that sent them on this journey together. Softening her expression, she reached out to caress his arm, her fingertips tingling instantly. "Or maybe, I don't really know the real you, do I?"

Sven remained statuesque, carefully guarded.

She imagined his brain working, calculating. Like he wanted to open up to her, and maybe he was about to, but he wasn't sure if he should. Could he feel that electric current between them, that thrilling connection? She sent a silent plea: *trust me, it's okay.*

A heavy sigh escaped him as he turned away from her, her outstretched hand falling away from him. "The truth—" he stumbled over the words, visibly breaking down his walls as his shoulders sagged, "—is there is a lot about me that you don't know, yeah. That you never got the chance to learn, before setting out with me in this new, difficult world. That's why I did not want you to come with me."

She froze in place, horrified by his confession. *I should have never asked. I'm not prepared for this answer.* They were a burden for him, she could hear it in his tone, he regretted bringing them with him. She was only meant to be a one-time fling. Sairha's heart hurt in her chest, a stabbing sensation with every slow beat. *No, no, no...* Was the air thin?

"But—" he turned back and grabbed her hand into his, "—there is something about you that I cannot resist, that I cannot stay away from. When I first spotted you in that crowd of people, I felt...drawn to you. And now. Sometimes you'll make a sound or movement and I find my inner-self responding to it. Surely, you've noticed? How easy it is for me to give in. For my body to take over my thoughts and wrap around you, to hold you, and be around you so effortlessly. So naturally. Like...like I was meant to be with you."

The atmosphere around them disappeared. She could not pull her gaze away from him, not even to blink. Seconds ago, anxiety told her he probably regretted having met her. That was not how she thought the rest of the confession would go. Her heart still ached, but in a different way. It pounded in response to hearing the things she felt echoed back to her. Sairha had never once dreamt of a moment like this, and yet, it was so dream-like that she did not believe it was real.

Reality returned with a squeeze of her hand. There was air as she learned to breathe again. Eyes dry, she blinked and could see clearly, noticing that Sven was still staring at her, concerned, as it dawned on her. He was as nervous as she had been.

"Well, say something," he chuckled.

This was her chance. He opened up to her and wanted her response. Her throat was parched, hoarse, and she struggled to think about what she had wanted to tell him. Blank, her mind kept drawing a blank. It all disappeared, and how could it not after his speech? It was now or never, even if she could not think of the right way to say it, she had to try.

Sairha exhaled, summoning courage. "Sven, I'm sorry."

His brows pulled together, confused.

Crap, I'm messing up already; she fretted but continued anyway. "I'm not used to this. There is so much going on in here—" she laid her hand on her chest, her heart threatening to jump out, "—that I have wanted to say to you, but it is never the right time, and I can never think of the right words. Even now. Ugh, what am I saying…"

He was patient with her slow pace and his thumb massaged the top of her hand.

She sighed. Maybe if she did not look at his handsome face, the fading daylight making his tan skin glow, or his eyes with that hint of a smile in them. Even his perfect lips were a distraction. She looked down at his hand in hers, wondering if her hand was sweaty, it had to be. *Focus, Sairha.*

"I have never been good at expressing my feelings, especially...intimate feelings. S*trong*, intimate feelings. I cannot even look at you right now because my words escape me and I feel numb." She blurted a lot of it out, and despite what she said, she lifted her gaze up to him. "I *do* notice it, I see how easy it is for you. For you to reach out for my hand, or how you know when I need your presence by my side, even a quick smile. The other night when you wrapped your arms around me...I melted inside because it was exactly what I had wanted but didn't know until it happened. Even if I had known, I would never have dared ask because...because I just wouldn't."

His expression lent to understanding.

Another deep breath. She closed her eyes again, allowing the words to flow from her. "I really care for you. A lot. More than I ever let on. And I'm sorry—" Her chin was lifted and supple, warm lips pressed against hers. It was a gentle kiss, yet so much was said within it. He understood her, he forgave her, and most of all, he accepted her.

His arm slinked around her waist, pulling her closer, and deeper into their kiss.

Her hands found their way to his hair and released it from the rubber band. She raked her fingers through the long strands. *So satisfying.* Heart aflutter and lightheaded, she knew she was safe in his embrace. Relief radiated inside of her. It was freeing to speak aloud what was in her. Even though there was much more she could add, and better words she could use, he understood what she had meant to say.

Out of breath, they transformed back into two separate people.

"Wow." Sairha rubbed her cheeks that now burned from more than the sun.

Sven chuckled. "Come on. Let's head back to camp." His arm still around her waist, he kept her close as they took their time walking back.

"Sven," she kept her tone light. The nurse's voice in the back of her mind still whispered through her daze. "Why *are* you so energetic today?"

His arm tensed around her. "Do you believe in mystical things? Like the healing power of moonlight?"

"Um…" Sairha tried her best to not sound surprised, and full of disbelief, causing her voice to come out flat. "No. Can't say that I do. I believe in modern medicine and the healing power of rest. What I've studied, you know, as a nurse." The healing power of the moon? That sounded like some hippy talk that her grandparents used to drone on about or the herbal-heads that lived in her hometown. Sairha was into provable facts, to which there was no real evidence of 'moonlight healing'. Sven did not come off as either of those types. What was he talking about? "Are you sure you aren't dehydrated?"

He laughed at the puzzled face she must have worn. "It's a full moon tonight, and I feel really optimistic. Look how far we've already come, with little to no problems. We're doing great. And I want to keep it that way by avoiding the towns at night."

She could not deny that it had been a really successful few days. Although it did not make much sense to her, Sairha could at least appreciate Sven's enthusiasm. "You know what? We do have this saying in the medical field." She pretended to be thinking, tapping a finger to her chin. "Something like…full moons bring out all the weirdos?"

"Aw, hey now. Weirdo?" he scoffed at her teasing.

"Who's a weirdo?" Cassandra interrupted as the two arrived at their camp.

Despite Cassandra having taken a nap, Sairha noted the enlarged, dark circles under her eyes. An exhaustion she guessed that would linger until their destination's end. "One of those 'you had to be there' convos, Cas. But long story short,

Sven is convinced the moon has healing powers and *that* is why he has been so chipper," Sairha said matter-of-factly, teasing him and his theory even more. "I think he's dehydrated and delirious."

Cassandra looked Sven up and down, then Sairha, then back to Sven. She apparently did not find it nearly as funny as they did.

Sven lowered himself onto Sairha's sleeping bag and stretched out. Closing his eyes, he waved his hand. "Whatever, you two. Believe, don't believe. It makes no difference to me. Wake me up when the sun goes down. Just need a quick little power nap."

The women looked at each other quizzically, before speaking in unison. "In like twenty minutes?"

He did not respond.

The sun had long since disappeared when Sairha could no longer take the ache in her bones. She curled up next to Sven and stared up at the ever darkening sky. One star twinkled, or maybe a planet, she mused, calling to the others. A little smile spread across her face, her gaze slipping from the sky to Cassandra who had failed at staying awake. *Someone should keep watch.* Maybe she could just lie there for a little bit longer, then force some moxie into herself. Sven needed the rest.

His arm wrapped around her, warming her wherever it touched... And her eyelids grew heavy...

A chill ran along her exposed body, disturbing Sairha's peaceful slumber. Groggy, she couldn't bring herself to properly cover up. Instead, she rolled over to snuggle against Sven but found him missing. No wonder she was cold. She knew he often had trouble sleeping, but it was rare that he got up and left her. "Sven?" she mumbled.

"Shhh, go back to sleep," his whisper came on another cool breeze. "I'm here, you're safe."

Satisfied he was near, she rolled over and fell into a near-dreamless sleep. Stills of her mountain home appeared, realistic down to the melodic howl of a wolf. She longed to be there, in the forest.

"Sairha! Wake up, it's time to kick rocks. It's a new day."

When she didn't respond, or make any movement to get up, she was left in peace. Rays of early morning sunshine started to cook her alive like a baked potato. Hadn't she just fallen back asleep? Throwing her arms out, Sairha shielded her eyes from the brightness. The ground wasn't the best bed, but at least the undeniable fatigue was gone. The stress of the hospital was insane and taxing, but it did not compare to traveling endless miles in the sun daily with the only relief being the hard ground she dropped onto at night. She would never feel truly rested, not until she got home. Something tickled her ear, then tickled *inside* her ear. "What's the big idea?!" she freaked out, swatting furiously around her head.

Sven was crouched next to her, his grin mischievous, a long blade of grass twirling between his fingers. The guilty party.

"Ugh, you jerk. I was *sleeping*, you know." She pushed him playfully.

He laughed and stumbled a bit to the side. "Come on, sleepyhead. Time to get ready. Cassandra is restless. She really wants to get to that town." He picked up her boots and turned them upside down, making sure there were no creepy crawlers inside.

A town. With renewed hope, Sairha got ready in a hurry, but also relishing every second alone with him she got. Yesterday's confessions felt like a burden lifted from her, replaced by an overflowing adoration for the man. Even as he tossed her shoe an inch from her face.

"Right, I want to get there too. Where did she go?"

Sven sat beside her with an open can of peaches, a fork

protruding from it. He offered her some and, as if on cue, her stomach growled. She dove in with a mumble of gratitude. The sweet canned fruit was damn delicious and helped satiate how parched she was.

"She probably wandered off to do her business in private," Sven said offhandedly. He stuck his own fork in, grabbing a few slices.

She rolled her eyes, but his silly comment reminded her. "Oh hey, did you get any sleep last night?"

He paused mid bite and stared at her for a moment before he shrugged with a half smile on his face. "Don't you worry about me. I feel great. I wandered around but stayed near enough to watch over you guys." He wrapped his arm around her shoulder, holding her close. "No big deal."

"I woke up in the middle of the night and you weren't there. It was weird and eerie," Sairha grimaced. "I was worried."

"Aw, hey," he murmured against her hair, resting his head atop hers. Somehow, beyond all reason, he still smelled good. Like fresh turned garden dirt and ginger roots, mixed with the salty tang of sweat. "You know I'd never let anything happen to you, right? I will always be watching out for you. Even if you can't see me."

"What makes you think I need you watching over me?" she teased before chewing on another peach, relaxing into him. "You know, with all of this training you've been giving us, we probably won't need you much longer."

"Oh, yeah? You think so?" He chuckled.

"Just watch. I bet you a hundred bucks we impress you when we get into town." She beamed a big, cheesy grin right at him.

"I bet you'll surprise even yourselves," he whispered in her ear, lips brushing her lobe, sending shivers down her spine, longing in her soul. If Cassandra had not walked back to them, there was no telling what Sairha would have responded with. Instead, she greeted her friend by offering her the fork laden with fruit. "Hey, you!"

Cassandra waved away the food, shifting back and forth on her feet, visibly anxious to leave. The sun was bright behind her, forcing Sairha to squint to see better. Maybe she was imagining it, a sort of glow about her, as if Cassandra had been rejuvenated overnight. *She must have slept better than me*, Sairha thought, only a little jealous. *Although... No, that's silly.* She side-eyed Sven, thinking upon their conversation about the full moon.

"Can you two hurry up? I finished my daily morning meditation and I'm ready to go!"

"You meditate?" Sairha and Sven asked at the same time.

Eyes rolling almost fully back into her head, Cassandra let out an exasperated sigh. "Of course I meditate. I need some daily escape from this new hellish lifestyle. And it helps keep me from throwing up witnessing all the lovey dovey crap you two display."

A furious blush spread across Sairha's face. She hadn't thought there was that much physical attraction going on between her and Sven. But, if it was making Cassandra sick enough to meditate into a better mood, perhaps Sairha would kick up the PDA a notch. Setting down the food, she finished tying up her boots and popped up more spritely than she thought possible. "Let's go!"

CHAPTER SIX

On their borrowed bikes, Cassandra led the way to town, more than willing to show off that studying the map had not been a waste of her time. Sven followed close behind with Sairha riding on the back, giving her time to contemplate the bet they had made. It was a small glimmer of fun in such a bleak situation. *Don't let me down, Cas,* she thought, looking ahead to her friend. She saw it before it happened; the bike chain coming loose, beyond worn, then falling apart in the wheelhouse.

Cassandra fishtailed, gripping the handle tight to regain control, but she was going too fast. The back tire locked, kicking up a trail of sand that Sven swerved to avoid. In the sandstorm, Cassandra let out a yell followed by the sound of her crashing. Panicked, Sairha jumped off their bicycle and ran for Cassandra, Sven hot on her heels. "Cas!"

"I'm okay," Cassandra choked out. The dust settled to reveal her entangled in the bicycle, rubbing at her side. The back wheel was long gone, handlebars twisted beyond repair.

There was no salvaging the hunk of metal. "Just scraped, I think. Nothing...feels out of place," she said with a wince as Sairha helped her sit up. Sven tossed the broken wreck out of the way. Unconvinced, Sairha tested Cassandra's ankles, wrists, and legs before allowing her to stand. "What are *those*?" Cassandra pointed with her chin.

Sairha turned her attention away from Cassandra, at last satisfied she wasn't seriously injured. Large animal prints lay around them, in a nonsensical path. Sairha squinted, brain searching out the locked away knowledge. "They look like wolf tracks."

"Wolves? Out here?" Cassandra audibly gulped.

Sven knelt beside Sairha to look at the tracks as well. "These are way too large to be an average wolf. Looks like they lead away from the town. Still...I don't like it." He rubbed his face, looking exhausted, and stood. "The bike is totaled. It's okay, I didn't want to announce our arrival riding up on them anyway. Let's get in and out of there as fast as possible."

Both women nodded, sobered by both the accident and the unusual tracks.

Hour later the town came into view. Wary of anything, or anyone, hidden around the area, they crept about cautiously. Two weeks of seeing not a single soul, yet Sairha dared to hope that they would come across someone soon. Someone trustworthy, safe. She wanted to ask questions, compare what they had seen, and what had happened the night that everything changed in the world. Some sign of normalcy, of life. Glancing at their dirty clothes, greasy hair, and faces, she wasn't sure anyone would trust *them*.

They entered through a short two street neighborhood. Sven made sure to stick to one side, with less debris and cars abandoned in the driveways, rather than walking in the middle of the road. They passed several homes that looked more than deserted, walls crumbling and doors torn off. Some with the windows blown out, glass on the lawn, their curtains limp in the dead air.

That's so weird, Sairha noted.

She paused before a house with unusual markings along the yard. It appeared someone had dragged a three-pronged pitchfork through the ground in two rows, shoulder width apart. With a pounding heart, Sairha diverted her path onto the lawn, close to the drag marks. She crouched, eyesight never leaving the windows as she did, afraid something would pop out of the house. Even though Sven was right that the large tracks didn't follow through to the town, visions of the dark creature in the hotel popped forward in her mind.

Everything remained still, quiet, no sign of movement.

The long lines started at the base of a window, trailing down to where they ended at her feet. Kneeling on the ground, she noticed there were smaller lines within the main ones. *Almost like...* Sairha lowered her hand, making a c-shape. Nausea hit her as her hand and fingers fit near perfectly inside. She dragged her hand down, making the same strokes with some effort. Shaken, she jumped to her feet and backed away, wiping her dirt covered hand.

"Let's go," Sven murmured, resting his hand on her shoulder.

Joining up with Cassandra, she pointed towards the center of the street. A shoe lay on its side beside a covered manhole, tied and knotted. If there was any cheer in the women, it was snuffed out by the scene in the neighborhood, the desire to sleep in a bed dashed away with it. They left the small neighborhood behind. The mood was somber as Cassandra navigated towards the one and only grocery store, keeping them close to the walls of buildings. The last, single, spark of hope left in them that the store hadn't been picked over.

At the doors, Sven and Cassandra stayed on one side while Sairha moved to the other. They paused, listening for signs of danger. Sairha willed her heart to slow down, along with her racing mind, to focus. Cassandra's breath was haggard, distracting, but Sairha pushed herself to hone in more. Sven sounded calm, his breathing quieter than normal. It seemed safe, so she reached over and slowly opened the door. It let out a soft squeal as she pushed, the hinges old and rusting. Sairha winced, but took a deep breath and peered inside. The view was disheartening, an absolute wreckage of a mess inside.

The trio went inside one by one and had to be more than careful with their footing. Boxes and cans littered the floor, along with money, and bags of groceries that had been discarded. A putrid, rancid smell wafted around them. Fruit and vegetables molding on their shelves, their rotten juices dripping to the floor.

Cassandra broke the silence with her stifled gagging noises.

Sairha's stomach did some twisting and turning of its own. She wanted to turn tail and leave, find another place that did not reek so bad, or look like a tornado had run through it, but Sven was behind them. He waited for their next move. She stepped lightly, careful to avoid anything that would make her slip. The last thing she needed was to smell like decayed fruits and moldy paper-bags. They already reeked from lack of showers.

Once past the chaotic mess of the front area, she decided to head to the snacks and see if there was anything to salvage. The aisles were a little cleaner, although most of the shelves were bare. A few colorful boxes lay discarded on the ground.

Cassandra let out a heavy sigh that reengaged her gagging, then stopped herself by burying her face in the crook of her arm. Once recovered, she picked up an empty box. "Well, shit." She shook it, discouraged. "Did they leave us anything?"

Sven wasted no time looking through other boxes further down the row. He tossed aside empty ones and when he did find a box with goodies inside, he ripped open the top and tossed the bags into his pack. Cassandra followed suit on the opposite side.

Deciding Cassandra and Sven had that aisle taken care of, Sairha left them to find another row to search. *What I wouldn't give for some chicken wings or a grilled steak.* Her stomach growled in agreement. It was weird how snack foods had become their actual meals. She wondered if she would ever have a fresh salad again or a crisp, juicy apple. For now, she found the chip and soda aisle. Ransacked, but something further down caught her eye; shiny, metallic bags flung on the top shelf. Excited, she made a dash for the packages.

In her hurry, she took a wrong step into spilled liquid and went spiraling out of control. It felt like slow motion as she flapped her arms around, attempting to keep herself upright. Her foot caught on something, and she crashed head first into the shelving. The thin bar, holding what little soda bottles were left, broke loose from the impact. Sairha fell back into the sticky, dark mess on the floor and had to shield herself as the bottles fell all around her. One knocked her on the head, forcing her back onto her elbows, a headache blooming instantly.

Sairha's heart raced as she undertook a survey of her body. Nothing felt broken, her tailbone and elbows were sore, bruised at best, and she could tell a bump was forming on the top of her head. She would survive. Sticky syrup seeped into her clothes. Her boots were worn thin from their travels, and not skid-proof like her hospital shoes. But it was the fact that she had lost her focus, let her guard down, that really upset her. On the day she was trying to impress Sven no less.

"Yuck." She tried to wipe some of the goop off and noticed a tremble in her hand. She could hear Sven and Cassandra coming for her amongst the hissing of bottles that air and soda were escaping from.

Svan reached her aisle first but came to an abrupt stop when he saw her sitting on the ground. A look of pure shock crossed his face, the color draining from him.

"I'm okay. I just slipped," Sairha called over.

Cassandra came up beside Sven and her face contorted from surprise to disgust. Turning away, she placed her hand on a shelf to steady herself and doubled over, releasing vomit all over the floor.

"Woah, Cassandra. It's not that bad, I'm okay!" Sairha stared, alarmed.

Sven made his way towards Sairha, more mindful than she had been. He toed away bottles in his path, never taking his eyes off of her as he crouched down and offered his hand. "Sairha, you...you need to get up," he said, obviously struggling to stay level headed. For a split second, he glanced to the side.

Sairha did not see what the big deal was. She had tripped, knocked over soda, and was now soaking in a pool of the stuff. Nothing she couldn't shake off. Although the stuff on her hands did feel *strange*. It was warmer than she would have expected and thicker. With Sven acting weird and Cassandra heaving up what little breakfast she had, Sairha felt a small panic start in her chest. *What did I fall in?*

"Sairha, don't," Sven cautioned. "Don't look. Just...just take my hand and let's go get you cleaned up."

Senses returning, the sugary sweet scent was tinged with a familiar metallic afternote. The panic in her tightened, and against her better judgment, Sairha looked around at the pool she was sitting in. Blood swirled together with the soda, and a sort of black syrup, in the areas her presence had disturbed. She needed to know, needed to find what she had tripped over. She was just out of reach for Sven to grip her, pull her away, and keep her from seeing.

With a shriek, Sairha darted away from what she found as fast, and slippery, as she could. A severed...arm...of some sort lay across from her. At least it looked like an arm, one that had been ripped away from the upper middle. Pale gray, paper-thin skin pulled taut over bones of abnormal lengths, black blood pooled at the exposed end. The elbow had an unusual amount of excess, wrinkly skin. As if that was not terrifying enough, clutched in its three claws, and a short fourth one on the inside, was a shoe with a severed foot still inside.

The small amount of food in her threatened to vacate Sairha's stomach. The stickiness on her fingers and palm, the sickeningly sweet smell. She could not find her breath, her chest was tightly constricted. Spots darkened her vision, so she shut her eyes tight, wanting to keep everything together. She wanted to get out of there as fast as possible. She *needed* to calm down. She needed...she *wanted* to find her happy place. A sudden memory brought forth a breeze, upon it the scent of pine and the sound of birds singing. Her childhood home; the cabin in the woods. She needed to get there.

"Sairha."

His voice pulled her out of the memory, away from that sense of safety. Sven had gotten close enough to scoop her up. He was careful with her sore body, somehow able to avoid falling in the mess himself. Once clear, he set her down and encouraged her to walk if she could. As if in a protective bubble, Sairha was barely aware of being guided out or Cassandra next to her, still covering her nose and mouth.

The warmth of hands on Sairha's face burst that bubble. Pain in her back and elbows screamed at her as the numbness melted away and an awareness that Sven was talking crept back. "Are you sure you're okay?" His thumbs brushed her cheeks, his gaze reaching inward for her soul, and in return she saw concern and fear inside him.

She didn't like it.

Flinging his hands off her, Sairha took a step away from the both of them. "I'm fine. I said I was okay," she snapped, trying to mask the trembles that were bubbling beneath the surface. Avoiding their stares, she hyper focused on scrubbing her hands on the legs of her pants. Rubbing them up and down until they burned from the friction. It took everything in her not to gag, she had never felt so disgusting in her life. She was soaked in the mixture from the waist down, it felt like it had seeped into her pores. Would that sickening smell ever come out?

"That..." Sairha took a gulp of air to steady her rapid pulse. "That was an...an arm. *An arm!* Some weird...mutated... clawed...arm. Oh god, and the..."

The severed foot in the claws flashed in her mind and she shook her head to clear it away, if only temporarily. With another deep breath, she looked up at the cloudless sky, willing her mind to go blank for a moment. She knew she needed to get past this to be efficient again. Her body cried out to lay down and wallow.

No time for that.

"Okay, I'm ready. Let's get going." Without looking back, Sairha headed towards the end of the desolate town.

Cassandra caught up to her first and reached to grab her elbow, but Sairha wrenched it away before she could get any of the slime on her. "Sairha, we should probably rest. You look like hell," Cassandra fretted.

"No, she's right. We *should* move on from here immediately. This was a mistake." Sven came up on the other side of Sairha. The sincerity in his tone only powered her more to get this place far behind them.

"She is not okay! *Look at her*. She's covered in—" Cassandra couldn't finish her sentence. She paused to lean against a telephone pole and dry heaved again. When she had finished, and out of breath, she continued. "Gross. Sairha. You should not have wandered off from us like that. What were you thinking?!"

Sairha shrugged. "We needed to get going, we can't wander around a grocery store like it's Sunday morning. I went to see if there were any chips left, figuring maybe people left some, thinking it would go faster if we split up."

At least, it was supposed to be, Sairha thought with bitterness. *What a stupid mistake that was.*

Cassandra lifted her hands in frustration, motioning back behind them. "Split up and crashed into...into that—"

"Hush," Sven hissed, cutting Cassandra off, somehow understanding that Sairha did not want to talk about it.

Sometimes Sairha wondered if he could read her mind. She hoped he couldn't, at that very moment, because everything inside her was crying like a child, frightened and hiding, in need of her security blanket. In need of her mom. Her tough gal attitude was a facade to try and push past it, to cope.

Is this the world we live in now? Body parts left to ooze? Not just humans, but unimaginable creatures? What was that? The thoughts ran through her mind almost as fast as the pace Sairha now set. They passed by the rest of the town; a second neighborhood similar to the first, with windows destroyed and rubbish littering the streets. Cars left with doors wide open, windshields cracked. A dark diner with formica tables in the lot, sparkly red barstools piled against the shattered door. If anyone was left alive, they never showed themselves.

They came to the end of town, after the 'Thank Y'all For Coming' sign and found a lone gas station. Determined to come away with something, Sairha made a beeline for it.

Moving closer, she pressed her wet backside against the wall and listened. It was difficult to concentrate, her mind hyper aware of the feeling of her soggy pants. And why they were soggy. *Get over it already,* she scolded herself, pushing the door open then slipping inside.

In the blink of an eye, the atmosphere changed. Sairha's arm was yanked behind her in a tight bind as something cold pressed against her throat. Fear gripped her as she tried to force her eyes to adjust to the darkness. A hot breath down her neck told Sairha the attacker was much taller than herself as well as stronger with that kind of grip. A misshaped figure came into focus. Not one, but two someones stood in front of her, holding steadfast to each other. Two sets of big, frightened, dark brown eyes peeked through messes of long, black hair. Identical twins, not much older than twenty, if she had to guess. Matching blue nail polish on their soft tan hands. One was visibly smaller than the other, the only difference Sairha could make out, aside from clothing.

The cold item pushed closer to her throat, sharp steel biting ever so slightly into her flesh. A knife, a rather large one at that.

"Who the hell are you?" demanded the person holding it, a baritone voice in her ear.

Sairha inhaled sharply, in pain, her arm twisted tighter when she didn't answer right away.

"Sairha!" Cassandra gasped when Sven and her stepped inside.

"*Be still,*" Sairha managed to hiss, knowing she absolutely did not look okay, locked in a tight hold by a mysterious man. She averted her eyes to direct her friends' attention towards the twins. Sven's gaze, however, never left the knife on Sairha's throat.

"Look, I'm sorry if I startled you," Sairha talked towards the twins, but her words were for the man holding her hostage. "My name is Sairha and these are my companions, Sven and Cassandra. We honestly mean none of you harm."

The knife loosened from her throat a smidge.

Sven was stock-still, worry etched across his face, eyes darting from her to the man behind her. She had made him concerned for her twice in one day, less than an hour between incidents. *Guess I really lost the bet now,* she mused. *Depending how this ends, I might not have to admit it.*

Sven shifted his weight, uneasy, and showed his empty hands in a non-threatening gesture. "We really do not mean you harm. Are you guys okay? Are any of you hurt?" With a grimace, he looked away from Sairha and nodded at the twins.

Cassandra remained by his side, protected, shell shocked into silence.

"How long have you been in here? Did anyone..." Sairha looked down at the twins' feet. Relief poured in when she counted all four, but could not move her head with the knife so close to check out those of the man's. "Did anyone get attacked?"

The taller girl made a soft noise and moved away from her sister. "My sister, her leg was cut pretty bad."

"I can help her," Sairha offered with a small smile. "I am a trained nurse. If you guys would trust me, I could have her patched up in no time. I promise we won't hurt you."

The situation was tense, and yet, Sairha felt calmer here than she had a few moments ago in the grocery store. Which was ridiculous, she knew. What harm could an unknown severed arm cause her that would be worse than her throat being slit or her arm broken?

The man removed the knife slowly from her neck.

Stepping away from him, Sairha angled herself to get a good look at her former captor. She spotted the silver beaded chain around his neck that dipped down into his shirt, identification tags hidden beneath. A tall, Black man built like a Greek god in military clothes. The muscles that rippled beneath his soiled and torn green ribbed tank were taut, and Sairha became aware of how easy it would have been for him to have severely hurt her. She followed his movement downward as he put his long knife back into its sheath attached to a utility belt. He wore baggy camo print cargo pants, secured tightly at the ankles by worn-in combat boots. Even though he had let her go, he was ready to fight at any given moment. Impressive and intimidating. No wonder Sven and Cassandra had frozen as soon as they took in the situation.

Glad that she had not been silenced permanently, Sairha turned her attention to the twins, focusing on the one that was hurt. Offering her hand, she hoped it looked cleaner than she knew it was. "Shall we get you looked at and cleaned up?"

The girl looked to her twin, who nodded, and then took Sairha's hand to be led outside the shop.

Sairha cleaned up the girl's leg, while the rest of the group finished rummaging around the shop. Everyone was on edge, except for Sairha who was in her element. She cleaned the long, shallow gash along the back of the girl's calf, thankful for the hindsight to have grabbed a first-aid kit from the hospital. It was easy, comforting work for her brain.

"My name's Angie," the girl whispered, her voice high in pitch, reminding Sairha of a mouse. "And my sister is Brenda."

"It's nice to officially meet you." Sairha smiled, wrapping gauze around the wound. "And the man you're with?"

"He goes by Cook." Sairha caught Angie's quick glance towards the shop door. "My sister and I were robbed, that's how I got hurt. We probably would have been killed if Cook hadn't come to our rescue. That was two days ago. We stopped here to look for water to clean it and because I couldn't stand the pain anymore."

Sven stepped outside, immediately positioning himself beside Sairha, and at an angle that meant he could view the door as well. His body language was still tight with tension. Cassandra and the other twin, Brenda, emerged with their bags a little fuller looking than before. Cook followed behind, scanning the town beyond, alert and ready for danger.

There had to be some way to lighten the situation.

"The good news is, you'll live," Sairha said cheerfully, packing the supplies back up.

"What's the bad news?" Angie crumpled into herself, her face wrought with fear.

Her twin rolled her eyes and came over to help her up. "The bad news is you'll live to see another day in this hell hole." Brenda's deeper octave made her words sound harsher than she probably intended.

Sairha winced and the group fell quiet, an invisible line dividing them. No one volunteered to come forward and propose what needed to be said. "We should stick together." Sensing the twins would follow his direction, Sairha looked at Cook directly. "Until our paths separate, that is." Prickling along her neck suggested Cassandra and Sven's focus were on her, but she didn't care. She'd said it before to Sven, there was safety in numbers, and they couldn't argue against that. Despite his perfect stone mask, Cook was clearly thinking along the same lines.

"Alright." He swung a green rucksack over his shoulder.

"We'll go with you, for the time being. But don't try to pull a fast one on any of us. I'm trained to kill."

The twins did not say anything, only gathered their things.

Sven slid his hand inside of Sairha's and gave it a squeeze. She wondered if he made a show of it intentionally or if it was a pure gesture, but relished the comfort it brought her anyway. He had nothing to worry about, she felt the same electric attraction to him as she did the first time they touched hands.

"Let's get going," Sven said with authority in his tone. "I want to get this place far behind us."

Cook nodded and the two led the way, the former easily matching Sven's pace.

As they left, out of the corner of Sairha's vision, she caught a slight movement in the middle of the street. She turned her head to get a better view. Nothing. Maybe she hadn't seen the manhole sliding open. Maybe it was a trick of her mind, delirium or exhaustion. Still...

"Yeah," she mumbled. "The farther, the better."

It *was* time to put some distance between them and the tragic town.

THE SUN HAD long since set when the newly formed group stopped. An unspoken agreement pushed them to add as many miles away from the town as possible. Angie's sore leg was temporarily tolerable with ibuprofen from the medkit, the lack of visibility in the growing darkness being the only reason for stopping. Sven found a field surrounded by a barbed wire fence and wild bushes to rest their weary limbs.

Making camp, it was obvious the twins were ill-prepared. Brenda had a messenger bag of a small, fashionable kind and

Angie had nothing. Sven offered his sleeping bag to them, though they protested, and it took him insisting that he did not use it, seeing as he cuddled up with Sairha most nights. They finally accepted it, set their bedding off to the side of the group, and looked almost relaxed while brushing each other's hair. Cook setup close to them with a thin, steel-gray wool blanket, and a rolled camo jacket that matched his pants that he used as a pillow. It looked uncomfortable to Sairha, but Cook plopped down and closed his eyes right away, clearly well used to the rough lifestyle.

Cassandra laid beside Sairha, looking worse for wear, and went to sleep immediately. Sairha frowned and mentally noted the sickly pale coloring of her friend's features. She hadn't talked about their travels that day, or what they would do tomorrow, not even a peep of complaint about aching muscles.

Sairha frowned. *Maybe Cassandra suffered more trauma from the grocery store incident than I did.* A faint current spread across her flesh when Sven came up and wrapped his hand around hers.

"Come on," he said in a hushed voice, tugging her away.

"Where are we going?" Though it did not matter, she would follow him anywhere. "What about Cassandra?"

"She'll be okay. We won't be out of sight from the camp." He glanced towards the newcomers. "We're going to hunt out some dry wood. I think a nice campfire will turn the mood." His fingers laced through hers.

Sairha liked the sound of that, even if everyone else was near asleep. They had not had one campfire the entire journey so far, the early fall still warm enough at night. She looked around at all the bushes and, in the distance, spotted some old bare trees. She pondered if it was the added cover that made Sven feel comfortable enough to light a fire, or if he really did believe it would cheer everyone up.

"I wish that we had some new clothes for you," she heard

him mutter. He sounded sympathetic but also frustrated. If only he knew how she felt about it.

"Aw, do I smell *that bad*?" she teased, knowing full well she did, and pouted.

He laughed when he stopped and saw her. With little effort, he pulled her into his arms, one hand on her lower back and the other pushing some of her hair away from her face. His soft lips brushed against hers, their noses bumping as he did, and softly replied, "Yes, a little bit."

A shriek of laughter escaped her, and she gave him a playful push. He pulled her back, planted a quick kiss on her lips, then let her go again. Pretending to be mad, she marched forward. "Come on, let's find that firewood then. We can burn my clothes, and I'll just become a nudist!"

Picking up dried wood, Sven never strayed too far from her. She did not complain, she enjoyed his company. It was rare that they had alone time. She realized they started the day off alone together and were finishing it alone, which should have made her happy. Yet, the day's events lingered in the back of her mind. What she could have done better played over and over, like a melody on repeat. "Hey Sven," she called out, picking up a stick. "I lost the bet, right?"

Sven snorted but said nothing. His arms were laden with enough wood to start the small fire as she added to it. There was a moment of peaceful quiet in the wild until he spoke next. "Sairha. You are a lot tougher than you let on, you know? And a lot smarter than you think."

She looked at him curiously but remained silent to allow him to continue.

"What you said to Cassandra, about needing to hurry along the scavenging and choosing to split up. You were right to do so, even with what happened. That was calculative thinking, something a leader would decide." There was no teasing, or joking, in his tone and his face was tight with sincerity. "The way you handled the situation at the gas station? Wow." He shook his head in disbelief.

Sairha sighed, seeing it another way. "I was reckless, not impressive," she said with a harshness that surprised even herself. Not undeserved. "I ran in there without really listening. I could have... He could have killed me. I was too focused on moving past that whole...grocery store...severed arm incident. I stormed in, again, and it almost cost me my life. I feel like you try to teach us so much and I just don't retain it."

Even in the dark, she could see the softness, and compassion, his features took on. She did not deserve any of that, and turned away from his view, trying not to shed tears of anger over the stupidity she felt.

"You may have run in there reckless, but here you are, admitting your mistakes." Sven closed the gap between them. "Sure, that man got the best of you, but he's trained by the military. He has spent years learning how to be silent and get the drop on people. You have had simple training from a hack job like me for what? Two weeks?" He reached out and rubbed her arm. "And you defused the situation easily, effortlessly. You took control, you got everyone to remain calm and join forces."

She took time to digest what he had pointed out. All she could do was learn from it, do better, and be more cautious of her surroundings. "You're right," she agreed. "Maybe I am a little too hard on myself. I'll try not to kick myself around so much."

"Don't try too hard. It should be natural to be kinder to yourself." Sven smiled, then headed back towards camp.

Sairha felt lightened from the burden of being a screw up. Sven's push to see her self-worth showed her how critically her brain had been wired. Hospital life was overanalyzing situations, thinking of scenarios and possibilities that could have made them more effective. It would take work, not only being more aware, but also releasing the guilt from mistakes; things she should have been doing as a nurse as well.

Sven took the wood they had collected and set up a stack in the center of the camp. There were enough rocks around that he used to form a circle to keep the subsequent fire tamed.

"Want the matches?" Sairha reached for her pack, remembering they'd snagged some before leaving Sabueso de Oro.

"Nah." Sven shrugged, and Sairha watched as he put dried grass and some crisp leaves on top of a thick, flat piece of wood. Thin stick in hand, he began whittling away at the dry pile. His hands shimmied back and forth to create friction with the bottom one he held still with his feet.

It was fascinating to watch; she'd never seen anyone start a fire like that. Sairha was not the only one staring at this artform happening. Cook opened an eye, ready to take over if Sven needed it. And the twins, who still sat close together on their borrowed sleeping bag, were mystified. Sven ignored them as he made quick work to ignite a spark of fire, never slowing.

Sairha took a second to look over at Cassandra, to see if she had stirred as well, but she continued to lay with her back to the group. A quiet cheer went up from the twins. Sairha turned back as Sven gave his creation a gentle puff of air to coax the ember into being. She noticed Cook looked relieved, relaxing back against his makeshift pillow, though he never took his eyes away from Sven and the fire. She cleared her throat to draw his attention her way. "Cook, is it?" She felt awkward asking.

He chuckled a bit, friendliness visibly washing over him. "It's Alexander Cook. But, yeah. Everyone calls me Cook, military thing and all."

She nodded with a soft smile. The feel of his hand twisting

her arm lingered in the back of her memory, but she was determined to move past that. They needed to all get along and stick together, something inside told her so. "We came from a small town down south, *Sabueso de Oro*. Cassandra and I—" Sairha nodded back towards the sleeping woman. "—met when I moved there a year ago to study abroad as a nurse. And I met Sven only a few days before all of this craziness happened with the world. Him and I are actually from around the same area. When he said he had to get home, I took the opportunity to have safety in a small group and travel back home as well. Back to my family, hopefully unharmed."

Cook looked between the two of them; whether he was suspicious or sizing them up, who could say.

Sairha wondered if Sven was okay with her revealing so much right away, without really knowing the others, but this was part of her strategy *to* get to know them, by opening up with honesty and tentatively receiving some in return. She wasn't stupid however; she wouldn't divulge too much information.

Cook tilted his head, as if thinking what he wanted to say before he spoke. Leaning up on his elbow, the light of the small fire danced across his face. "Alright. Sharing time it is. I was visiting some family while on leave when—BAM —the whole world went dark and every electronic *in* the world stopped. What a crazy silence that was. Decided I could not wait and wanted some answers, so I set out on foot to get back to my military base. I came across these two by accident." He nodded towards the twins. "I stopped in a small town, only a little bigger than the one you found us in, and heard a commotion going on. There were men shouting, screams and crying. My training kicked in, and I went to check it out."

"Oh my god, he was brave," one of the twins piped up. Brenda, Sairha recalled.

"So, *so brave*," the other, Angie, agreed as she shook a little in her seat. Her sister's arm went around her to calm her obvious anxiety.

"I got into an altercation with the men. Three of them, some thugs trying to take Brenda's bag," Cook continued, ignoring the admiration from the girls.

"He beat them up!" Brenda interjected, dissatisfied with his modesty. "They were threatening us with big knives. I tried to push Angie away, to get her to escape. But one of those low lives grabbed her bag and..."

Angie sighed, looking away from them.

Sairha's eyes went to her bandaged wound.

"I'm not ashamed. I beat one of them to a pulp and the other two limped off, dragging their buddy with them. I could not just leave Angie and Brenda alone, especially with the little one's leg like that." The last part was spoken with such tenderness, leaving no doubt that he had a weak spot for people in need. "We had stopped for some more water and were looking for a first-aid kit in that shop when you surprised us."

"Surprised *you*?" Sairha almost laughed.

Sven, who had remained quiet the whole time, looked up from the fire he was poking at. Somberly, he addressed Cook. "Did you stop at the grocery store, by any chance?"

Sairha involuntarily shuddered and closed her eyes, reliving that horrible scene again. When she opened them again, Cook was staring at Sven with matched intensity.

"Yeah, we did. I went in, leaving the girls outside; when I saw there was *nothing* of interest, I led them out to the gas station instead." Cook's expression was harder than it was seconds ago.

Sairha realized what he was implying. He *had* seen the severed arm but spared the twins the details. She was both glad and envious of them. There was no question what her nightmares would entail that night. The only monster those two would know in their dreams would be the villainous humans who took advantage of the world going to hell.

"Where are you heading towards, if you don't mind me asking?" Sairha decided to change the subject, for all their sakes. Sven took her hint and leaned back beside her, his hair tickling her arm. She brushed its softness away.

Cook shrugged. "San Dayo."

Sairha glanced at the twins; it was clearly written on their faces that they went wherever their savior did. At least until Cook tired of them, she guessed. She leaned forward to hold her hands out to the heat. It was comforting, despite the night being warm enough. The smell of burning wood was a pleasant change of sensory stimulation. "Sounds like we're going the same way for the most part. Why not keep on with us? Until our paths go separate ways."

After Sairha's disastrous day, it only solidified in her mind that Cassandra and her were too much work for Sven. Bicycle crash, the creature's bloody arm, stories of dangerous looters. Who knew *what* that arm belonged to, Sairha did not want to find out. But if she eventually did, it was a good idea to have more back up.

Cook stared at her, a smile slowly unfolding along his face. Something about Sairha seemed to amuse this guy, and she sort of liked that. They had only known each other a short while, yet Sairha felt like she could trust him. Maybe even with her life someday. He looked away, at Brenda and Angie. Brenda gave him an expression that could only be described as questioning. Maybe she couldn't see the point of staying together. Angie nudged her and two sets of brown eyes turned on Sairha. It was a good idea to have someone who could mend them up, Brenda couldn't argue with that logic, could she?

"Sure, why not?" Cook turned back to face Sairha.

She grinned and snuggled against Sven's shoulder, his head resting atop hers. Exhaustion, but also a sense of contentment she hadn't felt since before the explosion, encompassed her. "Great, it's settled then. We'll head out together again in the morning."

CHAPTER SEVEN

Cook's combat boots left a perfect line of trail, followed closely by Brenda and Angie's clumsy foot falls, then Cassandra at an exhausted, slower pace. She'd awoken pale in complexion and had kept to herself most of the morning, shrugging off Sairha's concern. *Other than that, everything so far is going good,* Sairha thought to herself about the ragtag caravan. Any doubts she may have had about joining forces dissolved away. She hoped Cassandra would perk back up after a while but made a mental note to check in on their break. There were still many miles of the day's journey to be covered before that.

Slowing down, to fall beside Sven who brought up the rear, Sairha nudged his shoulder. "Hey, there, mister. Whatcha doing all alone back here?"

Sven shrugged and smiled, though it lacked any feeling. "It's kind of a nice change, being in the back. Not leading." He tossed his hair back, taking a long second to look over his shoulder. Like he was waiting for something to happen, something to come from behind them.

She glanced over her shoulder as well, dread filling her when her imagination sparked. She could almost see a nonexistent manhole in the middle of the sand, three gleaming claws sliding the lid open. The manhole, the severed limbs, the pools of blood. It was time, she knew it was. Time to stop lying to herself. "The back is important, especially with how large the group is now," she agreed, watching out of the corner of her eye for his reaction to her next comment. "And that creature I saw back in the street."

Sven, ever the master of his emotions, held on tight to his aloof stance. However, she kept her sight set on him, prolonging the silence. He all of a sudden visibly let his guard down; shoulders drooping, face solemn, as he let out a sigh. "Yeah...I saw that, too. As we were leaving."

"It's weird that we never see it, just glimpses. Or..." She shuddered. "What do you think it was? I'm not an animal expert, but I've never seen anything like that."

He shrugged again. "I...don't know. Something we've probably never seen the likes of."

"Do you think..." Sairha steeled herself mentally, reverting to her practiced monotoned, objective mentality. "Do you think that's why we have seen so many desolate spots? That whatever this creature is, there's many of them and they're... hunting us?" Sven remained quiet, though Sairha noticed the tightness returning to his body. For his sake, she let the question go unanswered and shifted direction. "What about Cook?" she murmured to avoid being overheard. "He seemed like he saw something but didn't want to talk about it. How long can he protect those girls from what is happening in this world, you know?"

"That's why I decided on the campfire last night. The smoke helped mask the stench of blood on you," he confessed.

Sairha's eyes widened, insecurity setting in.

He waved his hands around in a frantic attempt to ease her worry. "Not for us! It really isn't that bad. It was for whatever that creature is. I didn't want it to have a scent to follow."

Warmth drained from her face as a chill swept over her. The thought that an unknown thing would follow them, because she accidentally doused herself in its blood, terrified her more than she cared to acknowledge.

"Cook must know something," Sven continued, clearly trying to move the subject along. "We should get him alone and talk to him about it, since he won't say anything in front of Brenda and Angie."

"Okay, sounds good," was all Sairha could manage in response, wishing for a hot shower to appear in the middle of nowhere.

***

ANOTHER CAMPFIRE BLAZED in the center of their camp that night, and Sairha made sure she sat closer than comfortable to it. It wasn't so bad; the smoke smelled like fresh wood and sagebrush. If that wasn't pungent enough, she wasn't sure what would be. The night before, staring into the flames had made Sairha feel safe and at ease. Now she looked into them, and the arm of the creature twisted out, morphing into misshapen shadow creatures. Yellow, hungry eyes glowered at her in her nightmare, despite having never caught a glimpse of the face. She needed to keep her mind busy, keep it distracted from those visions.

She glanced over at Cook, seated on a tree stump, cleaning his knife. Behind him, the gentle rise and fall of the twins' chests indicated their slumbering. After the nightly change of Angie's bandage, and some over-the-counter painkillers, Angie had curled up exhausted with Brenda soon beside her. Poor thing was sore but never once complained. It had been Brenda who voiced her concern for her sister's discomfort, loudly at that. Sairha smiled a little, thinking of her own kid sister and how she would do anything for her. Like traveling on foot across the desert to see her again.

Cassandra plopped down in a heap. She claimed to feel better, though her pale complexion had not left. With the fear of what had transpired during the first meeting wearing off, Cassandra had agreed to make an effort to stay awake and get to know the newcomer.

Stick in hand, Sven crouched beside Sairha and jostled the logs around, arranging them into a formation more to his liking. "Cook," he said after a while, glancing across the flames at the other man. "You know a lot more than you let on, I bet." It was spoken like more of a challenge than an observation.

Sairha rested her hand on his leg, giving it a light squeeze of warning. *Be kind.*

Cook stared back at him, his face a perfect blank slate. "I have no idea what you are talking about," he replied in a flat tone.

Sven narrowed his eyes.

Before either of them could puff out their machismo more, Sairha decided to intervene. "We want to talk about what we *all* saw in that town while still respecting your decision to protect those two's innocence on the subject, that's why we chose to discuss it now, while they sleep. Please. Did you see...anything unusual...along your travels?"

With it being evident that neither Sven nor Sairha would drop the matter, Cook sighed and rubbed his head, defeated. "Alright, I guess we could cross reference." He moved closer to them. The usual sparkle in his coal-colored eyes was gone as he looked from Cassandra to Sven and finally Sairha. "That town was not the first time I saw them, those creatures. I've been calling them bonebags because, well, that is what they look like." His words came out slowly, like recalling it caused a bad taste in his mouth.

"You've actually *seen* one? Like, out in the open?" Cassandra gasped.

He nodded. "Yes, unfortunately. I was on leave from the military for two weeks to visit my mama and family. My sister just had a baby, the first grandchild, so the whole family came around. It was a great week until *that* one night... We were all barbecuing in the back of my mama's house. Us men were outside, watching the grill and having some beers. The women were inside, talking stories and fussing over the baby. I remember everyone was laughing at some joke my brother-in-law told while we were finishing our last round of drinks for the night, but I was looking up at the sky. Mama lived in the suburbs, and there were less streetlights and traffic noises there. Especially compared to the noisy military base I had been calling home for over a year. The sky was so beautiful, every star was out twinkling, shining bright." He paused and took a moment to look up at the sky.

Sairha could have sworn she saw the shimmer of tears, but it was gone when he turned his gaze back upon them.

"Then suddenly, everything went silent. It was like someone had shot off a flash-bang grenade in the area. A bright, white light blinded me, followed by some high pitch whistle, and gone in an instant. I felt lightheaded and there was intense pressure in my ears. As if in slow motion, I watched my beer fall and shatter on the ground, soundless." His fingers tapped, restlessly, on his knees. "I remember seeing my brother-in-law run into the house, to check on my sister and their baby. I went out into the neighborhood, to take surveillance, to see if anyone was hurt. What I saw was...life changing, *world changing.*"

Sairha sat on the edge of her seat, enthralled. Cook's tale cast a spell over them, and despite knowing that it couldn't possibly end well, she was desperate to hear it through. She had been knocked out after the incident and was eager to learn what happened during that time. Beside her, Cassandra chewed at her nails as she listened, her eyes wide. Only Sven seemed unchanged, patient with the slow pace of the story.

"The neighbors had also gone outside to see what had happened. Most of them elderly folk. But what I saw beyond the safety of our fence was not what I expected." Cook rubbed his brow as he spoke. "I saw these...these unusual creatures, crawling out a deep crack in the road. They were tall, even on all fours. They had skin as pale and gray as the moon, pulled tight enough I could see the bones underneath. Except...where the limbs bent and the saggy neck with too many folds. The arms were extra long. The back legs short and weak looking. All of this was strange, for sure, but when I got a good look at their heads..."

Cook shuddered involuntarily and leaned closer to the fire, bathing in its golden light, warming his somber expression and hands.

"Their heads were huge, twice the size of a human's, and the face...terrifying. I have never seen anything like it. They had this long slash of mouth, from side to side. And the eyes... Well, it was dark, and I couldn't see anything for eyes. Just dark areas where they should be." He paused and looked down at his large hands, opening and closing, as if he held an invisible weapon. Or maybe wished he had. "Three long hooks, like fingers, and a little one on the back side like a thumb. That they used to drag...to drag my mama's neighbors off. I saw one knock a lady across the head, heard something snap, and watched as the creature tossed her like a babydoll off into the darkness. I never felt so terrified in my life. I had to get back to my family. I had to warn them."

Dread sank into Sairha. Was she shaking? She looked over at Cassandra, who was frozen with her hand clasped across her mouth. Never had Sairha come close to imagining such a thing. Even Sven shifted uncomfortably, looking away out into the dark desert.

Cook cleared his throat in an attempt to push back his emotions. "I was too late. Only by a few seconds. Too late to save them. When I went to go through the back door, I nearly ran into a creature finishing off my brother-in-law, thankfully with its back to me. My training kicked in quick, and I pressed myself back against the wall. Peering inside, I hoped to catch sight of my family." He paused, choked up. Seconds ticked by slowly before he was able to start talking again. "I saw my sister…what little was left of her, her hand was outstretched…across from her a blood-soaked baby blanket…I almost threw up. There was no time to grieve, though, the creature was moving again. And it was quick, impossibly quick. I ran out. Scrambled off the deck and crawled underneath. The deck's boards shifted, and I knew the creature was making its way out the back, where I was. My heart pounded in my ears as I shimmied further back, but I kept my face to the opening. If it was going to find me, I wanted to see it coming."

Cassandra gasped.

"One long arm came down onto the ground, then the hind legs. It slumped down onto its hunches. And the noises I heard next… They still haunt me." He murmured the last part.

Please, no. Please do not say it. Sairha gripped Sven's arm around her waist, holding her steady. Strong, empathic emotions threatened to bring tears to her eyes. Crying would do nobody any good, especially Cook who was so close to breaking down himself. Inhaling deeply, she shut her feelings down.

He shook his head, unable to continue. His lips were pressed together tight, visibly fighting with his inner self.

Cassandra reached out her hand and clasped his gently in her own. "You don't have to finish," she whispered.

He looked down at her hand, as if surprised that she was even there, and was brought back to them, to the present. The tragedy of the past was left dwindling in the crisp campfire air. Despite the intensity of the moment, he half smiled and rested his other hand on top of Cassandra's. "You guys need to know the rest. I can tell by your faces that this is more information than you have to share." His features took on a brave soldier's hardness, his voice became unwavering in strength. "That dirty bonebag, when it lowered its other arm, my mama's limp body was in its grasp. I started to turn away, to not look, but what it did next was so appalling, I could not turn away. It had no trouble as it ripped through her clothes, tore her flesh to shreds. Into little pieces using its teeth. Thin, needle-like, glistening teeth. Thousands of them. Like a goddamn paper shredder, it wrecked through my mama. And the noises it made after…slurping…"

Covering her mouth again, Cassandra paled to a sickly color in the firelight. A trained nurse, the gruesome description was compartmentalized into the part of Sairha's brain that wouldn't allow her to be sick.

Cook's eyes shuttered, taking one last staggered breath as he neared what was hopefully the end of his tragic story. "When there was nothing much left, it used those long claws to snap the bones and dig inside, extracting stuff with a long, almost snake-like tongue. Jutting in and out of the bones."

"The marrow," Sairha whispered.

He nodded.

Sven pulled Sairha closer. This was so much worse than she could have imagined. *It tore her flesh to shreds. It eats the marrow inside.* The image of what looked like an exploded middle section of a human in the hotel room came back to her in vivid clarity. Her thoughts shifted to her friend, wondering if Cassandra recalled any memories of her own from that time. They had never talked about it, maybe now would be the time. These creatures sounded more horrendous than any beasts she had heard of. Before, they had been shrouded in mystery, silent stalkers in the shadows. She had only seen an arm up close and personal. And that alone had shaken her. Now, she was mortified. Her heart ached for his loss, and as awkward as it might seem, she was glad that she had insisted Cook come with them. No one should be alone after experiencing that.

"The creature left, but I waited until morning, after the sun had long been up, and it had been quiet for hours, until I crawled myself out from under the deck." Cook let out a deep breath, his muscles relaxing a little as he did. Sadness etched his tone, but inner strength, the will to survive, was stronger. "When I left mama's, I found that a lot of the other houses looked similar. Bloody messes left behind. Somehow, I was the only one, either everyone was killed or some got away, I hope. The lack of people was deafening. I grabbed my bag and headed to the airport. Only to find nothing worked; no electronics, planes, cars, cellphones. All dead. I set out on foot, intending to get back to the base I'm stationed at. Shortly after, I met the twins as they were trying to fend off those thugs." He took a second to look back at them, still sleeping peacefully. Two girls who never left each other's presence, who were always within sight of him. The trio's closeness made more sense, the urge to protect a clear force that drove him.

"I made sure we stayed out of inhabited places at night, seeing as those bonebags only come out once the sun's gone. I only ever saw signs of them in towns, so best to avoid the towns all together. But we needed a first aid kit. Where you found us, yeah." He nodded to Sven. "I saw that scene in the grocery store. We weren't there when it happened, but I hope that bonebag bled out and died a painful death in the sunlight."

"Hmm… So, it wasn't you who fought it off," Sven murmured, shaking his head. "My guess is whoever got that swing at its arm also lost more than their leg that day."

A shudder ran through Sairha, his words evoking another horror film-esque scenario in her mind. "None of us have seen as much as you," she admitted to Cook. "I've only seen the creatures in mere glimpses, in dark areas where you can't be sure if your eyes are playing tricks on you. I thought I saw something, almost spider-like, in a hotel stairway. I had the feeling that it was following us, but we managed to get outside in time. And then…" She made the quick decision to not mention the border control building, since she wasn't even sure herself what she had heard. "Then in that grocery store, I was the one who found the severed limb with the foot wedged in its grasp."

Cook's face broke into what looked like a painful grimace, his mouth opened wide and his eyes crinkled tight. Something unexpected happened. Laughter, full hearted laughter erupted out of his mouth. He slapped his knee, tears welling up not from sadness but from laughing too hard. "Yeah, I'll say you found it alright! Girl, when I first saw you, you looked like you rolled around in a mud wrestling battle to the death with one. And smelled like…well, I can't even describe the stench."

A hot flush rushed over Sairha, probably the shade of a beet. She smacked Sven's arm. "You told me it wasn't that bad!"

His own face red from the silent laughter he had been

holding in, Sven lifted his hands up to protect himself. "I'm sorry! I'm sorry, really I said that to make you feel better."

"Hmph!" Sairha pouted and looked to Cassandra for some moral support but found her friend of no use either.

"Why do you think I've had to stay so far from you?" Cassandra chuckled. "I'd probably still be throwing up."

Scrambling to her feet, Sairha flipped everyone off with her middle finger before storming off. She overheard the three of them laughing more, and Cook called to Sven, "Looks like you'll be needing a new sleeping arrangement." She couldn't help but sneer at that as she kicked off her shoes, soiled pants, and scooted into her sleeping bag.

"Looks like it," Sven replied, the sound of a smirk in his voice.

JOKES ASIDE, Sairha awoke snug in Sven's arms when morning light came. He must have slipped beside her, and as warm as he was, she did not stir but instead curled into his embrace. Not a bad way to wake in the morning.

There was no conversation as they packed up the camp. The intensity of the night's storytelling lingered like a miasma. Cook had given them a lot to mull over. He resumed the lead with Cassandra close beside him. Sairha and the twins hovered around the middle, leaving Sven to bring up the rear.

The silent trek gave Sairha too much time to reflect. Learning more about the kind of man Alexander Cook was internalized all of the things she had taken for granted before. Similar to him, she had entered a career field of protecting people, though after only a handful of years being a nurse, she had become desensitized and bored. It was no longer about helping, simply a job she went to. Even studying abroad had been a failed attempt at rejuvenating something long dead inside of her. She'd left her mom and sister, and what little friends she had, behind to chase some sort of purpose in life. It had seemed like she had nothing to lose except herself and her career. A pang of shame tugged at her thinking about them now, about how precious her family actually was to her. Them and *him*.

She glanced back at Sven.

His head was lowered as he walked and he, too, looked deep in thought.

Her heart went aflutter. She wouldn't have ever guessed their little weekend fling would have turned into more. Would it have if the world hadn't been ripped away from them?

Shaking herself of the 'what if' scenarios in her head, Sairha turned her attention to the two ahead of her. Cook and Cassandra appeared to be hitting it off. The brunette was animated as she told a story, flinging her hands around. Cook obliged her every so often with a nod or a laugh. *She must be feeling better now,* Sairha thought happily. *I'll let them have their moment alone.*

"Hey, how's the leg feeling today, Angie?" she asked, picking up the pace to walk beside the twins. She couldn't help but notice she'd used her professional voice but was thankful for an easy topic starter.

Angie's face lit up with a bright smile in welcome. "It's doing so much better, thank you. I seriously cannot thank you enough. And a lot of the soreness is gone. I don't know how I would have survived without your help."

"It was an easy fix." Sairha shrugged, trying to avoid any more compliments. "It really was a simple cut to clean and close up with the right supplies. I'm just glad we caught it before it got infected."

Angie nodded, but her smile dimmed. "If I had just given those men my bag, instead of creating a struggle..."

Brenda let out a loud, exaggerated sigh beside her sister, and rolled her eyes, "You stood your ground. And what have I told you about standing your ground to bullies?"

"Yeah, I know...but I still lost and got hurt. The souvenirs from the music festival were in there and my clothes. Everything. And now we have—" Angie hung her head, her short, dark brown braids dropping against her shoulders. "—nothing."

Sairha felt bad that they had been targeted but could see how easy it must have been. They were young, cute, defenseless looking girls. If Cook had not shown up... "How old are you two, if you don't mind me asking."

"Old enough to be on our own," Brenda said, side eyeing Sairha. It was obvious who the ringleader of the duo was.

"We're twenty," Angie offered, nudging her sister and whispering. "We can trust her."

Sairha cleared her throat. "A music festival. Wow, that sounds like fun. What one did you go to?" There were only two she knew of and both were held in the desert. The appeal of being hot and sweaty in the middle of the desert without a shower never appealed to her. She could almost laugh at her situation now. If only she were out there for music, not to find her family.

Brenda's face lit up and she talked excitedly. "First time going to Brachella. And man, was it just as crazy and fun as everyone says it is! It was so hot, and packed with people, but you hardly notice because you are just there. Feeling the music. Swept up in it." Brown eyes glazing over, she mentally disappeared into the memory of her experience.

Angie nodded in agreement. "It was great."

This explained their attire of shorts and light, flimsy tops.

Brenda started up again, talking about the bands that she loved and how bands she didn't like before ended up being her new favorites because 'oh my god, they were so good live'. Angie piped up once in a while too.

"Sounds like a once in a lifetime thing," Sairha replied during a pause in Brenda's cadence of information. Her smile faltered when she realized the gravity her words held. The truth of the current world. Would they ever enjoy live music again on such a big scale as a festival?

"Yeah!" they simultaneously agreed. The fact that it was the last festival on earth, for who knew how long seemed to go over their heads. "I'm glad we got to go. We almost did not," Angie added.

"Oh?"

"I got really sick beforehand," Angie confessed. She glanced at Brenda, who said nothing nor made any indication to stop sharing. "I'm the younger of us. Brenda was born four minutes before me. Mom had a hard time getting me out, turned out I had my cord wrapped around me pretty snug."

"Like a feather boa, mom always said." Brenda's tender gaze on her sister conveyed more than words could say. The twins chuckled, then fell into a somber silence.

"We'll probably never see her again," Angie whispered.

"I don't care." The harshness in Brenda's voice caused Angie to flinch and even Sairha felt the tension shift. "I stole our mom's credit card to get us bus tickets to attend the festival. But she canceled it, and kind of disowned us, before I could buy us tickets back home. And they wouldn't accept my card since it didn't match my ID name. I didn't have time to go get it changed before we left. So, we were hitchhiking to the coast, to see the ocean instead. Maybe be movie stars. Well, before...*that*... and Cook rescuing us."

"We wanted to be somewhere we fit in better," Angie explained.

Sairha thought about what they were telling her, a glimpse into their lives at home. How Brenda took the big sister role seriously, even when getting the two of them into trouble. But there was a deep love there, a nurturing side. It reminded her of her own sister, although the roles were a bit reversed. Her little sister Alison was the troublemaker, always trying her hardest to follow Sairha's footsteps. Looking where she was now, she wouldn't wish that kind of grueling journey on anyone.

"I have a younger sister," she said, deciding to open up in return. "Her name is Alison, she's a spitfire. A real bat out of hell, my mom says. I'm on my way to find them, see if they are okay." She looked up at the cloudless sky. The brightness hurt her eyes a bit, and how much she truly hoped she would find them ached inside of her again. It was easy to be distracted by everything, by her feelings for Sven, by the dangers that lurked in the shadows, and day to day survival. It was when she allowed herself to really think about them, and how they used to be, that she missed them more than she could bear.

"Hey, you'll find them, don't worry." Angie placed a hand on Sairha's shoulder.

Sairha gave her a half-hearted smile and a single nod of her head. The three women walked in a comfortable silence for the rest of the day.

Velvety night touched the horizon by the time the group agreed to stop. Everyone was beyond exhausted. Sairha was setting up her sleeping bag, when a gentle tug at her elbow drew her attention away. Brenda motioned to follow her behind a nearby bush. Looking anywhere but at Sairha, she mumbled, "Listen, I wanted to personally thank you again for what you did."

"Really," Sairha waved it off, caught off guard. "It was no big deal. I'm trained in that sort of thing. I'm glad she's doing better."

"I know, it's just... It means a lot. She isn't the strongest person, she isn't built for this kind of life. Mom always took care of her health needs. Me? I was just the clown who came to cheer her up. I felt so helpless when she showed me how severe the cut really was." Brenda fumbled inside her messenger bag for a moment. She pulled Sairha's hand out and placed black fabric on top of it. "I'm not sure it'll fit you, but I want you to have my spare pants. They're kinda...dirty but..." She eyed Sairha's disgusting jeans.

"Are you sure?" Sairha was stunned. The act of fixing up Angie's wound was something she would have done for anyone in need. It wasn't a hassle at all. But to Brenda, her actions said it meant the world to her. As much as she wanted to refuse the offer, Sairha could not deny that she had been longing for fresh clothes. "Thank you."

Without another word, Brenda gave a quick nod and dashed off to finish helping with camp set up.

CHAPTER EIGHT

FOUR DAYS PASSED WITH NO ISSUES DESPITE THE QUICK, BUT methodical, pace that Cook set for them. Their energy had dwindled to near nothing, and even Cook and Sven, who the women joked had the tolerance of camels, were visibly fatigued. The previous night they hadn't bothered with a campfire or staying up to swap stories. Instead, they had lay on their makeshift beds, either falling asleep or talking in hushed voices to their neighbor. Sairha had suffered intense nightmares of being chased by disfigured creatures every night since Cook's story. The sky in her dreams was always dark, with billowing clouds of smog poisoning the air, and the sun never rose. Sven tried his best to soothe her, but as soon as she fell back asleep the nightmare would start again. The one-armed creature chasing her until the real morning light rescued her from slumber. Then it was back to walking.

With feet like lead, she dragged herself along behind everyone else. Sven stayed beside her, concern pulling the corners of his mouth downward. He reached for her arm and slinked it through his, which gave her some physical support that she was glad to accept. "The nightmare again?" he asked softly.

The warmth of his body beside hers, her arm linked with his, helped her feel safe and secure. *They were only dreams*, she reminded herself, but couldn't help a bitter after thought. *Dreams based on reality now.* "I've had these dreams for a while, where I am always running, exhausted, out of breath."

"I remember, you had one the night all of this happened."

Sairha nodded. "Yes, but it's different now. I'm running. Running because those creatures are chasing me...those *bonebags*."

Sven sighed. "I hate that name. Sorry, continue."

"The sky was dark, thick with smog. I could breathe, but I could tell it was poisoning the air," she said, looking up, half expecting to see her nightmare come to life. "When I could not run any longer, one of the creatures caught up to me... It had one arm." The last part was spoken barely above a whisper.

Sven said nothing but Sairha felt her hand being squeezed, his hand covering hers.

Waving ahead of them caught their attention. Cook was hailing them, and they picked up the pace.

Cook led them to the edge of a short cliff. Below was a bare road, if you could call it a road with its near-white, crumbling pavement and potholes with shrubbery growing inside. Sven and Cook crouched as they neared the lip, Sairha following suit, and he pointed at a graying farmhouse inside a squared-off area by a decaying fence.

A mixture of emotions ran through Sairha, but excitement overpowered her concern and caution. Maybe she was delirious, but she wanted so badly to inspect the place, as decrepit as it was. A hope beyond all hope that there was running water and a soft feathered bed planted itself in her mind. She turned to Sven, eager for his input.

He stared at her, mouth tight, then looked back down at the farmhouse. "Let's go check it out," he conceded, tugging his hand out from Sairha's and stepping up to Cook. They gave each other a knowing look, some unspoken agreement Sairha couldn't decipher.

"Ummmm, *hello*. Angie can't climb down this cliff with her busted up leg!" Brenda butted in.

Cassandra peered down the side. "It's hardly a cliff. More like a...sloping hill. She'll be fine."

"Still!" Brenda cried out and looked to Sairha for help.

"Angie is starting to feel better," Sairha offered neutrally.

"No, I'm okay guys," Angie protested. Poor thing probably did not want to be a problem for anyone.

To ease everyone, Sairha crouched to inspect Angie's stitches under the bandage. "...I guess I would feel better if you did not risk damaging it. Your injury is closing up nicely, but it doesn't need more strain than necessary."

"This is definitely necessary." Cassandra huffed and turned a longing eye at the house.

Before another word could be spoken, Cook tossed his bag down the edge, then scooped Angie up and onto his back. "Hold on tight," he ordered, and after she did, he climbed down with trained ease.

Cassandra and Brenda stared after them, fascinated.

"That's one way to settle it," Sairha laughed with a shake of her head before swinging her leg over to start the descent. Sven offered his hand to help, only letting go after she was securely out of reach, then helped the other two down.

Sairha landed on the bottom with a thud and wince. All this walking was wearing the soles of her boots down. She rushed to help Angie slide off Cook's back, the young girl's cheeks rosier than ever. Chivalry was still an awe-inspiring thing, even in a world like this. She could not tell if Brenda and

Cassandra were envious or awestruck as both flocked to Cook, asking if he was okay and commenting on his strength, with little concern for Angie's injured leg.

Sven jumped down beside Sairha, his braided hair thumping against his chest from the impact. "Alright, Cook and myself will be the first to check the area out," he said with a strong, authoritative tone. It seemed like he was avoiding eye contact with Sairha.

A good thing since she stared at him in quiet astonishment. *What about me? Haven't I proven myself?* He had said her gas station mistake was a learning experience. It seemed trivial, but she wanted to be the one to scope the place out with him. Up until that point, they had experienced everything together.

"The rest of you will stay here and wait for the signal." Sven pulled Sairha aside and whispered, "If anything happens to us, you take the girls and run. As far as you can."

Understanding came to her and she gave him a solemn nod. There was something else in his intense stare, something she could not read, and instead of saying it, he leaned in and surprised her with a deep kiss. The connection electrified her whole body. Her eyes closed, relishing the spontaneous intimacy. It was over too soon as Sven and Cook left for the farmhouse that time had forgotten.

Sairha watched, breath shaky with anxiety, as they hopped the fence and stole onto the patio, quiet as thieves. They stood, listening for some time, until Cook opened the door and Sven slipped inside. The door closed behind Cook, hopefully quieter than the pounding of Sairha's heart. The length of time the two were out of sight was excruciating. Out the corner of her eye she surveyed how the others were handling the situation. Brenda had her legs up against her chest, while Angie absentmindedly massaged her injured leg. Cassandra lingered farther off to the side, wearing an expression of deep thought.

Minutes, that felt like a lifetime, passed with nothing but anxiety ticking away, what-ifs of the worst kind piling up. She should have gone with them.

"Oh, there it is! The signal!" Brenda shouted, jumping up with excitement. She stopped long enough to help Angie up, then dragged her twin towards the house.

Sure enough, Sairha spotted Sven waving at them, and relief flooded her like a tidal wave. "Cassandra, let's go!" she called, snatching hers and Sven's bags, trailing after the twins.

SAIRHA AVOIDED TOUCHING the grime ridden walls covered in a thick layer of dust. Cobwebs filled lonely corners, their spiders long gone, allowing all variety of bugs to scurry in the shadows. The farmhouse had been evidently abandoned much longer than a handful of weeks. Rounding a corner, a horrible stench accosted her. Panic gripped her, the smell reminding her of the grocery store incident.

Cook and Sven stood in a disheveled living room, no monster limbs to be seen, staring at the ground behind an outdated, worn couch. "This is the culprit," Cook said, his shirt pulled up to his nose as a protectant. He kicked a corner of a large rug.

Sairha stared, disgusted yet transfixed, as it flopped over with a moist 'plop'. Red mold was eating away at the fabric from underneath, consuming an indistinguishable body of something once furry beside the rug. "Let's get it out of here before we're all poisoned." She swallowed hard, fighting the taste of bile in her throat. The two nodded in agreement and pushed the couch away while Sairha moved a dusty armchair next to a wood burning stove.

Cook and Sairha worked together to get the rug rolled up

and outside the house after Sven used a disintegrating curtain to dispose of the bones and fur. The rug fell apart when it hit the ground after they heaved it off the porch, clouds of dust and hollow bug shells flying out. Sairha took a moment in the fresh air, her sweaty hands resting on her hips. The sun blazed in an unforgiving, cloudless sky. Though she was exhausted, there was a sense of rejuvenation, if only mentally, to be sheltered in an old, empty home.

"I feel like I might get some rest tonight." Cook started to lean against the patio railing then thought better of it.

"I know, right? Maybe the beds won't be too bad," she joked, though it really did not matter to her anymore. She would take a filthy, dirt covered bed over the ground any night. Together they walked back into the living room. With the rug gone and windows wedged open, it was more bearable.

"Should we pick our rooms next?" Cassandra asked, clapping her hands together.

Sairha shrugged and Cook smiled.

"We can't stay *here*." Sven pushed off from the wall he was leaning against, his expression a combination of disbelief and repulsion. "This place is a safety hazard."

"Then why even let us come in here?" Cassandra snorted, rolling her eyes. Sweat dripped down her forehead, towards her eye, and she smeared dirt on her face wiping it away.

They stared at Sven, confused, waiting for an explanation. "Hey!" Brenda skidded into the room, out of breath, her cheeks rosy. She waved her hands to convey everything was okay when everyone took up a defensive stance. "Angie and I were wandering around the back—"

"Alone?!" Cook took a step towards her, eyebrows raised. He turned his head, searching out Angie. "You can't do that! What if something happened to you?"

She chuckled under his scrutiny, rubbing her arm. "Oh...

well, we didn't mean to go alone? But listen, we found this shed-like area, it was a stinky outhouse. So gross. But across from it, the jackpot!"

"Well, out with it," Cassandra snapped, exasperated.

Brenda shot her a quick glare. "We found a *shower*."

"That's great and all." Cassandra motioned around at the decaying house. "But I highly doubt this place has much to offer in the sense of running water. It's a dump. Who knows how long it's been abandoned."

Sairha cleared her throat, not used to hearing Cassandra be so impatient. Not one to usually be catty, Cassandra's contempt for Brenda dripped audibly from every syllable spoken. They could not travel together if the two were at each other's throats. *Maybe I'll have a talk with Cassandra, see what's bothering her.*

"No, it would not." Brenda put sass into not only her voice, but also the way she jutted out her hip. "However, it is a farm. And some farms supply their own water and fuel. You know, like a *well?* Angie's waiting at the door. We need a big, strong man to work the hand-pump!"

Cook wiped away his raised eyebrows, replacing the concern with exhaustion. "Of course you do. A shower, even a cold one, would really turn my day around." He motioned for Brenda to lead the way. With a quick, smug look at Cassandra, she disappeared around the entryway with Cook in tow.

"While Cook handles that—" Sairha gestured towards the kitchen. "—why don't we go see if there's anything to salvage?" She smiled at Cassandra, hoping the prospect of food would ease the tension lingering in the air. And it was an excuse to get her friend alone, something the two women hadn't been able to do since before the explosion.

With a heavy sigh, Cassandra stood. "Let's go."

When she left the room, Sairha motioned for Sven to give them a moment, mouthing an apology.

Appliances older than them, and a faded burnt orange and vomit green color scheme, it wasn't hard to tell what era the kitchen was from. Sairha grumbled at the old electric stove, useless, along with a fridge her grandmother would have had. "Anything in there?"

Cassandra threw the door open and shook her head. "Nope." She looked in the freezer, quickly slamming it shut, but not fast enough to keep the reek of rot from wafting out. She shuddered before rushing to the sink and started dry-heaving.

"Okay, that was worse than the rug," Sairha gagged as well once the smell got to her. Hoping the cabinets had more to offer, she reached up and opened the closest one, afraid to look. When she did dare a glance, joy bubbled within. "Look!"

Cassandra walked over and nodded, a small smile on her sickly-pale face. She pulled down one of many canned foods. "Better than nothing, I guess."

Beans, so many cans of them, and corn, and green beans. Sairha poked around in the other cupboards until she found the spices. "Maybe Sven could get the wood burning stove going and we could have a hot meal for once. My grandma had a recipe called *Cowboy Stew*. How's that sound?" She smiled at Cassandra.

Cassandra hopped onto the counter to sit. "Could be good."

There was no pleasing Cassandra it seemed; however, her poor attitude would not bring Sairha down. Getting all the things together, she decided to pry into the sudden bad mood of her friend. "Hey, you doing alright?" Met with a long silence, Sairha glanced over. Cassandra inspected a can of beans as if it was the most interesting thing ever. Either avoiding the topic or punishing Sairha for who knew what. The attitude was ebbing at Sairha's patience. *If she's going to pout about something, might as well put her to work.* Sairha handed her an old can opener with a fixed stare.

"I don't know. My stomach's been a bit weak since the grocery store incident, and I'm exhausted," Cassandra at last said, cranking the can opener.

"I noticed." Sairha set a large pot on the counter and poured in different spices. She took the opened can from Cassandra and poured its contents inside. "This trip has been... not what we thought it would be. Our diets are shit, to be honest, and sleeping on the ground sucks."

"*To be honest,*" Cassandra mocked. "Well, being honest then...The twins annoy the hell out of me." She crossed her arms, her full bottom lip jutting out. "Brenda especially. She's so bossy and sassy and like, 'look at me, Cook, look at me!'. And my feet hurt. *All the time.*"

Sairha couldn't help the loud snort that escaped her, quickly clearing her throat to disguise it. Side eyeing her friend, she mentally tossed around the question she really wanted to ask. "I promise, the twins aren't that bad. You said it yourself, you're just really tired and it's making you sensitive."

"Good news, everyone!" Cook's tall frame filled the kitchen doorway, his positive energy vibrant like sunshine after a storm. "We won't have to smell each other's stinky asses tonight!" He grinned from ear to ear, until he caught sight of the cooking pot, and stepped into the kitchen to glimpse inside. "Look at that. You found something worth eating!"

"Ahem." Sven's exaggerated throat clearing drew their attention away from the night's dinner. "We really need to be getting out of here. Put more miles behind us before the sun goes down."

Everyone looked at Sven in the doorway, confusion on

every face. Tension stiffened shoulders, having followed Sven into the kitchen. Sairha could not find any words to say, surprised was an understatement. She hoped he would say 'just kidding' but the seconds went by in silence.

"Um, excuse me?" Cassandra finally spoke. "You really think we're going to leave here today? *Not. On. Your. Life.*"

Cook nodded in agreement. "Yeah, not to be rude, but there is no way any of us can handle anymore today. The last few days have been grueling and I, for one, need a break or *I'm* going to break. And the twins need the rest, especially Angie."

"Why would you want to leave? We have a roof over our heads for once," Sairha piped up, trying to sound reasonable in her perplexed state. It felt wrong to ignore his suggestion, but it also did not feel right to give up the sanctuary of the farmhouse, mildew and all.

Sven's eyes narrowed into a sharp glare. "You guys want to know the truth?"

"The truth?" Cook scoffed, like it took everything in him to not yell at Sven.

"Yes, the truth," Sven spat out. "While you have been leading the group, I have been bringing up the rear and—"

"Is this some sort of leadership, macho man, pissing contest?" Cassandra interrupted.

"No." Sven lifted a hand to his brow that had started twitching from irritation. Sairha had never seen him this way. Rude, chaotic, borderline desperate. "No, it is not. It is nice to not have everyone's well-being solely on my shoulders for once. You can't even fathom how stressful it's been."

Sairha frowned; their restful evening was not going how she hoped it would. She looked at Cassandra who stared open mouthed at Sven, about to say something, something sassy and regrettable, Sairha could tell. There were mixed thoughts on the matter in her own head. They were all tired. Maybe he didn't mean it to be that harsh, but it stung to hear he had been silently stressing over taking care of them.

"That's not the point I'm trying to make," he rushed through, shaking his hand as if he could wipe away the confession. "The point is, we *are* being followed. It's not safe to just sit around, taking showers and fixing up a house. A house that is quite frankly a death trap in many ways."

There was a sound of sharp intake from Cassandra, and Cook tensed beside Sairha. Only she had been prepared for what he was saying. A quick flashback of the nightmares she had suffered and all the happiness of before slipped down the drain. She wasn't even sure a hot meal could warm the coldness inside after hearing that news.

Sven sighed and stood up straight, his body less tense. "We should really keep putting those miles behind us because I'm not sure how far behind the creature has fallen."

"A *creature?*" Cook shook his head, hand clenched, but Sairha could tell it was to hide the shaking, not out of anger.

"Yes, it's been following us since the town." Sven's expression was one of forced calmness. "It probably exhausted all of its meal options there. We could have lost it a while ago, but at the pace we have had to go for the twins... Our only saving grace is that being out this far has forced it to find shelter during the day. Hopefully, it is the wounded one."

Cassandra's gaze narrowed on Sven before she spoke, as if calculating exactly what to say. "So what you are saying is, it *might* be following us. Maybe close by, maybe not. I'm sorry, but if it's wounded and can only travel at night, I would rather be in a house than out in the open." She hopped off the counter and headed towards the hallway. "I'm going to see if it's my turn for the shower."

Cook's face hardened, but his fist unclenched. "I'll get wood to secure the place for the night." He rested his hand on

Sven's shoulder, giving it a tight squeeze. "We'll take turns keeping watch tonight, alright? And I'll take the first shift so you can get some rest."

"I don't...want to leave either," Sairha mumbled after Cook left, feeling awkward as she stood beside the stove, avoiding looking at Sven.

There was nothing he could say or do. They had voted against leaving the house, voted against him. Even her.

She flinched, listening to him stomp out of the kitchen.

IMPROMPTU STEW SIMMERING on the wood burning stove, Sairha explored the rest of the farmhouse, her nerves on edge. She claimed one of the bedrooms for herself and enlisted Cassandra's help clearing out the dust. Together they forced the old window open a crack before Cook boarded it up. The fresh breeze, and a little sunlight, chased the gloom of the room away though Sairha remained uneasy. No one had said anything about the argument in the kitchen, nor had anyone seen Sven since. She finished up by herself, putting all the linens on a clothesline in the yard to air out before dinner.

Sven returned for dinner, claiming he had walked around the property, checking its security. Other than that, dinner was silent and not very good. But it was hot, and they hadn't eaten an actual meal in a long time. Having a full stomach solved at least one of their problems. Sairha contemplated bringing the pot along with them, but it was impractical. Spices and utensils were easy enough to shove into a backpack pocket, but a heavy pot would wear her down. And water was scarce to clean it with. *When I get home, I'll have all I need.*

After dinner, the shower rotations continued with Sairha, who was eager to feel relief from the grime of traveling.

Despite the tepid temperature, she relished every drop of water, watching the dirt drip down her body and onto the stone ground. Taking extra care to scrub her skin where the creature's blood had penetrated through her clothes, she almost rubbed herself raw with the bar of soap. The water ran clear and a transcendental high to be clean again freed her mind of monsters and blood.

We did need this, she thought, drying off with a questionable towel. Sven's disappointed, aggravated face flashed in her mind and a conflicted pit shifted in her gut. *I hope he isn't mad.*

Anxiety grew from that pit as Sairha dressed in a nightgown she'd found. When she reached for the backdoor's knob, it twisted on its own, and Sairha was suddenly face to face with Cook. "All yours, buddy." She smiled, moving out of his way.

Cook laughed and patted her on the shoulder, then gave her a once over. "Dinner was not bad, not bad at all. Sure beats all the dry goods we've been rationing. I told Sven I'd take the first watch and I meant it. You two get some rest." He looked away from her, somewhere off into the distance, then stepped off the porch. His hand slid from her shoulder as he mumbled, "Could be a long night."

Sairha stood for a second and watched him, wondering where he disappeared to when he got that look on his face. She knew he had seen some dark times recently, but what had he experienced before, when the world was still there? Had he been in combat? Seen families torn apart from manmade wars? Did he kill someone? She could never imagine asking him outright but hoped to one day earn more of his story.

There was a stillness to the house when she stepped into the empty hallway, a quiet change from sleeping in nature. For a moment, she wondered if she'd be able to rest without the sounds of everyone's slumbering breath and the chirp of insects active in the coolness of the night. Opening the door to her room, she nearly jumped out of her skin, spying a shadowy figure on the bed. Her hand fluttered to her chest, physically trying to calm herself. "Sven. You startled me."

"Hmm?" He was slow to turn his head away from the window, like he might be afraid to miss something, but when his sights landed on her, a small smile pushed his somber expression away. "Sorry," he chuckled. "This is a pretty nice little room. Very…innocent like." The way his eyes traveled over her body, twinkling in the filtered moonlight like a hungry wolf, suggested he wasn't talking about the room.

A blush raised her temperature under his gaze. Feeling self-conscious, she wrapped her arms around herself.

He laughed at her reaction and fell back onto the bed, a cloud of dust flying up around him. Coughing, he waved at the air in front of him. "That was not a good idea," he choked out.

Sairha smirked but the emotion behind it died off, the weight of underlying anxiety making itself known again. She had to ask him, even if the answer wasn't what she wanted to hear. "Sven."

He looked over at her with an eyebrow arched in response to the unsure tone of her voice. "Yes?"

"Are you still mad at me?" Before he could reply, she hurried to answer his questioning expression. "Because I disagreed with you tonight."

With an audible sigh, he sat up again, angling to face her better. "No," he said, then groaned in frustration. "I mean, yes. At first, I was upset. Not only did no one heed my caution, but also the two people I trusted most to consider my advice just threw it out the window. Like old laundry you two didn't feel like dealing with. You and Cassandra seem so eager to follow Cook, a near-stranger, blindly and wholeheartedly, so yeah, it stung a bit."

"We followed you blindly," she said, quietly, dropping her head. She gripped herself tighter, holding what little of herself she could together. "And you've proven yourself to us, so I get where you are coming from. I'm sorry we made you feel discarded."

"Come, sit by me," his voice was lighter as he patted the spot beside him.

She did but was at a loss for words. If she could go back in time, she would have tried to find a better way to... well, was there even a better, gentler way to disagree with someone?

Sven slid his hand around her shoulders and pulled her in close, the contact warming her. "It hurt that *you* did not think my plan was as important. But that's okay. You do not always have to agree with me, you know." He rubbed her arm gently. "We're still new, still learning how each other works and thinks. It's normal to have disagreements and arguments. The important thing is that we talk through it. Like we are now."

Sairha looked up at him, and he met her with a smile.

"It was good that you disagreed with me. It made me stop, think about the situation, and the others here with us. Sometimes I need a reminder to look at things another way." He grasped her hand in his. "When I stormed off, I needed that alone time to think. The gaggle twins do need to rest. Cassandra, too. It will be good for us."

Confused, Sairha tilted her head. "The *gaggle twins*?"

The laughter that erupted out of Sven filled the space around them, cleansing away the tension. He ran a hand through his hair, a sheepish look on his handsome face. "Yeah, that's the nickname I may have sorta gave the two." Because Sairha's unamused, clueless expression didn't change, he let out a nervous chuckle and added, "Come on, it suits them. Those two are always together, following Cook around like he's a mama goose. And the chatter!"

"The chatter?" Sairha shook her head in disbelief, but a smile started to creep in. "Angie barely even speaks."

"You have not overheard the many hushed conversations between those two like I have. They chatter back and forth nonstop." He groaned, feigning exhaustion from talking about them.

"Okay, whatever you say," she teased, rolling her eyes.

He rested her back on the bed, and she smiled up at him, as he caressed her cheek with one hand, keeping himself propped up with the other. As if in slow motion, he leaned down and whispered, "Please, keep challenging me, keep me on my toes." A soft plea upon her lips. "Keep me always thinking of other ways."

Arms around his neck, fingers in his silky hair, Sairha pulled him down for a deeper, real kiss and closed her eyes. "I'll try."

CHAPTER NINE

Morning light filtered through the boards on the window, waking Sairha from her deep slumber. Seeing the ceiling instead of the open sky was surreal. Her bones didn't cry out in pain and her neck wasn't stiff. There had been no nightmares, no dreams, nothing that left her confused and dazed after waking. It was the first peaceful sleep she'd had in a long time. A sigh of utter bliss escaped her. Beside her, Sven's chest rose and fell as he still dozed, a rare thing as well.

He must have been more tired than he let on, she thought.

They had fallen asleep wrapped in each other's arms, Sven with his face nuzzled against her neck as she stroked his hair. She did not remember falling asleep, only sinking into content relaxation. The talk they had lifted a weight from her. Thinking back to the reason she had built up the anxiety in the first place, she could almost laugh. It only showed that their relationship was still new, despite how much they'd been through together.

Our relationship.

Although it was small in comparison to what was

happening around them, calling it a relationship was exhilarating. Sairha felt like she could face whatever lay ahead with Sven by her side. With him, she had found courage and strength in disaster. She would have never left Sabueso de Oro. As much as she wanted to believe she had been adventurous before, taking a hospital job in another country was about the only bold offer Sairha had chased after in her life.

I never would have met you if I had stayed in my comfort zone.

She kissed his cheek and wiggled to get out from under his embrace. Once freed, she watched him for a few seconds, surprised he remained undisturbed. *He's never slept this soundly. I'll let him sleep a little longer.*

Dressed in a pair of overalls she'd aired out during the night, she stepped out of the room and heard a murmur of conversation drifting from down the hall. She picked out the deep octave of Cook's voice mingling with Cassandra's softer one. Refreshed and ready to join them, Sairha headed their way but stopped when she overheard Sven's name. Though it was wrong and childish, she stood out of sight to listen in.

"There's just something weird about that guy," Cook said.

"I told you. He was acting so strange the day before we met you guys. All hyper and stuff. He practically ran laps around us. How much energy can one person have after walking the desert for as long as we have? He says it's not safe but disappeared yesterday for hours."

The sensation of being stabbed in the back pained Sairha. Betrayal and anger boiled inside her, her hands curling into fists at her side. *After all that he has done for us. Ungrateful—*

"Eavesdropping?" Sven snuck up beside her.

Her heart pounded twice as fast. "*Shhhh!* You spooked me," she hissed. The talking in the other room had stopped and Sairha second guessed going in there.

Sven gently gripped her by the elbow, ushering her into the

living room, and smiled. "You never woke me up," he directed at Cook. Cook wore a blank expression, not an ounce of guilt or sheepishness to be found. Cassandra avoided looking their way, Sairha noticed.

Cook finally shrugged, returning the friendly smile. "I had company some of the night. Brenda couldn't sleep. And then neither could Cassandra. We all took turns. Figured you could use a night off."

Sairha wondered if there was something more at play with Cassandra and Brenda. Like a silent power struggle over who got more of Cook's attention. When she looked over at Cassandra, though, her train of thought evaporated, and she couldn't prevent the sour face she surely wore. *How could she talk about Sven that way?*

"Great. Let's get going then. We have to make some serious distance today." Throwing his hands up in defeat, Sven left the room.

"Where'd you get those clothes?" Cassandra asked, standing up in no hurry. She twisted and turned, then stretched up.

"I found them in a closet," Sairha grumbled, not in the mood to talk. The thought of mentioning what she'd overheard popped up, but she pushed it aside and decided on leaving as well. On her way to the kitchen for supplies, she caught a smug glance between Cook and Cassandra.

FOR THE FIRST time since meeting Cook and the *gaggle twins*, Sven took over leading the group. 'Determined' was an understatement. His hustle was reminiscent of when he had taken control of the chaotic escape from the hotel after the earthquake.

Sairha noted how when Cook led the group it felt very uniform, like a military march with a set pace and in line, two by two. Methodical, less grueling. Sven, on the other hand, did his best to keep everyone together while he stayed only a few steps ahead. Cook said nothing about the leadership change and kept up with the vigorous pace. That was, he hadn't said anything to her. Being grouped close together meant everyone could hear each other's conversations, which was minimal, and this kept Sairha from focusing too much on how tiring the new pace was.

Sunset was normally the cue for when they would stop and set up camp for the evening; however, that time had long since passed. Stars twinkled to life, in a rich denim blue sky, with no change to the strides Sven made ahead of them. *He's going to keep us going all through the night,* Sairha realized. The twins grumbled about walking in the dark beside her. To her left, beads of sweat glistened on Cassandra's forehead, exhaustion painted on her features. Sairha frowned and moved up beside Sven, clearing her throat as she did. "Do you plan on stopping any time soon?"

He glanced at her but did not slow down. "Nope," he replied, then thought about it a bit more and added, "We should not, is what I meant to say."

Appalled, Sairha tried to remain calm, yet her voice cracked as her next words came out. "You must be joking. You have herded us further than we have ever gone in a single day. It's time to rest, they are all exhausted."

"Sairha," Sven started, aggravated as he turned to look at her. He must have caught sight of the ragtag group and saw how spent they all were. He sighed and lifted his hand to halt them to a chorus of thankful groans. "I guess this is as good as any place," he muttered to himself.

"Thank you." Sairha turned and went to help the others setup camp, eager to be away from his scowl.

Stretching with a yawn, she let her gaze wander over the camp. The twins were laid out on their shared sleeping bag, Cassandra busy laying large rocks for the fire, and Sven... *Where'd he go?* Panic threatened to ensnare her as she searched the area for a sign of him. She nearly jumped out of her skin when Cook appeared in front of her laden with a stack of firewood.

"Whoa there. Did I scare you? Sorry," he chuckled and knelt down to start arranging the wood.

"Have you seen Sven?"

"We went together for wood but had to venture a bit out to find anything decent. We must have gotten separated. Maybe he needed some space."

Yeah, sure. Sairha reached into Cassandra's backpack as she thought about what to say. Sven's absence opened an opportunity to approach the divide starting in their group. She couldn't let it slip by. "I had thought that there would be safety in numbers," she said, tossing him a box of matches. "That joining forces would be a good thing."

Cook focused on coaxing the fire to life before he responded, then leaned up and smiled at her. "It has been good. We're all different minded persons, who might not always agree. There is bound to be some sort of friction in a large company."

"I know," she admitted, more to herself. The words were being driven into her like a nail on a board lately. Twice now, someone had reminded her about it being okay to have different opinions. Deciding against confronting him after all, Sairha let it go. Cook and Cassandra were free to think what they wanted about Sven, it wasn't her duty to make everyone agree with him, or even like him. A shiver swept over her, and she looked beyond the fire again. "He shouldn't be out there alone. Where do you think he went?"

"Probably scouting out the area for any danger," Cook said without so much as a second thought, his assured attitude barely easing her growing concern. "I'm sure he won't be gone long."

"Maybe we should go—*What was that?*" The snap of a twig close by caught her attention. Her heart leapt, her eyes straining beyond the firelight. "Sven?"

Cook jumped to his feet when there was no reply. Light reflected off his long knife as he pulled it from the sheath on his hip. No one made a sound, desperate to pinpoint where the noise had come from. The twins sat motionless, frightened deer in headlights. Cassandra stilled beside the now large, crackling fire, her breathing ragged. Sairha wanted to call out again but something in the pit of her stomach warned against it.

More snapping drew their attention to the opposite side of the camp.

Sweat pooled in Sairha's tightened fist. Just because she lacked a weapon didn't mean she wouldn't go out swinging. An idea popped into her head and she forced herself to calm down, willing her heart to be quiet so she could hear better. She had never tried this technique in a heightened situation and knew closing her eyes would be a bad idea. She took in a deep breath and the world around her became sharper, clearer.

A low rasp, like someone gasping for air, came from the dark.

And instead of two foot falls, she heard the third fall of a much larger foot, with toes that dug into the earth with each step. Whatever it was walked around outside the fire light, pacing back and forth, as if surveying the group.

Then it stopped.

Anxiously, Sairha looked over to Cook for guidance. That was when she heard it. The sound of exertion as the creature lunged forward. "Cook! Look out!" she screamed.

Her warning came just in time. He rolled out of the way, crashing into the twins, as a shadowy, long creature landed where Cook had stood before. The thing hissed at the fire light and backed away. Sairha gasped and it turned towards her, ready to charge. The creature in full view for the first time, with its attention set on her, left her frozen in place. She should have run, but her limbs were heavy as lead.

Her gaze traveled along the tall beast, taller than any of them, and the way its skin glistened, almost translucent, in the fire light and clung in an unusual way to the skeleton of the creature; pulled so taut it looked painful, except for the knees and elbow joints which sagged into folds that swayed as the creature turned. A drooping neck dangled to and fro, the face of the thing sending a chill through her bones. Sairha had pictured glowing, yellow eyes and a disfigured snout, fangs even.

What was in front of her was much more terrifying.

Empty eye sockets stared at nothing, paper-thin flesh covering the holes, and yet, it felt like they burned right into Sairha's soul. Its two short slits in place of a nose opened and closed as it breathed her scent in. Its slash of a mouth cracked open along its perfectly circular head, tongue slithering forward, tasting the air. Goosebumps crawled up Sairha's arms, seeing the light gleaming off thousands of needle-like teeth, when it opened its mouth wide enough to swallow a human head whole. Now she understood, the body in the hotel that was shredded to impossible pieces. Cook's story.

The creature leapt forward, one long arm with three thick claws extended to grab her. Sairha's instincts kicked in and she swerved out of the way. It stumbled, struggling to gain balance again, a black, bloody stump where its other arm should have been.

The one from the town. Sven was right, it was following us, she thought.

Like a gorilla, it used its front, oversized arm to right itself. The back legs were short, spring like, and it used them to push itself around. It was ready to launch again. Sairha glanced to her right where Cassandra watched, horrified. The only other option was to run out into the darkness. Her heart pounded, panicked at the notion of being unable to see when this creature would come for her. Who knew what else was out there. As wounded as it was, Sairha doubted she could outrun it.

This is it. I'm done for. She braced herself for impact. *I only hope my sacrifice will allow the others to escape while the thing desecrates me.*

A chilling, deep howl carried on the night air. Ferocious growls, along with footfalls from several paws, followed after. Dust filled the area, making it hard to see what was happening. Sairha heard Cook yell at the twins to stay beside him through the sounds of a feral fight breaking out in their camp. Yanked from behind, she stumbled and fell backwards. Cassandra held her close, her heart beating fast against Sairha's as they crouched beside a bush.

The growls intensified and, every so often, a yelp of pain would resound louder than the growling. The creature's hisses became harsher, the rasp in its throat turned into guttural hacking. For just an instant, the dust settled enough for Sairha to catch a glimpse. The creature was pushed back against the fire pit, flames blazing at its backside. Driving it back were six enormous wolves, steaming drool dripping down sharp fangs as they snarled. Sairha was awestruck by what she saw.

Out of the darkness, leapt a massive black wolf, knocking the creature back into the fire as it landed on top of it. A blood curdling screech erupted from the creature, forcing all of the humans to cover their ears, the pitch near high enough to cause damage. It was cut short when the black wolf pierced its teeth into the creature's exposed throat. The wolf gave an aggressive shake until, with a horrible ripping noise, it pulled away with the creature's flesh in its mouth.

Ink-black blood oozed out of the creature as it strained to escape the flames. It seemed too weakened from the fight and previous injury to save itself. The stench of melting flesh filled the air, a putrid smell unlike any other. Its short back legs squirmed in vain to find the ground again, while its single long arm reached up to the sky. Blindsided by the attack, it struggled to accept its doomed fate.

Cook was up in a flash, a shimmer of metal in his hand, and with a silent jab, he dealt the final blow into the creature's head.

The body stopped moving, the fire crackling and popping as it consumed its prey.

Cassandra buried her face into Sairha, who sought out the others. The twins were huddled together behind Cook who stared at the sullied knife in his hand. Whimpers escaped the two young women, their faces still terror-stricken. It was not the ablaze, dead creature that they looked upon in fear.

Sairha stared at the pack of wolves who stood across from them, malicious intent obvious with their raised hackles and bared teeth. Cold, amber eyes stared right at Sairha, and the black wolf opened its jowl, dropping the torn flesh onto the ground. Much to her disgust, she watched as the wolf lowered its head and devoured the flap of neck. When it had finished, it lifted its head and growled at Sairha. The other wolves were quick to join in. Two gray wolves snapped their teeth at the twins, eliciting a shriek from Brenda as tears streamed down

Angie's cheeks. Cook tightened his grip on his knife, ready to fight another battle.

A lone howl in the distance caused the wolves to halt. One by one their heads shot up in the direction from whence it came. The large, black one was last to pull its gaze away from Sairha. As if summoned, the wolves darted into the darkness without a sound.

"Is it over?" Cassandra dared to peer over Sairha's shoulder.

Sairha looked at Cook and then at the shriveled body of the creature in the flames. "No," she croaked. "This is only the beginning."

"Thank goodness no one was hurt," Cook gasped, worrying over the twins like a father.

Sven. Sairha untangled herself from Cassandra, scrambling to her feet. Panic tightened her chest, her heart locked in a vice. *Where is he?* Digging her heels into the earth, she made to dash out into the desert but was tugged back against a hard surface, strong arms wrapping around her.

"Are you *crazy*?" Cook exclaimed, holding tight to her.

Bewildered, Sairha fought against him. "Sven is still out there! He hasn't come back. I-I *need* to go find him." She shoved at his arms in her frenzy. "He might be hurt!" When it was apparent he wouldn't loosen up, she let out a cry of anger and did the only thing she could think of. She bit him.

Cook yelled in surprise, releasing his hold.

Freed, Sairha scooped up a fiery stick and ran. The makeshift torch gave hardly any light, but she was thankful for her quick thinking once she was enveloped into the night. It shed its brilliance far enough to see the ground in front of her and anything she might find. Like a body. A knot twisted her insides, a painful thought that Sven might have been killed by that creature. Another worse image appeared of him being consumed by the bloodthirsty wolves. It was the obscene kind of motivation needed to force her feet to go faster, despite the frantic stumbling it caused. "Sven!" she called out, desperation dripping from her voice.

Her footprints mingled with other ones, and she realized that she was going in circles. She needed to broaden her search further. Glancing back to see if anyone from the camp had followed, she found she couldn't see where the camp was. It didn't matter, she decided, not until she found Sven. Even if the torch's fire was starting to get too close to her hand, holding the stick sideways, Sairha hoped to prolong its life long enough. "Sven, where are you?" She called out again then whispered, "Please, be okay."

Shadowy movement ahead of her made her heart leap. Quiet as she could be, on high alert, she approached. There was growling and her hands shook. Sairha's foot snagged on a rock and sent her flying. With a thud, she landed face first, scraping her hands and chin on the hard ground. Wincing, she tried to see through the dust she'd created. Her torch lay beside her, and her palms stung as she reached for it. A low growl by her ear made her pause. All the blood drained from her face as six pairs of wolven eyes glared down at her.

"Well, well, *well*. What do we have here?"

She turned to see who was talking, then immediately wished she hadn't. The scene was too confusing, yet fascinating, like a car wreck. She was unable to stop staring. A rough looking man stood before her. He was tall and was completely naked. The fire's light shone on his muscular chest, his skin a deep reddish-brown. She did her best to avoid looking at his manhood as she lowered her gaze, then gasped, swiftly scooting away from him. Thick, black fur coated his legs from the thigh down. Instead of knees, his legs dipped back and formed downward into skinny canine-like calves, ending in large paws. A bushy tail twitched behind him.

The large, black wolf.

Only he would not be a wolf for much longer.

As she watched, the fur on his legs dissolved off him, the canine hind legs transforming into that of a man's. He growled in pain as his tail fell away from his body, disintegrating before it could touch the ground.

"What...What are you?" Sairha tried to keep her voice steady, but it was no use. Her whole body trembled in fear. A cold, wet nose pushed against her neck and sniffed, and she shuddered involuntarily. This was it, she'd survived the creature attack only to be devoured by hungry half men, half wolf people. She squeezed her eyes shut.

"What do you *think* we are?" the now full human asked, his tone taunting.

She dared a peek at him. The fact that Sairha was terrified to death by them seemed to please him, for his grin was wide and there was a mischievous glint to his amber eyes.

"What's going on here?"

Sairha's heart vaulted in her ribcage. *That voice.* She knew that voice very well. She searched in the dimming light to find his face, desperate to see him alive and unharmed. Her sight landed on its target as he pushed two wolves out of his way. A shudder ran through her, dumbfounded again by what she saw.

Sven glared at the group of wolves, shirtless with his dirty jeans on, then at the other man who stood a hair bigger than him. Some unspoken conversation happened between them, and the other dipped his head in acknowledgement. Sven's feet were bare, human.

His face...

It was the sharp wolf eyes that struck her first. Then the

furry, pointed ears atop his head that melted away as she watched. His hair was short and white but growing longer and darker at an alarming rate.

He looked down into the center of the circle and gasped. "Sairha? What are you doing out here?"

"Are you..." Sairha choked on her words, unable to stop staring at his changing face. Her body screamed, aching from shaking so violently. The air felt too thick, too heavy to breathe. "Are you a...a werewolf?"

The other man smirked.

Human in appearance now, Sven's normal, *human* eyes widened. "Sairha." He reached down for her with a very human hand. "I can explain."

She recoiled away.

"You weren't supposed to find out like this."

Unable to grasp what was going on, unable to breathe, Sairha's world felt like it was crumbling, her reality shattering like glass. There was too much impossible information to take in. The adrenaline that had fueled her finding Sven was gone as everything went black around her.

Either the fire had gone out or she had lost consciousness.

CHAPTER TEN

P<small>ANTING, HER CHEST HEAVED IN SPASMS</small>. R<small>UNNING AGAIN, RUNNING</small> harder than she ever had before. Something was behind her, something that meant to do her harm, that much she knew. It was dark. Why was it so dark? If only she could see, maybe she could hide. She tripped. There was no time, it was right behind her. Forcing herself up, she ran once more, but her muscles were sore and heavy. She could feel its hot breath on the back of her legs. Its teeth nipped at her heels. She tried to avoid it but fell again, this time unable to get back up. A serrated grin greeted her when she rolled over to look at her assailant. Blistering, steaming saliva dripped down its maw and onto her face. Amber eyes bore into hers, penetrating to her soul, tainting it with its malicious intent. The wolf's grin opened wider as it moved forward, about to snap the fatal blow. A scream was trapped in her throat. She didn't want to die...

"Sairha. Sairha, wake up!"

Cassandra's voice, along with hard shaking, woke Sairha just in time. The nightmare left her breathless, and it took several minutes to compose herself. Cassandra's face was twisted with worry. Confused, Sairha sat up abruptly. The world spun, making her nauseated, and the early morning light temporarily blinded her. "Ugh, my head. How did I get here? Where is everyone? Are we all safe?"

"Woah, calm down. You were having some sort of terrible nightmare," Cassandra soothed, wrapping her arms around Sairha in a tight embrace.

"I was," she murmured, then winced. Her head pounded with every word she spoke. She took in a few deep breaths to stop the spinning, then cringed. A rancid stench, like sour milk combined with burning tar, assaulted her. The earth solid once more, Sairha covered her nose with her hand and surveyed the camp.

Cassandra and her rested atop a sleeping bag, some distance from where steam simmered off blackened logs in the firepit, the source of the foul smell. There was an outline of ash and bones leftover from the creature that had died. Oversized pawprints littered the dirt surrounding it.

The twins were close by, curled up together, still asleep. She couldn't find Cook anywhere, but his military bag was packed and ready to go next to them. Sairha frowned.

Cassandra followed her gaze and shrugged. "He was restless. Said he couldn't sleep thinking there were more creatures out there. So, he's been walking around all night. I only fell asleep out of pure exhaustion and had nightmares too. What happened to you out there?"

It really hadn't been a dream then. Being attacked by the creature, coming face to face with it. *Then I did leave the camp. The last thing I remember was...* Sairha tried to recall what she had been doing and why her head hurt. Everything before she left the group was clear, afterwards was foggy. "Where's Sven?"

Cassandra pointed over to the horizon. "He carried you back here. You knocked your head pretty bad out in the dark."

Sairha lifted her hand to the back of her head and winced. Sure enough, a bump had formed, tender to the touch. *That explains the dizziness.* She found Sven where Cassandra had pointed, a lone figure illuminated by the sun as it ascended over the desert. Normally a longing to be near him would stir inside her. Instead, she felt something like...uncertainty. Something...unsure. A feeling she had never associated with him before.

"Sairha," Cook called as he rounded a large bush, coming back into the camp circle. A relieved smile spread across his face, to which she gave a slow, embarrassed wave in response. "You scared the hell out of us last night. Running off on your own," he scolded, without an ounce of actual malice. "Don't ever do that again. We gotta stick together in this mad, messed up world, okay?"

She nodded. "Yeah, okay."

He offered his hands to help both her and Cassandra up.

Her eyes widened at the faint teeth marks on his arm. "About that..." she started sheepishly, taking his hand and standing. Embarrassment over her violent reaction flooded her.

He waved it off. "It's okay. I get it."

They both gazed down at the charred remains in the pit. The barren face of the creature haunted Sairha, with its hollow eye sockets. The way it had listened and tasted the air. She felt sick thinking about it but knew every detail of that encounter would stay with her, with all of them, forever. "So, that creature...that...that was the same thing..." Sairha could not bring herself to finish her thought, to mention Cook's deceased family.

"Yes, the same. Now you guys all know." His voice was grim, and his eyes darted towards the twins, then back at Cassandra and Sairha. "You all met the bonebag creatures. Up close and personal."

Cassandra put her hand on Sairha's shoulder. "Did you see it was missing an arm? It had to be that limb you found."

Sairha was not interested in talking about that again. In fact, she realized that she was tired of talking about the creatures altogether. Everything she thought she had known about the real world was proving to be illusions, illusions she was grasping to hold onto. And when she thought about that arm, with the severed foot... Needle-like teeth sunk into the human flesh in her mind's eye. Her imagination was too clear, too vivid, and it made her nauseated. "Let's pack up," she said, putting an end to the conversation. "Lest we attract any more of those things."

By the time the campsite was packed up, Sven had returned. Sairha turned away from him, pretending to tie her boots. He helped Cook destroy the evidence of their campfire, kicking unscarred dirt over the blackened area before tossing the rocks back out into the open.

Spreading out the ashes of that creature, Sairha thought as she watched.

The silence between her and Sven was a welcome one. She needed more time to think, to try and clear her fuzzy memory. To make sure that what she thought she remembered was really the truth or if she had imagined it all while unconscious. Exposing Sven for what he might be to the others was not on her list of things to do. Especially if there was the slightest chance it wasn't true. Finding that out would require her to talk to him and she was not ready for that.

Sairha tried her best to concentrate on things she knew to

be real instead. Like the dirt beneath her boots as the group marched along. The sun beating down on them, its intense heat making her sweat. The way her backpack straps scratched at her hands when she tucked her fingers in to relieve some of the strain. She was also keenly aware of how close Cassandra walked beside her now. The bitterness that had started at the farmhouse had dissolved completely after their encounter with the creature. She bumped into Sairha, grabbing her hand to stop her. Sairha looked over, confused, and Cassandra nodded towards Sven.

Hand up to halt the group, Sven's gaze swept over them. Sairha noticed he avoided lingering on her any longer than the others. "Last night—"

Sairha tensed.

"—I'm sorry I wasn't there when you guys needed me." The corners of his mouth were pulled down. "While I was out scouting the area, I ran into some of my friends. They had formed a search party to come find me."

Cassandra raised her brows. "Really?"

"Yes, they were worried about me and brought news of my family. I told them I wasn't going to just leave in the middle of the night. That I had you guys waiting on me. So, one of them stayed behind to travel with us."

Cook grunted and rolled his shoulders back. "Sounds good. We could use more numbers, after last night, so long as they have their own food and can take care of themselves."

"Trust me, he can handle it." Sven sounded relieved and he glanced at Sairha, silently pleading, begging something of her.

Was it understanding? Was it for her silence? A slow nod of acknowledgement was all she offered him before walking forward again. The sun forced her to squint, trying to spy the mystery friend in the distance. A figure leaned against a boulder in the direction they were heading. She wasn't sure how to act, but knew to keep her wits about her, to keep her sanity in check. The situation was unsettling.

"This is my good friend, Leroy," Sven said when they got closer.

"We meet again." Leroy's tone was teasing as he focused on Sairha, mischief making his onyx eyes dance. A flash of gold made Sairha step back.

The wolf. She let out a sigh of disapproval, but squared her shoulders and stood tall as recognition kicked in. He wouldn't see her vulnerable ever again.

He was fully clothed this time, thankfully, with no wolf parts to be seen. In plain jeans, hands stuffed inside the pockets, and a stark white t-shirt he looked like just another guy. His black hair was cut short, sides shaved into a well-blended fade, with a longer top that stood up like he had just rolled out of bed.

Sairha turned away from him, wanting to get away from his stare.

"A puppy!" Cassandra pushed past Sairha, nearly knocking her over, and knelt down to coax the animal out from behind Leroy. A snout poked out, curiously sniffing at Cassandra. Sairha's eyes nearly popped out of her head as a fluffy, furry *dog* scurried forward and nuzzled Cassandra's hand. With white and gray fur, it could pass as a husky. The paws were huge, though.

"Yeah, that's my boy Sawyer." Sven smiled at Cassandra, but Sairha caught the side-eye towards her. Perhaps trying to gauge Sairha's reaction.

"Sawyer. That's funny. I love when dogs have serious human names." Cassandra snorted, focused on petting the happy beast. Sawyer leaned heavily against her, rubbing up like a cat.

"Right. Just...suited him, I guess." Sven chuckled.

Sairha wondered if anyone else noticed how awkward it sounded. Confused more than ever, she longed to ask Sven to be straight with them, yet she knew it was not the time. They needed to have their own private talk, and the group was still shaken from the attack.

Leroy roughed the young wolf's ears up. "Little rascal. Didn't even notice him tailing until we were more than halfway gone from home."

Sairha watched Sawyer's ears fall back, ashamed, looking sorrier than any real dog ever could. She moved her hand out towards him for a sniff, like she would for any dog she wanted to befriend. His wet, cold nose pressed against her palm and inhaled deeply, which provoked a soft smile out of Sairha. *You're not so scary*, she thought, looking over his features as she stroked along his neck. His fur was softer than she could have imagined. She liked him already, he seemed like a gentle soul. Leroy, though, she was not as eager to get to know.

The hairs on the back of her neck rose. Turning, she half expected to find the guy scowling at her. Instead, she was met by an expressionless Sven watching their little interaction.

"No! I will not calm down!" Brenda burst out, shrill voice catching everyone off guard.

"Hey, what's wrong?" Cook reached to give her arm a rub, but she moved away.

Trembling, her dark eyes honed in on Sawyer, the look of terror plain on her face. "We were attacked by wolves *last night*. How do we know that isn't one of them? Look at that *thing*."

Sairha heard a low growl rumble deep in Leroy's chest, his muscles taut. Sven moved his hand out in a barely noticeable gesture. Their dynamic was unlike anything she had seen before. Would Leroy listen to anything Sven told him to do?

"Don't be silly," she spoke up, coming to her feet. Her heart pounded with the quick decision to cover for them. She wasn't good at lying. "He's just a sweet little pupper, not a dangerous wolf. Trust me." As soon as those two words left her mouth, she wished she could take them back.

"Trust you?" Brenda mocked, looking Sairha up and down, sizing her up.

"Hey," Cassandra stepped in between them, towering over Brenda. "If Sairha says trust her, you trust her. She's from the woods, and dirt roads, probably running barefoot with bears. She knows what she's talking about."

Dammit, now I've roped my friend into lying, too. Sairha kept her face straight, but on the inside she was a mess of emotions. The fear Brenda showed was exactly what she had felt the night before, and even now, she wasn't sure how she was holding it together.

Angie tugged on Brenda's arm, an attempt to get her to stand down. Brenda regarded Cassandra for a while, then conceded with a snort. Her trembling had slowed until it stopped all together, perhaps accepting the falsehood to some degree.

Sven placed his hand on Sairha's shoulder and gave it a squeeze. She hoped he knew that *she* deserved the truth, at the very least. "Those wolves are long gone, we made sure of it." His voice was soft, meant to ease the tension. Beside him, Leroy grunted, but didn't say anything. "Let's head out. We need to continue making good strides." With a clap of finality on the subject, he resumed the lead with Leroy beside him and the pup following close at their heels.

Conversation was all but dead, no more talk of wolves or what had happened the night before, no taking the time to introduce themselves. A long, quiet walk with an occasional excited bark from Sawyer when he ran ahead of them. It gave Sairha too much time to create more questions in her head. The truth was right there, it was so close to her, she felt like she might implode. She wasn't sure why she needed Sven to tell her himself. Maybe she didn't trust herself, she was a woman of logic and facts after all. She thought of her friends. They deserved to be told too, by Sven, not her. Silent, trudging along, Sairha grappled in a mental battle for clarity in her overcrowded mind.

SHADES OF GOLD and pink colored the sky when they stopped to make camp, a reprieve from the late night before with the threat of a creature at their heels. Knowing she shouldn't, but needing the peace and quiet anyway, Sairha ducked away from the group. Not too far, just enough to be left alone. She was exhausted and the bump on the back of her head throbbed. A constant reminder that something unusual had happened the night before. *Thump, thump, thump. Wolves, wolves, wolves.*

Her thoughts were conflicted, the long trek doing nothing to help untangle them. Which was worse: the horror of being face to face with one of those blood drinking creatures or seeing wolves melt away into men? And then there was her... friend... Sven, who was also a wolf under human facade. The creature and the wolves fighting replayed over and over like a film in her mind. The sound of the creature's throat ripping when the black wolf locked its jowls around it. The gleam of the wolf's teeth, sharp and precise. Black blood and flesh sizzling in the flames. She did not need to recall the smell because it lingered on her. On all of them.

"There you are."

"*Shiiit.*" She jumped, hand fluttering to her already racing heart.

Sven peeked his head round the tree she'd hidden behind,

hands in his jean pockets, a sheepish expression on his face. "Can I sit here beside you?"

She shrugged, scooting over on the log to give him space.

They sat in silence for a while, watching as the sun sank past the earth. There were so many questions to ask, Sairha struggled to find a way to start any of them. She wished he would tell her what was going on, that he would own up to it all without her having to speak. Without revealing the utterly crazy idea in her head. A heavy sigh left her lips. His hand grazed hers, warming it as he did, but she pulled away. "Sven, I don't even know where to begin." It took every ounce of courage for her to say even that.

"Ask me anything. I promise, I swear, I will answer anything," he responded fast, almost desperate sounding.

"Where do I even start!" Sairha exclaimed again, frustrated. Pain seared her skull from the outburst. "How about my head?"

"You fell on a rock when you fainted," Sven confirmed.

She thought it would be a relief to hear, but it was not.

"You fainted shortly after I arrived. I carried you back to the camp." He rubbed his arm, offering her a lopsided smile. It was obvious he wanted things to be okay, to be the way they were. "I had my friends go, but Leroy insisted on staying. So, I told him to wait for the morning before meeting up with the group, figuring there had been enough excitement for one night."

In an effort to remain calm as she spoke, Sairha took a deep breath before speaking. Nothing she was about to say felt sane. "How considerate, it was a bit overwhelming being attacked by a hideous, terrifying creature and then vicious, giant wolves showing up."

"Sairha, I am so sorry I wasn't there. I had gone out to circle the camp and make sure all was clear. I knew it was anything but safe, just didn't know how close the thing actually was. When my pack showed up—"

"Your pack? *Your* pack?" Sairha blinked several times in disbelief, trying to absorb the information of a *pack* and that Sven was a part of it.

Exhaling loudly, he leaned forward, resting his elbows on his knees, and ran his hands over his head. "Yes, *my* pack. I am the first born son of the leader of our pack, like my father, and his father before him. My lineage goes far down the line as pack leaders. My grandfather is still alive, so technically speaking, he is still the leader. But the younger wolves follow me and my lead when I'm home."

The pounding in her head amplified, and she pinched the bridge of her nose to relieve some of the pressure. "People don't run in packs, Sven. People do not just turn into wolves. It's—it's—" she stumbled over words as she did the logistics. "Why, it's impossible. Anatomically impossible. I can't even begin to imagine where... or how..."

"Hey, hey, hey." He reached over to massage her arm. "Try not to think about the how. You will only stress yourself out. I cannot explain how we go from one mammal to the other. It is simply how we are. You saw it, as much as your mind might try to block the unusual out. Your knowledge of how the human body works is being challenged, but you saw us, in various forms of transformation with *your own eyes*."

"I don't know what I saw," she lied to him, to herself, looking away.

"Don't be stubborn. Talk to me." He was gentle as he pulled her back to face him. His rich, light brown eyes shone with tenderness, willing her to open up. "Saying it out loud might help you understand. Retrace your steps."

He was too distracting, so she closed her eyes and tried to recall the night's events. "I remember... My chest hurt, I had ran so hard to find you. My adrenaline was still high after that creature attack. All I could think about was finding you. I was so worried about you!"

"I'm sorry." He tilted her head down and kissed her forehead, easing the furrow between her brows. "Please, continue."

It seemed to be working, her mind felt clearer, more rational as she talked about the experience. "I shouldn't have put myself in danger, leaving the group. But I couldn't leave you out in the dark. Admittedly, I was frantic as I ran. I tripped over a rock and found myself surrounded by wolves. The same ones who had attacked that creature. And then... a deep, mocking voice, laughing at me. I was confused why there was something so human sounding amidst wolves." Sairha paused and shuddered. She had thought it was the end for her twice that night. Her eyes widened a bit and she cleared her throat. "He was human and naked, but his legs..." She needed that mental push, a push to break the wall that blocked her from believing. "They were the hind legs of the black wolf. Like, actual wolf legs. All the way down to his claws. And right before my eyes, they changed, *melting* off of him. Before I could comprehend what was happening..." She took a deep breath in, then a long, shaky exhale.

The fear of being ripped to shreds. Mind uncomprehending what she saw. A press of a cold, wet nose on her neck. Then, her heart singing out when she heard Sven's voice.

"And then I saw you. With strange ears and strange eyes... A stranger behind a familiar face. That's when it all went black."

He placed his hand on her knee, thumb circling softly. "That's when you fainted and hit your head. Do you understand what we are?"

Sairha wasn't sure she understood anything anymore but nodded. "Yes, I think so," she said, barely above a whisper.

"We are wolfshifters, Sairha. Your kind call us werewolves. We are purebloods, born of wolfshifters who were born of wolfshifters before us. Most of us are strong-willed and can control our turns whenever we like. Our bodies break and grow new bones. Human to wolf, wolf to human. Yes, it is painful. We have keen senses, like scent, hearing, sight. Our human forms harbor some small resemblances to our wolf forms." He paused, a look of relief replacing the desperation, probably because her reactions had been calm so far. "I'm sorry I didn't tell you. It never seemed like the right time."

Anger sparked inside of her, and she moved away from him, scowling. "*'Never the right time?'* What about the other week? During the full moon. That's why you were so erratic, right? And all that talk about believing in the moon's healing power! I was so *dumb*. You could have told me then." Shaking, she brushed away hot tears that threatened to spill down her cheeks. Standing abruptly, she no longer felt like she could tolerate being near him. "I may be having a hard time grasping this all, but why you couldn't tell me probably hurts the worst. More than you could imagine. I would have gladly kept your secret, Sven, if only you had trusted me enough to tell me in the first place."

Stunned helplessness contorted Sven's facial features and his shoulders slumped in an admission of defeat. He was between a rock and a hard place, like she had been placed when covering for him.

She didn't care. She didn't like being lied to or being forced to lie.

"Sairha, I couldn't tell you. This is my life, a serious secret I've entrusted to no one outside of our pack. I barely knew you."

The rude awakening was served; a low blow that knocked the wind right out of her. Near a month together in life threatening situations meant nothing to him, it hadn't earned her that level of trust. "And I don't know you at all," she whispered. Feeling colder than the desert at night, she walked away from him.

CHAPTER ELEVEN

THE GROUP WAS DISJOINTED AS THEY TRAVELED TOGETHER, BECAUSE Sven's friend Leroy was anything but pleasant to be around. He had a waspish demeanor that kept everyone on edge, complaining loudly. The group was too slow, they should be making better time than they were, they could push themselves harder. Sairha had the strong desire to bite back: *We can't all be wolf people.* However, for the group's sake, and to prove her point of being trustworthy to Sven, she held her tongue. There were more important things on her plate to worry about.

Like marrow-sucking monsters.

And Cassandra who walked beside her, each footfall heavier than the last, eerily quiet. Concerned, Sairha looped her arm through her friend's to provide support. "Hey, you doing alright?"

"Yeah, I'm just really beat." Cassandra shrugged, leaning into Sairha's shoulder in mock rest. "Hold me so I can sleep while standing?"

Before Sairha could reply, a gray and white streak of fur

squeezed in between them, almost knocking them off balance. Her gaze followed Sawyer along his crazed, zigzag path up to Sven and Leroy, darting between them, then zooming around in circles up ahead.

Zoomies.

"Me too," Sairha sighed, resting her head on Cassandra's. "Just gotta keep going." Though she had known it wouldn't be easy, she and Cassandra had really underestimated how ill-suited they were for the long trek. Sven had known and had tried to leave them safe in Sabueso de Oro. Wondering what would have happened if they had stayed, she glanced at Sven ahead of them. She had maintained barely speaking to him. It was childish to hold a grudge, she knew, but it was proving difficult to forgive him. Instead of trust, tension grew between them. Sven should have told her the truth from the beginning of their journey. The only things Sairha knew of wolfshifters was from the horror and young-adult romance books she and Alison used to consume together. Two very conflicting genres. She had never once felt in danger being around him, yet they were as far from high school melodramatics now as was possible.

Sairha looked down at her feet, no closer to clarity than before, and wished for half the energy Sawyer had. Clumsy puppy tracks ran between the human boot prints but beside those, half trodden, were larger wolf prints. How had she not noticed them before? She looked ahead, up at Sawyer. His tail wagged as he walked between Sven and Leroy, tongue hanging out as he panted. She wondered how much of him running circles around all of them was puppy play or intentional. Were the other wolves leading them?

Frustrated, she took a deep breath that ended in gagging. A rancid stench filled the air. To their left she spied a crumbling drop-away. They were walking atop a canyon.

I'm so over this, all of it. Tossing her bag down, Sairha decided to do something about it. "I think it's time we stopped." Everyone seemed to be in agreement when she looked around, until she got to Leroy and Sven. Sairha sent a silent dare for either of them to challenge her, to say otherwise. Sven said nothing, only setting his own bag down in compliance, much to her surprise and satisfaction.

Cassandra let out an exaggerated groan, sat on the ground, and closed her eyes. She remained motionless, silent and peaceful, while sweat dripped down her forehead.

A loud huff of irritation came from Leroy, and he crossed his arms. "What? We're taking orders from you now?"

"We're all tired," Sairha replied, trying to keep the venom out of her tone. She really wanted to put him in his place, but he conceded with a scowl and stomped far away from her, muttering about women and their feet.

There's one small victory for the humans. Sairha smirked to herself. Spotting the twins nearby, she went over to inspect Angie's leg. "Let's have a look and see how that's mending, shall we?"

Angie nodded, a look of gratitude upon her face, and stretched her leg out. The fresh, pink scar stretched from her calf to her ankle. Her lips were cracked, crusted with blood. The dark circles made her eyes look sunken.

Sairha refrained from making a comment or showing visible concern. "The wound looks good, really good," she said instead. "You will have a scar, but hey, all the cool chicks do." She gave her best reassuring smile and stood up.

"Thank you," Angie croaked, her throat sounding drier than normal. Ever in tune with her sister's needs, Brenda was quick to dig around in their backpack for something to drink. They sat together, Angie's head resting on Brenda's shoulder.

Wanting to avoid arousing anyone else's attention, Sairha

locked eyes with Cook then gave a curt nod towards the horizon. He stood back up, reaching for the sky in a deep stretch, before he casually followed her out of ear shot from the group. They stood in silence, looking out at the changing scenery. She could see to the other side of the canyon and what lay below. A mucky, pitiful ravine was the source of the foul stench, stagnant at the bottom. Swarms of mosquitoes hovered above the murkiest puddles.

"What's up?" he asked, stuffing his hands into his pockets. "You've been on edge lately. I've wanted to ask, but you never seem to be left alone."

"I have been a bit tense," she admitted, then sighed, releasing some of the tension by the simple choice of confiding in him. As much as she could, that was. "I've been really out of it. Everything is weighing heavy on me, the state of the world, getting home, how tired we all are. Monsters. And to top it all off, that *guy* is really getting on my nerves." She nodded back towards the camp without looking. She did not want to see that scruffy looking *mutt*, who was probably watching her every move, judging her.

"Do you...want a hug?" He reached out, and with her nod of consent, wrapped his arm around her shoulder, rubbing her arm.

She sagged into the act of affection. It was a soothing notion, restoring her inner calm. "I just want this journey to be over, Cook." The sun created shadows of the jagged rocks poking across the ravine, a sign they were nearing the mountains. Even after spending weeks walking in it, the desert held a magical kind of beauty at sunset. Save for the stench. She kicked a pebble over the edge, and a few smaller ones slid down with it, leaving a dirt cloud behind them. She felt comfortable, safe beside Cook. Like they had been friends their whole lives.

"Halfway there. Need to check the map, but I think we'll be parting ways soon. My military base is within a few days' march at this pace." He sounded like he was forcing enthusiasm into his voice.

Sairha tensed at the news of them splitting up. "Yeah, this pace. Angie and Cassandra, they aren't handling traveling all day long very well. Cassandra, I've never seen her so unanimated, so uninterested in conversation. It's not like her at all. Angie's leg is healing great, no infection. But I've noticed she's been looking paler, sickly."

Cook said nothing and simply stared out at the canyon, his hand applying gentle pressure on her arm. Probably thinking the same things she was; what could they do about it? Until they got to their destinations, there was nothing to do but keep the hustle full force on their travels, even if it seemed to make things worse. Time was of the essence when supplies were scarce, and monsters were around.

A soft yip from behind reminded Sairha they needed to get back before the others got nosy, and she pulled away from Cook. Moisture on her cheek made her realize just how much she had been holding in. The stresses of their journey were all piling up, and now that she had to keep secrets for Sven, too, the pressure was only increasing.

They turned back to the camp and she watched as Sawyer ducked out from under Leroy's arms, then bounded towards her. She wasn't sure why but the pup's goofy grin, along with his eagerness to be near her, brought a small smile to her face. *Oblivious to the concerns that haunt us.*

"Thanks for listening, Cook," she said, brushing away her tears as she bumped into him playfully. "You're a good friend. I'm glad you almost killed me and thought better of it."

Mock offended, Cook shook his head and groaned. "Don't mention it. *Ever.*"

Sawyer padded up beside her, his paws quiet on the dirt, and his nose cold as he nudged her hand. She wondered if he was the one who had sniffed her neck that night. They rejoined the group, no one asking why they had left, and started setting up the camp.

With little around to make a fire, Cassandra improvised with a few candles set up in the center of the group. As dim as they were, it was better than nothing and gave them all something to sit around. *Nobody wants to sit in the dark after that attack,* Sairha thought, staring into the dancing little flames. Sitting on her sleeping bag, knees pulled up against her chest, she found comfort petting the wolf pup's head. With fur so soft, it was near hypnotizing to run her fingers through it.

"You two are getting on alright," Sven commented, kneeling on the other side of Sawyer. He playfully roughed the pup up. Sawyer used his wide paw to push away from the teasing. There was clear adoration as Sven switched to scratching between Sawyer's big ears.

"Is he...your little brother?" Sairha kept her voice low in an effort to keep the conversation private. Maybe, also, testing just how well his 'keen hearing' really was. Sven's hand faltered for a split second then continued to scratch, a soft smile on his face as he nodded. She looked down at the pup who seemed more than comfortable between the two of them, resting his head on his front paws. "He's great," she choked out. Watching Sven with his brother, as unusual as it was, made her really miss the old days when she used to get along with her sister Alison. Made her miss her even when they didn't. She knew now how much those moments actually meant.

Sven's hand covered hers on the back of Sawyer's neck. His hand was warm, and she let it be. "Why is he... Why isn't he..."

Sairha tried to figure out the best way to convey her thoughts but gave up.

"Why is he still like this and we're humans?" Sven chuckled a little as Sawyer let out a low growl. "Shhh, you know we all go through it too, Sawyer." He looked up at Sairha. "I don't know if you can handle the strangeness of it."

"Try me." What could be weirder than the guy she liked being half wolf?

"Alright then." A hint of a smirk graced his lips as he considered her for a second. "When a young wolfshifter, like us, comes of age we have to go through a rite of passage, *the turn*, before we can change forms at will. We start out as humans, though there are rare cases, and once our bodies reach adulthood it is up to us which path we take. But *the turn* is when we transform into our true wolf form and learn everything about being a wolf, in the safety of a pack, and we stay in that form until we are mentally strong enough to turn back."

Sairha looked down at Sawyer who moved his head to her lap. "How long have you been a wolf then, Sawyer?" she murmured, rubbing his head as lovingly as she would her own pet, or sibling in this case.

"Quite a while now," Sven commented.

Sairha picked up on the subtle sag of his frame. "I'm guessing there is some sort of time limit then." A little of the anger she had housed towards Sven dissolved. Could she fault someone who was protecting his family and their way of life?

Sven's fingers stroked the top of her hand tenderly. "Yes, you have a year to master the transformation. Or you will remain a wolf forever, losing your human side to the animal. We've lost good people to *the turn*. The time of a full moon is when we are the most powerful, as you've already guessed. It's our best bet, the easiest time to transform. That is where the werewolf myth comes from, more or less. Other than being nocturnal. Sawyer… He's coming up on eight months now."

Sairha tried not to look surprised, but she couldn't help as her eyes widened. Scooping up his fuzzy muzzle, peering into the pup's face, she spoke with a stern voice, "You listen here, mister. Don't you like being human, too? You will surely give your brother gray hair before his time. Well, his human form anyway. If he looks anything like you, I guess you don't need to worry about his wolf going gray."

A loud, bark-like laughter left Sven.

It had been a long time since she had heard him laugh like that, and it was contagious, causing Sairha to crack a grin as well.

"Shh, did you hear that?" Leroy, who had been silently watching close by, hissed. He sat straight up, face concentrating, alert, ready for a fight. A snarl deep inside curled his lip.

Sawyer's ears flattened back as he growled and rose, also taking a defensive stance. The gray and white fur along his back was raised.

"There's something out there." Gold flashed in Leroy's eyes as he stood.

Sven jumped to his feet, throwing his arm out to hold Leroy back. *"Don't,"* he commanded.

The candles were snuffed out by a rush of wind that swept over them, casting the group in complete darkness. A blood curdling scream shattered the silent panic. Sairha's heart stopped, looking in the direction of where Cassandra was. "Cassandra?!" She tried to force her vision to adjust, but they were taking too long.

"Sairha! Help me!" Cassandra's cry came from farther away, and the sounds of a struggle resounded all around them. "The creature! It's got me! Help, please!"

Sairha threw herself upon her bedding and fiddled around

until she found what she was looking for. Armed with a long kitchen knife she had taken from the old farmhouse, she set off like hellfire in the direction of the shrieks. "I'm coming for you, Cassandra!" Her eyes began to adjust, and she could almost make out what was ahead of her. One of the creatures, much larger than the one before, fought to keep hold of Cassandra who twisted and turned in an attempt to free herself from its grip. It was dragging her to the canyon's edge, and Sairha was not willing to bet the thing couldn't jump that gap. There was no time to think. Behind her, the others yelled, but she couldn't hear what was said. With each step in pursuit her heart pounded. A deep breath, knife in hand, she launched herself from the ground and landed on the back of the creature.

Surprised, the creature's wail pierced through the night, ringing in Sairha's ears. Her grip around its neck tightened, determined to not let go but also avoid its wide mouth, and its needle-like teeth that would tear her to shreds. Its baggy neck flap was like smooth leather under her hand. She knew the time frame was short before it would throw her off.

"Run!" she screamed at Cassandra.

She watched her friend scramble to get out of the way. *Now or never,* she thought as she lifted her hand in the air, loosening her hold on the creature. The thing flailed about in a panic as it tried to reach up for her, teetering back and forth. The blade gleamed in the minimal moonlight just before she struck with all her might at the creature's temple.

The creature found the back of her overalls and hooked its claws inside, shaking. She lost hold of the knife, the last anchor she had, as the creature's dying grasp was just strong enough to toss her off.

All of a sudden she was soaring. Soaring through the air and nothing but the night sky in her vision.

What happened? What happened to the air? Why can't I breathe?

Sairha grappled with reality. Her collision with the ground stole the air right out of her. Immobilized, she looked up at the twinkling stars, and in her confusion, she wondered why they would not help her.

The pained, shrill cries of the creature brought her back to the predicament she was in. She still could not move, could barely breathe, as it came towards her, the dark figure with its long claws thrashing blindly at the ground. The knife in its head was oozing black, steaming blood.

A gurgling gasp and the air returned to her lungs, and with it the ability to scurry out of the way.

The creature's claws opened and closed, trying to find her. Legs weakening with every step, it lowered closer and closer to the ground.

On hands and knees, she crawled backwards, away. Before she realized it, she was dangling off the side of the canyon, her fingers dug deep into the earth in an attempt to keep herself up, like the claws that reached for her. If the creature did not kill her, surely she would slip into the ravine, breaking bones all the way down, and drown in a puddle of filth, before being eaten if the creature was still so inclined.

She grunted, struggling, reaching for anything to help pull herself up.

The edge started to give way.

The creature neared, painfully slow, mouth opening wide.

A long howl, deep and chilling, sounded nearby, right before a black blur tackled the angered creature.

Engrossed, Sairha watched as the creature attempted to lift one arm to throw the wolf off. The wolf was there to finish what she could not. Sharp canine teeth sunk into its shoulder, stopping it mid-reach, jerking it around viciously. In slow motion the creature wobbled, then swiped weakly at Sairha one last time before toppling over. It lay flattened, with the wolf on top of it, biting at its neck. Its right arm stretched towards her, digging its claws into the dirt for stability, then stopped. Lifeless. Dead.

Rocks slipped beneath her foot hold, reminding her of the danger she was still in, inching further down the canyon wall. "Help," she called out to the wolf, desperate. He turned his amber eyes on her as he licked his chops clean of blood.

"*I got you.*"

Warm hands grabbed her by the biceps, pulling her forward, then gripped her shoulders for a better hold once she was closer. Sairha looked up into the face of her rescuer, Sven, who was concentrating on pulling her up and avoiding causing the cliff's edge to crumble more and take them both down. A second set of smaller hands clutched Sairha's shirt and helped pull her onto the flat surface.

All three of them panted, their efforts overexerted.

When her heart rate calmed, Sairha glanced over and smiled to see Cassandra.

"You almost died," she cried, flinging herself onto Sairha. She wrapped her arms tight around her, so tight it felt like she'd never let go. "You almost died *saving my life*. Who does that?"

"Your best friend?" Sairha replied with a soft laugh, resting her head atop Cassandra's. Exhaustion crashed into her like a tidal wave.

"It must have been following the other one's trail," someone's voice carried, disrupting Sairha's slumber.

Blinking, she again had the out of place sensation of being

well-rested. She avoided thinking of the night's events. Cassandra was still in her arms, snuggled close, on a sleeping bag. She smiled and stroked her curly brown hair. After a few moments, she wiggled free as gently as she could. Cook was close by, clearly agitated as he cleaned up his bedding. Leroy lounged beside him, looking as lazy as could be with nothing to pack.

"I don't care what that bonebag was doing, it was too close. It completely took us by surprise," Cook muttered. "Again."

Leroy shrugged and tried to keep his grin under wraps. Something about that man really creeped Sairha out, and by the looks of it, Cook was also turned off by Leroy's presence.

A sharp pain throbbed in her ribs when she straightened up. She winced and suspected a cracked or bruised rib was the direct result of landing hard on her back. The pain caused her to recoil from her stretch. Instead, she gave a small wave to Cook who stared at her with awe written on his face.

"Is there anything you won't do that isn't completely crazy?"

"Hmmm... I've never wanted to jump out of a plane," Sairha said with a thoughtful tone. Her gaze wandered to the canyon, to the foul ravine, to the scene of too many close calls. She was surprised to see Sven out there, his back to the camp. She admired his long black hair, pulled into a ponytail, as it shone in the morning light. After a quick nod to Cook, she headed towards him. Her attention was drawn downward to the ground where finger and claw markings marred the dirt in all directions. Visual evidence of the fight. Nearing Sven, she cleared her throat. "Hey."

He said nothing but reached for her hand, clasping it in his when she slipped hers in. Bringing it up to his face, he caressed the back of it against his cheek. His tenderness caught her off-guard, though was not unwelcomed, along with the electric-like tingles from his touch.

"Sven..."

"I almost lost you last night," he murmured, finally turning his sights upon her. There was affection, but also anger in them. "What the hell were you thinking? That was the craziest thing ever!"

She stared at him, speechless at his outburst, then stammered, "I...I don't know. I *wasn't* thinking."

"That's for sure! Running after the beast?"

"It had Cassandra," she said defensively, confused that he didn't understand. "You would have done the same thing if it had taken Leroy or Sawyer. Or me even."

Disbelief raised his eyebrows well into his hairline, and he turned away from her, staring back at the canyon.

Frustrated, Sairha looked along his line of vision and inhaled sharply. They faced the edge where she had almost fallen off. The whole lip was cracked and sunken in, a wide crescent-shaped chunk missing, several small holes from where her hands had dug for purchase all around. Black blood coagulated into dirt clods.

Wow. I was that close to falling to my death?

At the time, it felt like slow motion. In the morning light, the bottom looked even farther than she had originally thought. Being faced with her near doom she now understood Sven's reaction.

It was hard, but she tore her gaze away and searched the area. Not seeing what she was looking for, she broke the silence. "Where'd the body go?" Did she even want to know? Thinking back to when she had watched with disgust as the black wolf devoured the flesh of the first creature, a vision forever burned into her memory, she wasn't sure.

Sven wrapped his arms around her, startling her out of

deep thought, and pulled her into a tight embrace. He groaned and rested his head on top of hers. "We tossed it into the ravine."

"That's a relief, I thought maybe...your friend..." She trailed off, not wanting to say it out loud nor ruin the moment. She closed her eyes and leaned into him, arms slinking around his waist. It had been so long since they'd held each other. The strength his arms provided her was reassuring and her body relaxed inside the safety of him.

"I didn't realize how much you meant to me," Sven confessed, his head nuzzling against hers. "Until you were almost taken away."

She gave his waist a tight squeeze. "I know, I'm sorry," she whispered back.

He sighed and loosened his hold on her, letting out a quiet laugh as he held her at arm's length, inspecting her. "What am I going to do with you?" His smile faltered, then an exasperated groan escaped him when his gaze shifted back to the camp. "What am I going to do about *them*? They all saw Leroy transform last night, there is no way we can talk ourselves out of that."

"Maybe no one saw," she suggested half-heartedly. She watched Cassandra and Cook rationing out food, catching the little smile her friend gave the man. The twins were sitting as far away from Leroy and the wolf pup as possible. Maybe it was in her head, but Sairha thought she caught Brenda glaring in her direction. If she had, it was gone within a blink. Now the twins knew she was a liar. They all did.

"I'll tell them you didn't know," Sven said, perhaps also having seen the glare.

She said nothing, unsure if adding another lie would be beneficial or not. There might come a day when she would have to tell the full truth, but for now, she'd follow Sven's lead and play none the wiser. The trust was already thin enough in the group. She watched as Leroy, with a mischievous grin, walked over to the twins, waving a hello. He reminded Sairha of a cartoon wolf poorly fitted into sheep's clothing. The girls got up, terrified, and ran over to Cook. Disgusted, she looked back at Sven and raised a brow. "I don't think your friend Leroy likes people much. Especially women. Especially *me*. And although he left an everlasting impression on me, it wasn't a good one."

Sven shook his head, his jaw tightening. "He *did* save your life. Twice. He may be rough around the edges—" Leroy's laugh at the reaction he got from the twins was loud and obnoxious. Sven closed his eyes. "—really rough, but he is a good person and a loyal member of our pack. He's my second in command and would never let me down."

Irritated, Sairha rolled her eyes. "*You* saved me last night."

"No, I only pulled you up. Leroy was the one who helped you kill the creature," Sven said, evening out his tone. "Please, try to be more careful. You have more courage than you realize, which can be dangerous."

"Dangerous for a human, you mean?" She hadn't meant to put so much spite into the sentence and immediately regretted saying it. Before he could reply, she spoke as she gripped his hand. "You've taught me how to survive. Now, how about protecting myself and those I love? Teach me."

"Sairha." Surprise stole the tension, but he did not look put off by her proposition and even chuckled as he headed back to camp.

He didn't say no, she thought with determination, moving to catch up to him. If he didn't want to, she supposed she could always ask Cook, what with his military training, but given the way the two acted around each other, she doubted spending a lot of time with him would go over well. Sven's only choice was to teach her himself.

She clasped his hand in hers once she caught up and gave it another squeeze. Their relationship wasn't perfect, but neither was the world they had to navigate it in now. Almost dying put a lot in perspective. Like forgiveness.

CHAPTER TWELVE

Sairha fell to the ground with a thud, banging her elbows and butt on the hard clay-like sand. Wincing, she sat up and rubbed her arms, out of breath. Sweat poured down her face and back, it plastered her hair against her skin.

"Good. Again." Sven offered his hand.

She pouted, but accepted his help and planted her feet once ready. A slight bend in her knees, she put her hands up to defend herself from another attack. They were awake before the others as the sun rose above the mountains in the distance, its newborn rays soft and gentle. Unlike Sven's hands, firm and tough as he took a swipe at her, which she narrowly dodged with a quick swerve backwards. They circled around slowly, neither taking their eyes off each other.

After dealing with the controversy of them being wolves, the group had made headway leaving the canyon far behind. Sven and Leroy marched ahead of everyone, deep in conversation for hours, while the rest of the gang trudged along behind. And at night they went off to shift, no longer having to be secretive, and patrolled the perimeter. The early mornings had become *her* time with Sven. Vigorous, exhilarating training, using muscles she had never felt before. Although she had impressed everyone with her bravery by attacking the creature, it was evident that Sairha's fighting talents only emerged in extreme situations. Time and time again Sven threw her down with little to no effort.

Tightening her hand into a fist, Sairha mentally prepared to advance.

"Ah." Sven slapped her fist. "Open hand, less chance of breaking all the tiny bones."

"Oh, right." She shook her hands loose, then without blinking, swiped towards Sven's left. He rolled his shoulder back, her hand passing right by him, and grabbed her other arm, pulling her into him.

"Too slow." He leaned in and planted a kiss on her lips.

"No fair," she smirked and stomped on his foot. Once released, she sent a swift chop to his upper arm. "Gotcha. Finally."

"Alright, alright. I concede!" Sven feigned being wounded and hobbled to their water bottle. There wasn't much left, they'd need to find supplies soon. "I think you've got the makings of a pretty spunky fighter in you, Sairha."

She let out a snort, wiping sweat from her brow with the sleeve of her shirt. "Thanks." Washing away the dust in her throat with a splash of water, she eyed him to gauge his reaction. "This is great against other *humans*. But what about monsters?"

He visibly flinched, looking away to the camp. "We'll get to that, I promise. For now, the basics. Speed will always be your greatest asset, even against the monsters. Come on, the others are waking up."

He has to know more than he lets on about those monsters, she thought to herself, following him. *Cassandra and Cook suspected back at the farmhouse but haven't said anything. Up until we joined Cook, he's always been one step ahead of those things. We barely survived those attacks, and he's holding off on teaching me how to kill them. More secrets...* Her fists tightened at her sides. *I won't let them keep us in the dark.*

A NEW MOON made the sky a velvety black, with twinkling blimps of stars scattered along its surface. It was serene within the light of a decent campfire that Cook had made. Sairha thought about the state of things, and what she had come to accept rather than fight against. She didn't miss her cellphone or laptop, there was no pressure of posting to social media, or keeping up with high school friends, and she wouldn't miss the endless ads for things she didn't need. Although traveling by vehicle was more convenient, the nights were peaceful without cars honking or airplanes soaring overhead. She was as far from being the nurse who arrived in Mexico a year ago, her focus solely on running a smooth emergency room. Now she was scavenging for supplies, trekking across the land, and learning to protect herself.

"Hey, *hey*. Did you hear me?" Cassandra fidgeted beside her.

The irritation in her tone brought Sairha back down to earth, away from the exploration of old versus new. "Oh, sorry. What did you say?"

"You. Are. Hopeless!" Cassandra made sure to say each word painfully slow, like it might have more effect that way. "When do you think the guys will be back?"

Making sure to take as much time pronouncing each word as Cassandra had, Sairha replied, "I. Don't. Know."

Cook chuckled, adjusting some of the logs with a stick. The twins were fast asleep as usual, anything to avoid Leroy and Sawyer.

"Why? Ya miss us, honeypot?"

Cassandra yelped and clung onto Sairha.

Leroy was the first to appear out of the dark, his big, toothy grin revealing he had intended to scare them. He ran a hand through the top of his shaggy hair as he clambered over them and sat down on the log set across from them, his long legs all but touching his chest from being so close to the ground.

"You wish," Cassandra hissed. "Don't call me that. Whatever that even means."

Leroy snorted. "A sweet lure into a deathly trap."

Before either of the women had a chance to register that, the familiar dampness of puppy nose nudged at Sairha's hand. It was unnerving how quiet they were. She smiled and massaged between Sawyer's ears, the feel of his fur becoming more comforting than her favorite childhood blanket. As she continued to pet him, Sairha searched the dark terrain for Sven.

"Hey," he whispered, his arms wrapping around her from behind. She leaned her head back against his chest, the tightness in her body relaxing as he scooted behind her.

"Did everything go alright?" Cassandra was the first to ask, anxious. "Did you see any more of those...*things*?"

Leroy let out an agitated grunt and crossed his arms.

Sven shook his head. "Nah, we didn't see any signs of them or anything really at all. They shouldn't come out this far into the wild without a purpose."

The hair on Sairha's arms stood straight up, and beside them Cassandra shifted uncomfortably in her seat again. The comment solidified Sairha's suspicion that Sven and Leroy had to know more about those creatures. To be able to go out into the darkness, ready to meet one of them and battle it, fearlessly? There had to be something they were holding back. A quick glance at Cassandra, who gave her the nod of approval, and then at Cook sitting silently nearby, Sairha dared to ask what they all were thinking. "What *are* those creatures?"

Sven's body tensed around her.

"What makes you think we know anything about those things?" Leroy spat on the ground. He was unpleasant when he wanted to be, which seemed to be all the time, but his reaction was too quick, too knee-jerk.

"Leroy, come on," Sven sighed. "Give it a rest."

"What? You can't actually expect them to understand."

"Excuse me, wolf boy," Cassandra hissed with an expert level of sass in her tone. "We've seen enough horror and fantasy films to be open minded, okay? Ever heard of *'vampires'* or *'ents'*? Hell, I bet Sairha here has even read books that weren't turned into rad movies with hot, latex bodysuit-clad actresses in them."

Sairha closed her eyes and shook her head as she tried desperately not to laugh. It was hard to take the woman seriously when Cassandra used pop-culture fiction as examples. At least she was seeming more herself again.

"Vampires *are* real." Leroy stared, unblinking, at Cassandra.

She gaped at him, clearly having never thought that if wolfshifters were real, that vampires might be too.

"They deserve to know the truth about the Marrow Eaters," Sven said with an air of authority.

Sairha, Cassandra, and Cook wore matching faces of surprise at hearing the creatures' true name. None of them said anything as they waited to see if Leroy would give in.

"Whatever. Be my guest, Sven. They already know about us

being wolves, why not tell them all the secrets?" The grump lifted himself from the log and stretched his large body out on the hard ground. The fire doused half his face in shadows, increasing the foulness in the scowl he wore as he closed his eyes.

Sawyer curled into a ball at Sairha's feet and wrapped his tail around himself. Even in his young wolf form his face showed signs of unease. Sven unraveled himself from her, walked over to the fire, and crouched down in front of it. Everyone watched him, save for Leroy. The light from the flames brought out Sven's features even more than usual, his light brown eyes intense, focused.

Her heart skipped a beat, watching, waiting.

He took a deep breath.

"All we have are legends, passed unto us from centuries worth of believers. Where would we be without those legends? How the Marrow Eaters came about has been handed down throughout many generations, so far down that no one can recall when it first was spoken.

"The Marrow Eaters were not always bone crunching, bloodthirsty beasts of the night. They were once thought to be superior to all creatures that breathed, thus called the Superior Beings. As old as the moon from which they used to draw their strengths. Delicate skin that shimmered in the moonlight, like the underside of a moth's wing. All knowing, wide luminescent eyes. It is said they could make out the detail of a tiny caterpillar, on the highest of branches, chewing at an apple. The Superior Beings were intelligent, yet at the same time, simple. Tall, graceful, with long arms they used for balance, to keep them steady on their thin legs. Pointed fingers, not claws, used for digging.

"As herbivores, they had amazing gardens. They worked hard tending nature in the daylight hours, but come the night, they would dance and bask in the glow of the moon. Recharging themselves, for they never slept. They lived in harmony with the creatures around them, such as our kind, the wolves. Superior Beings spent a lot of their time learning from other species and teaching in return. Life was good for all. Until humans."

Sven paused and tilted his head downward, casting his features in shadow.

"Most of the now-called *paranormal* beings had no change with the coming of humans, however some of us would end up changed forever, such as shifters who until then were happy as what they were. The Superior Beings are said to have had it the worst.

"Curious, they worked along with man, teaching the simple Neanderthal how to nurture the land and harvest the crops. To follow the moon cycles and dance their moon dances. But something changed in the Superior Beings, something chemically reacted from spending too much time with humans."

A soft whine came from below and Sairha rested her hand on Sawyer's head as he curled closer to her. The night air itself was chilled with a breeze, regardless of the fire emitting heat for them. Looking at her friends, they were just as transfixed on the tale as she was.

"Well. What happened to them?" Cassandra piped when Sven took too long of a pause.

Sullen, he shook his head. "One night, the wolf elders summoned the strongest of our kind to the human-village, feeling that something was amiss. What they saw haunted them, most of them unable to ever speak of it again. They found the village settled in an unusual fog on a new moon night. Much like this one."

As if on cue, everyone glanced up at the sky and its absence of the moon. Even Leroy took a peek. Some of the stars twinkled brighter, and Sairha wondered if they also were listening.

"All of the humans had been slain," Sven whispered, his voice taking on an eerily low octave Sairha had never heard him use before. "Ripped to shreds, their insides destroyed. And when they found the culprits, they were creatures beyond recognition. The Superior Beings had been physically and mentally transformed. Once peaceful, they had become soulless, blood-consuming creatures of the night.

"Some think in a gruesome attempt to not be tempted by the humans, the Superior Beings gouged out their own eyes. Some say the reason they cannot go out in the sunlight is because they are ashamed of what consumed them while others think it is the actual change in diet.

"The wolves, who were once friends of the creatures, were forced to choose and ultimately decided to banish them, locking away the Superior Beings forever. To protect the last humans from extinction." Sven bowed his head, his hair falling around his face like a curtain. "That is what we know of the Marrow Eaters."

A quiet stillness lay over them. Processing the tale, Sairha ran through ideas of how the Superior Beings could have had such a vicious reaction to humans. *Maybe like a dramatic allergic reaction...*

"You guys *locked* them away?" Cassandra was the first to come out of the lull. She placed her hands on her hips. "Why? Why didn't you all just...I don't know...*kill them*? If they were such a threat."

Leroy grunted and leaned up on his elbow to glare across the fire at Cassandra. "That's what's wrong with you humans. If something goes against your idea of normal, kill it and be the surviving race."

Sven let out a heavy sigh as he stepped over Sawyer to

reclaim his seat beside Sairha. "Calm down, both of you. We could not kill something that had once been like our brothers. We were hurt that they would turn on another kind, especially ones that seemed so similar to them in nature. It was not up to us to destroy them from the face of the earth."

Cassandra hummed in thought, then, quick as a whip, issued another retort. "Okay, but you banished them and now they are free. Where the hell did you even send them? Obviously not somewhere secure enough."

Leroy let out a humorless laugh. "Locked 'em away right under your feet. Sealed beneath the earth, immortal beings left to starve in the dark. Alone. Forever."

Sairha could see this would turn into a roundabout argument with no end; Cassandra was annoyed, bordering on angry, and would take everyone down with her to feel better. "Come on, let's all get some shut eye. These are legends, who knows why anything happened the way it did. What we do know is, we have a lot of walking to do tomorrow," she interjected before another impossible question could be asked. Standing up, she fixed her gaze on her friend. "Us humans need to prove our own worth. We've come a long way from those first ones."

"You can say that again," Cook muttered as he left for his bed.

Seeing she had been silenced, Cassandra took the hint and begrudgingly went to her own sleeping bag.

Sven grabbed hold of Sairha's hand for a brief second. She wondered if he was appreciating her words or just the effort to avoid fights between the group. She smiled at him, unsure of how she herself felt about all of the information, then pulled her hand away. It was a lot to think about, and she was both mentally and physically drained.

AFTER HOURS OF RESTLESSNESS, Sairha lay wide awake at what must have been an ungodly hour. The sky was beginning to lose stars to the approaching dawn but was still dark enough to slink about without disturbing anyone. Maybe relieving her bladder would also relieve her mind. Ducking behind the designated tree, she paused when hushed voices reached her ears from beyond the camp. Leroy's was easy to pick out, the other too low to be distinguishable. *Who is he talking to?* She didn't want to make eavesdropping a habit, but her instincts encouraged it, and she inched closer.

"How much longer are you going to stay here and play house?" Leroy's tone was laced with agitation.

"It's not playing house," Sven whispered back, calmer than Leroy.

Sairha prayed they wouldn't hear her rapid heartbeat. This was not the kind of conversation she wanted to overhear.

"Look, you know as well as I do that these humans are holding you up. You could easily be back with the pack if you just..."

Sven let out an irritated groan, and Sairha imagined him pinching the bridge of his nose. She was saddened to hear her secret fear spoken out loud, the one she had been ignoring ever since finding out that he was a wolfshifter. She had tried to ignore how much faster it would be for him to wolf-out and run home, without them following him, needing him. What convinced her otherwise was that he seemed happy to be around them, to be around her. Even if she and him did seem to walk a tight line to keep the happiness.

"Your grandfather, he isn't doing so well. The seal being broken, the explosion releasing the Marrow Eaters, it really messed with the elders. Not only our pack either, or our species," Leroy said, a little gentler, maybe out of sensitivity to the subject.

It was quiet for a long time. When Sven spoke again, Sairha had to strain to hear it. "I won't leave her."

There were some rustling sounds she couldn't figure out, but Sven's words warmed her, making her feel a little bit better. He wouldn't leave her, he couldn't. But why didn't it feel reassuring? Hearing it from him, as indirect as eavesdropping was, should have been the confirmation she needed. Was he actually training her for a different reason?

"Come on. Her friend, Sven. Pretty soon—"

"I know, I know. I do not want to think about that right now. Just... just leave me be for a while, I need time to think," he said with finality.

"Love is the ruin of reasonable thinking," Leroy grunted.

It was in the extended silence that Sairha realized she had been clutching the neckline of her shirt, holding her breath. Her mind raced through a flurry of different thoughts: *He needs to think? What friend are they talking about? Cassandra? Cook? What do either of them have to do with this? He wouldn't...Sven wouldn't leave me...right?*

A tightness in her chest warned her that a panic attack was near. She needed to get away before they heard her gasping for air. Careful to keep her footfall quiet, Sairha waited until she was out of earshot before darting as fast as she could back to her sleeping bag beside Cassandra.

Cassandra rolled over and rubbed her eye groggily. "Sairha? You okay? Is it time to go already?"

"No, shhh. I had to...uh...go to the bathroom," Sairha whispered. She needed to steady her breathing somehow. *He sounded like he wasn't planning on leaving,* she repeated over and over as she laid down. *I won't leave anyone behind, we have to stick together...all of us... I will just have to ask him tomorrow what his plans are. No more secrets between us.*

Rolling over, scooting as far into her sleeping bag as possible, she inhaled through muted, shuddering gasps. Unsure about anything and near tears.

CHAPTER THIRTEEN

Sairha was a ball of nerves waiting for the right moment to speak with Sven. She didn't want to approach him in front of everyone, and he hadn't woken her up for practice as he usually did. There was also the matter of figuring out *what* she wanted to say and how to say it without giving away that she had eavesdropped. Again. What sort of trust would that imply? She would be upset if Sven ever admitted to listening in on one of her private conversations.

But I would never have secret conversations to begin with.

The desert had to be getting to everyone. Between the heat and dust that coated their clothes and lungs, their walk was spent in silent misery. Even the gaggle twins refrained from talking much. Sairha lagged behind the group, needing time to think and avoid spreading her sour mood. Once in a while her gaze drifted up towards Sven and Leroy, Sawyer alongside them, his ears pricked. His alert behavior, a clear sign of listening into their conversation, made Sairha's suspicions grow stronger. She hated feeling suspicious, especially over someone she thought she could trust, but the more she thought about it, and his past actions, the less things stacked up in favor of Sven. He seemed to be a man with more secrets than she realized.

"Hey, what's going on back here?"

Startled out of her thoughts, she half smiled at Cook who had fallen behind to match her pace. His expression showed concern as he leaned in and nudged her with his shoulder. "You look just as glum as the other day, if not more so." He spoke low, keeping the conversation for their ears only.

She wanted to open up to him, to confide in him, because damned if she didn't feel comfortable in his presence, but what could she say without giving too much away? Without sounding like a crazy girlfriend riddled with anxiety? Instead, she made a show of adjusting her backpack straps in an exaggerated act of being uncomfortable and tired. She fiddled with the broken strap, securing it tighter.

He pressed his lips together and continued to stare at her until she couldn't take being under his scrutiny anymore. "There's no getting anything past you, is there?" Sairha let out a little laugh as she shook her head, nudging him back. "How did I ever get so lucky to find you?"

"Only took the end of the world and your lucky stars to introduce us," he said with a wink. It was short lived as something caught his eye, causing him to frown with a heavy sigh.

She followed his gaze ahead, landing on the back of Cassandra.

Sairha wasn't sure what to make of Cook. He seemed like a perfect man; intelligent, humorous, and concerned for others. However, when it came to what he was feeling, there were absolutely no clues to follow. He never showed any interest beyond surface level friendship towards the two women vying for his attention and made sure to pay equal attention between them, like a father with too many kids. Though, she supposed, that's all anyone could offer in a new world full of monsters. She had noticed that she was exempt from the father-like treatment, instead treated more like his equal.

"She's been acting weird," he mumbled, giving Sairha reprieve from her own troubles.

"Has she?" She thought over the last few days. Had she been so self-involved that she had missed something amiss with her friend? "Well, she was almost killed by a Marrow Eater. Could put things in perspective for anyone, even someone as happy-go-lucky as Cassandra," she offered with a shrug.

Cook showed he was dissatisfied by her answer with a scrunch of his nose. "I can tell it's not trauma from a bonebag dragging her away. She's tougher than that, Sairha. That story last night, she was fired up more than necessary. And I mean, sure we all were shocked, and a bit peeved, that the bonebags could have been done away with from the beginning. But her? Cassandra was ready to shake the shit out of Leroy."

"Who isn't?" Sairha snorted, but she considered the evidence that Cook had laid out for her. Cassandra did seem like a bomb ready to explode for no reason. And at the farmhouse, she had mentioned being overly irritated. She could smack herself for how obvious it was. "It's probably close to *that* time of the month for her, Cook. Her hormones are all out of whack, and there's an annoying guy practically asking for her wrath, so she lets it all out." Sairha grinned at him, not knowing if that was really the case. It did make sense. Sairha herself was almost out of birth control, which would mean the return of her dreaded period unless they happened upon a pharmacy soon.

Realization washed over Cook's expression, and he cleared his throat. Without saying a word he stopped, dropped his sack to the ground, and knelt on one knee as he dug inside. "Ah ha!" He held a golden wrapped candy bar up.

Sairha's eyes widened, and she smirked. *Chocolate. If angels exist, they would be singing Cook's praise. That or he is one.*

He winked again and popped up, heaved his bag over his shoulder, and jogged to Cassandra.

Sairha watched the exchange, a soft smile pulling at her lips. Cassandra tried to reject the offering, waving her hands in front of her, but Cook insisted, pushing it towards her. Some agreement Sairha couldn't hear must have been made for Cassandra took the bar, unwrapped it, and snapped it in half, then handed one piece to Cook. Sairha's smile broadened.

Ahead, she caught sight of Sven and Leroy in a heated argument again. "I wish more problems could be solved with chocolate," she muttered. Depression shook its ugly head at her. Were they arguing about him leaving again? She wanted answers.

"I still can't believe you guys can turn into wolves," Cassandra said after a mouthful of canned beans, pointing her spoon in Sven and Leroy's direction.

They had made camp in a clearing, protected by a few trees clinging to life and tall, dry grass. Having plenty of kindling around, they made a fire and indulged in a hot meal. Even something as simple as beans warmed in cans lifted their spirits.

Leroy rolled his eyes and let out a snort. "Of course you can't."

"It's not like she got to see you transform." Cook's tone was defensive as he pegged Leroy with a hard stare. "She was being dragged off by a bonebag."

An involuntary shudder ran down Cassandra's spine, and she muttered about not talking about it again. Sairha rubbed her friend's thigh, glaring at both men.

The twins had stayed awake for hot food, and Angie now stared wide eyed over her can at Leroy. Out of terror or awe Sairha wasn't sure. "D-D-Does it hurt?" Her small voice was barely audible over the crackling of the fire.

Leroy looked at the twins in surprise, as if he had never seen them before. "What?"

"She asked if it *hurts*," Brenda spoke out the words with some venom, her low tolerance for them more than obvious.

So much for a peaceful moment, Sairha thought, sighing.

"Oh, I heard what she said, princess," Leroy said, making sure to add false sweetness to his tone. He tapped his ear with a finger. "Excellent wolf hearing. What do you think? Imagine, *and you can't*, how it feels to have every bone in your body broken and, in the same instance, regrown. While your skin melts off and also regrows. But instead of hair, thick fur spouts out of your follicles. Your jaw re-aligning, elongating, and sharp teeth—" He chomped down, making his teeth click loudly, "—protruding out. Your ears stretch upwards and are suddenly attuned to even the sound of a cricket jumping. On top of all this, a new limb, your tail coming right out of your a—"

"Leroy, that's enough," Sven interrupted, looking exhausted by his friend's taunting.

With a crooked grin, Leroy shrugged and leaned back on his elbows, making eye contact with Angie as he did. "You could say it hurts a bit."

Brenda turned further away from his line of sight and pulled Angie closer to whisper in her ear.

Cook shook his head at the twins but snuck a quick glance at Leroy and Sven, perhaps seeing them in a new light.

Cassandra raised a brow. "Is Sven, like, your alpha or something? You seem to heel at his command a lot." Sairha wanted to disappear, the tension was thick, and Cassandra only wanted to stir it more.

Sven cleared his throat so loud, there was no mistaking that it was to keep Leroy in check. "We do not use those kinds of terms in our pack. Too much toxicity and egotism surrounding them. I am the next chosen leader, though anyone could campaign to lead instead."

"I'd like to see them try," Leroy snorted.

Tired of Leroy's attitude, Sairha stood and stretched, deciding to deal with her irritation by practicing. She walked far enough to not hurt anyone, but still within view of the firelight. Twisting this way and that, she worked tirelessly for an hour on the evasive moves Sven had shown her. The monster in her mind took form, a larger than life black creature with a wolf-like jaw. She swung her arm out in a jab, and her elbow popped. A curse fell from her lips and her brows knitted together as she rubbed her sore joint. None of it felt natural to her, as she struggled with her footing, with being swift, with being quiet.

Her annoyance towards Leroy fueled her practice, her mind continually whispering that it was his fault there was a rift between her and Sven. Also whispering that she wasn't good enough, that she would never be good enough. It told her to give up. Who was she up against the terrifying Marrow Eaters? Against wolves?

Cold tears ran down her flushed cheeks, when she realized what her real problem was.

Jealousy.

She was jealous of the bond Sven and Leroy had, that

connection beyond human. He was Sven's most trusted companion, not her. It was an emotion she had never felt before in past relationships. It scared her. The trip was supposed to be about finding her family and yet it had turned into something else. Was she losing sight of her goal, of herself, because of it? But she couldn't do it without Sven, survive in the wild. She didn't want to. The ache in her chest was a throbbing reminder of why she had avoided dating while working on her career.

Light footfalls from behind caught her attention. She turned and bumped right into Sven's chest. Taking a step back, Sairha was quick to brush her tears away against her shoulder.

He eyed her hand on her elbow and reached out for her arm. "Did you hurt yourself?" His eyebrows pulled together when she shied away, but he said nothing.

"Just didn't stretch enough, I guess." She moved her arm around, showing him she was fine.

"You are getting really good." He shoved his hands in his pockets, perhaps getting the hint that she didn't want to be touched. "I was watching you for a little bit. And you even heard me approaching."

"You let me hear you." She rolled her eyes, trying to avoid looking at him. Her heart was a mixture of confusion and longing. It hurt her to turn away from him, but she also needed a little distance to sort herself out.

Sven's laugh was soft, in no way mocking her. "I did not. Why are you out here alone anyway? You should be resting with the others."

"I have a lot on my mind. Being alone seemed the best way to deal with these things," she confessed, rubbing her neck. Her hair was pasted to her skin with sweat. What she wouldn't have given for a hot shower. She looked over at the camp where everyone was settling down; the twins curled up together on their bed, Cook stretched out close by to them, and Cassandra's head lying atop the map she had been reading. She wasn't ready to go back to them yet, and she realized this might be the only time to talk to Sven alone. A lump lodged in her throat.

Sven looked at the camp as well. They both caught the glint of Leroy's watchful stare. "Come with me." He grabbed Sairha's hand, pulling her into the dark.

She stumbled a little but kept pace with him, tiny pinpricks of tingles surrounding the areas where his flesh touched hers. They came around a large boulder that kept them out of view from the campsite. Out of breath, Sairha leaned back against the rock and looked up at the stars as she adjusted to the night. The feeling of eyes upon her caused her to look back down. Down into Sven's light brown eyes, filled with intensity. She mentally steeled herself, afraid of breaking her resolve. He obviously hadn't dragged her out there just to stare at the stars together.

A groan escaped him, and he ran his hand through his hair, pushing it away from his face. "Sairha." Reaching for her arm, he seemed to have thought better of it. Instead, he placed his hand beside her head on the boulder, leaning in close. "What is going on with you?"

"*Me?*" Sairha asked, taken aback enough that the fiery spell his stare had over her broke. "What about *you?*"

He remained tight-lipped, letting the silence between them grow.

She wished that for once he'd open up rather than letting her bare her soul. That was all she ever did, this time it had to be his turn. Her stomach was a knotted mess and the lump in her throat was impossible to swallow. Sairha hoped the helplessness she felt on the inside was not plastered on her face, although his sharp intake of breath alluded that she was failing horribly at masking those feelings.

"Sairha, it's not that simple." His features softened, eyes pleading for her to understand. "I am being pulled in so many directions right now. I can't guess what's going on with you, or with us."

Sairha closed her eyes, bit back the bitterness on her tongue, and tried to tame her raging thoughts. "It can be simple. Talk to me, tell me what, or who, is pulling you where you don't want to go." She tried to sound sincere, full of kindness, but all she could think of was the wedge that Leroy had successfully planted between them.

Sven's focus sharpened as he regarded her. "Who?"

She nodded back towards the camp and stared at him, prepared for the worst reaction. "Leroy."

He said nothing, but she could almost see the shock hidden behind his straight-laced expression. Her hand lifted of its own accord to rest on his chest. His heartbeat was rhythmic against her fingertips, somehow calm. "You have been torn between the two of us since he showed up. He doesn't like me... Right?" she ventured, her voice low.

He sighed again, something he did so often lately, and rested his head against hers.

The quiet lasted only a few seconds, yet it felt so long to Sairha as she awaited his reply. Would he defend his friend? Or confirm her suspicions? *Please, just be honest with me.* A silent prayer.

"I have a lot of responsibilities as the future leader of the pack, Sairha. My grandfather... he is not doing so well. My time to fully take over is near. This is why I had to leave as soon as I did, why I... I wanted to try and leave you two back there, safe in that condo." Sven's words were strained. "Leroy is...

concerned. He's concerned I'll abandon everything, all of my responsibilities. It's not that he doesn't like you."

Sairha made a noise of discontent at that last sentence. An excuse for bad behavior. Leroy had been nothing but rude and condescending towards her and her friends. It was impossible to take that any other way. "I'm sorry about your grandfather."

"Thank you." His eyes briefly glistened, but he blinked it away. "Leroy does not like any humans, to be honest." He withdrew his head from hers and lowered his arm as well. His hands forced themselves into his jeans pockets, and he took a moment to look up at the sky. "He got distracted once, by a human, and abandoned everything. That's why he's so focused on me, not only so I don't fall down the same path, but because he does not want me to experience the consequences he suffered."

Sairha pushed herself away from the rock and gripped Sven by the shoulders, her face hard with sincerity. "I would *never* make you choose between myself or your pack, Sven. Never. I would walk away myself, no matter how painful, if it meant you did not have to choose. That wouldn't be fair to you. Please, be open with me, tell me these concerns that Leroy, or even you, might have. Haven't I proven myself? Shown my loyalty to you this far?"

He caressed her cheek with a smile; soft, but sad. "I know you would never make me." Something remained unsaid upon his lips, his thumb gently stroking her, leaving goosebumps along her flesh. He pulled her close, his lips brushing against hers. "When did you become such a force to be reckoned with? You are so much stronger than you let on, Sairha. Stronger than you even know."

Before she could fathom an answer, his lips pushed against hers. Gentle for but a moment before her response elicited fervency. It had been so long since they had kissed like that, free and full of passion. It took the breath right out of her, draining her mind of all negative thoughts. Every sense came alive, tingled. The little noises around them started to sound like a song; the grass shifting as Sven shuffled her back against the boulder, the sound of their heavy breaths as they parted for air, only for a gasp or two, and their accelerating heartbeats. Crickets added their string quartet. Maybe even the stars joined their love song.

Sven's mouth moved from hers and left a fiery trail of kisses along her jawline, to her neck, and collarbone. He slid his hand up into her hair. A throaty moan escaped her, which only goaded him on more. His free hand slid under her shirt to cup her breast, tickling her a little as he did. Wrapping her arms around his waist, she pulled him rough against her.

Neither of them had realized just how much they longed for each other in the intimate way. To be touched. To be kissed. To be needed and devoured. It was beyond all control, the need to be together right then, under the blanket of night.

Afterwards, they lay in the tall grass, half dressed, with giddy grins on their faces. Sven yawned, holding Sairha close to him. She snuggled into his bare chest, tilting her head to kiss the sensitive spot beneath his chin. "We should head back," she whispered.

He stirred but refused to open his eyes. A groan was his only response.

She chuckled but let him be, wanting to cherish the closeness for as long as she could. And the way his body fit against hers, like it was made for her.

When they did slink back to the slumbering campsite, Sairha was relieved that no one else was awake. Sven gripped her hand, pulling her back to him, and kissed her. With a broad smile upon her face, she went to get a few hours of sleep.

"Tch."

Sairha glanced at Leroy lying nearby, however he appeared asleep with an arm over his eyes. It was hard, but she refrained from making a rude face at him. She curled up beside Cassandra, nodding off easily for what little of night was left.

Sairha walked beside Sven in the lead, Sawyer lingering around her other side. All morning, they had stolen glances at each other until one of them noticed and stopped to grin. Feeling lighter than the day before, she bumped into Sven playfully. He rolled his eyes but grabbed her hand. Behind them, out of the corner of her eye, she saw Leroy's sour face. Although she guessed he would never warm to her, she felt better about the situation and ignored most, if not all, of his complaints. After hours of walking, she could not ignore the ache in her feet. "Hey, why don't we all take a breather and eat something?"

"Sounds good to me." Cook dropped his bag and stretched.

"Alright, a quick break," Sven agreed. "I want to look over the map with Cassandra again and see if we can't find a place to stop for supplies." He half-hopped the short distance to the brunette, like he had all the energy in the world, and together they plotted their path.

Someone snagged Sairha's elbow before she could sit. Half expecting Cook, she met the cold gaze of Leroy. "Oh, *you*. What do you want?"

"So polite," he teased with a smile. He released her elbow and produced something hidden behind his back. A clean, shiny kitchen knife with its black, polished wood handle.

Her kitchen knife. The one she used to kill the Marrow Eater.

She reached for it. "Thanks. I thought it was lost to the canyon."

"Ah, not so fast." Leroy brought the knife back to himself.

Sairha narrowed her eyes.

"I only saved this piece of crap relic because it turns out you aren't half bad with it." He twisted the knife in his hand, blurring the line between insult and compliment. "Which is good. You'll need it."

What does that mean? Cautious this time, she reached again for the knife. "Thank you," she said, unsure if she meant it. He flipped the knife handle out towards her. Wrapping her fingers around the handle slowly, like he might rip it away again, she took it back into her possession. "I think."

"No problem! I'd hate to leave a human defenseless."

Slipping her knife back into its place in her backpack, Sairha made her way over to Sven and Cassandra.

"What was that about?" Sven mumbled, nodding towards Leroy.

Unsure about the exchange herself, Sairha shrugged. "Just some...helpful advice, I guess."

Shielding her eyes from the sun, Sairha surveyed the large service station in the distance. Nothing moved along the horizon, appearing safe. But if there was anything about this new world she had figured out, it was that looks were deceiving. "That's the place?"

"Yup." Cassandra nodded, squinting too.

It had taken the better part of the afternoon to get there, veering more east than their normal route took them. Ominous doubts filled Sairha, many scenarios about what could go wrong playing out in her mind. A glance at Cook and Sairha knew she couldn't be as lucky as the last time they did this. Sven wore a determined, tight-lipped expression. Features softening, perhaps feeling her gaze, he gave her a half smile. "Let's get going."

Quiet, prepared for a fight, the group neared the building in single file. "Do you smell that?" Leroy hissed, moving closer to Sven. Sawyer's hunches raised, ears straight up.

"Yeah," Sven whispered.

Sairha's eyes darted all over the place, inspecting every shadow she could, anxious of what could be hiding. "Smell what?"

Sven wrapped his hand around hers, leading them towards the back. The door was wide open, motionless. They paused, waiting a few minutes to see if anything stirred. Cook brought up the rear, keeping watch behind them. Sairha mentally recalled the training Sven had given her, where her knife was, and just how fast she could run. *At least we have three half-men, half-wolf people with us.*

Making a circle with his finger in the air, Sven sent Leroy and Sawyer in first then followed after them. Grabbing Cassandra's hand, Sairha went along with the unspoken plan. The twins and Cook trailed close behind as they all entered the silent service station.

Spotted areas of light and shadow created an optical maze inside. Every window was a gaping hole, devoid of glass. Shelving units were tipped over, their assortment of items scattered about the floor. Ransacked. A low, long whistle bounced off the walls. "All clear," Sven breathed. "Everyone spread out. Let's find what we can and get the hell out of here."

Cassandra pulled free of Sairha's hand to light a stub of a candle. "Good thinking," Sairha whispered and together they moved down an aisle. Picking up a box, Sairha was surprised to find it full. Cassandra bent to grab another, giving Sairha a look of shock as she shook its contents. "Maybe we'll find some full water bottles too," Sairha said with a spark of hope. Yet, something seemed off about the place.

"Girls, stick close." Cook was on the other side, the twins not far from his sight. "If anyone sees anything, holler," he called out for everyone else to hear.

Farther in, debris pooled at Sairha's feet, making shuffling along near impossible. Cassandra stomped through, picking her legs up high. Disgust contorted her face anytime trash brushed against her, and she sent an empty can flying across the building. "Oops, sorry." They both winced as it clattered into the dark. Sairha glanced at Cassandra, and they hurried to find where it had gone.

"Woah!" Sairha snagged Cassandra by the arm in the knick of time, preventing her from falling into a pit. "Careful."

"What is that?" Cassandra hissed, holding her candle up to try and see.

"I don't know, but let's get the others." Sairha turned, placed her fingers between her lips, and whistled. In no time, they were joined by the rest of the group. They lit a few more candles in an attempt to see how far it went. Sairha's heart dropped to her gut seeing the cavernous pit running the length of the station, extending out to the front. It wasn't a hole at all, but a crack in the earth, a near perfect split, similar to the one they had seen in Sabueso de Oro. What probably crawled out of it made goosebumps crawl along Sairha's flesh.

"That explains the smell," Leroy grunted, kicking a bottle down into its depths. It disappeared, echoing as it crashed into the walls, until the sound faded, giving no indication of how far the bottom was. "Marrow Eaters. Lucky for us, long gone."

He jumped the gap to the other side, a feat no human should have been able to make, and Sawyer followed.

Sven glanced at Sairha and gave her a reassuring smile before he leapt over as well. "We'll look around this side for things."

"Be careful!" she called.

Scouring their half of the store, they neared the front and the tension Sairha felt loosened a smidge. Nothing had climbed out to grab them, they managed to restock their supplies, and they hadn't encountered any gruesome scenes. She pushed the metal frame of the door open, knocking away concrete debris, the glass crunching under their feet, as one by one the group exited, wary of the extensive crack they were following outside. The brightness of the day blinded her momentarily. When her vision adjusted, Sven waved at her from the other side.

"Hey! We found a bunch of water," Brenda said, lugging a plastic wrapped package of water bottles out the door. She tripped over some of the disheveled ground, crashing into Cassandra, who tumbled back against a gas pump. It creaked and groaned, tilting back from the force. Cook jumped forward, pulling Brenda back, then reaching for Cassandra. When Cassandra pushed off from the pump, a shrill, metallic shriek resounded through the area. It wobbled like a cup on the edge of a counter, until it was dislodged, and toppled into the crack, banging along the edges as it did.

"Fuck, that can't be good," Cassandra muttered.

"Hurry," Sven hissed from the other side, throwing his hand out.

Eyes wide, Sairha stepped to the edge and reached, ready to attempt the leap. Their fingers nearly touched before a rumbling shook the ground, jostling the group. Even Sven and Leroy struggled to keep their balance. Panic-gripped

Sairha, and she looked around frantically, until Cook grabbed her by the shirt and dragged her away from the opening. Shimmering heat rose from below, followed by a thunderous explosion that sent them flying back. Flames climbed upward until they tasted the sky. It took what felt like forever for Sairha to comprehend what had happened and to regain her senses from falling flat on her back. Ears ringing, she flipped onto her hands and knees, choking down the toxic plume of smoke that surrounded them, burning her eyes.

Sven!

Wobbly, she stood with the aid of a crumbling pillar, searching desperately through the haze for a sign of him. She tried to scream his name, but the smoke brought on a coughing fit. The ringing in her head intensified, making her dizzy.

"Sairha!" his voice barely pierced through. And in a brief moment of clarity, she saw him across the way, his face pinched tight in worry. He mouthed something she couldn't make out. Black started to fill her vision, the dizziness taking over again. Leroy clawed at Sven's shoulder with his hands, dragging him away from the explosion. The world spun and she blinked. They were gone. The flames shifted and she saw Sawyer, standing alert, staring at her until something called him and he turned. A secondary explosion shook the earth again, and Sairha toppled over. Pressure clogged her ears, her eyesight near gone. She attempted to lift herself but crashed face first back onto the ground.

THIRST CLAWED at her throat like a papercut, waking Sairha with a grimace as she tried to swallow. Her head throbbed, every muscle ached, and her eyes stung to open. Pieces of what had happened came back to her and she bolted upright. "Sven!"

"Careful," Cassandra hissed. Her soft hands wrapped around Sairha's shoulder, offering support. "Take it easy."

"Sairha," Cook's voice was etched in relief as he came into focus. "We were worried about you."

A groan passed Sairha's lips. Rubbing her head, she felt around for any cuts or bumps. "Is everyone okay? Brenda? Angie? Cas, you okay?"

"Yeah, yeah, I'm fine." Cassandra's gaze darted to Cook. They shared an understanding in their exchange that Sairha didn't get, but dread started to build inside her. "Everyone is fine. It's just..."

"We haven't seen Sven, Leroy, or Sawyer since the explosion," Cook finished.

The rotation of the world stopped at that moment, hearing those words. "That...that can't be. I saw them. I saw him, he was okay. He was—" Emotion choked her, chest tightening, head swirling, remembering his face as he screamed for her. Leroy had tugged at him, had pulled him away. "How long? How long has it been?"

Cassandra chewed on her bottom lip, her blue eyes glossy as she avoided Sairha.

"A day," Cook muttered. "I went back to look for... Well, all I found was wolf tracks. No bodies."

Sairha pulled away from Cassandra. "I... I need to be alone. We'll wait. We'll wait here for them." Her voice was firmer than she felt inside. She wanted to break down. Instead, she turned away from her friends to avoid seeing their reactions. There was nothing she wanted to see reflected on their faces, she could not handle any form of sadness or pity. Seeing that would break her. And right then, all Sairha wanted and needed was to keep herself sane, keep herself convinced that this was all a bad dream.

Sven had to come back. He had to come back for them, for her. He would never leave her. Would he?

Her hand lifted on its own and wiped away moisture on her cheek. She pushed any lingering tears back, shutting her eyes to sleep some more.

He will come back for me.

CHAPTER FOURTEEN

Lost in despair and denial, Sairha could not bring herself to leave the unknown area, fueled by a near empty supply of hope that Sven would come back for her. Cook had taken the women away from the destroyed service station, back to the route they had mapped out. They made camp with their backs close against a wall of large boulders and a patch of deciduous trees, leaves turning brittle and yellow. Part of Sairha wanted to go back and look for them. Deep down she knew it would be fruitless. A cold lump wedged in her chest, so tight it made every breath sharp and painful, indistinguishable between a panic attack or heartbreak.

The day was not yet over when she crawled into her sleeping bag, pulled its softness up to her nose, and fought back tears. Reinforcing her emotional dam, she heard whispering nearby.

"What are we going to do? How much longer does she need?"

"I don't know."

Cook and Cassandra must have thought she was asleep.

Sairha frowned. She was depressed, emotionally distraught, and above all, drained. Why couldn't they understand? She could hardly bring herself to move, let alone pack everything up, pretending she was okay. Her depression cocoon was peaceful, its soft fibers warmed her, comforted her. It wouldn't leave her after promising to be with her. Maybe hiding in her cocoon would transform her into something new.

"Sairha?" Cassandra's soft call was full of sympathy.

Sairha remained silent, unmoving, as if asleep. She couldn't talk to them yet.

"It's no use. She isn't ready," Cassandra sighed.

"We can't wait here forever, Cassandra." By his tone, Cook's patience was wearing thin.

"Come on, Cook. Leave her alone for one more night, please."

Burning hot tears started to blind her thinking about what they had said. One more night? That was all they were willing to give her, when her heart had been ripped out and trampled on by wolven paws? The memory of Sven caressing her cheek replayed in her mind over and over, the way he smiled when she looked at him, his long hair as the wind blew through it. Everything was going to remind her of him. She would never have a moment of peace because in those quiet times she heard his voice, smelled his scent, or tasted a lingering kiss. It took every ounce of her dwindling energy to contain that threatening panic attack. How was she supposed to move on?

In one fluid movement, she threw the sleeping bag off and darted outside the circle of campfire light. It was dangerous, near suicidal, to go out alone. She didn't care. She ran until her lungs were about to burst, until her feet could no longer carry her, until her vision was forsaken by her despair. Until she could no longer hear Cassandra yelling her name.

She leaned against a tree trunk as she struggled for air, clutching at her chest.

Calm down, Sairha, you have to calm down. It won't pass if you cannot calm down.

Too late.

Breathing only came in shuddering gasps, her heart threatening to rip out of her. A sharp pain in her abdomen signaled the curdling of her stomach, and she turned to the side as the vomit rose. Stomach acid burned her already sore throat and the backs of her eyes and nose, as she purged the nothing that was inside.

After a while, she rested her cheek against the rough bark of the tree, feeling calmer. Breathing came easier but her heart still raced. She willed it to slow down, to give her a break. Slow, thin tears fell, dampening her cheeks. Crying again, always finding cracks in her dam. Her brows furrowed, hearing his name in every heartbeat. *Sven. Sven. Sven.*

"Grrr.... How could you!" Sairha slammed her fist against the tree, bark splintering off. Rolling one after the other, her small tears turned into thick crocodile ones, soaking her neck. *"After all this!"* Her voice was hoarse from throwing up, but she had to let the anger out. "After everything we've been through. Nothing! It meant nothing to you?!" Her lips quivered and with a final fist slam, she turned and slid into a sitting position. Knees pulled up to her chest, she sobbed unbridled, allowing herself to feel the emotions she had bottled up. Abandonment, unworthiness, fear, but most of all, the shattering of her heart. She drowned in it. She felt all of it from the core of her being to the very outer edges of her existence. Sven had left her, when he said he wouldn't, and there was nothing she could do about it.

"You know, I did not ask for this," she called out to the dark night sky. "I was fine. I was perfectly fine on my own, living my life the way I was. I did not ask for *ANY* of this." She lifted her arms, gesturing to the area around her, to the crazy, hurtful life that engulfed her now. The tears dried into salty stains on her cheeks. Even though no one was listening, and she was alone in every sense, she had to say her truth out loud. It was like a weight falling away from her shoulders, off of her back, leaving in its wake nothing but numbness.

"I was not looking for someone to complete me or rescue me. I was independent and confident. I was *fine*. So what if I distanced myself from anyone remotely interesting in a romantic way. And yet—" She paused, biting down on her lower lip, as her mind flooded with memories of soft kisses, hand holding so warm and comforting, verbal pick-me-ups, and smoldering glances. "—and yet, you came around and messed it all up."

Growling out of frustration, Sairha punched the tree again and again, then kicked it. She did not want to remember the way his light brown eyes had looked, peeking out from the tangled mess of his hair when they first woke up. Or the way his arms fit around her waist and drew her close. Or the sound of his laughter. Pebbles at the bottom of the tree rolled under her feet, causing her to nearly slip. Irritated, she picked a handful up and chucked them into the distance. Yelling with all her might, she threw the last rock as hard as she could before, exhausted, she allowed herself to fall into the dry, patchy grass and curl into a fetal position. *How can your heart hurt and feel missing all at once?*

The sky was darkening when she unfurled herself and rolled over, stretching tense limbs. The familiar stars burned bright above her, and as angry as she wanted to be, she did not feel like they judged her but simply observed in silence. They were only, afterall, empty, cold rocks like herself.

"Never again," she promised.

THE SAME CONSTELLATIONS stared downwards at a valley miles away from Sairha as blurred figures ran across it. Three sets of padded paws left no sound on the soft grass below them. Tongues dripped saliva as the beasts panted with every heartbeat, every step forward, pushing themselves faster. A welcome breeze blew through their thick furs, keeping them alert of any danger ahead. They had not rested in two nights, and they wouldn't until reaching their destination.

He didn't want to leave her there alone, without him, hurting. For hurting she surely was if she felt the way he did and he was dying inside. He didn't want to leave her, but as he was constantly reminded, his grandfather's time was limited. The only relief from all the guilt he found was being in his wolf form, muscles stretched to their full extent, the dirt under his claws, and senses heightened, working more efficiently than in his human form. The wolf was not tied down as emotionally to anything other than existing. It was a release he needed.

Sven's heart pounded more in his wolf form, reminding him it was still there, not left behind with Sairha. He breathed in deep and welcomed the scent of pine that was approaching. They had traveled far enough away to wash the scent of her from his fur, though he could never forget its sweetness.

As he led them past the valley and onto the path to their territory, Sven wondered if he would ever again see the woman who had captured his heart. However, he knew, deep down, she would not want to see him. Not after his betrayal.

Emotionally spent, Sairha dragged herself back to the camp, guided by the brilliant glow of the campfire. A shout in the distance froze her, putting her on high alert, and she hoped it was her imagination.

There it was again.

The sound of yelling ahead of her, bouncing off the large rock formation.

Her heart pounded as she made her way towards it as fast as she could. *I should have never left them.* The rocks kept her hidden, and it was easy to slink between them. Her footfalls were light, mindful to avoid attention. As she neared, the sounds of a scuffle grew louder. Two sets of feet shuffling back and forth, kicking up rocks, along with heavy grunting. She flattened herself against a pillar in the shadow and inched forward.

A scream echoed through the canyon.

Brenda. Fear coursed through Sairha. *Calm down, calm down.* After taking a few deep breaths, Sairha continued to inch around, seeking a better view.

"SHUT UP!"

A man covered head to toe in filth gripped Brenda by the wrist, shaking her like a ragdoll. The lower half of his face was covered by a bandana, eyes black like coal, looking every bit deranged. Off to the side, Angie cowered with her hands covering her mouth. Tears rolled down her cheeks, while another rough-looking man dug through their belongings behind her.

Shit, Sairha panicked. *Looters. Where is Cook? Cassandra?*

Sairha sought them out with a sweeping gaze. Relief filled her when she spotted Cassandra's mop of brown curls, kneeling on the ground over Cook's still body. Dread ran through Sairha's veins, cold like a sheet of ice. *Please, don't be dead. Don't be dead,* she pleaded, looking around, unsure of what to do. Without Cook, Sairha wasn't convinced she could take on two looters herself. Angie was in no shape to help, Brenda was being held hostage, and there was no way to get Cassandra's attention from so far away without alerting the looters. She needed a plan, and she had precious little time to think of one. Spotting her sleeping bag and pack to the side of the camp, Sairha had an idea. Quietly, she crept to her stuff and reached down for the hidden knife.

"This broad ain't got shit!" The guy going through Angie's bag yelled in frustration and pushed the meek girl out of his way.

"There was another bag over there, it looked heavy," the other guy called back, his hand still tight around Brenda's wrist. Her eyes shimmered with unshed tears, but her face was a fierce scowl looking up at her captor. He dragged her around as if she was nothing, the dirt flying up around them as he did. "You're kinda pretty when you're mad. Maybe we'll take you with us, keep me warm at night," he sneered at her. The defiance was erased off of Brenda's face, replaced with fear, and she tried to claw free, but his grip only tightened as he laughed.

The other one neared Sairha's hiding spot. This was her chance, and she wasn't going to waste it.

"Hey, you cocksucker! Unhand the girl right now, or your friend won't live to see a new day."

Everyone stilled.

The bandana man turned his head slowly towards Sairha, who stood with her knife held against the partner's throat. Surprise lifted his eyebrows up into his greasy hair.

It had been a small opportunity to catch the looter off guard. Sairha held him tight, with one of his arms twisted behind him, his head stretched back against her shoulder. The stench emanating off him made her empty stomach roil. She could feel the grains of his facial hair against the blade when he gulped. Her heart was loud in her ears, but her head was clear, like she could see everything from every angle. "Brenda, are you okay?"

Brenda stared at Sairha, wide eyed, and nodded. "Yes, but I can't feel my fingers," she called back.

"I said release her, scum. And give back all you stole from them," Sairha demanded, not taking even a moment to be shocked at the courage in her voice.

The other man let out a bitter laugh. "You wouldn't dare, you ain't got it in ya."

A challenge? She hadn't expected that. Squaring her shoulders, her face hardened, grip tightening on the man's arm, yanking it back further until he cried out. His throat pushed against her knife, eliciting a trickle of blood. "Try me, asshole!"

"Geesh, do as she says!" her captive croaked.

Bandana man remained unmoved.

Before Sairha had time to decide what to do, there was a loud thud that filled the mere seconds of silence, and she watched as Bandana man let go of Brenda, sinking to his knees. His eyes rolled up into his skull, face wiped of expression, then he timbered to the ground. Cook's hunting knife stuck straight out of his back.

Cook. Sairha's heart skipped a beat seeing her friend standing a few feet back, glaring at the now dead man's body, Cassandra safe, and stunned, behind him.

Brenda scurried to them for protection, barely containing her sobs.

The man in Sairha's arms took advantage of the distraction. He attempted to shove away from her and yank his arm free all at once but had not counted on her sturdy stance. She jerked from the force, crimson red coating her knife as the man fell back against her. Sairha pulled her hand away, quick as fire, and flung him off. He tumbled to the ground, grasping at his neck, trying to keep from bleeding out.

"Oh, no!" Hand shaking, Sairha dropped the bloody knife and fell to her knees beside him. "You'll be okay. You'll be okay," she chanted, trying her best to cover the wound with her hands. The blood flooded out of him, too much, too fast. His soiled hands smeared her forearms as he pulled at her to help, his beady eyes silently begging. Frantic, she yelled, "Quick! Somebody get my med kit! Get something! *Get anything!*"

"Sairha," Cook's voice was a calm contrast to hers. He nudged her shoulder.

She hadn't heard him come up behind her. "What are you doing? We have to help him," she pleaded, but allowed herself to be moved out of the way. Cook placed his large hands over the man's wound, his face serious, as he muttered something then slid those hands to the sides of the man's head.

Crack.

SAIRHA CHECKED Brenda for serious injuries, while Cassandra walked around picking up the items the looters had tossed. Twice Sairha's sights shifted over to where the bodies lay covered by their own coats, blood staining the dirt around them. A hand on hers brought her attention back to Brenda and she tried to smile. "Other than some bruising, you'll be fine."

Brenda nodded, but her eyes lacked their usual shine.

Bruising and some mental trauma.

This time the thud of heavy boots announced Cook's arrival before he knelt beside them. "How's the arm?" he asked Brenda, extending his hand out for her.

"I'm told I'll live." She obliged, then winced when he touched it, helping her up. "Thanks, Sairha."

Cook and Sairha watched Brenda walk to Cassandra and help pick stuff up. "I'm glad you made it when you did. I don't want to think about what would have happened if you hadn't," Cook whispered.

"What happened?"

"The guy with the bandana came out of the rocks, creepy as all get-out, and demanded our food. Obviously, I wasn't going to allow that. I tried to talk to him, see if we could help him in some way. We got into a fist fight; I was winning until I felt something hit my skull. The bigger dude attacked me from behind, I guess, and I was down for the count."

Sairha remained silent. If she hadn't left the group...even though there were four of them to the two robbers, the women had no idea how to handle themselves in that sort of situation. It could have ended fatal if she hadn't had the element of surprise. Maybe she was an important asset to the group after all.

"Hey, where'd Angie go?" Cassandra called out.

Brenda stood up straight and looked around frantically. "Angie? Angie, where are you!"

Cook and Sairha stood, scanning the area, only to find it empty. Dread was a seemingly permanent pit in Sairha's throat. The young woman had been right there a moment ago.

"I'm over here," Angie's soft voice called, popping out from between a crack in the rocks. She motioned for them to follow her. "I found something." Squeezing between tight spaces and winding through a natural maze, she led them to a completely sheltered opening. It was littered with scraps of clothing and blankets. Flies swarmed empty cans of food that had been tossed anywhere. "I found some people, actually." Angie stepped aside to show a woman sitting with a small child curled in her lap.

The boy had light copper hair and cheeks full of freckles and scratches. The woman was older, with fiery, red hair graying at the roots. Dark circles lined her eyes and there was a healing split on the side of her lip. She stared at them with a mixture of worry and helplessness.

No one moved or said anything, save for a soft whimper from the boy.

Sairha willed herself forward, nerves be damned, and extended her hand down to the woman. "I'm Sairha," she said, never breaking eye contact. "We won't hurt you." Whether it was the gentleness in her tone, or maybe the kindness she tried to convey, the woman grasp her hand.

"My name is... my name is Emily," she said quietly and pulled her son forward to face the group. "This is my son, Connor. Are... Are those men..."

"They're gone," Sairha finished for her. "They won't hurt you ever again."

Emily's lip quivered as she nodded, tears starting to pool. Relief from the nightmare of being their captive visibly relaxed the tired lines on her face.

"THINK WE COULD STAY HERE TONIGHT?" Sairha whispered to Cook. Her first reaction had been to leave; the scent of blood, strong on the air, would surely attract a Marrow Eater or coyotes, but it was getting to be late in the night and the group was exhausted, to say the least.

He surveyed the rocks surrounding them. "It seems safe enough. By the look of things, the looters had been here a while. Even if something is out there, I think they'd have a helluva hard time getting in here. Besides, there's plenty of fresh meat to feast upon out there."

That thought made her shudder.

"What are we going to do about them?" Cook set his bag down, his expression calm as his gaze casually swept over the mother and son.

Sairha also looked at Emily who lay beside Connor, reading quietly, on a bed of worn blankets. "We could... offer to take them with us."

Cook raised his eyebrow.

"We aren't heartless. Those two have seen the dark side of the times." Sairha shrugged, crossing her arms. "Look, they have a wagon of their own supplies, too." It was hard to see in the shadows, covered in grime and dust, but there was a fabric-folding wagon with two gallon jugs of water inside. "They could be an asset to us and maybe we can help them find a safe place to settle or something."

"Settle? You really think we'll find a place like that?"

Sairha looked back at Cook, surprised. "Yes. Why? Don't you?"

"I don't know what I think anymore," he admitted, scratching at the stubble on his cheek. "That *is* a nice thought."

"That there's safe places is a dream I have to hold onto. Along with believing my family is alive." Sairha forced back the negative thoughts that threatened to strangle her. "There's got to be some place safe for everyone."

When she pictured that safe place, it was with Cook by her side as well, not just Cassandra. They weren't supposed to stick together long, yet Sairha could not see her life without Cook. The way he treated her like an equal, was a soundboard when she needed, and most of all, a strong protector. It was then she realized parting with him would hurt, and she didn't want to do it. Hadn't she suffered enough?

"I think," he took his time to speak, putting his hand on her shoulder. "You should hold onto those dreams as tight as you can." He pulled away, the tenderness ending just as quick as it had come. "Alright, they can come with us."

With medkit in hand, Sairha crossed the small space and knelt in front of the woman and child. She gave them her friendliest smile. "Hey. If you two don't mind, I'd like to look you over."

"Why?" Emily asked, alarmed.

Sairha kept her practiced nurse's smile on as she spoke. "Because that's what I do. I'm a trained medical professional and whenever anyone new joins our group, I like to give them a basic check up." When Emily did not move, Sairha had to rethink her approach. For some reason, her mind went straight to *him*. To how much she had wished he was honest with her. "Look," she lowered her voice. "There are creatures in this world now. Ones that follow the scent of human blood. Any fresh wounds would be a beacon for them. I have to protect everyone, not just you but also—"

"Your people. Okay." Emily finished with a sigh, looking at Connor. She gestured for him to come closer. "You can start with him."

"Hi, Connor." Sairha smiled when he stood in front of her, leaning against his mom. His shy demeanor was going to be a challenge, but she'd had enough experience with kids to know a sure fire way to win them over. "My name's Sairha and my favorite dinosaur, in the whole wide world, is a brachiosaurus. What's your favorite dinosaur?"

Connor's grin widened across his face. "I love dinosaurs! I have five favorites."

"Oooh, tell me all about them. And with your permission, I'm going to make sure you don't have any cuts that need bandages, okay?" She set the medkit down, unzipping it, but never taking her focus away from Connor.

Connor nodded excitedly, stepping in front of Sairha, and started listing impossibly long dinosaur names.

He passed her checklist with only a few bruises on his arms and scabbed over, superficial scratches on his face. There was a twinkle of innocence left in his pale green eyes that the hardships of the world hadn't stripped fully away. He played with Sairha's medkit, when she turned her attention to Emily.

Emily was curvaceous, a full-figured woman Sairha was sure had been a beauty in her time. It was now hidden underneath layers of dirty clothes, her hair lacked natural sheen, and her skin was dry as paper. Her spirit was sadly more beaten than her physical body. When Sairha looked over her arms, she found similar bruising to Connor's, plus some that ran up her legs and disappeared under her skirt. Sairha's heart cried out for the mother, but she didn't ask. When it was evident that neither had any open wounds, she closed her medkit, satisfied. "You guys are all good. Nothing a little rest won't heal. We want to extend protection to you. If you like, you can come with us on our journey."

Emily started to speak but thought better of it and clenched her fist. Something like gratefulness tried to shine through but fizzled out before it could break through.

Sairha stood up, brushing dirt from her pants. "Think it over tonight. We'll be leaving in the morning."

Later, alone in her sleeping bag, Sairha stared up at the stars and the fake smile melted away. The emptiness amplified, echoing throughout her. Her hand was as heavy as a rock as she opened and closed it, remembering the feel of her knife against the looter's throat, the sound it made as his flesh was sliced open.

I killed that man...

The aroma of sweet and spice, filling the small area, roused Sairha from her troubled sleep. The promise of a good breakfast forced life into her tired limbs, and she sat up. Emily sat beside a small camping burner, stirring a pot bubbling above blue flames. "Mmmm. What's cooking?" Sairha asked, forcing gratefulness into her voice. She walked over to inspect, grappling with a new anxiety of attracting unwanted attention from potentially dangerous humans.

The older woman looked up at her and pulled the lid off, revealing steaming, hot oatmeal. "I know I probably shouldn't have, but I thought you all deserved a hearty breakfast," she murmured, glancing at her still sleeping son. "For saving us, that is. And for taking us with you."

"It smells great, thank you." Sairha smiled and patted Emily's shoulder. "Be careful with your water from here on out, okay?"

Emily nodded and handed Sairha a bowl from their wagon.

With a steaming bowl and two spoons in hand, Sairha went over to where Cook was just sitting up, rubbing sleep from his eyes. "Hungry?"

"That smells freaking great," he said through a yawn, then scooted over for Sairha to sit.

"There weren't enough bowls for everyone, so you'll have to share with me." She winked and handed him his spoon. They both dipped in at the same time. Sairha opted to blow on her oatmeal, whereas Cook shoveled it into his mouth hot as hell. She laughed when he both winced and moaned in happiness. The flavor was simple, yet amazing. A little bit of cinnamon and honey, like eating a cinnamon roll again from her grandma's kitchen. It warmed Sairha inside and out, momentarily sweetening the world around them.

After eating her fill, she curled her knees up, resting her chin on them. Her eyes closed, but her mind continued to race. "I had nightmares all night."

"Anything in particular?" Cook asked softly.

Hot tears came and her throat had a lump in it she could not clear away. "I killed that man," she forced out. Saying it aloud gave no relief from the guilt that weighed heavy.

Cook's spoon clattering into the bowl upset the quiet of the space. "No, you didn't, Sairha."

"I could have saved him, you should have let me save him." She looked up at him, the tears escaping, sliding down her cheeks. "I've never killed anyone before. Not like that."

"Sairha." It sounded like he struggled with how best to respond. "You could've used the whole medical kit on that man, but he was a goner. You shouldn't dwell on this. It was an accident. He moved when he shouldn't have, and you know that. You were defending yourself, and us, your people. A kill or be killed situation that you tried your best to handle. When you can't save everyone, you protect your own and that's what you did."

Sairha wiped her cheek on her shoulder, sniffling as she did. Killing a bloodthirsty monster seemed so different. It was in the heat of the moment, survival. But killing a human? Her own kind? It hadn't previously occurred to her that she might have to kill to protect herself. The harsh reality of the world they were in now did not sit well with her. "It could have been avoided," she whispered.

Cook shook his head and looked out beyond them. The twins were sitting with Emily and her son, laughing and enjoying their breakfast. Cassandra lay asleep still. "It was him or us. If he lived, he would have done this again and again. I understand your guilt, but you'll have to learn to let go of it. Like I did after my first war." He tried to keep his tone soft, but it still came out harsh. He stood abruptly. "I'm going to wake Cassandra so we can pack up." Before leaving, he glanced over his shoulder at Sairha. "You didn't kill anyone. I did. But someday...you might have to."

His words lingered long after him, making Sairha somehow hollower inside. She knew he was trying to help, that he was right, but it didn't make her feel any better. She wasn't sure she should feel better. The world wasn't a great place before the 'end of days' stuff happened, but now she knew firsthand how dark some people really could be inside.

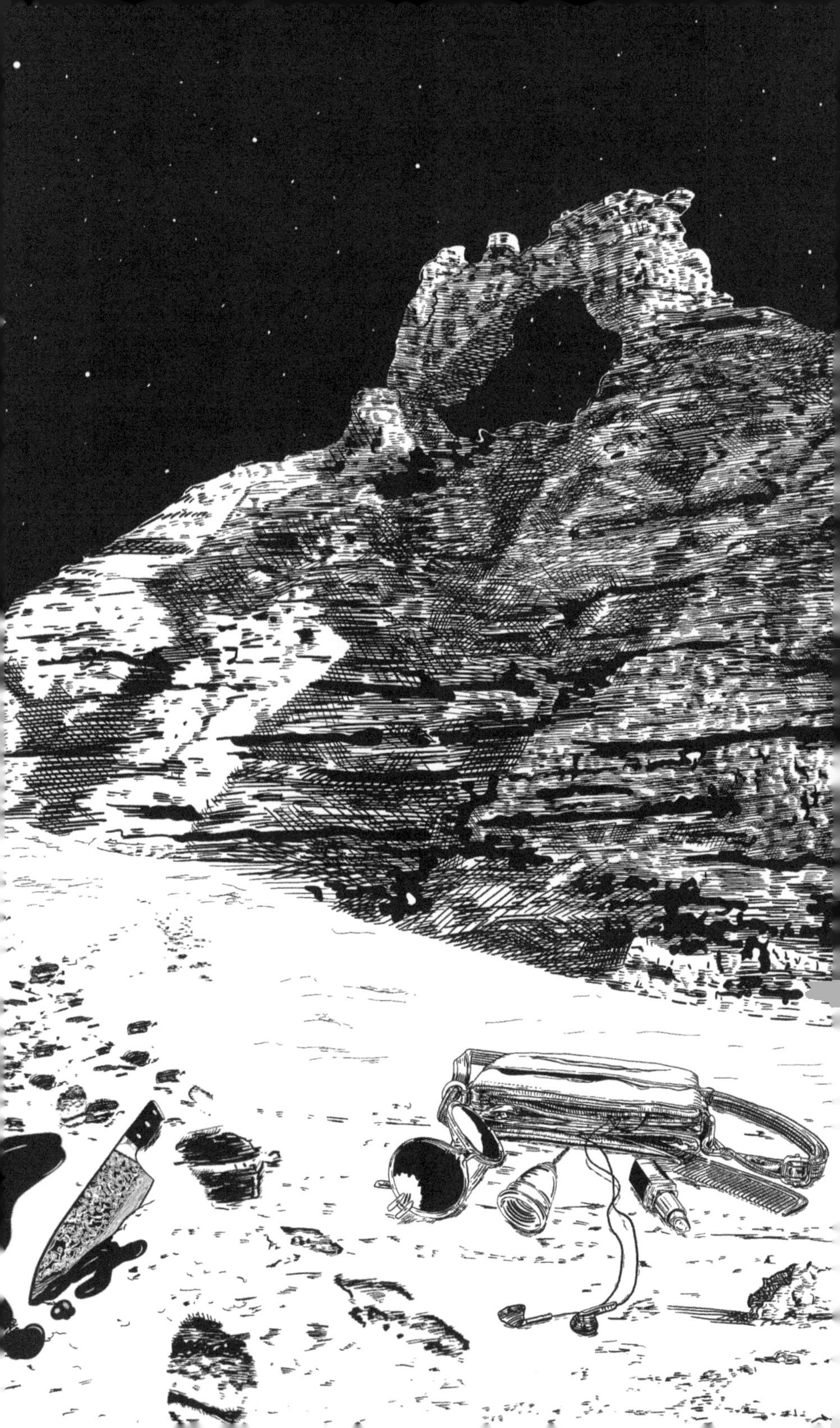

CHAPTER FIFTEEN

A whistle snagged Sairha's attention out of the melancholy trenches of her mind. She had been mid-rolling up her sleeping bag when the sad thoughts crept up. Cook and Cassandra waved her over, the map laid out before them. Sairha finished her packing and went to kneel beside them. "What's up?"

"We're near ready to go," Cook said, giving Sairha a pointed look. "We just need to know which way."

Which way? Glancing at the map, she cringed inwardly at the service station marked on it. Wounds still too fresh to revisit. Following the trail up, they were nearing forks in the roads. One, coming soon, was a direct shot to San Dayo. Her eyes darted to Cook.

"I think we should go this way," Cassandra said, moving her finger along a path that would take them through a city. "It looks like the easiest, fastest route to your home, Sairha." She tapped the circled spot, their end goal, Lake Hulahoe. "But, there are other routes if we still want to stay out of the cities. Up to you."

Up to me?

Her head spun over the options, and losing Cook so soon, the twins along with him. "Let's... I... I don't know." Not making a decision seemed the safest bet to her. Letting someone else make the decision an even smarter idea. A city meant an opportunity for more supplies, but also possible threats.

Cassandra huffed, closing her eyes for a moment. Irritation quickly passed over her face before she locked Sairha with a stern stare. "This is your trip, Sairha. I said it before, I'll say it again, I will follow you to the end of the world. I trust you."

"We have enough supplies for now, so whatever you think. I trust you, too," Cook agreed.

Sairha stared at them both, overwhelmed by the endearing sentiments. The real question was, could she trust herself? With uncertainty in her heart, she leaned forward and tapped the route she wanted to take.

MORE AND MORE PATCHES OF trees dotted the scenery, a sign that they were nearing the end of the desert. As the days wore on, the old, broken road that they followed split into a three lane highway. Cars littered the pavement the farther they went, yet there were still no signs of anyone living.

"It's like a dusty museum for automobiles," Cassandra commented, when they stood atop a hill overlooking a formerly busy on-ramp.

"Or a graveyard," Brenda whispered.

"Stay close." Sairha tightened her backpack straps, adjusting the weight. It did look like a graveyard, and she didn't doubt there'd be bodies entombed forever in their metal mausoleums. She led the way single file through the labyrinth of cars, steering clear of any gruesome scenes, past doors left open, keys still in the ignitions, and windows covered in grime and debris. Rust was starting to set in, which seemed abnormally fast, and the sharp metal edges extended outward like claws, ready to snag someone who wasn't careful. Sairha and Cook were the only ones who dared to inspect the potential hazards, scavenging what could be found. Bandaids, hand sanitizers, sometimes a half empty water bottle or cooler with warm drinks inside and spoiled food. It was unnerving.

At the fork in the highway, they stopped for the day under the cover of an overpass. San Dayo and the ocean lay to their left and the metropolis on their right. The third, time consuming, option was an indirect road that would circle back to Sairha's hometown. She had chosen the route, uneasy about the choice, but questioned it now standing at the split, fear of the unknown amplified by seeing the state of the highway.

She ran a hand through her hair, scratching her head in thought. Why any of them trusted her with this kind of planning was beyond her. Was it not her just a few days ago crying on the desert ground, heartbroken, feeling the lowest level of despair imaginable? Who wanted to save the life of a vile roadside criminal whose death she still struggled with? Glancing over her shoulder to avoid catching anyone's attention, Sairha analyzed the ragtag group.

Cassandra and the twins stood at attention as Cook demonstrated self defense stances. He moved his hands back and forth, while showing them how to keep their feet light and springy. Curling her hands into fists, Cassandra moved in front of him to spar. A hearty laugh escaped Cook, and he adjusted Cassandra's hands to position her thumbs on the outside, tucked out of the way from breaking.

Sairha smiled, her mind comparing the lessons she had received to the new ones Cook had started with them in the evenings. His method was more uniform than... A grimace contorted her face, and she shook away the thoughts of *him*.

She was feeling mentally stronger with each passing day, like she could breathe again and keep herself glued together. The looters' attack had flipped a switch, making her realize the people in her group were too important to distance herself from, and that wallowing was a luxury no one could afford anymore. She clung to the hope of her family being alive and waiting for her, with a city looming in the distance between them and her. It was time to make the decision; take the long route around it or shave off days by cutting through?

Cook caught the curious way she stared at the group and instructed the others to keep practicing. He walked over to her secluded spot and clapped a big hand against her shoulder, giving it a squeeze. "Can I join you?"

Sairha gave a halfhearted smile and a nod.

"What's up? You look lost in space." He sat beside her and rested his arms on the tops of his knees. His presence had an immediate calming effect.

She shrugged, leaning forward on her knees as well. "Time to make a choice. We've avoided ever having to go into a city. Only visiting small towns. But now...I'm conflicted. What if there's more people out there who need help? Or who will attack us?"

Cook let out a low sigh, nodding in agreement. "I see. All valid concerns."

"I don't want to risk what we have. How will we know who to trust?" Sairha tried to hide the sound of helplessness inside of her, but she was at a loss. Her desire to be home begged to go the faster route, yet reasoning said it was a bad idea. "And... you said we'd travel together until our paths split ways. We're at that point, aren't we?"

"Don't..." Cook ran a hand over his face and looked around

at their camp. "Don't worry about us leaving yet. There's another way to my base after the city."

"Angie's leg is healed. I wouldn't blame you," she whispered.

He took the time to consider her words before he looked at her. Brows pulled together, a visible uneasiness settled on him. "If you want to go through the city, I'll go with you. I wouldn't leave you to do that alone. And I wouldn't want to take any supplies from you or Emily, either, so it's a great opportunity to see what we can salvage. Remember what you said to me when we first met?"

"There's safety in numbers?"

"There's safety in numbers," he repeated. "We got this."

A genuine smile graced her lips and Sairha rolled her eyes. "Alright, we'll go to the city. In the morning. Tonight we'll rest and I'll check everyone for open wounds. I'm sure with the training you've given us, we can take on anyone."

"Hopefully we won't need to. Which reminds me, I have something for you." Cook jumped up and jogged to his bag. He dug around for a while until he found what he wanted. "Here, for you. So you'll always have your knife handy." He dropped a black sheath onto her lap.

"For me?" Sairha picked it up, turning it around in her hand. There were worn leather straps looped through slits in the back. "You...made this for me?"

He chuckled, shrugging. "I found the empty sheath in a car. But yeah, I made those straps since you don't have a belt. You can attach it at the thigh, within hand's reach."

Tears welling up and a tickle in her nose, she looked up at her friend. "Thank you."

When the sun rose, they left for the city with a plan to use the daylight as a timer. Get in and out by noon, allowing plenty of time to put distance between them and the city before nightfall. As well thought-out as the plan was, Sairha still harbored unease regarding the decision of them all going. She pushed past the feeling and reminded herself that they always needed more supplies and that she needed to get home.

There was an eeriness around the neighborhood they entered, like an invisible fog, and it could not be shaken, not even by the soft morning light. Houses dotted the outskirts of the city limits, dark and seemingly abandoned. Sairha wondered if anyone was left alive, seeing some houses boarded up. Further into the city, tall buildings with shattered windows and unhinged doors surrounded them. A rancid smell wafting out from someplace unseen accosted them, making it difficult to remain quiet. Stifling a gag, Sairha covered her mouth and nose with the sleeve of her thin shirt. "What is that smell?"

"If I had to guess," Cook squinted, eyes red and watering. "It smells like gas fumes, rotting waste, and decay all mixed together in a giant microwave."

She chuckled at the precise description, then regretted it. "Whatever that earthquake was, it really fucked the whole world up, didn't it? Part of me was hoping it would be normal the closer to home I got. This is worse. And smells like what I imagine the Bog of Eternal Stench smells like."

Cook nodded to a road heavy with ownerless cars, down towards a lonely looking market store.

"This way and be careful. Try not to touch anything," Sairha whispered, motioning for the others to move ahead. Spotting Emily, she frowned. "The wagon." It would never wheel in between the mess of cars.

Cook wasted no time getting to the back of the line. He set Connor on the ground to walk beside his mom and picked the wagon up high above his head, like it was light as a feather. Brenda and Angie marveled at his strength audibly. Cassandra rolled her eyes, but smiled, as she walked beside Sairha. "Show off," she muttered.

"You like him, don't you?" Sairha asked, an eyebrow raised and a small grin on her face, picking through the easiest path.

Cassandra appeared surprised, but a sadness darkened her features and she said nothing.

"It's okay, you know," Sairha spoke softly. "It's okay to let yourself move on from what happened." The words struck her like a slap to her own face. A self-reflection, as she didn't know if Cassandra was struggling with her own depression. Cassandra could be hurting. They had never discussed if Cassandra saw or heard what befell the man she had been with when the earthquake happened. Even though she had not known Gregory long it did not mean that she wasn't grieving over him, or the peaceful life they had once known.

Cassandra waved her hand, shooing off Sairha's concern. "There's more problems to worry about than if I fancy someone," she replied, ending the conversation with a finality in her tone.

Feeling even more like a shitty friend, Sairha kept her mouth closed out of respect, the least she could do. Hopefully Cassandra would feel comfortable enough to open up eventually, maybe after their trip was done.

The wasteland of the city was covered in a thin layer of sand with no signs of disturbance in a long while. The farther they went, the more acrid the stench grew. Sairha wondered if the toxic air was going to have damaging effects on them. It was too late to turn back, however. The store loomed ahead with dust-coated glass that reflected their rugged appearances back to them between wooden boards. They crept by overturned shopping carts, the once shiny metal now rusty orange, bent outwards ready to rip through flesh.

A bead of sweat ran down Cook's forehead, but other than that he did not look perplexed by the load at all when they stopped outside the entrance. "This place is a ghost town," he murmured.

Cassandra shuddered and looked at Sairha, "Ugh, if ghosts are real too, I swear..."

"Hopefully it's as abandoned on the inside as it is the outside." Sairha pushed down the fear that threatened to ruin her resolve for supplies. "Alright, here's the plan. Brenda, Angie, and myself are going to go in and get whatever we can find. Cook will stay out here to keep watch with the rest of you."

"I'm coming." Cassandra stepped closer to Sairha.

Memories of the last time they had gone into a store together gave Sairha pause. The bloody scene had made Cassandra purge her stomach multiple times. "Are you sure that's a good idea?"

Cassandra pushed out her chin, tightening her mouth.

"I'll stay out here, with Connor and them, then," Brenda said, looking at her sister for a moment. She added to Sairha, "I trust my sister with you. Cook will need more help out here if anything happens."

Sairha was surprised but didn't argue. With nothing left to discuss, she pushed on the doors, careful to keep it as quiet as she could. Cassandra and Angie lit candles, ready to explore the unknown darkness. After a few excruciating moments nothing had come running towards them, so the three of them went inside.

Light poured in from the open doors, though it could not reach down the aisles. *Flashlights, I miss flashlights*, Sairha thought as her hand slid down her thigh, to the handle of her knife in the makeshift holster. She hadn't wanted to touch it since the looter incident, even cleaning the blood off had sent guilt down her throat in painful bursts. Now it felt like a lifeline, like the knife had always been an extension of her.

Unnerving silence greeted them, only their footfalls echoing in the emptiness. To the right were the food aisles, and to the left, the sundries. Sairha motioned for Cassandra and Angie to go to the food while she turned the other way. Restocking her first-aid kit was Sairha's top priority. If anything was going to take up room in her bag, it needed to be important. *Wandering off on my own, like a true Velma,* Sairha laughed to herself to calm her nerves, lifting the candle higher to see. The scene stopped her dead in her tracks.

Wiped clean, not even a single box of cough drops were left on the walls. Her hope sank as she turned to leave, then her foot hit something that went flying across the way. Crouching, lowering her candle, she saw what appeared to be a trail of medicinal items. "That's weird," she whispered and picked up the box, a picture of colorful band-aids on the cover. Another few swipes along the trail and she had bottles of supplements and aspirin. It was strange, and she knew it could potentially be a bad idea, but her curiosity was stronger, and she needed to find more things. The trail led her out of the aisle and around a corner into pure darkness. Sairha stopped and stared, calm for some reason, and waited until Cassandra and Angie showed up with their bags full and relief on their faces. Sairha motioned to where she wanted to go, and they added their light to illuminate the area. Without a word, she led the way further back.

At the end was a door and beside that, sealed tight, a pharmacy. Sairha's spirit soared until Cassandra grabbed her arm and shook her head. Pulling away, Sairha reached out. The pharmacy, if it hadn't been emptied as well, was the ultimate jackpot. With a deep breath, she twisted the knob.

Locked.

She cursed her luck.

"Who-who's there?!"

Sairha jumped back from the door. Cassandra grabbed at her arm again while Angie cowered behind them, her knuckles white from gripping her candle tight.

"Is someone in there?" Sairha called, continuing to ignore Cassandra's pleas to leave. "Are you okay? Do you need medical attention? Please, I'm a trained—"

"You shouldn't be in here!" The person responded in a nervous, rasp of a whisper from the other side. "You should leave, before anything bad comes."

Sairha fought back the urge to ask what and instead decided to try and reason with the person. "We'll leave soon, I promise. Why don't you come with us? We can protect you. Hello?"

Anxiety built up waiting for a response, and too much time had passed that Cook would be starting to worry. Sighing, Sairha turned to leave, but the creak of a pharmacy window stilled her. A plastic bag of pill bottles slid out the small opening. Carefully she took them and placed them inside her bag. She leaned down to look inside, and before she could see anything, a red first-aid kit was shoved through. "Thank you, you have no idea how much this really helps us." Another first-aid kit came out, but this time Sairha was ready, and she grabbed the hand pushing them out. "Come with us," she pleaded.

"No, no, no. No, I really cannot. It's safe. It's safer in here," the anxious voice said as the person tried to take their hand back. "You should go. Please, just go away. And don't tell anyone about this place."

"Sairha," Cassandra hissed, nodding back towards the glow from the outside world. "Let's go. We have people waiting for us, and this person obviously wants to be left alone."

With a heavy heart, Sairha released the hand after giving it a squeeze. Angie stepped beside her and pushed a bag of beef jerky into the opening. "In case you need something to snack on," she said softly, then turned and left with Cassandra.

"Wait," the voice whispered, before Sairha too had left the area. "Be careful. The East End is overtaken... They sleep in the tunnels." The slam of the pharmacy's roll-up window echoed throughout the empty store.

What does that mean?

A big city could have many dangers. Murderous gangs came to mind first, though she suspected it was worse than humans with sinister intentions. Hoisting her backpack up over her shoulder, Sairha tucked the warning away, deciding to keep it to herself. She couldn't handle a panic starting in the group, delaying them any longer than necessary in the city. All they had to do was avoid any tunnels.

The sun was hot and brilliant when Sairha emerged out the doors. "Let's get out of here."

Cook was loading up the snacks Angie had scavenged into his own bag. "Alright, we're ready. Did you get the medical supplies you wanted?"

She nodded and looked out onto the street, hoping they didn't need to continue East. There had to be multiple ways out of the city.

"Wait!" Cassandra yelled, startling everyone. She dropped her bag down next to Cook. "I forgot something!"

"Cas!" Sairha called after her, confused.

"I'll be right back," the woman yelled over her shoulder as she disappeared into the maze of aisles.

Cook shrugged, making no effort to stop her, so Sairha stayed put as well, though her nerves were on edge. She wondered what her friend could have forgotten that was so important to run back into the store alone. At least they knew it was safe enough.

Out of breath, cheeks flush, Cassandra re-emerged in no time. Dangling on either side of her were two large jugs of water. A quiet round of praise for Cassandra went around, and they lingered long enough to fill their water bottles. When they were ready to go, Cook hoisted the wagon up again, reminiscent of a strong man from a circus, and grinned. "Shall we?"

Sairha's gut was in knots as she nodded and led the way.

These people were the reason she kept going, and she'd be damned if she let anything befall them if she could fight it. Finding that lone human, locked away, reminded her how precious their lives really were these days. If she was lucky, she would find her family, too, and be whole again. No wonder *he* had been so hard on them all. It must have been terrifying to know what was coming after them and keep a level head. Sairha looked back towards the shop and noticed Emily and Connor had fallen behind. The mother crouched over her son beside a flattened truck, but she couldn't see their faces. Concerned, Sairha let the twins pass by then hurried to Emily. "Is everything okay?"

Emily startled and stood up straight with a wavering smile. "We're just tired, that's all. I was trying to give Connor a pep talk to keep his head up."

Sairha smiled at Connor, offering her hand to him. "We'll get out of the city in no time and then you can relax a bit. How about a piggy back ride until then?"

"Oh, that's not necessary!" Emily cried out, waving her hands back and forth.

Too late, as the boy accepted the ride with glee and clambered onto Sairha's back once she adjusted her pack to be worn in the front and had knelt down. "It's no problem. Ready, Connor?" Sairha shifted his weight to be more balanced.

"Forward march!" he giggled, pointing ahead.

Two hours later, they arrived at a fork in the road and a sigh of relief escaped Sairha. They hadn't come across any tunnels and were nearing the city's end. The road snaked off into two directions, tons of cars littered the road that continued downward, whereas the path Sairha wanted to take had only a handful facing them. It was a one-way street that veered north. "Let's go this way," she suggested, starting in that direction.

"Are you sure?" Brenda's tone was questioning, challenging. Or at least that's how it felt to Sairha as she paused. Brenda motioned towards the overcrowded street. "Seems like this is the way to go. What with the whole town having gone that way." Angie pulled on Brenda's arm, her eyes wide as she shook her head.

Cook took a quick assessment before adding his two cents. "I have to agree with Brenda on this one. That's a one-way road with hardly any cars, probably leading into another neighborhood."

Sairha shifted Connor's weight on her back and willed her foot not to tap in irritation. How could she convince them to go her way without freaking them all out about the possible threat of Marrow Eaters or looters?

A loud groan broke the silence as Cassandra put her hands on her hips. "Look at all these damn cars," she said, sounding really worked up. "If they didn't make it out, because of a traffic jam, then how the hell are we supposed to make it out? I don't know about you guys, but I don't want to zigzag in and out of a bunch of cars just to find the path blocked or something."

Well, that's one way to win the crowd over, Sairha thought, surprised by her friend's logical reasoning, and without even knowing Sairha needed help creating one. "Come on, it should be fine."

It was a relief when her way proved to be a lot easier, and Sairha was happy to see them make good time without more objections. After a mile, they came to a hill where they no longer could see what was on the other side. Weighed down by her passenger, Sairha agreed to let Cassandra and Cook scout ahead. Angie took over pulling the wagon, with Emily in the back to help push, slowed by the steep hill. Halfway up, Cook reappeared on the horizon and waved to signal that it was clear. His expression was wrought with eagerness, and Sairha couldn't help but wonder *'what now?'*

"So. What would be your worst nightmare?" he asked after she caught up to him.

She tilted her head, confused by the question. So many things haunted her nightmares. When they came up over the hill, she understood his meaning.

Cassandra's mouth was a tight scowl. "How about a dark, creepy tunnel?"

CHAPTER SIXTEEN

DECAYING IVY HUNG LIMP ON THE BRICK FACED WALL OF THE TUNNEL, its pitch-black entrance a menacing threat of secrets. Tunnels normally had lights that lit the way for safe passage but along the ceiling were only shattered housings where bulbs used to be. Sairha paced back and forth as she waited for Cook's return. He had volunteered to see if they could go around or possibly climb it. It was a hopeless venture, Sairha knew it, and was mentally preparing to have to brave the unknown darkness. Her heart raced thinking about what could be lurking in there. People, Marrow Eaters, other creatures that might be scarier, far worse than a Marrow Eater. Maybe even wolves. Her only spark of hope was that it was the North tunnel, not East.

"He's back." Cassandra stood and waved to Cook.

They were greeted with a sullen expression and shake of his head. *Damn, damn, damn.* Sairha bit back her chaotic thoughts and looked again at the tunnel before turning to the group. She hoped her face looked as brave as she wanted it to portray. "We have to go inside. It's the way out of the city. We will light a few of those big prayer candles and—"

"No, we can't!" Emily blurted out, looking from Cook to Sairha, her eyes pleading with them. "We can't go in there. There might be bad things in there. Please, there must be another way?"

Sairha glowered at Emily, upset at the woman's outburst and lack of sense to not raise panic in the group, the same panic she could barely keep down herself. She crossed her arms against her chest, fighting the urge to yell at the woman. "We have no choice," she snipped. Was she mad at the older woman's resistance? Or was it frustration at the lack of options?

Cook seemed to sense the heat radiating off Sairha and took over, standing between the two women. He slid his arm around Emily's shoulder, encasing the woman in his wide grasp. "Look, if we *had* another way, we would choose it. This is the only way." His voice was calm as he spoke.

Sairha said a silent prayer of gratitude for this wonderful man that she did not deserve in her life; her teammate, whom she would be lost without.

Emily chewed on her bottom lip, rigid in Cook's arm, but gave a single nod of acceptance.

"I understand," he continued and followed her gaze to her son who sat next to the wagon. Connor was oblivious to the situation as he played with a little, green army toy. "We will do our best to get through the dark as fast as possible."

"We must not stall any longer, however," Sairha chimed in, motioning to the midday sun. "If we could turn back and go the way we came, I would. But that is not a safe option anymore, we are racing the daylight."

Emily stared at Sairha for a moment, and it looked like

there was something she wanted to say, something that lingered on her tongue. Instead, she shrugged herself free of Cook's grasp and reached for Connor. "Come on, son."

Connor stood, letting out an audible whimper as he did. Sairha looked over at him, puzzled, but Emily picked the boy up and turned towards the tunnel. "Is he alright?"

"He's fine, just sore from all this traveling."

"Let's get rolling then," Cassandra called, heading into the tunnel first.

Sairha was more than ready to stop wasting time coddling the anxiety-ridden mother, as they needed to get out of the city limits. Brenda took over the wagon from Angie, Cook following behind to help push if needed. Walking past Emily with a final glance at the two, Sairha took her candle from Cassandra.

Bright flames shone through the clear glass jars, warming the tunnel in light. Angie held an emergency long burn candle in the middle of the group, and Cook brought up the rear with a safety glow stick that he attached to his rucksack. Abandoned cars were hiding spots for things, the light not near enough to unveil whatever may have been concealed. The group's shadows on the walls bounced around as they walked. No one dared speak a word, cautious to remain as quiet as they could.

What felt like ten minutes passed, and Sairha started to breathe again. They hadn't stumbled upon anything and, in the distance, if she squinted, she could see the daylight at the end of the tunnel. She looked back at Cassandra, then made eye contact with Cook, nodding towards the exit. His grin widened with enthusiasm. Something glimmered beside them, catching her attention, and her heart hitched as she veered close to a truck. The object was a silver pistol sitting in a small pool of blood. Streaks led underneath the vehicle, as if someone had been dragged away. Cassandra's eyes widened. Unable to hide her own shock, Sairha could only nod and motioned to keep going. Thankfully, her friend did.

Sairha tried to catch Cook's attention again without alarming the others. When he did notice her, she tipped her head towards the truck and then walked on, leading the group closer to the wall. Her mind screamed and begged for her to bolt, to get out of there. It took everything in her to remain calm. A hand grasped hers and Sairha squeezed Cassandra's, appreciative of the support. They just needed to make it through the last stretch, and they would feel safe in the sunlight soon enough.

The grip on her hand tightened, a slight tremor transferring through it. Cassandra's eyes were still wide, and she tapped her ear. At first, Sairha could not hear anything over their breathing, and she had to force her mind to slow down and focus. A raspy, wheezing sound came from somewhere ahead of them. It was quiet as a whisper but left no doubt that they were not alone. Memories of the hollow face of the Marrow Eater came back to Sairha in a flash, the sunken eye sockets and the too large mouth. Thousands of sharp, skinny teeth. The rasps were even in depth and timing, hopefully meaning the creature was asleep. Sairha felt sick to her stomach as terrible thoughts consumed her. Had she led them all to their doom? How deep of a sleep did these creatures go into? Would they make it to the end of the tunnel if they ran?

There was no time to turn around, or warn the others, they had to keep moving forward.

Passing another car, Sairha directed the group to the far left of the tunnel, as far away as she could from the noise. She was nervous though, remembering tunnels played tricks with directions of sound. Stopping, her light shone upon her worst fear. On the ground, poking out from under a van, was a long, thin arm with three claw-like fingers. It lay sideways with its back to them. If they were silent and quick, they could make it past, she knew it. They had to.

Her hand trembled as she ushered Cassandra ahead of her. Despite her fright, Cassandra took over leading the way. Emily followed her, no questions asked and avoided looking at Sairha, which she was thankful for. The last thing Sairha needed was the older woman freaking out before they could even pass the thing. The twins came next with the wagon trailing behind them. Her hand started to shake, the candle scattering shadows and light around them. Brenda side-eyed her but kept walking alongside her sister.

Cook opened his mouth to speak, alarmed that she remained behind, but Sairha pressed a finger to her lips and pointed at the arm. Understanding immediately flashed across his face and he nodded as he hurried by, hand at his knife.

CLANK

CLANK

The sound of the wagon hitting a crack in the road reverberated off the walls. Cook and Sairha froze, time slowed. The arm was still there, but it was impossible to calm Sairha's thunderous heart enough to hear clearly. Cook's hand hooked into her arm, tugging her forward. She couldn't stop looking, even as he dragged her along the rest of the tunnel. Then it all sped up. Everyone picked up the pace knowing that the clatter had been unfortunate. The light ahead of them grew bigger, closer. Sairha finally dared to look ahead and could see Cassandra's brown curls shimmering in the sunlight as she waved frantically.

Taking one last look back, before her eyes had to adjust, Sairha searched for the creature.

It was gone.

THEY TRAVELED HOURS AFTER SUNDOWN, Sairha and Cook pushing, encouraging them to go a little bit further. She tried to stay focused, but all she could picture was the Marrow Eater chasing after them. Along with the hours of a head-start they had, Sairha reminded herself over and over again that she had checked every single person before they had entered the city, a precaution she was thankful for enforcing. The more she thought about it, the more she had half a mind to force everyone to keep walking through the night as well. *I didn't understand before, why you were so mad we stopped at that farmhouse,* she sighed. *But I do now.* The argument that had ensued made much more sense, the scene playing out in her head, but in a new perspective. Angie's healing wound had been a glaring red path straight to them. *He* had been trying to protect them by staying far ahead of the creatures.

Emily stumbled, nearly dropping the dead weight of her sleeping son. Cook ran to her side and wrapped his arm around her for support. "Sairha, we have to stop. They need rest."

Biting her lip, Sairha looked over her shoulder at the group, then beyond them. Blackness of night hid any signs of the city, but a horrible feeling curdled in her stomach. Glancing forward, nothing lay ahead of them, no shelters or rock formations. Off the beaten road, to the side of them, was a patch of white birch trees. "How about over there?"

Cook nodded and led the way.

"Only the bare minimum," she told everyone, when they started to settle for the remainder of the night.

"I'm so beat! This is the longest we've ever been forced to

walk, longer than that guy Sven ever made us," Brenda whined as she rubbed her feet. Angie gave her a sharp look and elbowed her in the ribs. "What?" Brenda hissed, though she glanced at Sairha.

Sairha rolled her eyes. "It's fine."

But it wasn't.

It did pain her to hear anyone mention his name. It was hard enough how often she thought about him because of the situations they got into. She took a deep breath, preparing for what she knew had to be said. "I'm sorry I pushed you guys so hard today. I know you are all beyond exhausted." She looked from each tired face to the next. "We were lucky that we made it out of that tunnel alive." Letting that sink into the three who did not know the truth about the tunnel, Sairha considered the weight of telling them everything. When she looked at Cook, she remembered how he had hidden the truth from the twins about the creatures, just like Sven. The results ended with all the women unprepared when they came face to face with the monsters.

No more secrets.

"There was a Marrow Eater there." The words felt cold as they left her mouth. No one else spoke, the shock on their faces said it all. Brenda, Angie, and Emily had not even noticed.

"Those creatures that drain people's blood?" Emily broke the silence, her voice uneven, scared.

Sairha nodded. "Yes, those things. There appeared to be only one and it was sleeping. These things are attracted to blood, so we should be fine. I checked all of you before we entered the city, and we've put a lot of distance between us."

"Oh, god," Emily gasped, her complexion visibly paling in the soft candlelight. Her hand fluttered to her mouth.

Cook uncrossed his arms, reaching over to pat Emily on the knee. "We'll be okay."

The older woman shook her head, her fading red hair falling into her face as she cradled it and whimpered. "This is not good. This is not good at all."

"Heyyy, shh." Cook tried to calm her, glancing at Sairha, concerned.

"You have to protect us! You have to!" Emily grabbed onto his jacket, her hands trembling.

Cassandra jumped to his aid, pushing herself between the two of them. "Get a grip on yourself, woman," she scolded Emily who crumbled to the ground. "We're all in this together and we will be—"

"Shhh! Did you hear that?" Brenda's harsh whisper cut through the air. Her eyes were wide as she looked out into the darkness. Angie curled closer to her sister, terror on her face.

Sairha's hand went automatically for the knife at her thigh, her palm moist with sweat as she gripped the handle. Her heart quieted on its own and her breathing slowed. For a while, there were only the heavy breaths of those around her and nothing else.

Maybe it was a false alarm.

Cook looked away from Cassandra to Sairha across from them, his mouth forming words that Sairha could not make out.

She heard it before she saw anything, knowing right away they had been fools. The sound of dirt being scraped came from behind the twins. Claws, a lot of them.

"Get down!" Sairha screamed.

Too late.

One of the creatures sunk its claws deep into Angie and dragged her back to the trees. The night filled with her screaming, so much screaming. Shouts and wailing and crying. It was impossible to hear anything else. Sairha stood frozen in shock, unable to distinguish the multitude of noises.

Brenda joined the chorus of chaos by yelling for her sister as Angie cried for help from farther and farther away. To Sairha's left, Emily wailed on the ground, "My baby! My baby!" Cassandra struggled to keep Emily safe and out of the way. Cook grunted, beating on the side of a second Marrow Eater, trying to find any way to draw its attention away from Connor who lay under the creature's grip.

Everything felt like it was happening in slow motion. Where should she go? What should she do? Who should she choose to save?

Breathe...

Snapping out of it, Sairha went at a full run towards the Marrow Eater over Connor. "Cook!" she yelled over the mangled shrieks. He turned his head ever so slightly and seemed to understand. Pulling away, he laced his fingers together, creating a step up. Sairha shoved one boot inside and used the boost to launch herself onto the creature. She stabbed her knife into its shoulder for added support as she climbed, the creature hissed in pain as it reached up with its long claws to get at her. Sairha was already on top of it, the knife glinting black in the faint candlelight before she drove it down into the creature's head. With a shrill squeal of surprise, the creature tittered until it crashed onto its side. Another deep stab of the blade and the creature moved no more.

Sairha's breath came in ragged gasps as she rose from the slayed monster, yanking her knife free as she did. Adrenaline coursed through every vein, and a sick fascination pinned her attention on the ichor that oozed from the Marrow Eater's skull. Someone was yelling at her, and she had to force her mind to focus on what Cook was saying.

"Brenda and Angie! We need to go help them!"

She nodded.

Cook followed hot on Sairha's trail as she weaved in and out of the trees, Angie and Brenda's cries leading them. There was a loud crack, and the night became silent. Stumbling through the thick bushes, Sairha and Cook were in a clearing amongst the trees. A smaller Marrow Eater knelt over an unmoving body, its long claws digging inside her stomach. Bright crimson painted its mouth, the ground, her clothes. A literal blood bath. It took no notice of them, so consumed was it in devouring its victim.

Sairha turned herself away from the gore and searched for the other twin.

"Look, over there," Cook whispered beside her. Brenda was slumped against a tree to the side of the creature, eyes closed but still breathing. She had probably been flung back and knocked out, a snack saved for later. So that meant the body...

Sairha swallowed, fighting back tears. *Angie.* The sounds of the Marrow Eater slurping and rooting around the inside of the poor girl would haunt her forever.

"Help...me..." Angie gurgled weakly.

Sairha gripped Cook's shoulder, horrified, as Angie's head rolled to gaze sightlessly in their direction. The light that had once sparkled in those eyes was gone. But Sairha was not helpless, the blade in her hand reminded her of that. Fueled by rage and raw emotion, she pushed off from the ground and ran.

There was no time for the creature to register what had happened. She was upon it in the blink of an eye. No thought, no hesitation, she rammed her knife hard into the creature's hollow eye socket followed by a swift left hook that sent the surprised beast onto its back. With a fierce battle cry, Sairha jumped on top of the creature's chest, the sound of bones cracking under her boots. Her vision was red as fire as she yanked the knife down the creature's face and out of its flesh.

Raising the knife high, Sairha slammed it down into the chest of the Marrow Eater with all her strength. Over, and over, and over again she stabbed in different areas. Hot anger had her dripping in sweat.

Cook's hand on her shoulder, forcing her still, pulled her out of her frenzy. Gasping, she allowed him to take her away from the butchered monster. Her lungs ached, body shook, and a tingling numbness crept through her.

"It's okay, it's okay. It's dead now," Cook cooed onto her head as he held her close against his chest.

Tears slid down her feverish cheeks, while the adrenaline pumped its last burst, eliciting a final shiver. She leaned hard into Cook's embrace and would have stayed that way until feeling returned to her again but a rustling noise alerted them that they weren't alone.

"Angie?" Brenda's voice was hoarse.

Sairha pulled away to go to Brenda's aid. "Hey," Sairha croaked through the tightness in her throat. Brenda backed away from her, mortified. Looking down at her hands, Sairha realized why. Black, gooey blood coated her arms and hands, and she guessed her face was also smeared from the way Brenda wouldn't look her in the eye.

"Where's Angie?"

Choking came from behind them as if in response and Brenda was up, pushing past Sairha with force. "Oh, *no!*" she shrieked upon seeing what was left of her sister. She covered her mouth to hold back a sob as she knelt down. "Angie... oh, god. I'm sorry. I'm so sorry. Why did this happen to you?" She cradled Angie close, tears streaming down her dirty face.

The Marrow Eater had done irreversible damage. Her insides were strewn around her body, pelvis torn apart, bones crushed and licked clean, leaving her legs in an awkward, lifeless pose. Angie stared upwards and a soft smile spread across her face. Colorless lips formed words that Cook and Sairha could not hear, something only for Brenda. Sairha's lip trembled, her heart breaking as she watched the sisters touch foreheads. Between sobs, Brenda gave her sister a tender kiss.

A single tear rolled down Angie's cheek, and she shut her eyes for the last time.

CHAPTER SEVENTEEN

It took Sairha and Cook several tries to drag Brenda away from her sister's body. Upon arriving at the camp, another crisis demanded the last bit of sanity remaining in Sairha. Despite Cook's best efforts to get the Marrow Eater away from Connor, it had not gone without incident. Emily latched onto Sairha's arm with a vice like grip, dragging her towards the bundle of blankets where the child lay crying.

"Quick! Get the first aid kit." Sairha wrenched her arm free and fell to her knees beside Connor, immediately assessing the damage. The creature had torn long gashes in the boy's right arm, thin punctures on the exposed muscle. As gently as she could, she elevated his arm to slow the blood from flowing out. He let out a pain drenched scream and bolted upright. With light force, she pushed him back down. "Hold on, Connor, you'll be alright."

"Sairha, here!" Cook called.

The first aid kit flew in the air, then slid across the dirt to her. It was difficult to dig inside with one hand, but it was something she had been trained to handle, and her muscle memory kicked into gear. Pulling out the hydrogen peroxide, she twisted the cap off with her teeth and cleaned her hands first, wishing she had soap and water to spare instead. "This is going to help you," she said as calmly as possible. He shook his head back and forth, tears streaming down his terrified face. With a steady hand and a deep breath, Sairha poured the liquid onto the open wounds, eliciting more screams from her patient.

"No!" Emily jumped to stop Sairha from causing more pain.

"Keep her back!" Sairha yelled, eyes transfixed on Connor's wound. The peroxide bubbled along the torn flesh, mixing the smell of sanitation with metallic.

"Let me go! Connor!" Emily panicked from the sideline, wrapped tight in Cook's arms. He grunted from the effort, a worried mother's strength nothing to bat an eye at.

"How can I help?" Cassandra knelt down beside them, shaky, but willingness and compassion softening her haggard face.

Sairha glanced at her for a second, unsure if her easily queasy friend could handle it, then nodded at the kit. "See if there's a needle and thread. We need to stitch him closed." Connor stopped squirming under Sairha's pressure, his eyes rolling back into his head, and he went slack. *Oh, fuck;* she freaked out mentally and pushed one of his eyelids open, then the other. A sigh of relief escaped her. *Dilated. Only fainted, probably from the pain. He's lost so much blood, though.*

"Sairha, here." Cassandra nudged her hand, offering a thin suturing needle threaded and ready to go.

Bracing herself, Sairha made the first suture and thanked luck that Connor was out cold. She worked her way down his arm, the act of stitching skin together familiar work for her hands. When she switched to the other gash, something glinted in the fire light and she dug her finger in to get at it.

Connor awoke instantly and thrashed around, nearly causing Sairha to leave the object inside him.

"Hold still, Connor! Hold him, Cas, that's it. Calm, nice and calm. We're almost done, Connor. I promise." Hands still steady, Sairha did the best she could to finish amidst the boy's screams. Minutes later she stood, hands soiled yet again with blood. Cook released Emily and helped Cassandra up. Emily pushed Sairha away like she hadn't just helped him but was simply torturing the boy for fun. Blinking a few times, Sairha felt a squeeze on her hand. She glanced at Cook's hand wrapped around hers, which she didn't recall grabbing. Together, the three of them walked away from the sobbing mother holding her child.

"Will he be alright?" Cassandra whispered.

"I don't know," Sairha replied, feeling every bit permanently numb within.

No one slept much during the last hours of that night, all of them looking like apocalyptic zombies by the time they left for the day. Conversation was non-existent beyond checking to see if everyone was ready. Cook's eyes were puffy, having given up his night's rest to bury Angie in the woods, alone, while Sairha and Cassandra helped soothe Brenda to sleep. He marched beside Sairha mechanically for hours, a silent shell of himself. The sound of the child-laden wagon wheels, pulling on the road, ticked time away like the second hands on a clock. Rolling, cracking over pebbles, until at last the sun was ready to give way to night.

"Let's stop," Sairha decided aloud, turning off the road on top of a hill.

More and more patches of evergreens surrounded the

group, creating a sense of protection after what they had been through. Denser forestry lay ahead, leaving the harsh desert and unforgiving sunlight behind. Sairha's gaze crossed over the new horizon. Even though everything was painted in the gray of early evening, it was wondrous to see the landscape changing to the mountain terrain from her childhood. Yet the loss of the night before hung heavy on her shoulders, a bittersweet taste deep within at seeing how far they had come only to be beaten down so close to the finish line. What lay waiting for her hung by a thread, and Sairha was too numb to muster any hope.

Turning away from the view, she passed Cook as he worked on starting a fire. They would no longer risk being in the dark at night, not when there was finally plenty of wood. She nodded to Cassandra, who was trying to coax Brenda into eating something. Quiet sadness surrounded her, and her destination was no cheerier. Emily sat beside her slumbering child in the wagon, face etched in worry lines that aged her. Sairha knelt on the opposite side, devoid of outward emotion as she inspected Connor. Beads of sweat glistened on his brow, plastering his fair hair onto ashen skin. It didn't take touching him to know he was running a fever, but she pressed the back of her hand to his forehead anyhow.

"He'll be okay, right?" Emily croaked.

Sairha ignored the woman and lifted the boy's head, damp with moisture, and carefully poured water into his mouth. He groaned, then started coughing, and she leaned him to the side. The water came back up, a splatter of blood along with it.

Dammit. I tried, I tried my best.

She didn't want to think about it, didn't want to admit that he would be beyond lucky to survive the night, much less another day. After laying him back down, Sairha stood but avoided looking at Emily as she gave her instructions, "He needs rest, but you must make sure he stays hydrated. Give him some water every thirty minutes." She could not handle telling the sleep deprived mother the truth right now. Her own mental stability would crumble along with Emily's.

Seeking some solace, Sairha walked over and sat beside Cook within the warmth of his small fire. Cold gripped her, but she knew it was internal and that nothing could truly warm her. Not until she was home. They had lost the sweetest girl in this new hellish world, and they were about to lose an innocent child. This felt a hundred times worse than anything she had witnessed in the hospital. She hardly knew either of them, but that didn't make them any less important to her. They had become an unlikely group of survivors, traveling and caring for each other. *How much loss will we have to endure?* Rubbing the tension from her brow, Sairha pulled a small, thin object from her pocket and twirled it between her fingers.

Cook nudged her. "What's that?"

She held it up to the light, making the white needle-like object shine. "A Marrow Eater tooth," she murmured. "I pulled it out of Connor's arm."

Cook sucked in a breath of surprise, then leaned closer to look at it. "It's so... thin and pointy."

She nodded and palmed the tooth, then shoved it back into her pocket. *A memento of a terrible mistake,* she thought and it took everything inside of her to fight back tears. *First looters and now this? Why did it have to be this way?* Cook's strong arm wrapped around her, his military jacket heavy and warm on her shoulders. Releasing a shaky breath, she allowed her head to fall against his shoulder.

"I don't understand how this happened." Cassandra spoke up across from them, scowling at the fire. Brenda sat beside her, hand in Cassandra's lap, motionless, lost to the world. Cheeks cleaned of blood and dirt, but forever tear stained.

Cook shook his head, holding his hand up to silence her. "It doesn't matter. It happened. They were awoken when the wagon hit that bump."

"But how did they follow us? How could they catch up to us when we walked so far!" Cassandra was visibly upset, and Sairha knew they would never get her to quiet down. She needed answers, but no one had them for her. The rest of them were content to remain in silent misery, but Cassandra needed to vent and it was best to let her. "It isn't fair, it isn't right."

Emily left her spot at her son's side to join the group, avoiding looking at Cassandra and Brenda as she sat. Sairha noted the intense wringing of her hands, a justifiable nervous sign. She chewed on her bottom lip for a moment before pinning Sairha with her bloodshot stare. "I have a confession to make."

Everyone turned their attention to her, even Brenda glanced over at the older woman, although her gaze remained unfocused. Sairha hoped beyond all hope that the woman was not going to say something stupid. Grief was burdening on all of them, not just her, and they might respond unkindly, say something they didn't mean.

"It was my fault," Emily cried out, throwing her face into her hands as she began to weep.

Ever a firecracker, the scowl on Cassandra's face deepened as she snipped, "What do you mean it was *your* fault?"

"Back in the city, when we were starting to head out of it —" the woman could barely talk through her crying. "— Sairha, you asked if everything was alright when we fell behind. The truth is, Connor had cut himself against a car. I didn't think it was that deep, but..."

Sairha closed her eyes, hurting inside more than she thought possible from hearing the truth. She wished she had checked Connor when she suspected something was wrong.

Instead, she had trusted the woman to put all of their safety first, not just her and her son's. When she opened her eyes again, the scene had changed dramatically. Brenda jumped from her seat, soundless, and like a feral cat lunged for Emily. The two toppled over into the dirt with a surprised yelp and angry growls. Sairha watched, shocked, as Brenda rolled her hands into fists and planted a hard punch into the woman's cheek.

"How could you!" Brenda shrieked, rearing up for another blow.

Emily's arms went up to protect herself.

Cassandra looked ready to join the fight.

And all Sairha could do was watch it unfold, torn between her own anger and sympathy towards Emily.

Cook was the one who jumped forward to pull Brenda off. She kicked and lashed out, even as he dragged her away like an unruly school child. Sairha shook loose her immobility and helped Emily up, lifting her by the armpits out of the dirt, a spittle of blood trickling from her busted bottom lip.

"*How could you!*" Brenda yelled again, her arms flailing about in fury. "My sister is dead because of you! I'll never forgive you, never!"

"Shhh, shh. Calm down, Brenda, breathe." Cook's soothing, deep voice tried to reason with her, pulling her further away from Emily. Inhaling and exhaling loudly, Brenda settled herself and he stood her up, leading her towards the sleeping bag she used to share with Angie. With a quick maneuver, she darted under Cook's arm and aimed her sights on Emily again. Unfortunately for her, Cook must have been expecting something like that and caught her with little effort. He tossed her over his shoulder and brought her back to the sleeping bag. Together, they lay on the ground, Cook stroking Brenda's hair.

The sound of heart wrenching sobs filled the night as she curled up against him.

"I hope it was worth it, keeping the truth from us," Cassandra spat out as she passed Sairha and Emily. If daggers could have flown out of her eyes, Sairha had no doubt that Cassandra would have riddled Emily with holes.

Emily turned to Sairha, mortified. In spite of her own boiling anger, Sairha got Emily a gauze from the first aid kit. Emily muttered a thank you. Sairha stopped her. "You should have told me. Go spend time with your son, before it's too late."

Sairha left the older woman to her own mental anguish. As wrong as it was, she hoped her words stung, because the realization that she, herself, should have been honest with the group about the tunnel was not lost on her. She lay awake, overanalyzing the tragedy. The solution she came to, before the forgiving embrace of slumber took over her, was that they should have never gone into the city in the first place.

There was little surprise that Emily and her son had vanished in the night. Maybe even a little relief. She left a whole jug of water beside an extra bag of canned food but took the fuller one of the two first-aid kits. Cassandra looked down at the stuff, her arms crossed at her chest. "That woman," she growled. "She thinks she can just leave us to hide her shame? After all we've done for them."

"Let it go," Sairha whispered, kneeling down to shove the kit into her backpack with more force than she intended. "She was only trying to protect her kid. And, in the end, she is the reason he will die. If she wants to be alone, that's her choice." She picked up the bag of cans, hand shaking. Shame filled her over the fact that she was glad none of them would have to help bury another body, though she found just enough hope in her that Connor would survive. A shadow blocked the morning sun, and she handed the food to Cook's outstretched hand as he crouched in front of her. "We move on without them. And never forget the lesson we learned. No large groups in a city. We should make it to my family's cabin within a few days."

Cassandra grunted and looked over at Brenda, who was waiting for the others to be ready to go. "I don't think we'll ever forget what happened."

There was no cheer, no playful banter, no lightness of feet in the lull of marching towards their journey's end. Brenda remained silent, save for the sniffling during the day, and the heartbreaking sobs during the night. Sairha kept thinking of that night, kept dreaming of it and waking in cold sweats. Between that and Brenda's crying, she walked every day with only a few hours of sleep. Entering the forest by road, the four of them stayed alert, though they never saw another person nor Marrow Eater. Moving beyond exhaustion for three days, at last they were within eyesight of Sairha's home.

Sairha was the first to reach the top of the steep hill they climbed, following the familiar dirt road that curved, revealing a short glen below. Sun rays hit the cabin hidden between giant pine trees that surrounded the property, like it was a little bit of heaven waiting for them. Sanctuary. Overwhelming emotions of both happiness and fear choked her when she saw it. All thoughts of their difficult journey disappeared. *Please, let them be there. Please,* she silently hoped, willed, begged of any higher power.

"That's the place?" Cook stood next to her and rested his heavy bag on the ground.

Nodding, Sairha wrapped her arms around herself and took a deep breath to steady the queasiness that bubbled inside her. "Yes, I grew up here. I know it sounds silly... but... do you think anyone is down there?"

Cook remained quiet, which hurt Sairha more than she cared to admit.

"It looks just like the pictures you showed me, Sairha," Cassandra sighed, coming to a halt beside her friend. Brenda tried to look interested, lifting her brows, only for her eyes to fill with tears.

It really did look unchanged by the horrors they had found in other places. As if they had stumbled from a nightmare into a fairytale. Sairha's heart lurched, spying the dusty, forest green hatchback her mom drove. Right where it always had been. There was no way of telling, from where they stood, if the cabin had inhabitants in it.

"Let's head down. Cook and I will go first to make sure it's clear," she said as calmly as she could. Her nerves twisted, threatening bile in her throat.

The three nodded in acknowledgement and let her lead the way. Each step towards the glen had Sairha holding her breath and her hands shook the nearer they got to the door.

Mama, Alison, I'm home...

CHAPTER EIGHTEEN

Dust particles flurried in the sunlight after Cook kicked open the cabin door. Splintered wood lay on the ground, the house boarded up from the inside, stirring up hope in Sairha like the dust that tickled her nose as she stepped past the threshold. She gripped her knife tight, ready for anything, as her boots made loud thuds with each careful step she took through the otherwise silent home. When her eyes adjusted to the dim lighting, her heart sank.

The home was torn apart. Furniture turned over, pictures fallen off the walls, lamps turned on their sides with crushed shades. The sliding glass doors to their backyard were shattered from the outside, shards littering the wood floor. Deserted. Abandoned. Devoid of her family. No one rushing to wrap their arms around her in greeting.

Sairha sighed, blinking away tears, and acknowledged the bitter truth; she had been foolish to hope otherwise.

Walking farther in, she turned towards the hall. Cook reached out to stop her, but she avoided his grasp and went to inspect the rooms. She couldn't face them. *There has to be some sort of clue, a message, anything!*

The door to the master suite squeaked when she stepped inside. The room looked better than the living room, although it was apparent someone had left in a hurry. She kicked aside some of her mom's clothes strewn across the floor. The small desk across from the closet was strewn with papers, its lamp turned over. The only normality in the chaos of the room was that her mom's bed was made, something she had drilled into them as kids, that the beds needed to be made before leaving the house every day. A tingling numbness swept over her as she tried to process the loss.

Leaving her mom's room, she stood on her tiptoes to feel around the top of the door frame to her room. Her fingertips grazed the key, right where she had left it. She twisted it inside the handle and the door swung inwards. The room was untouched by time or current circumstances. Brighter than the rest of the house, the small rectangular window at the top of the wall had been left unboarded. Sairha sat down on the dusty bedspread, flattened from being made for so long, and looked up at all of her favorite books on their shelves, then her empty desk. She reached out and touched the spot where her family photo used to sit on her nightstand, the one left she behind. Being in her room felt like nothing had happened, yet outside everything had changed. She had changed.

She left the surreal feeling of being in her own room to check her sister's. When she got inside, she was surprised to find Alison's room a complete wreck. Her sister had painted the walls a dark plum and black since the last time Sairha had been in it, making the space seem smaller. The bed was turned upside down, flung against the closet. A nightstand was knocked over and magazines littered the floor, stepped on and torn into pieces.

What happened here...

As if righting the room could fix things, and could tell her where her family was, Sairha pushed the mattress back onto the box spring. It fell with a loud smack, a cloud of dust spewing out, and something flew up into the air. Snatching it, she turned the ripped paper over. Her sister smiled back at her, hugging someone who had been torn off. It was a photo Sairha knew well; the one of herself and Alison the summer before she left. A gut wrenching sob escaped her, and the tears fell, soaking her cheeks, the loss too heavy to contain within. She slid the photo into her back pocket, then set to work fixing the bed sheets and comforter. Righting what had been wronged in the room, but not in her heart.

Comfortable in Sairha's family cabin, the threat of the outside world eased for the group. Cook made sure the front door was secured again, as well as all the windows, and together with Sairha, they boarded up the back. He even set up some cans on rope, like they had done for bears in the past, around the property to sound the alarm. There would be no getting in undetected. Afterwards, he and Cassandra dug around the kitchen to see what food supplies were left.

It felt strange, and every muscle throbbed in pain, but Sairha relished sitting on her mom's raggedy old couch in the living room. She watched the fire she had built dance in the stone fireplace, wondering what had happened to them. There was no blood, no sign a Marrow Eater had been there. That only left two options; they had left of their own accord, and someone had looted, or they were taken not by choice. With no note to be found, only dead-end clues, Sairha worried it was the latter. If they were still alive, finding them would be near impossible. The fire offered no real warmth to her after those thoughts. She could hardly feel anything, she was so emotionally drained.

"I'm...sorry they weren't here." Across from her, Brenda sat in an armchair, curled up tight into herself. Her eyes were red rimmed from crying, and although her cheeks were dry, the tear-streaks remained. She hadn't spoken more than a mumbled acknowledgement when spoken to, and Sairha was worried she'd starve herself.

"I know this is nothing like what you went through..." Sairha felt awkward even mentioning it, their pains were vastly different. "But I am here for you, and they say misery loves company."

Brenda gave her only a short glance, eventually whispering a 'thank you' before pulling tighter into herself, burying her face from sight.

Cook and Cassandra entered the room, a large, speckled pot in his hands while she juggled mismatched bowls. "Grubs on!" he boomed, dishing steamed rice into the bowls. Cassandra shoved a spoon in one and handed it to Brenda. She grabbed two more and sat beside Sairha, handing her one. Cook took a deep inhale, his eyes closing. "Mmmm, thank god for gas stoves and 'never gets old' boxes of rice."

"Soy sauce?" Cassandra offered and pulled a small pouring bottle out of the apron pocket she was wearing.

Sairha's mom's apron.

Sairha half smiled and focused on her bowl. Two mouthfuls sat like lumps in her stomach, reminding her how hollow she felt. She pushed the rice around her bowl, unable to stop thinking. "What did I expect? Them to be here, waiting for me, with a tray of cookies or something? Silly of me." She tried to cover her sadness with a laugh, to break the tension she imagined her mood was creating, but it was empty.

Cassandra swallowed and stared into her own bowl.

Cook set his food down and looked directly at Sairha. "It's okay if you did," his normally loud voice was soft and quiet. "I think we all had similar hopes. That your family would be here, and that our own families are okay." He reached over Cassandra and patted Sairha's leg.

"That there are more people in the world other than us," Cassandra added.

He shrugged and leaned back against the couch, full lips pulling into a smile. "Well, if we *are* the last, I'm glad we found each other."

Sairha and Cassandra nodded in agreement. In honesty, Sairha wasn't sure how they would have survived without him after…well, after they were left in the desert on their own.

"We've had an exhausting day, and week. Hell, a month. How about we rest tonight? I've got the place locked up tight, and the rope traps will alert us if anything comes near the cabin. Tomorrow we'll figure out what we want to do." He looked between the three for confirmation.

"Sounds like a good plan. It's been so long since my head has rested on a pillow," Cassandra sighed and sucked on her spoon, looking happy just thinking about a peaceful sleep.

"I'd like to stay here for a while, at my fam—well, my cabin, if that is okay with you guys? As long as it's safe." Sairha looked to Cook, hoping he understood this was a different kind of break she needed. It wouldn't be her curled into a ball, ignoring them. Not again. There was no 'after this' for her. Getting home to her family had been it. Her future was as barren as her home had been.

"I go where you go," Cook said, then took a moment to mull it over. "We aren't anywhere near cities or civilization, where most of the bonebags seem to dwell. I'll scope out the area and we can make sure of the safety. It would be good for us all to get more rest than a single night."

Cassandra rested her head on Sairha's shoulder, as if to say she was there to stay as well. Relieved, Sairha took in a deep breath, right as the exhaustion hit hard. She would need a week of sleep to feel even halfway like a human again. With her friends in no hurry to move on, she had one less worry to hinder her falling asleep that night.

It was hard to open her eyes the next morning but, when she did, she was greeted by a familiar rectangular sunspot on the ceiling. Groggily, she looked around her room and wondered if it had been a bad dream. The sight of her knife on the bedside table reminded her how real everything was. It only felt like being a kid again, sleeping in her own bed in her old house, but in reality those innocent days were long gone.

Getting up from bed was slow work. Every inch of her body ached, made more apparent thanks to a comfortable night's rest. After a few stretches to relieve some of the pain, Sairha dressed in her old clothes, picking clean and practical, easy to move in garments. Jeans that actually fit and a tattered band t-shirt over a thermal long sleeve. "Not quite the professional garb I used to wear," she commented to her reflection.

"Pop punk, huh?" Cook's deep voice teased from the kitchen when Sairha passed by.

She smirked and threw up devil-horns, the universal hand gesture for being rebellious.

His laughter filled the cabin as he stirred a large pot on the stove.

Sairha smiled and sat at the breakfast counter on a worn stool. *Her* stool. "I saw this band live, you know." There was an air of pride in her tone. Her smile turned into a wince when she pulled at a knot in her hair. "First time I ever got punched in the face. Got stuck in a mosh pit. My mom was pretty upset, but she got over it when I wouldn't stop talking about how amazing the experience was, with a shiny black eye."

"Ooohhh, tough." Cook grinned as he ladled some of his cooking into a bowl. "Your mom sounds like a responsible parent. I'm impressed with how well she kept this place stocked up on durable food. Oatmeal for breakfast, with some strawberry preserves." He slid the steaming bowl over to her.

She relished the flavors of her first bite, thankful for something new to eat, swallowing the sadness talking about her mom brought up. "You have to be stocked up when you live thirty-ish miles from a grocery store. That's why we have a gas stove and a well." Even if Cook proved to be a better cook than her mom ever wished to be, seeing him stand in the spot where she used to, watching her two daughters eat, really hit Sairha hard. She continued to eat her breakfast with a lump in her throat that just wouldn't go away. *Maybe staying here is a mistake. Can I handle all of the memories?*

Cassandra poked her head around the corner, yawning, looking like she had a crazy night's sleep. Her brown curls were a rat's nest, and she still had sleep crusted eyes. "Ugh, why does it feel like I could sleep for a thousand years, and it still would not be enough?" She covered her mouth as she yawned a second time and slid into the seat beside Sairha's.

Alison's seat. But when Sairha thought on it, it seemed fitting. Cassandra was like a sister to her now more than ever. Warmed by the realization, she reached out and rubbed her friend's shoulder with care. "Good sleep?"

Cassandra let out a happy groan, nodded, and leaned into Sairha's touch.

Cook slid a bowl over to Cassandra, then leaned back

against the stove. "Now that you're both here. We need to talk."

Sairha set her spoon down, resting her hands beside her bowl. Her stomach did a flip at the seriousness of his tone. *One day. Can't we just have one day of peace?*

Cassandra pointed her spoon at him, "Shoot." She shoveled another bite into her mouth, not noticing how Cook's demeanor had changed. Sairha had.

"Brenda's gone."

"What?!" Cassandra choked, spitting oats out. She wiped at her mouth and looked to Sairha, then back at Cook. "Where the hell would she go?"

"I don't know, but I'm going after her." Cook pushed off from the stove. "Before you ask, I'm going alone."

"Sairha! Tell him he can't." Cassandra almost shrieked.

Sairha curled her hand into a loose fist to avoid the two from seeing her tremble. *This is my fault. I couldn't save Angie. Why would Brenda want to stay?*

"It's not Sairha's call. We don't know if there are Marrow Eaters out there," Cook responded, standing in front of them. "I don't want to risk losing either of you. I debated even telling you, but I want no lies between us three."

I wasn't here for my family.

"Then...then stay here! She left for a reason, right? Maybe she wants to be alone. Sairha. Why aren't you saying anything?" Cassandra snapped.

I can't protect them.

Sairha closed her eyes tight, fighting back the monstrous images that plagued her from that night, of the bloody Marrow Eaters burned in her brain, of sinew, bones, and torn flesh...

"Sairha!" Cassandra shook her, dashing away the dark spiral she was slipping into.

Slamming her hand onto the counter, Sairha stood. "You

can't search everywhere on your own. You don't know the area like I do. I'll check the trail behind my house, you go the way we came. Cassandra, you stay with me."

Sairha was met with a hard stare from Cook, but when she made no sign of backing down, he conceded with a nod. "Alright. We'll meet back here in two days. She got a head start on me, but I have to try. If I don't find her, it's just us three."

Sairha let loose a shaky breath.

We have to try.

COOK LEFT after breakfast was cleaned up, with his hunting knife and rackbag, which felt more ominous than Sairha liked to admit. She did her best to remain calm on the outside as they saw him off, saying a silent prayer that he would find Brenda and they'd return unscathed.

Lingering on the porch until Cook had disappeared from sight, the sun was warm on Sairha's skin. She ran her hands through her hair, releasing some tension with an audible sigh. It surprised her more and more how much she was coming to terms with things beyond her control, moving past the bad to get to what needed to be done. All thoughts about what happened with *him*, that had crushed her soul, now seemed small compared to the things they had endured without *him*.

"Thanks for loaning me some clothes." Cassandra's voice pulled Sairha out of her self-reflection. She stepped beside Sairha and stretched. "Ow. My ribs hurt from not sleeping on top of rocks last night. You ready?"

Sairha chuckled at the joke and looked Cassandra over. Something was different about the woman, something she couldn't place. She had lost a bit of weight the last month, but otherwise looked better than she had while traveling. *Probably* two good meals and rest on a real bed. We'll all be looking better within a week. A clean change of clothes, wild hair tamed, and face washed also helped heighten the illusion of health.

"Come on, I'll show you the way," Sairha said, grabbing her friend's hand and tugging her off the porch, her knife secured in its sheath, strapped to her leg.

They checked that Cook's alarms were still in order around the property. Sairha stomped through the overgrown lawn, past the unattended raised garden beds, nearing the back fence. "That's where we keep the winter gear and—" she pointed to the plain brown shed they passed. "—knowing my mom, there should be canned fruits and vegetables. I think we'll be okay for a while here." That was, if Sairha could live in the present, instead of the past.

"Neat," Cassandra said, sounding uninterested. "Do you think Cook is okay?"

Sairha glanced behind her to see the very real concern on her friend's face. "It's only been about an hour. He's trained and capable, I have no doubt he's doing fine." They stopped close to the six foot tall fence and listened, Sairha peering through the cracks. The forest beyond was still, peaceful. Opening the gate door as quietly as possible, she stepped out first and motioned for Cassandra to follow. "Can I ask what's up with you and Cook?"

Cassandra's cheeks were a little flush as she passed Sairha. "There isn't anything there," she said with a shrug.

"Uh-huh, sure." Sairha narrowed her eyes. "This way."

"What? There isn't." Cassandra tried to sound convincing.

"If you think it's because he's interested in someone else," Sairha said quietly, picking her way through the brush until she found the pathway she was looking for. "You do not have to worry. I... I can't fathom ever feeling that way about someone again, to be honest." She blinked as the words hit her own ears, sounding far away and from someone else. It was the sad truth. She doubted she could ever heal enough from the heartache she suffered, an ache so intense she had abandoned safety concerns. She would never allow another soul to be that close to her, her life depended on it.

Cassandra followed, keeping her own voice low and the tone softer. "Sairha, what happened back there... I'm sorry. I am really, truly sorry. But you can't let that asshole ruin your life. You'll find love again. I know it."

Sairha didn't say anything; she couldn't. She was afraid that if she opened her mouth she would choke on her words and tears would escape the stronghold she had over them. Her time of mourning love was done. She waved her hand like it was no big deal, waving away the emotions that tried to emerge. "This isn't about me," she diverted back. "I'm serious, I think Cook does care for you. More than he lets on."

"Ha, ha, ha." Cassandra's laugh was bitter, humorless. "Sairha, I can't begin to explain what sort of trouble I would be for that man. I'm no good. Damaged goods."

"What are you talking about? You're amazing, Cassandra! You've grown so much, before he met you to now." Sairha stopped, facing Cassandra and gripping her shoulders, a soft smile painted on her face. "He would have been lucky to know you *before* all of this happened, even your wild girl ways. You've always been amazing. And I'm sorry if I ever made you feel otherwise. If he's someone you want to pursue, go for it."

Cassandra dug her hand into her pocket. "Sairha, it isn't just me anymore that someone would be taking on in this life."

Sairha's brows knit together, confused, but the pistons in her brain started to piece things together. Had she been blind to all the signs before? Blinded by her love, grief, trying to survive. Too busy to even notice? Self-absorbed. *Oh, it couldn't be... could it?*

Cassandra handed Sairha a plastic bag, a white stick inside, then shoved both her hands back into her pockets. She kicked at the ground, careful to avoid eye contact as she spoke. "There's going to be a... a mini me, I guess, in a few months. Assuming everything goes alright."

"Oh," was all Sairha could manage as she stared down at the positive pregnancy test.

All the things she had mistaken for being resistant to the new life, things that she had laughed about, or had thought it was just Cassandra being moody, flashed in her mind like a movie reel. Her, a trained medical professional, had missed all the telltale signs. Sairha was dumbfounded. It took her a moment to regain her composure, and when she did a true smile pulled at her lips. "Cassandra, this is great news." She threw her arms around her friend in a tight hug.

"Great? How can this be great?" Cassandra cried out, pushing away. Her face hardened, eyebrows scrunching together in a scowl. "What kind of a world is this to raise a baby? With creatures picking us off? Not to mention, how will we keep it healthy? Ourselves healthy? And then there is the most normal part of this, the thing won't have a father."

Such a burden to carry on her own. And where was I? Too busy with my petty problems. She felt like a jerk, leaving Cassandra to suffer alone. *But she isn't alone.*

"Cassandra, I'll take care of you. Both of you."

Cassandra's stern expression wavered, her bottom lip quivering as she searched Sairha's eyes. Seeking reassurance.

"We can stay here. We can make a life for you and the baby." She pulled Cassandra back into her arms and kissed her forehead. Cassandra was tense at first, then relaxed and held onto Sairha's shoulders. Even though she had no idea how they would successfully pull it off, deep down in her heart, Sairha knew it would work out.

They stayed like that for a while, locked in each other's arms with Cassandra sniffling.

A scream broke the silence that surrounded them, shattering the illusion of safety.

Alert, Sairha's attention snapped in all directions, trying to pinpoint where it came from. "Shhh." She pulled away from Cassandra and reached for the knife at her thigh. It was quiet for a long time, while Sairha and Cassandra shifted on their feet, scanning the area. The sunlight filtered through the trees, casting shadows, creating many hiding places. Cassandra backed up close to Sairha, whispering, "Do you think—"

Another scream bounced around the trees. Sairha's pulse accelerated, her palm sweaty against the knife handle. "It could be Brenda," she whispered. The sounds of a fight amplified, and, without another word, the two ran towards it. There was no time to think, Sairha was determined to save Brenda. *I won't fail her this time.*

The scene they arrived at was nothing she expected.

A Marrow Eater hissed from inside a cave, protected from the sun, black blood oozing from several punctures in its gray flesh. Across from it, in the daylight, a large tan wolf crouched with its hackles raised, growling. The two were at a stalemate, the wolf's focus never once leaving its opponent, the Marrow Eater biding its time, waiting for the chance to attack. Neither noticed when Sairha skidded to a halt a few yards away, yanking Cassandra behind a large tree.

"It's not Brenda," Cassandra hissed. "Let's leave."

Sairha counted to ten, slowing her racing heart, calming her thoughts. "We can't just leave," she reasoned. "If the wolf doesn't finish off the Marrow Eater, it'll eventually find us. It is too close to our home. Stay here."

"No!" Cassandra whispered, reaching for Sairha too late.

Keeping to the shadows, dashing from tree cover to tree

cover, Sairha made her way to the cave's opening undetected. The wolf let out a vicious bark that vibrated throughout the area before it launched itself at the Marrow Eater. While they were engaged in battle, she crept ever closer, pausing to make sure Cassandra was safe where she left her. The brunette peeked over, anxiety written all over her face. A yelp made Sairha turn back, just as the wolf was thrown against the cave's rock wall where it lay motionless.

Thump, thump, thump.

Heartbeat loud in her ears, Sairha reminded herself she could do it, she'd done it before, and ran forward at top speed. Dropping to her knees, she skidded across the ground, under the Marrow Eater, and stabbed her knife upward, slicing through its stomach. Jumping to her feet, reinforcing her hold on the knife, she readied for another go at the creature. The Marrow Eater shrieked, grabbing at its middle, while its insides slipped out of its grasp. It wobbled, cries losing volume, then toppled over in a puddle of black.

Sairha took a shaky breath and stood up, walking to the dying creature. Wary of its reach, she rounded to the back of its head and then drove her knife to the hilt, stilling the Marrow Eater forever.

"Fuuuuuck."

Ripping her knife out, knuckles white, she spun on her heel to face who had snuck up behind her. *What now?!* A scowl was on her face and she zeroed in on the figure that leaned heavily against the wall, one hand cupping his side. Before her was a man with flowing, shoulder length blonde hair, golden skin, and a smug look on his face. He was also very, *very* unclothed.

"Sairha! Are you oka—woah..." Cassandra paused, slowing to a jog as she took in the sight. "Who are you and why are you naked?"

Sairha closed her eyes. "He's the wolf."

CHAPTER NINETEEN

"The name is Travis," the man said with a dramatic fling of his hair. He looked both women over with hazel eyes, no apparent shame about his indecency. "And you are?"

Neither of the women spoke.

"Okay then. As much as I appreciate the help, I had it and you two shouldn't be out here."

Sairha rolled her eyes and put her knife away to pull her band tee off. She tossed it to him. "We can handle ourselves. You're welcome, by the way, for saving your *tail* from becoming Marrow Eater food."

His eyes flashed before he pulled the shirt over his head. "You know their names..." A statement, not a question.

"Yeah, we do. And we know what you are," Cassandra snapped. "We're looking for our friend, Brenda. Cute, black hair in a braid, big brown eyes, tall woman in her early twenties. Have you seen her?"

"Cassandra." Sairha shot a warning look to not give away too much information.

Travis laughed as he turned away from them and walked

out of the cave. He stood in a sun beam for a few minutes, taking deep breaths, visibly becoming relaxed. "Come on then," he called back, waving them forward. The women followed, Sairha watching warily as he went to a bush and grabbed some things. He slipped on some rough looking jeans, covered in dirt and with more holes than swiss cheese. After zipping up the fly, Travis clapped his hands together. "I haven't seen your friend, but let's go check in with the pack."

Blood pressure dropping, Sairha took a step back, gently nudging Cassandra with her hand. "No, we're good."

"Oh, that wasn't an offer, girly." Travis took a step towards them, producing thin rope from his pocket.

"Men's pockets," Cassandra hissed. "They hide everything."

"You don't need to tie us up," Sairha panicked, reaching for her knife slowly. "We'll go quietly."

He made a tsking sound and motioned towards her knife. "You know the world today. I wouldn't expect any less from you, either, if the roles were reversed. It's a safety precaution. Don't make me wrestle you to the ground. You all look like you just cleaned up and, to be honest, I'm beat. I just got knocked around by that monster, and it's a long walk to where we're going."

Cassandra looked at Sairha with worry. There wasn't much fight in her, and Sairha didn't blame her. The last thing Cassandra needed was to be knocked around in her state. Glancing at Travis, then her knife again, Sairha weighed the probability of winning a fight with a wolfshifter. Slim to none. With a sigh, she put her hands together and stepped forward.

"I am sorry about this," he spoke quieter, tying her hands. "You understand, don't you?" When he had finished, she clenched and unclenched her hands, testing to see how much give the rope had. There was no possibility of her fitting the knife's handle between her palms. Travis leaned in close, making her anxiety spike, and she closed her eyes tight. There was a soft inhale beside her neck. "You smell lovely."

What a weirdo, she thought. *I wouldn't even bother taking you captive. I'd kill you here and now for that alone.* Though when she tried to envision it, Sairha knew she could never outside of a life or death situation. She watched him carefully, ready to tackle him if he tried anything half as strange with Cassandra. He merely bound her the same, pausing for the briefest of moments.

"Let's go."

After the sniffing incident, he left them alone for the rest of the day, aside from giving the rope a rough tug whenever the women started to lag. Hours later, heavy footfalls and rustling stirred the bushes around them. Sairha and Cassandra huddled close together, expecting an attack, however Travis appeared unphased. Three large wolves jumped out and circled around them, growling and yipping. "Don't worry about them," Travis called back. He lifted the rope, smirking. "Found these two lurking in our neck of the woods. Taking them to the pack. Care to help escort?" They fell into one wolf on each side and one behind, once in a while growling if Sairha or Cassandra made eye contact. The back wolf snapped its jowl when Cassandra stumbled. It was nerve-racking to have them so close, but a few miles of them obediently following Travis, and the alarm wore off.

Sairha couldn't believe her rotten luck. She had hoped to never see another wolfshifter again, yet here she was being held hostage by some. And in the pit of her stomach, she worried about where they would be taken. Instead, Sairha focused on Cassandra who marched alongside her in silence. It was obvious Cassandra was exhausted, both physically and emotionally spent for the day. Cassandra licked her lips, making Sairha painfully aware of how thirsty she also was. Reminding her of Cook. Was he safe and far away? Had he found Brenda? If Cassandra and herself didn't make it back, would he come looking for them? He deserved better than that, better than two women who got captured because Sairha had made another bad decision.

Her thoughts dissipated when, amongst the last rays of sunlight, an A-frame cabin protruded out of the trees. The small group ascended the steep hill it was nestled on. Sairha marveled in both awe and chilled anticipation at the building, with its well maintained redwood walls and slanted rooftop covered in moss and foliage. The top blended near-perfect with the surrounding forestry, most likely impossible to spot from the sky.

As they got closer, Sairha realized what she had thought was a steep hill was actually the start of a mountain that the cabin's backside disappeared into, seemingly melded with the stone wall. She wondered if there was a drop off around the other side, and if they used it to dispose of trespassers, a dark thought that she made quick to shake herself free of.

They passed through a gated fence, made from the same sturdy wood, into a flattened clearing before the cabin. The closer they got, the cabin transformed into a lodge made to look small. Her gaze moved upwards, where a figurehead protruded near the roof's peak. A wolf mid-snarl, sharp teeth polished until they gleamed, wooden eyes glaring down at the onlooker. The craftsmanship was nothing less than impressive, and its message rang clear. Submit, or face the consequences.

Travis yanked on the rope, pulling them closer. They came to a stop a few feet in front of the entrance. A wide set of steps led up to a wraparound porch, double doors in the center shut. He let out an authoritative bark to the wolves behind the women, which sounded odd coming from a human mouth, and the wolves dispersed.

Sairha watched, wondering where they had gone, until the hairs on her neck rose. It felt as if someone was watching her.

"Well, bite me in the ass like an annoying little flea."

A gruff voice she had hoped to never hear again. A voice that made her blood boil just by its tone.

Turning ever so slowly, praying to be wrong, Sairha physically cringed when she laid eyes on the short, messy hair and the mischievous, toothy grin. "Leroy," Sairha said with disgust as she watched the self-assured male strut down the stairs towards her.

Dressed in simple khaki pants, and a white t-shirt that looked like it was trying to choke him, Leroy looked anything but pleased to see them. "Look what the mutts dragged in. The human that couldn't, Sairha, and her ditzy companion," he teased, arms crossed at his chest, a wicked twinkle in his eyes.

She growled, the fury inside of her passing boiling point. It was more than she could take to see him again and to be insulted on top of that? Salt tossed into a barely healed wound.

Without a second thought, Sairha let her anger take control of her.

She bolted right into him, knocking them both to the ground. Scrambling to stay on top, to pin him down, Sairha tightened her hands into fists and went for a jab before he could recover from the shock. Her bound hands made contact with his cheek and slid onto his nose. She felt it crunch under her force, his head falling back.

He grunted, a mixture of pain and surprise contorting his face.

"Sairha!" Cassandra yelled too close, yanked forward by Sairha's punch. She tried to stay away from the two on the ground but was tugged back by the rope. "Stop it, Sairha!"

It was hard to hear, Sairha was so engrossed in her anger.

Leroy recovered and put one arm up, blocking his face, but his other arm was pinned. She tightened her thighs around his waist, willing them to crush the air right out of him, trying her hardest to find an opening for another punch. She knew it was only a matter of moments before Leroy would gain the upper hand, but she didn't care. Any damage she could inflict would satisfy her rage.

"Do something!" Cassandra yelled to Travis and the small crowd of onlookers that had appeared. No one stepped in to help. With every movement of Sairha's hands, Cassandra struggled to remain out of harm's way.

"THAT IS ENOUGH!"

Everyone froze. The command echoed throughout the clearing and woods, startling all that heard it. Birds overhead flew away in a frightened frenzy.

It made Sairha's heart stop.

Leroy looked up from under his arms. "Dammit," he muttered under his breath, almost not loud enough for Sairha to hear.

"Leroy, get up. We do not behave like wild animals," a second, rougher voice called.

Leroy paled, his face instantly washed of any attitude, blank, blind obedience replacing it.

Cassandra scurried to her feet, then pulled the stiffened Sairha up by the arm. Sairha avoided looking towards the source of the voice. She couldn't. Her friend's eyes were wide, staring behind her head at the men the small crowd parted for, confirming what she knew.

Never would she have thought that she would wish to be anywhere else, with any other wolf pack, than she wished with all her might right then. Even fighting the Marrow Eater earlier seemed a more favorable situation than who she was about to face.

Close by Travis was barely stifling laughter, watching Leroy, full of shame, rise from the ground.

"Clean yourself up, we're needed inside at the council. And you," *his* voice snapped Travis to attention.

Sairha closed her eyes, feeling his presence near, and exhaled before opening them. Their eyes met. The once warm brown irises were cold as they locked with hers for a mere second.

Sven...

"Untie our guests, then get back to your post," Sven called to Travis, turning for the lodge.

Sairha glimpsed an older man, with a polished oak branch fashioned into a cane, climbing the stairs, shaking his head, long silver haired braids swinging as he did. Sven rushed to help the elder.

Leroy glared at Sairha from the porch, holding the door. He wiped at his nose with the back of his hand and it came away bloody. He couldn't contain the shocked look. She had knocked him a good one, even his ego seemed damaged. However angry that made him, he left without a word after the two went inside, the door slamming loudly behind them.

"Guests, huh," Travis mumbled to himself. He turned to Sairha and slid his hand down her hip, snatching the knife from its holster. "That was quite some show there, girly. Guessing you know our brute second-in-command. Old lovers, perhaps?"

Sairha remained quiet, although she wanted to headbutt Travis in the face for suggesting such a disgusting thing. All the fight in her was spent, her adrenaline squashed by the lack of acknowledgement from Sven. Travis held her knife too close to her wrists. Once released from the ropes, she rubbed the sore skin. Something for her hands to do while her mind remained in stasis. He cut Cassandra loose next, and Sairha was glad to see Cassandra's lips pressed tight to show she wasn't going to talk either.

"Suit yourself," he said, his tone light as he flipped the knife in the air and caught it by the handle before offering it to Sairha. "I like a girl with secrets. Maybe next time, you'll tie me up. Catch you around, girly."

They watched him walk across the clearing, quite chipper, then disappear around the side of the lodge. As if he hadn't dragged them there against their will and witnessed a fight of egos and fists. *Weirdo,* Sairha thought.

"Sairha," Cassandra whispered once sure they were alone, reaching for her. "That old guy...do you think—"

"Yeah, probably." There was not a single thought in her head that didn't revolve around Sven again. *This* was his territory. She hadn't expected him to actually live so close, a mere day's hike away. Could she continue to live in her home, knowing that? If Travis did not know who she was, did his grandfather? Did that mean Sven, Leroy, and Sawyer had never told anyone about them? About *her*?

Her heart felt like it would break all over again and she mentally hardened it the best she could. *He didn't even say anything to me.*

"Saaaairha!"

She did not have time to get a good look at who was calling her before a lengthy kid leapt from the stairs and wrapped his arms around her so tight she had to cough for air.

"Oh, Sairha. I've missed you!" His grip loosened as he looked up at her through black, curly hair. A young boy of about twelve or thirteen, if she had to guess, who stood at bosom height.

Her cheeks flushed a little, having someone she didn't

know so close against her, someone she did not recognize right away. When she looked down into his face, brown colored eyes stared back up at her, smiling, warmer than a spring day.

"Oh, you do not remember me?" He pulled away, feigned hurt washing his face.

She stared in wonder and could have sworn she was staring at a young Sven. The only difference was that his black hair was wild and curly as it fell around his head like a halo. "Sawyer? Is that... you?" she asked with caution, trying to avoid offending him further. He was a wolf the whole time they had traveled together. Seeing him as a human was a whole new, overwhelming, mind-blowing experience. "What happened?"

He beamed at her and crossed his arms over his chest. "I mastered the *turn*," he boasted, then faltered. "Well, I mastered it enough to turn before my year was up. It...wasn't easy. I couldn't have done it without my brother." A dark shadow took away the smile, and his eyes glossed over, lost in that trial of shapeshifting that neither woman knew much about. With a shake of his head, the light returned to his face and he went to Cassandra for a quick embrace. "It's good to see you, too!"

Despite her confusion, Cassandra hugged him back. "Wow, look at you... You're, uh, a real boy after all."

His smile was bright and pure as he nodded.

"I thought I'd never see you again," Sairha croaked once the shock wore off. Her eyes became heavy with tears. Even though it was like meeting a complete stranger, she found herself overcome with joy. Pulling him back into her arms, she held him tight, the embrace filling a hole in her heart she never thought would be satisfied. Seeing and knowing that he was okay, and that he was happy, was like a soothing balm.

The moment was over too soon when he squirmed away, quick to wipe his own eyes. "Don't cry, we're together again! I was sent to show you guys to your room, and maybe we can sneak by the kitchen to see what's for dinner. There's so much to see here." Sawyer spun away, leading them towards the stairs.

Sairha hesitated, glancing behind at the path out of there, then up at the snarling figurehead, before she climbed the stairs. She was not sure what kind of fate awaited her in the wolves' lair, and although Sawyer's smile was welcoming, she felt an unnameable heaviness start to weigh on her.

Cassandra halted. "Wait. We can't *stay*. We were brought here, rather roughly, to see if Brenda is here."

"Oh," Sawyer paused. "Brenda? She isn't here, I'm sorry. But you must visit for a while! Please, Sairha?"

Put on the spot, Sairha shifted her gaze from Sawyer's hopeful face to Cassandra's pleading one. She took in the shadows deepening across the yard, the forest itself cast in darkness. "It is getting dark. Let's stay one night. Sawyer, you said you have a room for us?"

"Sairha," Cassandra whispered under her breath. "What about Cook?"

"We'll be back by midday tomorrow." Sairha looked away from Cassandra, unsure about what was pulling at her to stay. Convincing herself it was for safety and nothing else.

"Well, actually," Sawyer mumbled, rubbing his head. "You can't technically leave until Grandfather says you can."

"What?" Sairha and Cassandra replied in unison.

With a wince, Sawyer looked at them apologetically. "Yeah. It's been the new rule ever since the world got messed up. We can't risk people knowing where we are and bringing looters or worse back here."

"Sawyer," Sairha sighed. "You know us. We aren't looters, raiders, robbers, or 'worse'. We wouldn't bring anyone or anything here."

"I know that." He hung his head with an exasperated

groan. "It's just how it is right now. But you'll like it here. You might even want to stay."

Cassandra shot a glare at Sairha who shrugged. What could she do about it? Nothing. They couldn't outrun wolves.

With a swallow of nerves, Sairha took the first step into the wolves' den.

CHAPTER TWENTY

"Maybe I don't want to go home," Cassandra joked as she lounged in a plush leather armchair. Enjoying the large sitting area in their oversized room, she appeared more relaxed than when they had arrived as she watched Sairha inspect the room. "This place is pretty nice."

"I guess," Sairha muttered, looking at pictures sitting on a shelf along the wall. Most of them were decorative photos of birds in contrasting colors against white backgrounds, but some were old black and white photos of the lodge. Little things here and there, like the gardens and trees, were different in the photos but the building remained the same in each one. She wondered how long the place had been in Sven's family.

Sven.

She moved away and plopped into the armchair opposite Cassandra. Needing something to do, she reached over and picked up one of the many candles on the table and sniffed it. Sandalwood and vanilla.

The room reminded Sairha of the ski lodge miles from her

home, albeit a much fancier one. Candles and oil lamps sat on handcrafted wooden tables, paired up with leather and wood furniture. Rustic charm. A deluxe bed in the corner looked like bliss covered in fluffy pillows, soft wool, and flannel blankets. Sairha had no choice but to agree with Cassandra's assessment: this place was impressive. The room was made more comfortable for them by a wood burning stove in the corner. Nothing about this luxury room made Sairha feel threatened or held against her will.

Nothing except the door being locked from the outside.

The main part of the lodge had been dark when they entered, much to Sairha's disappointment. Sawyer had ushered them down a cold, poorly lit, hallway into their room. He left them with promises of peeking back in once he had permission to show them around. It had been a long while since.

Cassandra groaned when she pulled her sore legs up. "Who would have thought we'd end up here." Her boots left dirt smudges on the leather as she untied them, a testament to their journey. "I don't think Cook would have guessed it. I do hope he's okay. Hey, you're a nurse. Are my nipples supposed to hurt this bad?" When Sairha didn't respond, Cassandra leaned over and nudged her shoulder. "Hellooo, earth to Sairha."

"What?" Her gaze drifted over Cassandra who motioned to her chest. A half smirk pulled at Sairha's lips. "That's normal in the early stages of pregnancy. Sorry, I've got a lot on my mind. Like, I wonder how long until we talk to the leader. Or how I don't want Cook showing up here. Oh, and do you think they'd sentence me to death or shake my hand if I end up murdering Leroy?"

"Oh." Cassandra tried to stifle her laughter in between words. "Okay, but did you see Leroy's face when you tackled him? He looked like a gazelle right when it notices a cheetah launching at it. I can't believe you socked him in the nose."

Sairha flung her hair back, a genuine, full smile plastered on her face. "That felt so good. Even if my hands hurt now, it was worth seeing that asshat in a little bit of pain."

"He probably isn't used to someone standing up to his snark," Cassandra laughed before sobering up. "Admittedly, I wouldn't want to be you right now. There must be so many emotions going through your head. I can't imagine them keeping us for long. You freaking saved that wolf-guy Travis from a Marrow Eater and dated the leader's grandson. Speaking of... Sairha. Whatever happens, whatever... *he* says... Don't forget how far you've come, despite what he did to you. Don't forget how strong you are."

Although she meant well, Cassandra's words cut through Sairha like a blade. There was no inkling of feelings left when Sven had looked at her outside. He had seen right through her, scraping the scabbed wound back open. She would never, could never, forget he was the one that had left them. *Her.* And yet, she still wanted him to acknowledge her. To apologize, to beg for forgiveness. Hell, to explain himself and his actions.

Putting her head in her hands, she groaned loudly. Her mind was a confused, lonely space full of self-doubt. She wasn't sure she could face him and his cold eyes again.

The night passed with no one coming to talk to them. Being in a secure location, and the most comfortable bed, did not guarantee a night's rest for Sairha. She awoke early, and anxious, and found the door still locked, causing her to pace around the room like a caged animal. It was some time before a loud yawn drew her attention to the bed. Cassandra looked like a little girl, surrounded by many pillows, her tight, curly hair disheveled as she rubbed the sleep away. "What are you doing?"

"Going crazy. I thought we would have had a meeting by now to talk about us leaving," Sairha ranted, never slowing her pace. "Nothing but silence."

Cassandra crawled across the blankets and hopped out, snatching a silver handled comb from the nightstand as she did, a matching hand mirror and brush beside it that Sairha hadn't noticed. "Has anyone delivered breakfast?"

"Food? Really?" Sairha rolled her eyes, then felt bad. She knew Cassandra had two main worries right at that moment: Cook's safety and the baby growing inside her. She glanced down towards Cassandra's stomach, imagining that it already looked a little swollen. It wasn't, not yet, but Sairha knew it would only be a matter of time if they kept her fed and healthy.

"I mean, if someone comes to bring us food, we can ask to see the leader then?" Cassandra ran the comb through a section of hair, thinking, then pointed it at Sairha. "Or whack 'em over the head with the mirror and flee."

"And be chased down by wolves?" Sairha countered.

"Considering our luck, it would be Leroy," Cassandra smirked. "Or that Travis guy who brought us here."

Sairha made a gagging noise. "No, thank you to either."

Someone knocked at the door and their playful banter ceased. A familiar boy's voice called from the other side. "Sairha? Can I come in?" The lock clicked and Sawyer peeked his head inside after they consented, his smile bright as he spotted them. A tray, laden with food, was in his hands. "I'm sorry I couldn't come sooner." He set the food on the table and sat in one of the armchairs, looking like he planned on staying for a while. He reminded Sairha of Alison, except less bratty and softer spoken. Her sister was a spitfire.

"It's alright. We understand," Sairha lied and jumped out of her skin when Cassandra snuck up behind her to dig into the platter.

"It's not that I didn't want to," he sighed. "I have special duties to do now that I am really part of the pack. And I was forbidden from coming to see you, anyhow..." He trailed off, looking away, and Sairha wondered if it was Sven who had told him he could not see them. She remained silent, picking at a fresh roll.

"Thanks for the food. Mmm, this is so good," Cassandra mumbled through a mouthful of apple, relishing every bite.

"No problem. We have tons of stored fruits and vegetables to spare, even after all this nasty stuff that happened to the world. Who knows when it'll get better. But it won't bother us much, up here in the woods, with our own gardens and livestock."

Cassandra made eye contact with Sairha, nodding towards Sawyer. Before Sairha could mouth the word 'no', Cassandra walked over and leaned against his chair. "Wow, food stores sound cool. I sure would love to see that," she spoke earnestly, admiring the apple in her hand. "Think we could go out and see it? Sure could use some fresh air."

Sawyer's eyes filled with excitement as he thought about it. "I'd love to give you both a tour. Fresh air *would* be good, especially for the baby."

Surprise overtook Cassandra's expression.

He blushed under her gaze and murmured, "Sorry, I can smell it on you. Pregnancy, that is. Women sometimes smell different when they are growing babies."

"Did you know? Before? When you were a wolf traveling with us?" she asked, still stunned.

"Yes, of course. Didn't you?" Sawyer was confused now.

Sairha watched in silence, realizing what Sven and Leroy had been talking about that night when they thought everyone was asleep. *Of course, another thing Sven knew and kept from me. A secret. So many secrets. And he left us, knowing she'd need help.*

Sawyer's question was innocent enough, but Cassandra's laugh came out harsh as she ruffled his hair. Sairha stuffed her hands into her pockets to keep from rolling them into fists.

"Let's go then! I'll show you around!"

They laced up their boots and grabbed a few snacks for the tour. Outside of their room Sawyer led the way, cheerful as he talked about the lodge he called home. The hallway was better lit and housed fifteen other rooms, all similar to the one Sairha and Cassandra were staying in, he explained. Sairha paused to inspect the smooth stone surface of the wall, unlike anything she had ever seen. It was impressive.

"It took my ancestors, like," Sawyer thought aloud, rocking back and forth on his feet beside her. "Ten years or something to complete this part of the stronghold. Pretty cool, huh? Protects the back of our home from intruders and the elements. Come on, let's go through the kitchen."

"What's this room?" Cassandra asked as they stepped around a corner.

"This? This is the Great Hall," Sawyer said matter-of-fact as he walked through the large room. "It's where all our big meetings happen. And movie nights. Well, when we had electricity."

Sairha and Cassandra gasped when they got the full view of the Great Hall. A massive room with a vaulted ceiling made it feel cavernous, and in the center was a square-shaped, sunken-in sitting area that could seat a hundred people. Fluffy lambswool pillows were scattered about, along with blankets that dangled off the side of the middle sitting section, making the room inviting. Heat came from behind them as they walked farther in. Sairha turned and gazed in wonder at a large stone fireplace that took up the majority of a wall. Confused, she took a few steps back. The fireplace, in actuality, was only connected at the top by the chimney. The sides of it were an illusion, hiding the hallway they had come from.

"Secret wall?" Cassandra whispered to Sairha.

Sairha responded with a slow shrug, awed by the clever design. "I guess so."

They picked up their pace to catch up with Sawyer right before he opened a large, silver door, a small porthole window in the center covered in steam.

When they stepped inside, they were enveloped in moisture and the scent of bread baking. The room was alive with busy action. Most were cleaning, while two older women made stacks of sandwiches on an enormous island in the center of the room, the top of it made from the same polished rock as the mountain. Hanging above them, from the slanted ceiling, were metal racks with copper, silver, and cast-iron pans. The trio passed by a butcher's carving station and Cassandra gagged at the raw meat hanging off hooks and blood-stained cutting boards. A girl with a stack of dirty dishes came bustling by, forcing Sairha to lean back against a shelving unit, the jarred herbs on it clanking together. Her gaze followed the young girl as she made her way to the sink, where she set them down next to her peers that were already washing a stack. They exchanged whispers, glancing at the newcomers.

"Here's the pantry," Sawyer whispered before he darted into a side room. He reemerged with a tin tucked under his arm and grabbed Sairha's hand in his own. "Come on, let's sneak out the backdoor before anyone notices."

It was too late, most of the people in the kitchen had stopped what they were doing to stare. Someone gave a sharp whistle, getting everyone back to work. Sairha wondered if any humans had been to this well-oiled fortress as she left the kitchen.

When the sunlight hit, she shielded her eyes with one hand

until a stone courtyard with a large fire pit in the middle came into focus. Beyond that, she spied rows of gardens and tool sheds. Sawyer tugged at her hand until she started moving again.

"I'll show you all the cool stuff! The gardens are getting close to harvesting right now, which means it's almost time for our Fall Festival. And I think you'll love the animal pens," he chatted excitedly.

While showing them around, he explained how things worked around there. Some topics he spoke about in depth, like about the Fall Festival not being as fun as humans made it out to be. It was just harvesting and hard work, all who were present at the lodge had to help. They did have a modest feast after and night activities; however, for lack of his own underage experience, he left most of it up to their imaginations. Sairha could not decide if she wanted to witness such a thing, her limited time with them in wolf form causing her to think perhaps not.

Sairha was yet again impressed by the overall property planning when Sawyer showed her the many different wells throughout the property. He did not know much about them, but she spent some time looking, getting ideas of her own. The filtering system mystified her, and she reluctantly left after Sawyer and Cassandra both expressed boredom.

No wonder Sven was so anxious to get back, Sairha thought, following the other two. *Everyone has a role here. This place is a tightly run ship, no room for slacking.* She glanced at Sawyer, his comment about Sven helping with his transformation still rattling around her conflicted mind.

They spent an hour feeding alpaca, goats, and sheep handfuls of alfalfa. It was a moment of relaxation and peace.

"Sairha." Sawyer touched her arm lightly. "I...I'm sorry we left your group behind. In the desert."

Sairha stared blankly at the sheep she was feeding, doing her best to hold back any emotion that his apology invoked. "We survived it," was all she could mumble and they fell back into a comfortable silence. It was a nice gesture on his side, but Sairha needed more than that and not from him.

Minutes later, Cassandra leaned back and gave Sairha a hard stare behind Sawyer's back, shifting her eyes several times towards him. Sairha understood too well what the signal meant. "Sawyer, do you know when..." She hesitated, hating to put him in the middle of something so serious, but he was the only one who had come to see them. "Do you know when we could talk to someone about leaving? Your grandfather, right? It's just that...Cook's waiting for us."

"Oh," Sawyer sighed, face crestfallen as he turned around and leaned against the fence. "Right. I was hoping you'd—oh, shit."

"Sawyer!" Sairha laughed. "Watch your language."

Cassandra turned, cleared her throat, and smacked Sairha's arm. "*'Oh, shit,'* is right. Don't look now."

Though it filled her with a sense of dread, Sairha looked over her shoulder. Her heart stopped and the air became hard to swallow. Sven was heading towards them, and guessing by his rigid stride, he was not in a good mood. A pang of regret coursed through her, wishing she had not let Sawyer show them around, had she known it would cause trouble for the young boy. Even with a scowl, Sven looked handsome with his long, black hair flowing freely behind him, dressed in black jeans and a green flannel shirt. It had been a long while since she had seen him cleaned up.

Keep it together, woman, she scolded herself. *Don't let him see an ounce of weakness in you. You've come too far.*

"Sawyer, what do you think you are doing?" Sven's tone was harsh, a glare directed at his brother.

Sawyer chuckled nervously. "Showing...the girls... around?"

"And who said you could let them out?" Sven tapped his foot, arms crossed at the chest.

Between that comment and not even acknowledging their presence *again*, Sairha fumed inside. She placed a protective hand on Sawyer's shoulder and stepped in front of him, face to face with Sven. "We waited all morning to speak to someone. It seems like we were forgotten prisoners rather than *guests*. Sawyer was being a gracious host, letting us get some fresh air, showing us around."

It looked like it physically pained Sven to turn his eyes from Sawyer to Sairha as she spoke. He pressed his lips together as he took a few seconds to think. "It was not his call to make, especially after I told him to stay away from you."

His words stung her something fierce, confirming what she had suspected, but Sairha kept her face even and calm as she listened. It was all she could manage to keep back the furious fire she felt like spewing.

"This is pack land, surrounded by all the members of our pack, he can't go against my command just because you show up."

"*Show up?*" Sairha blurted like an uncorked jar, astounded, bewildered.

Cassandra nudged Sawyer and whispered, "Come on, let's get out of here before Sairha reaches a new high octave." Sawyer looked confused but thankful for an escape from his brother's wrath. Before they left, Cassandra brushed her hand against Sairha's, sending a mental bit of strength to her.

An audible sigh left Sven as he reached up to massage the pressure points between his eyes.

Sairha attempted to calm down, but the longer he remained silent, the more she was alone with the thoughts in her head. Angry ones, the ones that had built up since he left her, *abandoned her*. The thoughts were jumbled up, but they were there, and they threatened to pour out of her like word vomit. The hurt, sadness, and uncertainty; they all screamed for vengeance. She knew if she blew up now there would be no stopping her, no one to hold her back.

"Look," Sven growled, then loosened his tense shoulders and started again in a flatter tone. "I'm sorry, but it's safer for you to stay in the room until the council decides what to do." His hand moved up, rubbing his forehead.

Do I really give him that bad of a headache? Or is he just trying to avoid looking at me? Sairha crossed her arms. "Oh? Decides what to do with us? How about let us go and leave us alone? We weren't hurting anyone, or anything, on my family's property. The only reason we ventured out in the woods, saving *your* pack member by the way, was because Brenda went missing."

Sven looked up at her and a frown pulled at the corners of his lips, a question written on his face.

That was not something she was prepared for, and it took her aback. She guessed at what he wanted to ask and was quick to look away, so he wouldn't see the tears that were building up. She shook her head. "My family wasn't there. It looks like..." She paused, and took a deep breath, before continuing. "Like they left in a hurry or were taken away, maybe. I'm guessing the latter after our own run-in with looters."

"Sairha—"

"No, don't you say my name in *that* tone. You have no right." Ice in her veins, she moved out of his reach. There was no way she could stay strong if he tried to comfort her, and right now she needed that distance from him, she needed to stay mad. It was like his presence sent magnetic waves to her, pulling and pulling. She had felt it when he stood near her the day before, and now there was that tug to run into his arms. For her own sanity, Sairha knew she had to resist. "You didn't even acknowledge I existed yesterday. Like we were nothing, like *I* was nothing. Nothing but an annoying human. Then you have us locked up in a room. For our safety. Like we didn't spend all that time training together, working together." Sairha hoped her voice didn't sound as shaky as she felt. There was so much more, begging to be let out, but she needed to steady herself. "You have no right to act like you care about me or my family."

His throat bobbing was the only movement he made, his face a perfect, blank mask. It took a while for him to even open his mouth to speak, and he did so carefully. "The reason... I ignored you is because no one knows about you, or the others in your group, except for Leroy and Sawyer. And I've made them swear a blood oath to never tell anyone. That's why it's not safe."

Sairha's heart fell. No wonder Travis thought she might have had a past with Leroy. Sven *had* kept his time with her, his feelings for her, everything about their experience together a tightly guarded secret. Pangs like tiny swords stabbed into her chest.

"Travis wasn't supposed to bring anyone here. He's new to the pack, a *bitten*, not really one of us. He thought he was doing us a favor, but we do not allow outsiders here. I'm sorry he brought you against your will."

"Yeah, well... Me too." She could no longer handle the confrontation and rushed past him, intending to find her way back to their room.

"Sairha, wait!" Sven reached out, wrapping his hand around her wrist. It sent an electric pulse right through her. She looked down at his hand and he quickly released her. "Please. I'm sorry, I don't want to fight. I wish you could understand, wish that I could explain why I did what I did. Do what I do."

Her heart thundered in her chest, in her ears.

"What I did was wrong," he sighed, looking down in admitted shame.

What's he doing... Sairha was torn right down the middle, torn between turning and leaving for good or staying to hear him out. A part of her longed for the answer, but what answer could ever be good enough? The truth was, and she knew it, she would never understand his choice, nor would she ever be able to forgive him for it, but she also wasn't sure she wanted to. Swallowing the lump in her throat, she spoke quietly. "I don't want to hear it."

Sven looked physically stricken by her words; his shoulders dropped and his strong resolve melted. He looked every bit defeated. "That's completely fair."

"I know...I know you are the pack's future leader, and there's a lot of responsibility on your shoulders. I know that Leroy's a big part of why you left, but that does not excuse it. You left me in a dangerous world." It was hard to not show emotion, to not tear up when thinking back on those first, lonely nights without him, when she was hollow inside. "You have no idea what I've been through since you left."

"My grandfather really wasn't doing good after the earthquake. You are right, I acknowledge that it's not an excuse. I was a coward, I should have been there for you, to protect you."

Sairha turned away from him, terrified her determination to stay strong would dissolve. "A lot happened after you left, a lot I wasn't prepared for... I killed someone, Sven." The words spilled out of her, like an emotional dam with a crack down the middle. She closed her eyes to fight back the tears. There was no stopping them, however, and a few trickled down her cheeks. "It wasn't like killing a thoughtless, bloodthirsty monster. This was a human being. Someone who had a mother, a father, maybe even a family once. Someone who turned to the life of a ruffian because of what this world is now." She wiped her tears with her shoulder, sucking in a wavering breath. It felt strange, also right, to confess to someone who wasn't there, who didn't know the situation one-sidedly, who hadn't seen the lifeless face after she had stabbed him.

One of several faces that haunted her.

The silence between them grew as she battled the overwhelming longing to feel his strong arms around her and hear his soft voice reassure her she had done what she could as she cried against his shoulder. "Because of me..." Her throat tightened. "Because of me, one of the twins was killed by a Marrow Eater. And a mother likely buried her son, alone and hurting, because of me, Sven. Because of choices I made. Because when you left, they all looked to me for answers." The coldness from those memories sunk deep within her.

"And you led them the best way you knew how. Yes, with a broken heart, but also a strong desire to survive and fierce loyalty. I knew you'd be okay, in the long run." Sven's response was tender, however the intensity of his words were not lost on her. "We are not so different, you and I. That's why I just can't get over you."

Sairha swayed in her spot, a gentle breeze blew past them, pushing strands of her hair onto her damp cheeks. Time felt paused for them. She had known his feelings to be true before, but it had not kept them together, it had not convinced him to stay by her side. What would make it different this time?

"Seeing you on my doorstep, on top of Leroy and beating the shit out of him—" he let out a soft laugh. "—it was like you had hit *me*. I had no idea Travis' group was going to bring you, out of all the people, here. I was knocked out of it, senseless, speechless. I thought I would never see you again." There was a slight tremor in his hand as he reached for hers again, waiting for her to either accept or reject the silent offer of affection.

She was immediately warmed by his touch, when their hands clasped together, and she took a single step closer. "Why am I your secret? Why doesn't anyone know about me?"

Sven took a moment to think, looking down at their hands as he moved closer. "There hasn't been an incident of turning a human, in our pack or any others we are aligned with, since we've started keeping to ourselves like a tight knit community. We've been successful at minimizing the ratio of bitten werewolves to born wolfshifters." He sighed. "The truth is, I shouldn't have been with you at all. My interactions with humans are supposed to be business only and limited. And I messed up, I met you and couldn't help myself. I...I was drawn in, pulled in almost, against my will. You are like a magnet to me."

She pushed her hair behind her ear as she thought about what he had said. Thinking back to that exact moment in the crowd when they had first made eye contact. She had felt called to where he was, like she did now.

But it wasn't enough. She hadn't been enough. Right?

"Sairha..."

She shook her head back and forth several times, backing away from him, away from the old feelings stirring inside. Cassandra had warned her, had told her to be strong, to remember how far she had come. It had been a positive warning against losing herself in the allure of romance again. "I...I want to go home," she whispered. "I want to talk to your grandfather. Arrange it, please. It's the least you can do for me." With that, she turned on her heel and ran for the lodge before he could call to her again.

CHAPTER TWENTY-ONE

"How was your talk with Sven? Did you say everything you needed to?" Cassandra asked when they were alone in their room. She walked around, wrapped in nothing but a plush towel, preparing for a bath. "I worry about you, but I know you can handle yourself. You always could."

Sairha crouched in front of the wood burning stove, tending to the fire while she thought about the questions. It took a while for the jitters from the confrontation to settle, and she replayed the scene over and over in her mind. Things she had wanted to say, things she wished she had said. Things she wished he hadn't said. "It was good," she responded after a while. "I think your bath is ready."

"Oh!" Cassandra darted for the bathroom. "I can't believe this. A hot bath. In a clawfoot tub, no less. Pinch me, for truly I am dreaming! If you need me..." Cassandra paused inside the doorway, her tone turning dramatic as she said, "*Don't*. I plan on soaking until I am wrinklier than a grape left out in the sun!" The door clicked closed with an audible sigh of relief from the woman inside.

Sairha shook her head, happy for a moment of pure peace for her friend to enjoy a luxury soak, while her own head swam with conflicted thoughts. A rap at the door startled her. "Come in?" She stood, waiting to see who would enter.

The blonde haired guy that had brought them poked his head inside. "Not indecent, I hope?" Travis called out, though a wide smirk painted across his handsome face said otherwise.

Sairha glared at him as she walked over. "What do you want? Came to bring me my shirt back?"

"Shit, right. Your shirt is being laundered, and I'm not here to tie you up for fun, that's for sure," he joked, then straightened up. His demeanor changed in an instant from playful to serious. "Before they send me off on patrol duty, I was sent to retrieve you for a meeting with the leader."

"Cassandra is in the bath, so he'll have to wait a moment." Sairha crossed her arms, standing in the path to the bathroom, in case Travis decided to amp up his creep level. She'd fought a Marrow Eater to save his life, but she wasn't afraid to take it herself if need be. Her expression must have conveyed that to him for he cleared his throat and avoided her gaze.

"I'm sorry for mistreating you," he said quietly. "Like I said, it was a precaution. I've already been ringed around the neck for it. But I meant what I said, you have to be careful in this life, careful of who you trust. As for your friend, I was informed she is not necessary, if she does not wish to be there. And I strongly recommend you do not turn down a meeting with the leader."

Chewing on her bottom lip, Sairha weighed the options. Sven had done what she had asked by getting her the meeting with his grandfather, yet she hadn't expected it to be so soon. With a nod, she knocked on the bathroom door and let Cassandra know she'd be back soon. Lead down another rock wall hallway, both of them remained quiet, and saw no one else. Travis stopped in front of an ordinary looking door and knocked to signal their arrival. Sairha choked down her rapid heart from her throat and took a deep breath.

"You'll be alright," Travis whispered to her then opened the door. He closed it after she stepped inside, leaving her in a dimly lit study with a roaring fire in the stone fireplace.

The walls were built in wooden bookcases, filled to the brim with all different kinds of literature. Some looked old with leatherbound spines, while others looked newer, factory made paperbacks. A library to make any bibliophile swoon. She walked onto an old, ornate rug and faced a matching desk and chairs set, where the older man sat, Sven and Leroy standing on either side of him. Right away, Sairha noted the nasal cannula at his nose, the tube leading down somewhere to a hidden oxygen tank. He looked ashen, his complexion nearly blending with his long, silver hair, nowhere near the strong leader he probably once was. Sairha realized she was being allowed a privilege to see him this way and dipped her head in a show of respect. After what felt like forever, he motioned for Sairha to sit in a chair across from him and she did, though on the edge.

"My name is Samuel, and as you know, I am the current leader of this pack." He spoke softer than he had the day before. "It has been brought to my attention that you and your companion were brought here wrongfully. We will remedy this first thing in the morning."

Sairha tried to keep her heart still, knowing that the old man could probably hear every beat. "Thank you. I hope we did not cause too much trouble. You will not be bothered by us once we leave."

"I have an offer for you, however," he said, pinning her down with a hard stare from his brown eyes. They were similar to Sven's and Sawyer's but held so much more wisdom than either of them yet possessed. He motioned to Sven with a wrinkled hand. "My grandson tells me you are a skilled nurse. The world being what it is, we could always use more with medical knowledge. You could stay here, be protected by us, but you'd be put to work and have to be part of the community beyond medical services. Everyone pulls their own weight, and then some, around here."

Leroy shifted in his spot, trying to hide the disbelief on his face, but Sairha saw it and knew this wasn't something the leader had discussed with his council. It was a more personal request than expected, considering his own health, but also a smart one for their community. Sairha avoided looking at Sven, of betraying an inkling of even knowing he existed in the room. Instead, she stared Samuel in the eye, as an equal, as a fellow leader. "What about my group?"

Samuel made a short chuckle, laying his hands on the desk. "What I offer you is very rare, as we keep humans far separated from us to ensure none of our kind accidentally turns a human. The more humans around, the higher the risk. Your companion is welcome, but we cannot accommodate more."

"With all due respect," Sairha started, not missing the tch from Leroy and subtle movement from Sven. "You wolfshifters are part human, too. How can you turn your backs on people who share the same earth, the same concerns, and hopes as you? My kind are becoming prey to these monsters, the Marrow Eaters. This is when we should unify, strengthen in numbers."

"Wolves have been protecting humankind since the very beginning. We locked the Marrow Eaters away, our brothers, to save the human race from extinction. Now it is because of one of your kind that they are freed. We are not turning our backs on you, we are standing back and regrouping with our own. When we can, we will lock them away again. But as far as rescuing and bringing humans back here to the safety of our dens?" Samuel crossed his hands, years of hard labor and work written into every deep line. "No. It's not unreasonable to want to protect our families above others."

His words rang true, harsh but true, and she knew she would do anything to protect her family, Cook and Cassandra. The new baby. Brenda, if they found her. She exhaled and looked up at him, "No, it is not. Then you will understand that I must politely decline your offer." She could not believe she said that last part, but she knew it to be true. "I have a lot to protect now as well."

"So be it," he nodded. There was a twinkle in his eye that Sairha imagined might be respect, or at least understanding. A weak smile graced his thin lips and he motioned for her to stand. "I want you both to join us for breakfast in the morning, then you may depart." Samuel motioned Sven forward. He went around the desk, careful to stay distanced from Sairha, and waited for his grandfather to finish. "I want you to show the members that we can all get along well enough to co-exist on the planet, on our own separate territories, of course. I want there to be no animosity between our pack and humans."

Sairha's stare was blank, shocked at his request, but also in awe that he would want to try to ease anyone's ill feelings. Although she did not like being at his whim, if she was to create her own community, she needed to see and do things from a political standpoint. "We appreciate it," she agreed, trying to keep her voice steady. "Thank you for your hospitality."

Dismissed by a weak wave of Samuel's hand, Sven held the door open for her and they stepped out. It took everything in Sairha to keep the trembles away. *Did I make the right choice this time?* She dared a glance at Sven ahead of her, leading her back through the hallways. His body language only read tense, as it usually was when he was trying to appear like a leader. She knew her answer was a slap to his face, a final blow of rejection. She had been dangled the opportunity to join them, to possibly be with *him*, and had turned it down. Nothing would speak louder than that decision to him. The chance to save her own kind had become more important to her than their one-time romance, she realized that now.

So why did it still hurt? Why did it feel like losing him all over again?

He stopped in front of the door she assumed to be their room but didn't reach for the handle. She watched his shoulders sag and dreaded the conversation they were going to have. "Sven..."

"I don't want you to leave," he whispered.

"Was that your idea? That I stay to care for everyone?" Sairha suspected as much. It was a valiant effort on his part, but he should have known she would have never agreed to be separated from the others.

"No," he said, turning around with the saddest expression, avoiding her gaze. "It wasn't my idea at all. I had no idea he was going to offer that. I just...Why? Why can't you stay?"

"If I stayed, what would that mean for us? Could we be together without consequences? Or would you pretend I didn't exist day-to-day then sneak into my room late at night?" Shaking her head, Sairha let out her frustration with an exhale. She lifted his chin to look into his eyes. "Cassandra and I have a life to get back to, to start setting up. Cook is probably worried about us, maybe even looking for us." She noticed how his face soured at the mention of Cook, but he nodded and said nothing. "We need to prepare for the baby." She gathered his hand into hers, rubbing her thumb over the top of his. "It's okay, *we* needed this. You and I can say goodbye this time. This is closure."

Pulling his hand away, he caressed her cheek tenderly then moved down to her chin and tilted her face upwards.

Stealing my move again, she laughed to herself before closing her eyes and the distance between them.

The kiss was delicate, filled with sadness and longing behind it. The taste of what once was and could never be. Not right now. Maybe never. Sairha let go of her restraints, they both knew this was it. Her arms wrapped around his neck, and she stepped backwards, him following, until her back was against the wall. It was over; their bitter farewell kiss melted into fiery passion. Their mouths parted, their breaths a heavy unison of gasps, until their lips locked again. It was happening so fast, their kissing made her head spin. Her hands slid down from his neck, feeling his shoulder muscles on her way to his hard chest. His body pressed against hers and it answered with a craving she had thought long dead. Intoxicated, Sairha moaned softly against Sven's lips as his hand gripped her thigh.

"Way to be discreet, guys." Leroy snorted from the hall's entryway. "I should have known what was keeping you."

Sven let out a low growl before pulling away from Sairha. "Dammit, Leroy. Let me fucking live, for once."

Taken aback at the snap, Leroy scoffed and shot a glare at Sairha before his face hardened. "I came to tell you, we need to go to the Great Hall right away. Serena's pack is here, with news, and Samuel has called a whole pack meeting."

Sven tensed, closing his eyes, and Sairha laughed inwardly. It was always something keeping them apart. Their goodbye kiss wouldn't be any different. He looked at her, his features a lot softer than a moment before, and sighed. "Stay in your room, please. I know you're tired of hearing it, but it's for your own safety. I'll... we'll see you tomorrow at breakfast, before you go."

"Of course," Sairha muttered, watching him leave again with Leroy instead of staying with her. She had made her choice to stay apart, one passionate kiss wouldn't change her mind. No matter how breathless it left her. She went to open the door, the handle turning in her hand before she could grasp it.

"You're crazy if you think we aren't going to go snoop." Cassandra smirked, slinking her arm into Sairha's. "If something is about to go down, we need to know."

THE VOICES of many people talking bounced off the walls. Curious but cautious, Sairha inched towards the edge of the fireplace's fake wall where she and Cassandra hid. Holding her breath, she leaned her head forward enough to see and not be seen.

The room was packed full of all kinds of human wolfshifters. They took up seats on the middle section, the floor, or crowded around the top level. Like an actual den, it was a place that comfortably accommodated so many of them for official pack business. It was intimidating. Sairha leaned back behind the cover of the wall and looked wide eyed at Cassandra. She had lost count at forty two heads, though she guessed there could be more.

Cassandra inched closer to Sairha and they traded spots so Cassandra could survey for herself. Careful not to trip, Sairha got as close to her friend as possible and motioned for her to crouch so they could both look.

"Pack members, settle. Quiet down," Samuel's voice echoed throughout the room, silencing the chatter. All bowed their heads in respect to their elder who stood tall in the center, his muscles taut as he gripped the cane for support. His back was to the kitchen wall, giving Sairha a good look at his side profile, along with the assurance that all eyes would be away from the fireplace. Samuel's complexion was rosier, nowhere near the alarming gray pallor of earlier. "We have some unexpected, welcomed guests," he began and, for a second, Sairha worried he meant them. They had been anything but welcomed.

It can't be us.

All the wolves' heads looked back up and the women ducked behind the wall again. "They bring news from the Paranormal and Human Interaction Council. Please, listen to them calmly and do not interrupt. We will be doubling up on space to accommodate our guests, as well. Kitchen duty will be adjusted. If you see our guests, immediately offer to help them with anything they may need."

Better reception than what we got, Sairha grumbled to herself. *What's this council he's talking about?* She leaned back over, just in time, to see Samuel sit between two other elders, Sven and Leroy above him. Sawyer sat with kids around his age, in wide eyed wonder. Again, the congress bowed their heads as the new pack stood.

There were six of them, all appearing in their twenties to mid-thirties, in clothing that stood out. Dark tan and brown leather, not quite like a biker club. Patches of pale dirt suggested they come from the desert south of there. They had matching leather belts with a medium sized bag and rubber gas masks attached to them. Sairha guessed that they used the belts like saddle bags to carry their clothes while traveling as wolves. A clever idea, though she was unsure about the gas masks. Recalling the stench from the city Sairha's group had last stopped in, she wondered if it was worse where they came from.

One stepped forward. Her muscular, bare shoulders

squared with pride, as she looked around the congregation, her expression carefully guarded. Chestnut colored hair cascaded down her back in tight curls, smaller pieces framing a soft, but stern, face and piercing, dark eyes. She had skin that screamed of sun-worship with its dark golden hue. Sairha marveled at the length of her shapely legs that carried her across the small space with panther-like grace. "Thank you for receiving us on such short notice," she spoke, her voice commanding attention in volume, with a feminine rasp. "As you can guess, my pack and I have traveled from Cin City itself to bring you this terrible news."

No mistaking she's the leader, Sairha thought. *They've traveled a long way up, this must be really important. And yet, nowhere near the feat we just did.*

"Some of you know me, for those who don't, my name is Serena. My second in command is Kerry, they were witness to the things I'm about to reveal."

Short cut, pale blonde hair flew back when Kerry stepped forward and tossed their head in acknowledgement, exposing one shaved side with a pink scar curving around the ear. With a mean scowl, they stood a solid pillar of muscle beside their leader.

"As you all have guessed, the treaty between the paranormal leaders and the human leaders was broken." She paused, turning around the half circle, creating a dramatic hush. She gave off a vibe that she was willing to take on any challenger, though no one posed a threat. "A human encroached upon the sacred lair, in which we locked away our former brethren, the Marrow Eaters, and released them. As per the agreement signed so long ago, all the things we've helped the humans create, and sustain with magic, have been stripped away when the seal broke. We have apprehended the culprit, but the damage cannot be undone."

A murmur washed over the crowd. Sairha's mind tried to wrap around the idea that there was real magic, magic that helped the world she had known, not just human scientific discoveries. There were so many questions she wanted answers to but knew she wouldn't get them. She peered down at Cassandra, who looked equally confused.

"It is time all packs join forces to protect each other, to help rebuild the world we once ran and regain everything we sacrificed for the humans who took us for granted," Serena continued. "We will no longer live in the shadows. We will no longer hide who we are. We will no longer *be* the paranormal."

Thunderous stomping on the ground echoed throughout the whole lodge, everyone displaying their approval, rattling Sairha to the very core. Not only was her kind being hunted, but was there going to be an uprising in these 'paranormals'? It mystified her how people who looked like them could so easily write the humans off as Marrow Eater feed. She sought out Sven, wondering what he would say or how he would react. Would he stand up for them? His grandfather stood and Sven came into view, once Samuel walked towards the younger leader. Seeing his blank expression disappointed Sairha, though she shouldn't have been surprised.

"You have confirmed everything we have heard through travelers, and we are in agreement that now it is time to step up." He motioned for Sven to join them, who immediately stood beside his grandfather. "Sven, Serena." The older pack leader took both of their hands, then addressed the congress. "We will move ahead with aligning the two packs."

The whole room erupted into cheers, whistles, and more foot stomping.

"*Shit*," Cassandra whispered and bolted down the hall.

Sairha glanced over to what had scared Cassandra off so

fast and caught Leroy glowering at her from across the room. She quickly ducked her head and followed her.

"Tonight, we celebrate!" Samuel's voice boomed from behind.

"HOLY CRAP," Cassandra breathed, back in their room. She plopped onto the closest armchair and fanned herself with her hand. "That escalated fast. What did any of that mean? There's a council? A treaty?"

Sairha walked over to the wood burning stove, lost in her own thoughts, shocked. She didn't bother to look at Cassandra as she replied. "I don't know, but that's the second time I've heard it was a human's fault the Marrow Eaters are hunting us. The pack leader Samuel mentioned it, too."

"So, some asshat ruined our lives? Thanks a lot." Cassandra shook her fist up at the ceiling in anger, then went back to fanning herself. "Hey, you okay?" She must have noticed how unmoving Sairha was.

Sairha kept reminding herself that she had decided she was done with Sven and the wolfpack. She wanted to take care of herself, of Cook and Cassandra, to save more human lives. Why did it feel like all the blood had drained from her? The inside of her went numb as she had watched Samuel hold up Sven and Serena's hands. "What do you think he meant by aligning with that other pack?"

Cassandra scoffed, then softened her tone. "I'm not sure. I warned you, Sairha. I didn't want you getting hurt again. You spoke to the pack leader, right? Can we leave? This place... it's nice, but it's toxic for you. And Cook is waiting for us, he might go crazy if we don't get back."

Shaking the image from her head, Sairha sat down in the

chair opposite her friend and slouched until her head rested on the back. "He offered me a position here," she said, holding up her hand before Cassandra could interject. "When I found out they had no intention of helping humans, I turned him down. We can leave in the morning, after a public show of breaking bread together, to keep the peace."

There was a long silence between them, until Cassandra jumped up from her chair and kicked Sairha's foot. "If it's our last night of being in this safe haven, we should go out in style."

"What are you talking about?" Sairha groaned.

"The party. Let's go crash it." Cassandra did a little dance in her spot, a wide grin spread across her face. "Like we used to do, before the real world went away and turned murderous."

Palming her face, Sairha groaned again then sat up, glaring at Cassandra. "You're pregnant, you can't go party 'like we used to'. And the last place I want to be is surrounded by a bunch of strangers who care nothing for our kind and where I might or might not see my ex with a very good looking equal counterpart!"

Cassandra crossed her arms, her foot tapping, clearly agitated with Sairha's answer. "Please, Sairha. I *need* this, I really do. When will I ever get to be like my old self again? When will we feel secure, safe from Marrow Eaters? What if... what if I die from childbirth? You... you can stay here. I'll go by myself, it's okay." She took a deep breath, then nodded and bumped Sairha's knee with her own as she went to leave.

The door opened, the heavy beat of festive music entered the room, and then it was gone with a click of the latch. Sairha exhaled, slamming her fist on the arms of the chair. As much as she didn't really like parties, Cassandra was right that this would be the last night they were in place so secure they could let their guard down. The last time she had let Cassandra go off on her own to party Sairha had regretted it and now there was a baby on the way. Sairha couldn't let anything happen to her, even if they were safe, even if she might see Sven with someone new.

Jumping to her feet, she made up her mind to go find Cassandra and keep an eye on her. *An hour tops,* she promised herself, slinking through the hallway. Laughter from the Great Hall made her slow down and creep around the corner, quiet as possible, to see what was going on. Three people walked by, two identical looking guys laughed and pushed each other in jest, carrying loaded boxes, while a pretty redhead walked beside them also in a jovial mood. She watched them exit the front door and turn towards the back of the property, then disappear before she slipped out the door to follow.

A massive bonfire was lit, and a lot of the younger crowd danced around it, playing and laughing with each other, sharing drinks. A small band consisting of a guitar player, flutist, and two hand-drummers created an upbeat melody. Long logs had been dragged into a circle surrounding the bonfire for people to sit on, buckets of jagged ice and drinks at the ends. After a deep breath and steeling her emotions, Sairha stepped forward, hoping to find Cassandra somewhere in the mess of people partying.

She squeezed her way past strangers who paid her no mind. It was her goal to go as unnoticed as possible and it seemed to be working. Everyone needed a carefree night it seemed. As she passed a group of people talking her arm was yanked downward, forcing her to sit on a log. Startled, Sairha turned in hopes of having found Cassandra but met the amber gaze of Leroy. He grinned at her, and Sairha's mood soured as she rubbed her arm where he had grabbed her. He leaned in close, his breath hot upon her ear, as he spoke over the noise. "What are you doing out of your pen, little sheep?"

She pushed away from him, rolling her eyes. An intoxicated Leroy was the last thing she ever wanted to experience. "It's a celebration, right? I'm here to party, obviously." Sairha shimmied her shoulders, but his unchanged face conveyed he didn't buy it. "I came for Cassandra. Do you know where she is? We'll go back to our *pen* once I find her."

Leroy's smile broadened and he lifted his hand, a glass bottle gripped in it, then tipped it towards the center of the area.

A couple moved out of the way as she followed Leroy's direction. People made space for somebody dancing on the other side of the bonfire. She groaned inwardly, hoping it was not Cassandra, knowing how much the woman loved to dance. However, it was someone else enticing the crowd with her wild and seductive moves. Serena bobbed around to the music, running her hands through her thick, curly hair, while her hips swayed.

Sairha gave Leroy a flat, unimpressed look.

He winked, leaned back on the log beside her, and watched with amusement.

As much as she hated it, she could not help but look over again. That's when she saw what Leroy had really wanted her to see. Sven sitting on a log, his hands clasped together, as he leaned forward and watched, hypnotized by Serena who swayed in front of him. Disgusted, Sairha turned away and caught Leroy staring at her. "I don't care," she yelled at him.

With a look of mock surprise, Leroy stood up and left without another word, heading over to Sven.

Worried that Leroy would point her out, she stood fast and shoved her way back through the crowd. She did not want Sven to see her, surely with a devastated look on her face. She did not want him to know she had even been there. Despite the anxiety it gave her, she took a second to glance back through the throng of people. Serena now danced with her focus solely on Sven, Leroy giving him a clap of encouragement on the back.

Sairha turned away, biting back the taste of bitter jealousy, grabbed two brown bottles with flip tops, and stormed back to the lodge. On the porch, she spotted Cassandra. "Done partying already?"

Cassandra gave a half shrug, a sad smile on her face. "It's not really as fun as it used to be. I guess maybe the world has changed too much. Or maybe I've changed too much. Either way," she motioned to the bottles tucked under Sairha's arm. "Looks like you got in the spirit." She smirked.

"Cas." Sairha half laughed, half groaned at the pun and opened the door for them. "Let's go back to our room. I think my kind of party involves trying out that claw-foot tub you raved about."

"Cassandra, you're awfully quiet. What are you thinking about?" Sairha asked, taking a swig of the cider she had taken. For a home brew, it was pretty good and was starting to give her a carefree buzz. She leaned back against the chair, dipping her head for Cassandra while she waited for the last bucket of water to heat to fill her bath.

"Thinking about what that she-wolf said." Cassandra's reply was quiet as she brushed Sairha's hair.

Sairha stiffened, having been trying to push all thoughts of the wolfpack leader out of her mind with the help of alcohol.

"If we really are being hunted to...extinction... then... Do you think we could ever have a place to stay more than one or two nights?" She rubbed at her belly subconsciously.

"I do," Sairha said with as much earnestness as she could

muster. She realized it was a different meaning to her friend to have somewhere safe to live. "I really do think so. We will find a place... a place like this. A place we can protect and that will protect us. You, me, Cook, Brenda, the baby... We will build not only a home, but a haven for anyone else needing protection."

Cassandra smiled as she nodded. "That sounds like a great idea. Rebuild a community of protectors and those needing protection. I think you can do it, Sairha."

"Me? It'll be *us*, together, because I am nothing without you and Cook. You guys are my family now," Sairha spoke from the heart, the raw honesty in her words warming her.

People had come into their group and left it, some because they were too weak, others because they were stronger than them, but when it came down to it, Cassandra and Cook had followed Sairha in complete faith. Even when she had been unfit, at her lowest point, and nearly got them killed by looters. It was her turn to repay them for their loyalty, to find a safe place for them to grow and, with any luck, find others to join them.

"Your hair has gotten long since Sabueso de Oro," Cassandra mumbled sleepily.

"Go ahead and sleep, Cassandra." Sairha chuckled and stood from the floor, heading towards the bathroom. "We need the rest for the journey tomorrow."

We'll need strength to defend ourselves from here on out, she thought to herself as she closed the door behind her.

As the steam from her bath wafted around her, everything that had happened over the last month came rushing forward. Meeting Sven, the explosion, begging him to take them with him on this crazy journey, and having no idea of what was out there. She wondered if she had known from the start what she knew now, would she have even ventured out of Cassandra's flat that day? Would she go through all the fear and uncertainty, through all the pain and heartache again? She set her drink down and looked at her once soft hands, transformed after carrying bags that were too heavy, gripping knives, and fighting with actual monsters. The calluses that had formed were badges of the new world.

Undressing, she dared a glance at her reflection in the mirror and was surprised by what she saw. An unnatural, unrealistic body. The way only a survivor of extreme events could look. But she was also in awe of the muscle she had put on. Arms toned, ready to stab into a monster. Solid legs that could last miles with no break. A back strong enough to pull not just her own weight, but others if needed. It was more than her hair length that had changed her appearance. The woman staring back at her in the mirror was no longer a lost, mundane soul going through the motions of modern life. Sairha was someone new, someone determined to do more than survive.

And she wasn't sure what to make of it.

When she turned away from the stranger in the mirror, and slid into the tub, the faces of those who surrounded her during her metamorphosis popped up. The ones she had lost along the way were more vivid than she liked. Although she wished her mind wouldn't, she thought of Angie. Not as she was in life, but as she was dying. Her graying skin, her eyes blind, and the creature with her guts in its claws. Try as she might, the better memories of Angie were lost under that horrifying one.

A knock at the door broke her thoughts, but not the grim expression on her face. "Come in," she called and pulled the shower curtain for privacy before submerging herself under the steaming water. It washed away her tears for Angie, who had deserved life as much as herself. For Connor, who was only an innocent, small child. Sairha pushed those dark thoughts away, knowing she should not dwell on things she could not change, which only brought back the personally unpleasant ones. Sven barely glanced at her that first day, their kiss in the hall, his face as he watched Serena dancing. It made her feel sick to see him look at someone else that way, but she tried to convince herself it was for the better. That it would be easy for him to forget her, and in turn she would be able to forget him, at least enough to move on with her life.

The lies we tell ourselves.

Her lungs screamed for air. She could not hide under the hot water any longer. When she popped up, gasping and blind, something soft brushed her arm and she jerked back against the other side of the tub.

"Shhh. You'll wake Cassandra."

Sairha gripped the edge and peered around the shower curtain, up at Sven, who held a towel for her. Cautious as she did so, she took the corner of the towel and wiped her face, careful not to touch him. "What are you doing here?"

He shrugged, smiled a little, then ran his hand through his loose hair, pushing strands away from his sad eyes. "I wanted to see you," he confessed.

"You're drunk," Sairha scoffed, though her tone did not imply she meant it. She, herself, was still enjoying the little buzz leftover from her drink. Her fingers tapped along the curtain's edge, holding it in place between them.

"No, I haven't had anything to drink," he replied, a little too fast. "Okay, well maybe a little. But I am not drunk, for sure. It takes a lot to get me drunk."

Layering her tone with agitation, she stretched back out to enjoy the bath and grabbed a washcloth to lather up. "You shouldn't be here, Sven. Shouldn't you be with your fiancée? Entertaining her?"

He did not respond, though his focus dropped to his hands that held tight to the towel. What could he say? Nothing would be acceptable.

Sairha found satisfaction in knowing that she had something over him, some knowledge he probably would not have shared with her, and yet there she was, privy to it. She knew and she let him know that she knew. It felt a little empowering in an otherwise uncontrollable situation.

"May I?" He offered his hand for the washcloth.

After some hesitation, she slid the shower curtain open a little more and handed it to him, turning so he had access to her back. Maybe it was the alcohol, maybe it was a morbid curiosity at what more he could say. He gently moved her hair away and started massaging with the washcloth. "It's not like I knew they would come, Sairha. I thought I would never see her again."

Sairha remained quiet while she leaned against her knees, allowing him to wash further down her back. So many mean, nasty things ran through her mind, things to make him feel hurt and betrayed too. But instead, she kept those thoughts to herself, reminding herself that she had to be a better person, and had to keep the peace. And deep down, she wasn't sure she actually wanted to hurt him.

"Your hair is getting longer," he commented when she still hadn't said anything. "I like it."

"Cassandra said the same thing," she managed. The small talk was too much to bear. She let out another sigh and turned to look up at him, preparing herself for what she was about to do. "We can't keep doing this. We *are* through, Sven. You have not one but two packs to lead and you don't need me."

"She's not my fiancée. We'll just be co-leaders. A fiancée is someone you choose, I didn't choose Serena. If I had my choice..." He trailed off, looking down at her, his features reading miserable. "All I think about is you. Even tonight, with all of the others around me, I couldn't help but wonder what you were doing, if you were okay, and I longed to be with you.

What if..." He paused, his throat bobbing. "What if I ran away with you?"

Sairha bit her lip, glancing away from him, heart hammering in her chest. "You didn't think about me when you left me in the desert to fend for myself with a broken heart. You chose your pack family over me. And... I've accepted it. Now I need you to do the same thing, to live with the choice you made." She leaned back in the tub, trying to keep herself from gripping the edge too hard, and remain strong as she spoke. "Cassandra and I are leaving in the morning, and it will be the last you and I see of each other." Sven opened his mouth to say something, but Sairha held up her hand to silence him. "Let's leave it at this. It's not our time, probably never will be."

A silence fell between them.

She broke the stillness as she stood up and climbed out. "I think you should leave." She took her towel from him and covered herself, still not meeting his eye, and opened the door. The atmosphere around them was stale, and she wished him to go already, before she lost her nerve.

At last he stood, taking one last look at her before he left. Crestfallen, dejected.

Once she heard the soft click of the bedroom door handle, she took a deep, shaky breath and leaned against the wall for support. After facing Marrow Eaters, looters, and having a knife to her throat, somehow telling Sven to leave was the hardest thing she had ever done. There was no going back, she had made her choice and hoped it would make her stronger in the long run.

CHAPTER TWENTY-TWO

Sawyer poked his head in their room the next morning, after knocking, and his bright smile greeted them. "Ready for breakfast? Then maybe I can show you the orchard we have. It's a bit of a hike but shouldn't take us too long."

Sairha placed her hand over Sawyer's, trying to smile but couldn't. She shook her head, "Cassandra and I are leaving after breakfast. It's time we found our own home, somewhere we belong."

He looked hurt by her words and croaked out, "But... you belong here, with us. I don't want you to go." He wrapped his arms around her in a tight hug and rested his head against hers. She felt him inhale, taking in her scent for his own memories. Like he had the first night they met, when he pushed his wet pup nose on her neck before she fainted. Both would be tender memories for herself as well.

Even though he pretended to be glad to have one last breakfast with them, albeit it in the dining hall with the entire pack and then some, Sairha could tell Sawyer was despondent about their departure. She kept the conversation light, asking him about what sort of daily wolf training he had nowadays. Some of the others that sat near them chipped in with their own opinions about training. Otherwise, a lot of the people were quiet, exhausted but in good moods probably from the celebration.

Sairha glanced around the dining room to see if Samuel was watching, pleased. Instead, she spotted Sven helping Serena with her food, engrossed in conversation. Leroy was to the left of him, taking his time eating, his sights set on Sairha. *One good thing about leaving, I'll be rid of you,* Sairha thought as she turned away from his scrutiny. Samuel was nowhere to be seen, but she hoped he had been informed of them holding true to her word, and that he was well.

When breakfast was over, they went outside to say their goodbyes. Sairha leaned down to fasten her knife back where it belonged against her thigh when a shadow stood over her. With a big sigh, she looked up. *What now?*

Leroy towered in front of her, arms crossed against his chest, his white shirt fitting too snug against his muscles. He looked like he would turn green and rip the fabric at any hint of anger.

"What do you want?" Sairha said in a bored tone. "Came to say goodbye? Wave us off?"

"Fat chance," he muttered.

Sawyer let out a nervous laugh and stepped between them. "Well, actually, Leroy has been asked to escort you off of our territory." He smiled, trying his best to defuse the tension. "To protect you guys, while you are still on our lands."

"You have got to be kidding me," Cassandra groaned.

"Nope, no jokes here. I'm all yours, honeypot. Get to leave the property for the day to usher you princesses off our land." Leroy sounded too happy about that last part. "Because I have absolutely nothing better to do, apparently."

Cassandra huffed.

Sairha rolled her eyes then turned to Sawyer, opening her arms up for another hug, which he obliged more than willingly. "You'll always be welcomed at my home," she whispered in his ear. Tears threatened to spill as she pulled away, giving him a final nod, but she held herself together as the three set out for the gate. She refused to take one last look at the A-frame lodge, with the beautiful wood walls, the hand carved wolf emblem, and anyone who might be watching.

"Did you enjoy the party last night, Sairha?" Leroy asked after an hour of walking, his hands in the pockets of his jeans. He stomped through the woods overgrowth without a care. The farther away they got, the more relaxed he seemed to be, despite the concern of Marrow Eaters in the woods. Something he and Sven apparently had in common, Sairha noted.

Sairha gripped Cassandra's hand to stop her from throwing a punch in his direction. Through the gritted teeth of a false smile, she replied. "Oh yes, loads of fun. You guys sure do know how to throw a backyard jamboree."

"It was a joyous occasion, after all," he teased. "More of us, less of you all."

She ignored him, knowing he would be dissatisfied if she didn't say anything, knowing that his sole purpose when around her was to antagonize, and tease, and poke, and push until she blew up. And she was in no mood to be at odds, or in a fist fight, with Leroy anymore. All Sairha wanted was to wash her hands of the wolfshifters and the drama that surrounded them.

"Leroy," Cassandra spoke up after a while. "What's that council and treaty thing the meeting was about?"

Leroy grunted, kicking up debris as he walked. "Wouldn't you like to know," he scoffed, then shrugged. "A long, long time ago our ancestors made a treaty with all creatures and humans. Pretty simple. We don't mess with your business and you all wouldn't mess with ours. As a show of good faith, we locked away the beasts we could not control, the Marrow Eaters, and eventually we all became so separated that your kind forgot who we really were. Started making up ridiculous tales about our kind as *myths* and nightmare fuel for naughty kids."

"You can't fault storytellers, especially if the treaty was created to keep yourselves secret," Cassandra reasoned. "And it's not like you *aren't* big, scary beasts. Right, Sairha?"

Sairha's head started to throb, she didn't want to be brought into another argument. "Maybe we can just not...be at each other's throats for the rest of the hike?"

Leroy came to an abrupt stop, stretching out his arm to halt the women. Sairha reached for her knife. Next to her, Cassandra readied herself for a fight, backing up to Sairha with her fists up. Without their own rustling through the forest undergrowth, Sairha heard the faint snapping of twigs behind them. She looked over her shoulder, jaw tightening.

Behind them, leaning against a tree, was the second-in command Kerry. They picked at their nails, as if bored. Their pale hair rested along their cheek in a sharp angle, giving an overall appearance of indifference, though their body language suggested otherwise.

Leroy growled but eased up on his stance. "*Don't* sneak up on me like that, Kerry. If you know what's good for you."

"Well, well, well. What do we have here?" A raspy, feminine voice called out. Serena stepped out from behind a different tree, hands on her hips, a coy grin on her face. Her dark curls were pulled into a sort of mohawk with two clips, reminding Sairha of a Trojan helmet. The she-wolf licked her lips and forcefully pushed past Leroy, her focus never leaving Sairha.

"What do you want, Serena? I thought you were in a meeting with Samuel and Sven back at the lodge," Leroy hissed; however he was less tense, showing his trust of the two.

Sairha was not as trusting and kept her stance ready to dodge Serena if she chose to attack. Cassandra never so much as lowered her hands an inch.

"I wanted to see who this tasty snack was that you are escorting so discreetly off property," she responded.

"My name is Sairha, this is Cassandra. We were mistakenly taken in and are leaving now. So, if you don't mind..." She felt naked under Serena's gaze, but refused to show discomfort....*move the hell out of my way.*

Serena narrowed her dark eyes, a flash of yellow to them. "I *know* who you are." She started walking around Sairha before grabbing a lock of her hair. She twirled the short strand around before letting it slide out of her grasp. "I know everything about you, more than you think."

Sairha stood her ground and tried to keep the surprise from her expression, wondering what all she knew. Sven said that he had only told two people, Leroy and Sawyer, all that there was between them. A flash of anger flared in her, assuming Leroy had told Sven's secrets. Swallowing down the possibility that perhaps Sven had revealed it himself.

"Then you know that they are leaving, under our protection. So, let *us* be on our way and *you* go back to do actual leader business," Leroy gritted out, obviously trying to keep his tone respectful, but firm.

"I have every right to know about the little side piece *my* future life mate, *our soon to be alpha*, has been running around with like a sick puppy," she growled back at Leroy.

It was Cassandra that stepped between Sairha and Serena. "Look here, you *werewhore*, you can't talk about my friend like that."

Kerry leapt quickly from their spot with a grunt, but Serena stopped her with a quick, halting motion. Serena bared her fangs at Cassandra. "What did you call me?"

"You heard me," Cassandra challenged and Sairha wished she hadn't.

Serena let out a snarl and lunged at Cassandra, ready to send a punch aimed right at her abdomen. Leroy moved quicker and took the blow to his side, his eyes hard and deranged as he stared her down. "You are out of line, Serena! I suggest you and your second head back right now, not another word spoken, or so help me I will get the *current* leader involved. These two are his guests and I am positive he would not appreciate any harm coming to them."

Kerry nudged Serena's arm, whispering, "Serena, let it go. Think of the alignment."

Serena's fist was still tightened as she matched Leroy's stare, her mouth stuck in a vicious snarl. When the blonde touched her arm again, Serena regained her composure and visibly shook off her anger as she brushed past Leroy, then with more force past Sairha.

Leroy watched them leave, even after they were out of human sight. When it seemed they would not return, he started back down the mountain, rubbing his side. "Goddamn, egotistical, stubborn headed leaders," he grumbled. "This is exactly why we stopped with all the bullshit archaic *alpha* talk. Goes straight to people's itty bitty brains."

"You alright?" Sairha looked Cassandra over, to which the brunette shrugged it off; she was fine, other than the shock of what had happened. They both jogged to catch up with Leroy who was still muttering as he stomped onward.

"Leroy," Cassandra breathed, a faint hint of teasing in her tone. "Did you just...do something...*nice* for me?"

Sairha grinned. He must have been really embarrassed for them to be able to see the faint rosy blush on his dark skin.

"It isn't right what she did," he huffed, avoiding looking at Cassandra. "I would never hit someone with-child. That's just wrong. She's always been hot headed and jealous, since they were kids, but I never expected that sort of low blow from her."

"Well... Thank you," Cassandra said with sincerity.

Leroy let out a huff, waving her off. "Yeah...you're welcome, I guess."

They walked on in silence after that, a little less angry at each other. Sairha did not have to like him, but she respected the stance he took against Serena, someone of higher authority, for her friend and unborn child. Maybe there was still some chivalry locked away, deep down inside of him. Maybe she hadn't gotten to know the real Leroy, the one who didn't have to do what Sven or any leader told him to, the one who had a mind of his own. But all they had left were the last few hours of the trek, and Leroy made no effort to speak to either of them, so she didn't bother, either.

The sun was well behind them, nearing the end of daylight, when Sairha caught a trail of smoke coming out of a tiny chimney. A sense of lightheartedness by the imagery overtook her, much different than the last time she had looked upon the cabin. This time someone was for sure waiting for them.

Cook. Home.

Cassandra picked up her tired pace, all but skipping down the trail with renewed energy. "Cook! He's there!"

Sairha was about to join her when there was a gentle tug at her elbow. Stopping, she looked back at Leroy, curious as to why on earth he would want to spend another second with her.

"Sairha, I know we have our differences," he said quietly, with no trace of anger or teasing in it.

Is he...apologizing?

She waited with a patience she didn't know she had for him, while he mulled over what he wanted to say next. It surprised her how he couldn't look her in the eye, like it was hard for him to do, and also amused her.

"We haven't gotten along much, but I want you to know that I never told Serena about you."

Sairha blinked. He'd had several chances, before or during the party or after breakfast before he had joined them. Somehow, though, she knew he was not lying to her. There were many things Leroy was, but she realized he had never been dishonest. Quite the contrary, he was brutally honest, and abrasive. She tilted her head to catch his eye. "I believe you."

"I did tell Samuel," he confessed, straightening out tall, no longer ashamed. "*He* is my leader and he suspected, so he asked me on pack honor. He asked why Sven was so distracted lately. I had to obey or pay the price, so I told him. And maybe I am jealous of you, in general. That level of trust and care you two built, in such a short time, that was something only Sven and I shared."

Shaken, she had to take a deep breath and count to three, letting his confession sink in. "I wouldn't expect any less from the most annoyingly loyal wolfshifter I've ever met. Goodbye, Leroy." With that, Sairha turned quickly on her heel, jogging to catch up to Cassandra.

"I hope our paths never cross again," she heard him call after her. "Take care, Sairha."

The sun dipped below the far off mountain range, shadows taking over the path. Sairha knew it well enough, from where they were, to navigate with ease in the dark. "You know, they say stress is not good for growing these things," Cassandra commented when Sairha walked up beside her. "Next time, no splitting up from Cook. We all stick together."

Sairha chuckled, shaking her head. "It's a baby, you know. You should probably stop calling it a thing or an it. Something more... motherly, perhaps."

Cassandra rolled her eyes. "Like what? Right now, I feel about as happy about it as a person does feeding a leech."

Sairha couldn't fault her friend, it was an unexpected surprise, one she could only hope that Cassandra would feel better about as their situations improved and the baby grew. The heaviness of the world was not lost on either of them, but she'd be damned if she couldn't carve out their own section of the wilderness for safety.

"I promise, once I start feeling the thing moving or kicking, I'll start referring to it as a baby."

"Fair enough," Sairha replied, bumping into Cassandra playfully. "When do you plan on telling Cook? No secrets between us, remember?"

"Uuugh," Cassandra groaned. "When the time feels right. Maybe next week. Maybe next month. Maybe after the baby is born."

The two laughed as they neared Sairha's property.

Cook wore a look of relief when he opened the door. Sairha and Cassandra echoed it back to him, seeing him unharmed. He reached out and grasped them both into his arms, creating a three-person bear hug. "I was so worried about you two." His voice was tight with emotion. "Get inside and tell me what happened."

"Brenda?" Sairha asked, afraid of the answer.

The corners of his mouth pulled down into a grim frown, shaking his head.

"...And that's all of it," Cassandra finished and leaned back. Sairha nodded in agreement, having let Cassandra do most of the talking, warmed by cups of steaming tea and the small fire.

The private conversations she'd had with Sven were still too fresh to recount aloud. She focused instead on the inspiration that the well-planned out wolf lodge had given her. The logistics needed a few confirmations, a glance at a map, and her best friends on board. If plausible, the idea would keep her far from packland, from any chance of running into Sven.

"What are the odds," Cook mumbled.

They fell into a comfortable quiet for a while.

"Well." Cook stood up after the fire had become nothing more than glowing embers. "I better put her to bed. The couch isn't that comfortable."

Sairha blinked and looked over at Cassandra, curled into herself, breathing lightly as she dozed. *That was fast. Tomorrow I'll propose the idea,* she agreed with herself. *For now, rest.* Cook leaned forward and scooped Cassandra up. Sairha stood, marveling at how good it felt to be back in his calming presence. The way he treated both her and Cassandra as respected individuals reminded her that good people existed.

Jostled, Cassandra looked up at him, confused then apologetic, and uttered a groggy *'thank you'*. Sairha followed them into the hallway, watching from the door, as he tucked Cassandra in. When Cook rejoined her in the hallway, she put her hand on his shoulder, sadness tugging at her heart. Brenda should be there with them.

In her own bed, she tossed and turned, wondering why Brenda had left them, without saying anything. She dared not think of the others, not again. Guilt ate at her, thinking of the lies and half truths she had told. Maybe she was the reason Brenda left.

Staring up at the ceiling, she realized she had gotten used to sleeping next to Cassandra. The quiet breathing of her friend drowned out her active mind. Having the bed to herself, the sheets were cold and the silence loud. Sneaking out of her room and into the master suite, she crawled into the opposite side of the bed beside Cassandra. Once settled, her eyelids became heavy, and her mind slowed enough for sleep's embrace.

MORNING LIGHT CAME, what felt like only minutes later, and Sairha found herself alone in her mom's bed. A weird balance of emotionally drained and renewed hope settled inside. It would be the first day of their new lives. She hurried getting up and ready, eager to find out what had happened to Cook the three days they had been separated.

Heading for the kitchen, Sairha's skin crawled seeing the front door wide open. She approached slowly, sighing in relief at the boards leaned against the wall, hammer and nail laid beside them. Cook and Cassandra sat outside on the small porch, looking serene in the early sunshine.

"Good morning," she said softly, and they scooted to make room.

"Someone is in a good mood," Cook chuckled and took a sip from the coffee mug in his hand.

Steam coiled up out of it and Sairha gave it a jealous eye, wishing she had tea. A mug was presented in front of her, and she wrapped her fingers around the warm ceramic, the scent of vanilla wafting out.

"I thought I heard you up, so I made you a cup while I

made my second one," Cassandra grinned, bringing her own drink up to her lips.

"Thank you." Sairha blew into her cup. "Did I miss anything important?" Her eyes darted to Cassandra, wondering if she had told Cook the life changing news. If Cassandra caught her meaning, she did not show any sign of it as she shook her head.

"No, we've just been enjoying the sunshine together," Cassandra replied. "But since you are here now, let's hear what happened to Cook after he left us. Did you catch up with Brenda? Is she okay?"

His sigh was a deep release, shoulders slumping ever so slightly. "It was not as dangerous as killing a Marrow Eater," he said, eyeing Sairha. "Nor as exciting as being kidnapped by wolves." He looked into his cup, thinking, then continued before they could get impatient. "Brenda had left before dawn, when she thought none of us would notice. Since I didn't want to leave without talking to you two, she got a big head start. I followed her trail for a day, back towards the city where..."

Sairha swallowed as a chill crept into her bones. It hadn't crossed her mind that Brenda was reckless enough to go out on her own, back to where her sister had perished. If they had suspected, Sairha would have never left her alone.

"Her trail went cold just before the end of the forest. Maybe she changed her mind," he shrugged. "Either way, I didn't want to search blindly, alone for that long. I was worried about you two. And imagine my shock to come back and you weren't here."

"To be fair, we weren't gone by choice," Cassandra corrected him.

They chuckled, but it was short lived. Sairha placed a hand on his shoulder for comfort. She noted the stubble on his normally smooth face that he hadn't bothered to razor off while they were gone. Was it because he had been too worried to care? Or maybe he was done with the clean cut military look.

"I must have walked three miles in every direction looking for any trail you two left behind. But there was nothing. Guess the wolves covered 'em pretty good." Cook scratched at his cheek as he spoke, as if feeling her stare. "I wasn't sure what to do, and rather than risk you both coming home and I'm gone, or worse, I attract a Marrow Eater to our shelter, I decided to stay here for the night and go find you in the morning if you didn't show. Or die trying."

"Aw, isn't that sweet?" Cassandra teased.

"Nah! You'd all do it for me, right." Cook laughed, but when they didn't say anything he fixed a stern eye on them. "Right? Right?"

Sairha gave his shoulder a gentle squeeze before removing her hand. She took a sip of tea, then muttered, "We'd totally let you die in the wilderness." Both women erupted into a fit of giggles at his over exaggerated disbelief.

The sun inched higher, their drinks down to the last sips, when Sairha ventured to speak aloud her idea. "What do you guys think about a ski resort?"

"Skiing? It's not even winter. And you're crazy if you think I'll climb a mountain for you," Cassandra huffed.

Waving Cassandra's comment away, Sairha leaned forward and pointed to the left of the forest in front of them. "About thirty miles that way, there's a small ski town with grocers and supply stores. Another five miles lies a ski resort that is always stocked up for winter."

"Oh, only thirty-five miles?" Cassandra asked, her tone mocking.

"Yep." Sairha grinned from ear to ear, looking between the two. "My mom has some old maps. It'll be tough; uphill and downhill a lot. But it could be worth the effort. We've made it this far. What's a little more distance if we find a place we can settle down, call our home, and start building that new life?" She shook a little with excitement as she nudged Cook, then Cassandra. "We could wait out the winter, living luxurious suite-lives in a cushy hotel. Then, come spring, we start a garden and greenhouse, another thing my mom has tons of books on. We build up perimeters. Permanent, reinforced ones." Sairha could tell she had them hooked, they were listening as they gazed off into the distant homeland she was painting. "I want to continue to find more like us, to protect, preserve the human race. Start our own safe haven."

Cook looked from Sairha, then to Cassandra, and raised an eyebrow. His dark eyes twinkled before he smiled. "Well, if Cassandra promises not to complain the whole trip there... I don't see why not? Yeah, *yeah*. I like this community idea, Sairha. Gardening, perimeters, abandoned ski lodge. Sign me up. I can train those who want to learn combat moves, too."

Cassandra's mouth tightened, brows furrowed; however, she could not hold the straight-laced face for long before giving into a smile.

Sairha nodded, glad to have them in agreement so effortlessly. "It's decided then. A new life and clean slate with my best friends. Save humanity. Kick ass."

"And what about Sven? The wolfpack?" Cook asked.

Sairha kept her sight ahead, thinking about how she wanted to respond. A sharp pang shot through her heart, but it wasn't aching to be fixed. It was just present, always would be.

"We can stick around... If you wanted to see if he would come to his senses about you," Cook offered.

Sairha gripped her mug tight and exhaled slowly, releasing the pain. "He already came to his senses," she said with a new calm. "And I turned him down. So, there is nothing here to wait for. I am ready to start this next chapter together. The three of us."

Cassandra cleared her throat as she lifted the mug to her lips. She spoke fast, as if ripping the truth off like a Band-Aid. "The four of us, eventually, in a few months."

Sairha snorted. *Well, that's one way of breaking the news.*

"What?" Cook spilled his coffee all over himself when he jerked forward. "What do you mean? Are you... So, that... Ohhh... That explains so much." He leaned against the house and put a hand over his eyes, mumbling about missing the signs. Cook's bewilderment had both of the women in loud hysterics for a while. When things calmed down, Cassandra shifted beside Sairha and wrapped her arm around her friend's shoulders. Sairha leaned into her, feeling at peace. A journey that had started out to find her family had ended with her finding herself. A second one would start, with two people she considered closer than blood, along with a purpose to fulfill in the strange, new, primitive world.

END

GLOSSARY

CAST

SAIRHA (S-air-uh)

Sairha is an emergency room nurse who worked hard to continue her education, choosing to study abroad. She hails from the outskirts of the small, lakeside town, Lake Hulahoe, in the California mountains. Introverted, determined, and often unsure of herself.

Likes: tea, studying, peace and quiet, the color magenta, and teriyaki jerky.

SVEN (Ss-ven)

Sven is a public speaker, touring underdeveloped towns to offer information on assistance. He hails from a rural county, deep in the woods, also outside of Lake Hulahoe. Outgoing, energetic, and ready to help others.

Likes: rootbeer, solitude in nature, the color sky blue, and running.

GLOSSARY

CASSANDRA

Cassandra is a self-proclaimed party girl who never really found the right career for herself, but tried. Although well-traveled, she was raised predominantly in Sabueso de Oro, Mexico, by numerous nannies, and sometimes her parents. Loud extrovert, can't sit still for long, and loves dancing until her feet go numb.

Likes: Chocolate truffles, chai lattes, the color red-orange, and nightclubs.

ALEXANDER COOK

Goes by Cook after getting used to being called that as a soldier in the army. Stationed in the seaside town of San Dayo, but his family is from South Sponal, California—not too far from the Mexico border. Thoughtful, quiet until he feels comfortable, then he's a conversationalist.

Likes: Sparkling lime water, small gathering bbqs, the color forest green, and helping others.

LEROY (Lee-roy)

Leroy is Sven's most trusted friend, the right hand man, and a rule enforcer. He doesn't remember where he came from, only that he became part of Sven's family at a young age and prefers to not leave their property. Sour, sarcastic to a fault, and a button pusher to see people's reactions.

Likes: nothing

SAWYER (Soy-yerr)

No matter how you meet him, Sawyer is always ready to offer a smile and befriend anyone willing. Also part of Sven's family, Sawyer comes from the rural forests of California. He prefers to see the brighter side of things and has seemingly endless amounts of energy. A precocious explorer, a charming mischief maker, and always happy-go-lucky.

Likes: Fizzy drinks, pumpkin pie, making new friends, the color blue.

GLOSSARY

THE TWINS - BRENDA AND ANGIE

Hailing from an unknown city in Nebraska, the twins were living their best lives at a music festival when they decided to stay in California. Brenda is the oldest (by a few minutes), tallest, and most outspoken, often hot headed. She is fiercely protective of her sister. Angie is petite, soft spoken, and observant. She keeps her sister inline with her gentleness, and often appears unwell from an unnamed illness. They are fondly known as The Gaggle Twins, thanks to Sven over hearing all their endless shared whispers.

Likes: Cook, gossiping, and musical festivals.

EMILY AND CONNOR

Connor. Not much is known about where they came from or who they even are. Emily keeps to herself, but enjoys cooking the meals when she can. Connor is full of imagination that keeps him occupied, especially with his toy army men.

Likes: Feeling safe, reading books, playing make believe together.

CREATURES

THE SUPERIOR BEINGS

Ancient, mystical beings only known in stories handed down generations. Every paranormal species has their own version, this account is from the wolfshifters. Superior Beings were described as intelligent, yet simple. That they drew power from the moon after working long days tending to nature. They were herbivores, who got along with all creatures. Tall and graceful, with luminescent skin and wide, knowing eyes. Faces often reminiscent of barn owls. They lived high up in trees, where they would sing with the birds the most lovely of songs. They enjoyed learning from other species, and teaching in return. Superior Beings taught gardening to all, but especially took interest in humans when they arrived on Earth. It is said that this was their undoing.

MARROW EATERS

Often told to the young as a scary bedtime story, the Marrow Eaters were described as monstrous creatures that lurk in the night, who hunt humans by the scent of their blood. They were locked away in an underground cavern system, after nearly decimating the human population. These creatures are known to move incredibly fast, on long front arms and powerful, short back legs. They have no eyes, and only slits for nostrils, along with a wide mouth that stretches across their perfectly round heads. Thousands of needle-like teeth line the inside, with a long, thin tongue. Their sagging throats often look red after gorging on blood and marrow. These creatures know no other desire than consuming, but are restricted by their need to hide during daylight. They were once the Superior Beings, believed to have been biologically transformed when introduced to humans.

WOLFSHIFTERS

Wolfshifters come from a line of beings that could transform into any animal at will. Eventually they lost the ability of many forms, sticking to just two. Human and animal. The number of different animal shifters are unknown. Wolfshifters appear as normal humans when they please, but retain some of their animal attributes, such as sense of smell, better eyesight and hearing, and stamina. In their wolf forms, they have varying pelts, are much larger than normal wolves, and can communicate with each other telepathically. Although a matured shifter can change upon will, they feel most called to the *turn* when the moon is full and will have boundless energy. The *turn* can be quite painful, even to the experienced, and most prefer to do it in privacy. A born shifter will spend up to a full year as their animal and must master the transformation within that year, or else become pure animal. This happens at different ages for everyone, when the inherited shifter gene becomes activated. There are two kinds of shifters; the born and what they call *the bitten*. It is rare for a bitten to maintain their sanity after their first *turn*, often resulting in feral behavior. Most shifters form tight communities to protect their kind.

LOCATIONS

The world in which Sairha and The Marrow Eaters live is set in an alternate version of our world. I've kept the names of the Americas and their divisions, the general scenery, but decided to create fictional towns and cities for a fresh experience when reading.

SABUESO DE ORO

A city inland of Mexico where Cassandra was raised and Sairha was continuing her education as an emergency room nurse. The city is a local and tourist favorite featuring nightlife, hotels, and a state of the art hospital. There is a farmer's market almost every day and the beach is only an hour drive away.

LAKE HULAHOE

A ski town in the Northern California mountains, with a lake at its center. Sairha grew up in this town, until her early teens when her mother moved her and her sister to the outskirts in the woods. There is a popular ski lodge, a handful of restaurants and grocery stores, and a small community college. The lake boasts warm swimming in the summer and plenty of fishing year round.

SAN DAYO

A coastal, central California town with military posts, San Dayo is a melting pot of people. Known for its fish tacos and great surf, along with a great job market. Cook was stationed there as a soldier in the army before he went on leave. The town has all the amenities of a small city, and then some.

CIN CITY

A metropolis city farther south, bustling full of life day and night. This city is a major hub for business, travel, and even vacation. Set in the middle of the desert, it has extreme heats and relies heavily on their short rainy season. There is a swift river that runs through it, coming from the Sierra Nevada.

ACKNOWLEDGMENTS

This book. There were so many road bumps, so many gates kept locked, and hardships that I could have used as excuses to give up. However, Sairha and the Marrow Eaters became so endeared to me, I pushed through. It took seven years to get to this point. And now, I can't believe it's in readers hands. WOW.

Big thank you to my kids, who allowed me the mornings to write and evenings to meet deadlines. Who held my hand, asked if I needed a snack, and stared at me in awe when I told them someday people would read my book. And for the endless cuddles. I love you. Thank you to my incredible partner, Allen, who sneakily talked about my writing to anyone who would listen. I love you. To my mother, who doesn't read my genre but was obsessed from the very first, very rough draft. Thank you, I love you. And to my mother in law, who not only helped watch the kids, but also read nearly all of my short stories. To my Papa George, thank you for all the bookstore and hot cocoa visits as I was growing up. I love you.

The biggest thank you to my best friend and partner in idiotic crime, Amanda Stockton. For listening to all my crazy ideas and reminding me that my characters could have moments that didn't move the plot. And for the freaking AMAZING book art. I appreciate you.

My other bestie, Molly, who crawled through the querying trenches with me, and who laughed and cried over Sairha and

Sven with me. This book wouldn't be as badass if it weren't for you. No, you shut up. I appreciate you.

Johnny, for always being a hyper-focused cheerleader and tech-guru helping at the drop of a hat. I appreciate you.

Stephen Black, thank you for always believing in me and my story, and for your editorial help, above all else. You really cleaned the heck out of this story. It shines brighter than a new tea kettle. I appreciate you.

I wouldn't be anywhere without my communities on Twitter, Instagram, and Discord. Too many friends to list, but: Stefanie, Natasha, Harlan, Rachel, Jae, Kota, Abby, Rose, Britta, Lawrence, Jon, Will, Dennis, Sean, Shawn, Chuck, Martin, and Jax.

And saving the best for last, thank YOU, reader, for taking a chance on my book. I hope you enjoyed it and will continue on Sairha's journey in book two.

ABOUT THE AUTHOR

Some wonder what it's like in author Alexis L. Carroll's head after reading one of her stories. Imagine, if you can, a party where Trent Reznor, David Bowie, and Guillermo del Toro are chatting while Alexis sits awkwardly in the corner jotting everything down. When not writing, she can be found in the salon creating colorful hair and swoopy fringe. Outside of multitasking careers, Alexis loves to explore new places and eat tasty food in the PNW, where she lives with her mate, two doppelgangers, and hellhounds.

Alexis loves to delve into the what-ifs of monsters and forbidden pets, interpersonal dramatics and self-reliance, as well as secret worlds in her dark fantasy and horror themes. She is the co-author of *Things Magical Under The Moon*, a collection of grim tales, and *When Her World Went Away*, an apocalyptic horror novel. You can find her on social media under the handle @alexisxstetic or on her website www.bloodbloomspress.com

Milton Keynes UK
Ingram Content Group UK Ltd.
UKHW031143121124
451094UK00006B/503